Praise

MENDERS

Weather Menders is a pioneering cli-fi novel that combines science fiction with time travel and spiritual fantasy in a unique and captivating way. The message is clear: we must act soon and be woke. Oh, and there's a telepathic time-travelling cat!"

—Dan Bloom, editor, The Cli-Fi Report

Debra Denker is delightfully fluent, evoking people and places with a radiant immediacy. *Weather Menders* is a remarkable feat of the imagination—and particularly appropriate for our times.

—David Michie, author, *The Dalai Lama's Cat*

Palm trees at Stonehenge, a world fallen disastrously out of balance. Tara, her cat, and her great-granddaughter struggle to set the earth back in harmony with the help of three mysterious visitors. This romp through past, present, and future will inspire and delight a wide range of readers—fantasy and sci-fi enthusiasts, feline lovers, and any one concerned about the future of this planet. The pace is fast and the stakes are high in this wonderful and diverting novel. Don't miss this last chance to set the world to rights!

—Susan McDuffie, author of the
award-winning Muirteach MacPhee mysteries

Palm trees now grow near Stonehenge. Nearby, a small group of humans hang on after decades of catastrophic climate change, global pandemics and economic collapse. So starts Debra Denker's engaging new novel, *Weather Menders*. It's part of a long sci-fi tradition of post-apocalyptic survival but with a twist: empathy and spiritual traditions matter. Denker adroitly weaves in Buddhism, Native American beliefs and other ancient practices as she takes us to particular political moments in the past. Her characters are intriguing, especially her 96-year old protagonist; her locales are beautifully described; and the story line is highly salient. This is a captivating book, a parable about hope and the power of love.

—NV Baker, author, *Vanished*, a novel

Debra Denker's earnest, yet whimsical novel reminds in no uncertain terms that humanity stands at a crossroads. We can either wake up, take control and chose to live in rhythm with nature and spirit, or continue to sleep at the wheel and allow billionaire elites to drive us into a disastrous, car wreck of a future. Written with a practitioner's heart, Denker weaves through her writing nuggets of wisdom that illuminate a path to a more grace-filled, hopeful future for all sentient beings that share this home called Earth.

—CJ Ondek, Writer, Editor and Dharma Hound

Weather
MENDERS

Weather MENDERS

A Novel by

Debra Denker

Paperback Edition published 2017 by Catalyst Artistic Productions
ISBN for paperback edition
978-0-9991252-0-5

Cover design by Marla Phillips
Back cover cat photograph by Max Underwood
Interior Formatted by

emtippettsbookdesigns.com

Also By
Debra Denker

Sisters on the Bridge of Fire:
One Woman's Journeys in
Afghanistan, Pakistan, and India
(a memoir originally published in 1993, reprinted 2001)

War in the Land of Cain
(a novel published in 2011)

*Dedicated to the happiness
of all sentient beings
everywhere in all the universes,
known and unknown,
and in all Timelines.*

What if Time Travel were real?

What if Time Travelers from 300 years in the future told you that there was a chance that you could prevent the catastrophic climate change, plagues, and wars that have shaped your world in 2050 by going back in time to key Pivot Points and ethically altering the outcome of elections that had been manipulated? What if failure would result in the destruction of the biosphere? Would you go?

In post-plague 2050 Britain, palm trees tower over the rice paddies of Stonehenge. Tara MacFarlane, a weary 96-year-old anthropologist originally from Taos, New Mexico, longs only to finish out her life in peaceful Buddhist meditation, and rejoin the great love of her later years, the humanitarian Scottish-Afghan doctor Xander, in a future incarnation. Suddenly one stifling autumn day Tara, her great-granddaughter Leona, and Leona's boyfriend Janus are faced with a trio of Time Travelers from a future alternate Timeline where humanity and the eco-system survived and thrived.

The fate of humanity and most of Earth's species falls squarely on the shoulders of Tara, Leona, Janus, and Tara's small gray cat, Georgie, who shows a surprising aptitude for telepathy. Time is short to reverse catastrophe that will bleed through into the alternate Timeline, and the three mysterious Time Travelers must determine the ideal Pivot Points by reading the Time Code vibrations off the great standing stones of Avebury. Unexpectedly joined by the brave and wise cat Georgie, the six plunge into the Time Circle of Stonehenge on their mission. Where and when will they go, and will they succeed in restoring the Earth and humanity to balance?

"Three will meet three,
and a portal will be.
The portal will lead
to wherever there's need,
to stop the greed,
so all will be freed."

—Leona the Shaman,
7 October, 2050

Chapter
1

22 September, 2050

**Avebury Encampment,
New Avalon**

As always when she first awakened, Tara wondered why she was still alive, and at age 96, even healthy and fit.

"Gran! Gran!"

That would be her step-great-granddaughter, Leona.

Tara stretched, pulled her long, white hair away from her sweaty neck, and attempted to curl back up into the relatively cool shade of the great standing stone against which she had fallen asleep.

"Gran!" Leona's voice was more insistent, finally irresistible.

Tara yawned a wide yawn at the same time as the sleek gray cat curled up at her feet yawned. She laughed and petted Georgie.

"Thank you. Did you sleep well?" Soft words formed in her mind. She looked at the cat's intense green eyes and blanked out what she thought she had heard. At her age…

Leona ran towards her excitedly, splashing through a rice paddy, her wild, dark, kinky hair spread out around her like a raven's wings. She was out of breath by the time she reached Tara.

"Careful," admonished Tara. "You'll get heat stroke running like that."

"I'm used to it. Remember I was born a lot later than you, Gran."

"Right, right, so your body is adapted to the heat, etcetera. What's all this *tamasha* about?"

The girl's hazel eyes glittered in her dark-skinned face, reminding Tara of the cat.

"Long story."

Tara smiled. "I've got time."

Leona settled down beside the old woman, seeking out the shade of the ancient dark stone.

"Where are you coming from?" Tara asked.

"The old Henge."

"In one day?" Tara marveled at the girl's energy. It was nearly 40 miles away.

"Most of it was on the canals. I didn't run all the way."

That's right. Tara still forgot about how many new canals had been dug as the waters had risen, extending the 18th century network as much of the West Country progressively turned into marshland, making foot roads impassable.

"Gran. There's people coming through the old Henge. Space men and women."

Tara sat up abruptly. "Leona, have you been…"

"No, Gran, no drugs, no moonshine. At least not recently."

"You're sure you're not dreaming? Even as a child…"

"Gran," Leona interrupted impatiently. "You're not listening."

"Okay."

"I haven't been able to talk to them. But they see me, and I see them."

"And the others?"

"None of the others can see them. Well, I think Janus does sometimes, from the way he looks, but he hasn't said anything."

"*I have seen them…*" Again, soft words in her head. She shook her head to clear it and looked at the cat. Georgie was staring at her intently. "*Cats do.*"

She scratched the cat's ears, assuming that her hearing a cat speak was a sign of impending dementia. She was a little surprised, and grateful, that she had avoided it this long. Perhaps she was not too long for this world. Leona was almost grown…

"Have you seen them before?" Tara asked the girl.

"Just like shapes, like mist, like ghosts."

"Always at the Henge?"

Leona nodded her head. "Always. Up till now."

"What's…" Tara stopped, squinting towards the whitish sun just dipping behind the horizon in the west. Georgie the cat froze, looking intently in the same direction. Three silvery figures advanced towards them, through the rice paddies, just as the dinner gong sounded from the Longhouse in the distance.

"Can you see them?" Leona whispered.

"I see something," Tara said uncertainly. "Just humans. But…Maybe they came all the way from the City."

As the figures advanced, she had time to observe them. She had the keen sense that they were observing her as well. She glanced down at Georgie. He was tense, expectant, but did not put his back up or hiss.

Clearly human. A little misty around the edges, but that could just be the late afternoon mists of what used to be autumn. Two men and a woman. Not quite space suits, more like the jumpsuits worn in *Star Trek* and other sci-fi films of her youth. Maybe that was the fashion in the City now. It was so rare that anyone came out into the depopulated countryside that she didn't know.

The three stopped about fifty paces away. Their whitish garments glowed slightly in the gloaming.

Leona crouched by Tara's side, like the long-extinct lioness that was her namesake, her eyes focused, staring the figures down.

"They followed me here," whispered Leona. Tara could feel her great-granddaughter shaking next to her. She wasn't sure if she herself was shaking as well.

"Welcome," Tara called out uncertainly. Her voice was surprisingly strong.

"Thank you." A human voice, male, deep. Not just a vibration or a thought in the mind.

"Do you come from the City? You are welcome to join us for dinner in the Longhouse. We don't have much variety, tuna, rice, a little greens…"

The man shook his head quickly. "No time now. You can see us? Both of you?"

"*And the cat,*" purred the soft words in Tara's head.

"And the cat," said the man. The other man and the slim woman remained silent.

"Yes," said Tara. She started to reach out towards the man's hand, to touch. The party of three backed off a few paces.

"No," he said sharply. "Not yet. This is still an experiment. So far it's you, the girl, and the cat. Good. We have to go."

Tara blinked. Leona and the cat stared at the place where the three had been. Lightning flashed purple-white and Tara could see footprints in the mud, which were quickly obliterated in the deluge that followed.

Georgie jumped onto Tara's shoulder and tucked himself beneath the oblong woven reed umbrella that she put over her head. Leona unfurled her own umbrella from her knapsack and the two humans and one gray cat slithered and slipped their way to the Longhouse.

As they entered the pool of fish oil light, Tara looked meaningfully at Leona.

"I know," said Leona impatiently. "They'd think we were crazy. I haven't even said anything to Janus."

Tara hesitated, the rain sluicing off her umbrella. "How often have you seen them?"

"This is the first time they've followed me," said Leona evasively.

Tara stepped under the thatched porch and shook off her umbrella. She thought she'd seen everything in her 96 years—wars, revolutions, terrorist attacks, the climate breakdown, the three Great Plagues. She'd seen Crop Circles in the old days when barley and wheat grew in these very fields, and she'd seen UFO's fairly routinely in her travels throughout the world as an anthropologist working on environmental restoration with indigenous peoples from southern Africa to Tibet to Taos Pueblo, where her maternal grandmother's ancestors came from. But she'd never actually spoken with Star Beings or inter-dimensional beings.

Her heart stirred with hope. Had they finally come to help, at this late date? Were the Prophecies that she had long ago dismissed as myths about to be fulfilled after all?

Chapter 2

October, 2017

Edinburgh, Scotland

"O*mmmmmm…*" The assembled Buddhist *sangha* breathed in as one with the Lama on the brocade throne at the front of the narrow room. Tara held her breath, visualizing white light at her crown chakra.

A soft, drawn-out, "*Aaahhhhh…*" Red light at her throat, crimson, warm.

"*Huuunnnngggg.*" The breath let out, blue light at her heart, visualizing the sacred Tibetan syllable burning in fire the color of the blue gas flame she had once seen at the sacred shrine of Muktinath, high in the Nepal Himalayas. Blue light seemed to permeate the room. She gazed through half-open eyes, down to the tip of her nose as instructed, willing her mind to still, fighting with thoughts, hopes, and fears.

The breathing exercise continued, the presence of the master lending both joy and gravitas, somehow making it easier to let go of the struggle. Tara breathed, attempted to concentrate, to dissolve the swirl of thoughts, worries, and fantasies in her mind.

"You'd think after 20 years of meditation that I'd be further along," taunted the words in her mind. But she smiled, dissolved the words, watched them drift away. For a moment she felt she was in a state of Samadhi, congratulated herself with momentary glee, then realized with chagrin that her awareness and self-congratulation were the very conceptual thoughts she was supposed to be avoiding.

The practice was over. The Lama was smiling, whirling his ever-present prayer wheel with the rainbow crystal a student had given him as a weight, as he conferred with Joy, his translator. Tara watched the animation on the beautiful young woman's face. Joy had unusual and exotic features, perhaps some mixture of Scottish, African or West Indian, and who knew what else, Tara thought.

"Rinpoche says please drink tea," Joy said at last, laughing.

"In silence?" asked someone.

The Lama shook his head, beaming love at everyone present.

"It's all right to talk now," said Joy.

Tara stretched as she got up from her cushion. At 62, nearly 63, she felt blessed not to have to ask for help. Unlike some friends her own age or even younger, she could still sit on the floor comfortably. Well, fairly comfortably. She was grateful for the yoga teachers in the various cities where she spent her time.

She made her way to the tea station. So did the tall, improbably handsome man who had been sitting like a motionless rock in front of her, apparently deep in Samadhi the entire time. As they nearly collided, she realized she was a little ungrounded.

"Sorry!" she said, embarrassed.

The man smiled, and put out his hand in a "you first" gesture. She sneaked a look at his left hand. No wedding ring. But then these days men didn't always wear one. She shook her head, annoyed at herself for still looking, much less at a meditation retreat.

She poured strong black tea from the teapot through a strainer into a proper china teacup, and added milk. They still did things right in Scotland.

No Styrofoam cups and tea bags here. A slight smile played on her face as she observed her actions and multitude of thoughts.

"It's not easy, is it?" said the handsome man. He had a slight Scottish burr, though his dark, slightly silvered hair and sharp features did not quite look Scottish.

She smiled ruefully.

"Well, that's why it's called practice then, isn't it?" he added as he poured his tea. "Sugar? Xylitol? Stevia?"

Tara shook her head. "You make it look easy," she blurted out, immediately cursing herself. God, Tara, a PhD and years of travel all over the world have not given you social skills.

"Me?" he asked in surprise.

"You're like a rock. In a good way."

He laughed as he backed away from the tea station to make room for someone else, cradling his teacup and saucer in his large hands.

"I've somewhat mastered the stillness of the body," he said. "But I've as much monkey mind as the next person."

She sipped her tea, trying to think of what to say next.

He balanced the teacup precariously in his left hand and held out his right. "Alexander. Xander."

She shook his hand somewhat awkwardly, finally remembering her own name.

"Tara."

"Ah."

"I've spent years trying to live up to the goddess. Still trying."

He gave her a dazzling smile. His greenish eyes burned intensely, perhaps as a result of the meditation. "You know what Rinpoche says, 'Cultivate Bodhicitta and rest in Nature of Mind.' The answer to all things."

"Indeed."

"You're American *sangha* then?"

"Born there. Still based in New Mexico. Albuquerque."

"Do you follow Rinpoche everywhere?"

"I wish! I travel so much I don't always get to see Rinpoche in the States, and I was just at an anthropology conference in France, so I came here."

Xander smiled. "Welcome."

The Lama was making his way back to the throne, greeting his students, hugging them, pressing his Third Eye to theirs in a way that most Lamas did only for other high Lamas and close family members.

Tara was momentarily enveloped in Rinpoche's love, and blissfulness enfolded her. Nothing else mattered as she felt the direct transmission of love and knowledge shoot through her Third Eye like an electric shock as the Lama held his forehead to hers.

She smiled as Xander bent down low to receive the blessing from the tiny Lama. After pressing his forehead to Xander's, Rinpoche looked directly at her and winked.

Tara's heart quickened, confused. What was that all about? Was Rinpoche implying something about her and Xander?

Tara attempted to concentrate on Joy's English translation, but let her mind wander—or rather, observed it involuntarily wandering—when Rinpoche was discoursing at length in Tibetan. She had been looking for her soul mate, more, her Twin Flame, all her life. Or at least since she was a teen-ager in Taos. She'd visited something like 70 countries and lived in about 20 of them. She'd had relationships, of course. Well, more like Karmic ambushes. She'd weathered them, mourned, kept teaching, writing, doing her development work, trying to make the world a better place. Since she had started studying Buddhism she had come to view her experiences as a chance to burn up Karma, and had come, over time, to accept the wrenching pain of loss and rejection, the repeated crushing of the ego that was intimate relationship.

And here she was, like a schoolgirl, almost giggling at a handsome man who looked to be around her own age and didn't wear a wedding ring. And her teacher, her beloved Root Lama, had winked at her.

After the retreat's final dedication prayers, it was time to offer the white silk *kata* scarves, along with cash offerings in red envelopes for the Lama, his attendants, and Joy.

Tara stood in line, her heart filled with love and gratitude. Her heart began to flutter uncharacteristically as Xander got in line behind her, his *kata* draped over the offering envelope in his outstretched hands, a grin of pure bliss on his face.

She heard the faint buzz of a cell phone on vibrate, and was aware of Xander slipping his phone out of his pocket and looking at it. Rinpoche looked up and nodded directly to Xander.

Xander tapped Tara on the shoulder. She felt an electric shock, similar to what she always felt when Rinpoche gave his blessings.

"Sorry, I have to leave urgently," he said. "Can you please give my offerings to Rinpoche and the others?"

"Of course. What about your *kata*?"

"Leave it in the pile. The blessing's in us, not in a piece of cloth."

"Okay…right…"

Xander smiled and pressed his hands to his forehead in prayer position, bowing to Rinpoche as he hurriedly backed up towards the door.

Tara chided herself. She still had that little hope, and what better place to meet a mate than in her own teacher's *sangha*? But there he went, and her flight home was tomorrow. She doubted Xander would show up at the *sangha* dinner after his hasty departure, so that was that.

Tara bowed low with devotion to make her offering, and Xander's. Rinpoche pressed his forehead to hers once, then twice. "For Xander," she thought she heard him say, though she wasn't sure, as he normally didn't speak English. She backed away blissfully, and put Xander's *kata* in the basket of scarves that belonged to the Dharma center. She fingered her own, a sumptuous long one that she had been presented with on one of her service trips to Tibet. It had the blessings of many Lamas in it. Thinking of Xander's reminder that the blessing was not in this material thing, she slipped it off and added it to the pile.

That was that.

Chapter
3

30 September, 2050

Stonehenge,
New Avalon

Tara slogged through the sodden grass behind a procession of ragged, rather exhausted members of her Longhouse. Leona was up ahead with Janus, but to her credit kept looking back to make sure her ancient Gran was keeping up. Not for the first time, Tara gave thanks that her body was mysteriously holding out. She smiled grimly under her reed umbrella. Perhaps it was good genes. Her present body's DNA was comprised of a not unusual mixture of Taos Native, Hispanic—which probably meant old Spanish mixed with some tribes indigenous to Mexico—and what they used to call Anglo in New Mexico. In Tara's case Anglo meant a passionate mix of mostly Irish with a pinch of Slavic, French, and Swedish.

The Weather Menders had called this Gathering after the deluge that had started at sunset on the 22nd had continued for eight straight days, and then strengthened. No more TV, no more Internet, no more satellites, so no way to technologically predict how long the storm would go on. It was rumored that satellites still fed information to the Elite in the City, who seemed to have preserved enough resources to shelter themselves, but had failed miserably at their last-ditch effort to fix the climate.

She didn't think the Weather Menders were doing much better. She viewed them as ragtag descendants of the Druids, though she doubted that most of them were more than dimly aware of the historical precedent. Especially their self-styled so-called leader, Seamus.

If there *were* genuine shamans amongst the Weather Menders, and some days she rather thought there were, including her own Leona, they didn't include Seamus. He had perfected the perpetually bedraggled look, and even in the rare times when the weather was bearable and not producing spates of rain, a faint to reeking smell of rice wine always wafted from his person.

As usual, Georgie the cat rode on her shoulder, on a special pad designed by Leona's mate, Janus. Georgie seemed to sense when one shoulder grew tired, and would gently shift to the other, taking care to keep under the shelter of the reed umbrella. He had been silent, neither a meow nor that strange imagined voice in her head breaking the silence on this, the third day of their journey through the unrelenting rain. But now he began to purr, and it was comforting.

The Weather Menders waited for her to catch up, thankfully not too straggling, thankfully not last. They allowed her, as an Elder, to enter the mist-shrouded stone circle first, followed by a few men and women only a decade or two younger than she. The Weather Menders chanted as they banged rocks together. Wood and skin drums were no longer practical in this humidity. At least the day had cooled enough that they were no longer sweating.

As was the custom, they set down their reed umbrellas as they entered the circle and stood bare-headed in the rain. Georgie leapt off her shoulder and found shelter under her discarded umbrella, licking furiously at his wet gray fur.

"*I don't like this custom,*" came the soft voice in her head. "*Stupid, if you ask me. No spiritual basis whatsoever.*" Oh oh, here we go again. Thankfully these delusions didn't seem to extend to any other area of her life and hadn't yet affected her usefulness.

"*Sorry,*" she found her mind murmuring back. "*I agree.*"

Leona and Janus, as the youngest, came in last and took their places at the center of the circle. Seamus waved around a long stick covered with shiny objects, bits and pieces of old CD's and DVD's.

"Weather gods, hear our prayer," he intoned.

The group of 28 repeated the refrain.

Seamus shook his stick and went on with the ceremony. Tara tried to visualize the rain stopping and sunshine returning to dry out the water-logged land. For a moment, she lost her train of thought and found herself remembering that today was San Geronimo Day at Taos Pueblo. She remembered the cool weather in northern New Mexico in the 20th century, the leaves on the aspens high in the mountains just beginning to turn a rich yellow-gold, the smell of pinon smoke, the sound of drumming, the dancers, the laughter of the river running from its source in the Blue Lake, the men climbing the greased pole and standing on top, precariously balanced.

"Leona, tell us what you see," cried Seamus' voice, ripping Tara out of her reverie.

"I see the rain slowing, stopping," began Leona. "I see…"

A flash of light, like lightning but not, revealed the three figures Tara, Leona, and Georgie had seen before. They flashed into existence in the center of the circle, right behind Seamus, who remained unaware of them. The male one who had spoken with her—who in this light Tara thought looked vaguely Tibetan—shook his head at Leona as the girl stared at him. He lifted a hand to signal her to continue.

Leona did not continue the rote speech of the ritual. Tara watched as her great-granddaughter went into a genuine trance. "I see the sun, I see the clouds drying, the land drying. I see the Balance returning. I see foods we have not eaten or grown for…all my lifetime, and beyond. I smell flowers, I hear birds, I see…I think they are called foxes? I feel…cold? I see the stars as a wheel, turning above this wheel of stone. I taste…foods I do not know. Carrots, kale…hmmm, spices I have only heard of, cinnamon, vanilla, chocolate. I am above the world…"

Janus reached out and grasped Leona's hand tightly, as if to keep a balloon from flying away. To Tara, Leona did appear for a moment to float. "I see the world restored."

Seamus impatiently shook his stick full of shiny discs, rattling them together. "The rain, what about the rain?"

The three figures that nobody else seemed to notice all raised their hands together, and the rain stopped abruptly.

"*Nice work,*" said the soft voice in Tara's head. She looked down at Georgie, whose head now protruded from under her umbrella on the ground as he gazed intently at the three figures.

Tara watched as Janus's gaze shifted, focusing behind Seamus, then snapped back to attention on the Druid's face.

Seamus shook his stick. "First the rain stops, then the sun returns."

On cue, the clouds began to part and long fingers of light stretched across the land.

"It certainly is green," thought Tara, somewhat irrelevantly. But then, it always had been, just a different shade, a rich, temperate shade rather than this yellowish, tropical green. She wondered what had happened to the areas of Earth that had been tropical, and to her homeland in New Mexico? Was it all desert now? Or did it matter? Perhaps everyone had died in the Three Plagues.

In salutation and supplication to the sun, everyone in the group raised their arms. Tara sneaked a look at Georgie, who blinked in the light but continued to stare at the three whitish figures. Was it her imagination or did they seem more, something, corporeal than they had before?

Or was the whole damn thing her imagination? The delusion of age?

As before, the three figures saluted and vanished in a blink. The man who seemed to be in charge waved in a way that reminded her, improbably, of her beloved Xander.

Perhaps she was approaching the other world, at last. Perhaps she was already entering the Bardo, the intermediate state between life and death.

The ceremony concluded, the group filed out and had their usual meal of tuna and rice in the surprisingly sturdy temporary Longhouse that had been constructed just outside the Circle by the young folks. Like a little girl, Tara licked her fingers, actually enjoying the tuna, as Georgie licked his lips and silvery paws.

Chapter
4

July, 2018

Findhorn, Scotland

Tara concentrated on slicing the large, sweet-smelling carrots, thanking them and those that grew them, and the Carrot Deva that was their spirit. She sliced carefully, diagonally, as an Ayurvedic nutritionist friend had taught her to do.

A voice, and a strangely familiar shadow against the light, almost made her include a slice of her index finger in the mix. She caught herself just in time, as she looked up to see Xander, the man she had met at Rinpoche's teachings last year, rushing into the kitchen.

"Sorry I'm late," he was saying to Michael, the tall red-haired Scotsman who was the Kitchen Focaliser today.

"If it was anybody else but you…" retorted Michael, jokingly lifting up the wooden spoon he was using to stir a delicious-smelling vegetable stew and shaking it in Xander's direction. With his free arm, Michael gave Xander a half-hug. "Welcome back. Let me introduce you."

Tara had come to Experience Week, something she had wanted to do for decades, fully expecting to be working in the famous Findhorn gardens, and had been surprised when the Service Department Attunement meditation had given her a clear vision of herself working in Park Kitchen. She had been honest with herself and the group about what she felt called to do, and had summoned Rinpoche's teachings on non-attachment to talk herself out of a subtly lingering disappointment. Now she was wondering if there was a higher purpose after all.

Michael made the introductions to the six people working in the kitchen that day, a group diverse in age and national origin, finally getting to her. "And this," he said with a flourish, "is Tara, all the way from New Mexico in the USA." Tara smiled tentatively, wondering if Xander would remember her.

Xander's face lit up. "Ah, the American goddess Tara from the *sangha* in Edinburgh."

She was glad that her skin was dark enough to hide the blush she felt rising. "Good to see you again," she said, attempting to sound casual. How were these things supposed to work?

Michael flung a blue cotton apron at Xander and said, "Get to work, mate."

Xander shrugged on the apron and fitted a purple cap over his hair. Tara watched out of the corner of her eye as he grabbed a brown chopping board out of the rack, set it on the stainless steel counter next to where she was working, and deftly started dicing white onions. In a few minutes tears were streaming down his face, and he was laughing. As the pungent fumes wafted over to her, she too started crying and laughing at the same time. Pretty soon all the people in the kitchen were laughing.

"The Onion Deva is a naughty one," said Xander, wiping his face with the back of his hand and ending up with bits of white onion joining the silver streaks in the dark hair that peaked out from under his cap.

There wasn't time for more than idle banter, as lunch for 85 had to be served by 12:30, but Tara found herself uncharacteristically peaceful in Xander's presence. Out of habit, she had been checking out the single men as soon as she had arrived at Experience Week. Several had seemed interested, and she was flattered, but they were all much younger than she, and she just wasn't up for a summer fling with a younger man.

However she had been enjoying both Taizé singing and the Sacred Dance festival, teaching some flamenco steps she had learned as a young woman, and demonstrating fancy shawl pow-wow dancing for fascinated Europeans who had never been to North America's Indian Country.

When she arrived at Universal Hall that night for the Scottish *ceilidh*, she was surprised to see Xander in a deep red plaid kilt. He was surrounded by a knot of women of various ages, and looked to be enjoying the attention. Her heart sank. Fool. To think you could compete with women half your age. If he's even single.

But as the pipers started up, Xander broke away from the group he had been talking to and made a beeline for her, gallantly holding out his hand.

"I don't really know what I'm doing," she said shyly.

"Nor do most people here. I have a feeling you're a quick study. Just follow my lead."

Something else she had never been very good at, either in dance or in life. Well, she'd give it a try.

She loved the music. She had since she was a child, though as far as she knew it wasn't part of her ancestry. Later she had come to attribute her love of Scottish music to past lives. There was no denying it. She felt at home here.

The leader taught the dances slowly, calling the steps out. She followed Xander's lead, wove under arms, continued along the circle, dancing sometimes with men and more often with women, since the numbers were nowhere near parity. She resisted looking towards Xander, but was sure she felt him looking at her. Oddly, she didn't feel nervous. A calm acceptance descended on her. If he was free, he was free. If he was interested, he was interested. If not, then not.

She was dancing with another partner when the pipers called a break. She flowed with the crowd out into the cool night air. She smiled at some of the people who were in her Experience Week group and gave them warm, sweaty hugs, but was thankful that no one seemed to feel the need to talk.

Music from multiple guitars floated up into the moon-fed night, and the sound of people singing Dylan in various accents, with great gusto. *Tangled up in Blue.* As she had been, most of her life.

A touch on her elbow. She moved, thinking she was in someone's way. Xander squeezed her upper arm. "Can I get you a drink?"

"Oh…sure. What do they have? I'm not much of a drinker."

"Well then no Water of Life for you."

"Water of Life?"

"Whisky."

"Oh, right. I suppose that's heresy in Scotland, but I really can't…"

Xander laughed. "Pint of cider? It's organic. A bit strong though."

"Thank you."

As she waited for him to return from the Phoenix Café with the drinks, she wandered towards a group of people singing around a picnic table. All ages, many nationalities, great joy in the singing. She joined in and got through a couple of tunes before Xander came back with two bottles.

"Come on," he said. "Let's go talk to the fairies."

He led her down winding paths until they came to a wooded place, far from the laughter of the crowd. They sat on the grass, their bare legs touching in the warm summer night.

For a while neither spoke. Tara sipped the delicious cider, watching the silvery moonlight dance through trees whose branches constantly shifted in the light breeze. She could swear she saw figures moving in the woods, figures that weren't human.

"Can you see them?" he asked quietly.

She shook her head. "Something. I don't know."

"You know that *Dakini* is sometimes translated as fairy."

"I've heard that."

"Or Sky Dancer. Maybe the same thing," he mused.

"And *Dakas*?"

"The balance. The male. The consorts of the *Dakinis*."

She suddenly felt shy, socially inept.

"Haven't seen you in the *sangha* in Edinburgh," he said. "Not since last year."

"I travel a lot, but I've had to be other places and the timing hasn't worked out to get back when Rinpoche was there. But I've seen him in the States. How about you?"

"Also traveling a lot. But he's in our hearts, like he says. 'Calling the Lama from afar' and all that."

"Can you?" she asked. "Call him mentally?"

"On a good day. In a good meditation. How about you?"

She laughed. "The same. So, what do you do, that you travel so much?"

"I'm a doctor. And an amateur reforester, which is what I've been doing here in the community for a number of years, when I can fit in a visit. I'm based in Edinburgh, but I volunteer with Doctors Without Borders. West Africa, and that."

"You must have seen some hard things. Ebola?"

He nodded soberly and sipped his cider. "What we do helps. That's why none of the epidemics have yet got out of hand. And you, dear *Dakini* Tara, what do you do?"

"I'm an anthropologist by training. I try to be useful. Needs assessments, that sort of thing. Conservation, biodiversity, cultural diversity. Projects to help indigenous people reforest, hopefully before it's too late."

They were silent, each contemplating the anthropogenic clock they and so many others were racing against.

He sighed deeply. "Impermanence. I guess we've all had our personal lessons in that too."

She nodded.

"My wife's name was Happiness. She was from South Africa, a refugee from apartheid. We met in Kenya. It seems a lifetime ago."

"Happiness. A lovely name."

"And she was. All the time, even when she was dying."

"I'm sorry."

"It was ten years ago. Luckily we both already knew Rinpoche. It made it easier. Still…"

"That impermanence thing is a bitch, isn't it?"

The two of them laughed ruefully.

"I have a daughter, Joy," he said. "You've seen her, she translates for Rinpoche."

"Joy is your daughter? She's a wonderful translator."

"She and her husband, Dawa, who is Tibetan, have a six-year-old daughter, my granddaughter Dechen." Xander pulled out his cell phone and proudly showed Tara pictures.

"A beautiful family," she said. "You're lucky."

"What about you?"

Here it comes. The admission that she'd never been married, never had children, didn't do anything that society or any of the three cultures she'd come from had expected her to do.

She took a breath. "My mother is still living. Her mother was from Taos Pueblo, and her father was from the Hispanic community. Mom is still highly regarded as a *curandera* who incorporates the Native Medicine ways as well. My father was an anthropologist of the old school. He was my inspiration. I hope I haven't disappointed them too much, not having children. Luckily my sister did."

The two gazed into the woods, looking at shadows that might be fairies dancing, certainly could seem so in this magical light.

He shrugged. "Not your Karma in this life. But Tara is the Mother of the Buddhas."

She laughed. "It's not the name I was born with."

"What then?"

"Tomasita Concha Garcia-O'Connor."

"And when did you become Tara?"

"Actually long before I started studying Buddhism. I was briefly in a commune in northern California, before I went back to school to become an anthropologist. I legally changed my name. My parents weren't thrilled. But now I'm, well, a little bit known, at least in my field, by that name."

"Quite well, I'd say."

"How do you know?"

"I confess to a Googling addiction."

Tara was momentarily taken aback. "How did you know my name to Google me?"

It was Xander's turn to be flustered. "Well I saw your name on the sign up list. It was an unusual name, and well, I remembered meeting you briefly." In the bright moonlight, Tara could see that his face had started to flush. "Anyway, it's not serious, the Googling addiction I mean, and I promise you I'm not addicted to anything else."

She was trying to think of what to say in reply when his lips touched hers, and his tongue entwined with hers, and she realized that her age and her long hiatus from lovemaking had in no way dampened her desire.

Chapter
5

7 October, 2050

**Stonehenge,
New Avalon**

Tara had stayed on at the Henge another week, along with Leona and Janus, simply enjoying the clear weather that had followed the Weather Mender ceremony. The sky was a pale, sun-washed blue, and the sodden land had begun to dry out. Best of all, the heat had started to abate.

Tara enjoyed leaning against the cool blue stones of the ancient stone circle, resting with Georgie in her lap when she wasn't weaving baskets, umbrellas, and Longhouse panels out of reeds. She was glad that she was still useful, not a burden. There was enough food to go around, as long as one didn't mind the sameness, but she wanted to earn her share.

Georgie played half-heartedly with the reeds she was supposed to be weaving, and she ejected him from her lap, laughing at his offended expression. She willfully ignored the words, soft as the cat's fur, that tried to form in her mind.

"Go do what cats do," she said aloud. "Go chase mice or something. God knows their population hasn't declined like everything else."

Georgie flattened his ears against his head and stalked off, pretending annoyance, then bounded between the stones and out of the circle.

Tara watched dreamily as Leona and Janus walked hand in hand into the circle, sweaty and disheveled. It was obvious what they had been doing, and Tara only hoped that Leona was drinking the herbal tea that had a pretty good chance of preventing pregnancy. She was so young, Tara thought wistfully, and yet right now the last of her line of Scottish, Afghan, Zulu, and Tibetan ancestors. A true child of these jumbled times.

Leona had so far listened with an impassive face to all the "repopulate the Earth" lectures by Seamus and some of the other "spiritual leaders." The girl had quietly come to her Gran to ask if there were ways to postpone what seemed inevitable. Leona said she wanted to just have some fun for a while, which made sense to Tara. And as far as Tara was concerned, the new society that had formed in the wake of the population collapse seemed in many ways just as patriarchal as any other society in the past 5,000 or so years. Perhaps it would still evolve into the partnership society so many cutting-edge thinkers had envisioned in her youth.

A streak of light from the direction of the City, what used to be the huge metropolitan area of London, cut the blue-white sky. The Elite still had some rockets and shuttles, though God only knew where they were sending them. Oddly, this one seemed to double back on itself and head right back to the City. She held her breath, waiting. Would it explode? She blessed any sentient beings who might be on board.

But it seemed to turn slowly, parabolically, in the sky and then go back exactly the way it had come. Strange. She'd not seen that before.

Leona and Janus were watching too, hands up to shade their eyes.

"Maybe it's beginning," said Leona with a grin.

"What?" asked Tara.

"You always talked about the Prophecies. How the Star Beings would come to help us in need, when we had raised our consciousness enough."

Tara flung her long white braid to one side, and Georgie suddenly streaked into the circle and batted it. She played idly with the cat, flipping her braid back and forth as she spoke.

"Sadly, Leona. I think those stories are just myths and legends. If it hasn't happened by now..."

"It doesn't mean it won't," said Janus.

Tara was surprised, as the boy rarely spoke. At least to her, or in public. Man, she corrected herself, young man.

"At my age, it's hard to keep the faith," Tara said.

"Gran," said Leona, "you have to keep the faith. You're practically the only one alive who remembers the old stories."

Tara laughed. "Thank you, I think."

"So you must be alive still for a reason."

Tara didn't say anything. Again, she felt that odd feeling, that she had no idea whatsoever why she was alive. She didn't necessarily want to leave her body. Life was not unpleasant, not like it had been during the Plagues and years of loss. But she felt like she was marking time. She'd taught Leona a lot about a lot of things, stories from all over the planet. Janus, the shy orphan, had listened intently and seemed to be taking it all in as well. But the task seemed endless, surely something she couldn't complete before her body, or her mind, gave out, whichever happened first.

"Leona, have you seen..." Tara began.

"No, Gran. Why do you think we're still here?"

"I thought perhaps to take care of your old Gran?"

Leona kissed the old woman on the cheek and teased the cat with a long reed.

"You've got the whole encampment to take care of you. You're a valuable resource. You have the Memory."

Tara laughed, surprisingly light-heartedly. "Leona, I don't know why, but sometimes you remind me so much of your great-grandfather."

"Who you loved with all your heart, and still do. So that's a good thing."

Tara reached out and hugged Leona, and smiled at Janus. "You," she said, "take care of her if I do leave."

The quiet young man nodded vigorously. "I love her. I want to have babies with her. Well, once we are sure that the changes are over and they can survive. No point in repopulating the Earth like they're always going on about unless we're pretty sure that the kids will make it."

Tara looked at him thoughtfully. He was not well-educated—almost no one was anymore—but he had good sense, and a healthy dose of intuition. And perhaps could see the Beings. If they'd ever come back. If they'd even existed. Were they products of the rain and mist? Fairies? Interdimensionals? Star Beings? Or a group hallucination born of hope?

"Wait!" A voice sounded clear and loud, inside her head, and outside her head. Leona lifted up her head, startled. The cat froze and crouched by Tara's side. Janus looked back and forth, his long dreads whipping beside his head in a growing wind.

Tara thought of the stories of Crop Circles, how on rare occasions someone witnessed one of the complex patterns being made, how lights and energy and some kind of wind all seemed to converge and then depart, leaving a pattern in the crops in their wake.

The three humans and cat all stared at the very center of the circle. A pattern that had not been there was etched delicately into the grass, three spirals in a triangle. Old Celtic, amongst other things. Also on the petroglyphs in New Mexico, and if she wasn't mistaken, sometimes found in southern Africa.

"What the f…" Janus started to say, and stopped himself.

Tara laughed. It was somehow endearing, after all they'd been through, that a young man would try to avoid swearing in front of an Elder.

"Yes, Janus, what the fuck?" she said evenly.

Georgie stalked around the pattern, sniffing, but not stepping on it. The grass was not as long as the wheat and barley had been in the days of Crop Circles, but just like in those, the blades were bent rather than broken or damaged.

"Gran, what does it mean? What did it used to mean?" asked Leona.

"So many things," she replied uncertainly. "The Triple Spiral stood for the Triple Goddess—the Virgin or Maiden, the Mother, and the Crone or Wise Woman. The three times, and birth, life, and death. The Buddhas of past, present, and future. Choices…"

Tara thought of Prophecy Rock on the Hopi Third Mesa. She had been taken to the sacred site by Grandfather Thomas, an old Medicine Man who had spoken at the UN, delivering the Hopi message of doom and hope to the

"Great House of Mica on the Eastern shore where the nations come together to solve world problems without war." Together they had offered tobacco and prayed that humanity would make the right choice, the good choice. But collective humanity hadn't, at least not soon enough.

"I don't know," said Tara, shaking her head in wonder. "Why that symbol, now? Do you suppose it has anything to do with the three Beings?"

Leona stared at the spirals in front of them, in the center of the circle. Tara could see the girl's features altering, almost dissolving, as she entered into a trance.

"Three will meet three, and a portal will be," Leona whispered. "The portal will lead, to wherever there's need, to stop the greed, so all will be freed."

Leona seized Janus' hand, then Tara's. All three joined hands, the gray cat in the center of their little circle purring loudly, in comfort, joy, and anticipation. They stayed like that till the sun set, then made their way to the Longhouse in silence and hunger.

Chapter
6

July, 2018

Findhorn, Scotland

Just before dawn, Tara tiptoed into the room she shared with a young American woman, Tiffany. Who, of course, woke up.

"Out with the fairies?" Tiffany asked mischievously.

"Sorry to wake you up." Really, the woman was young enough to be her daughter.

Tiffany stretched. "At least somebody's hooking up. That is so cool, especially at your age."

Tara sank down on her bed, pleasantly sore, a smile on her face in spite of herself.

"Yeah, it is pretty cool."

"Is it that handsome older dude?"

Tara threw a pillow at her roommate. "Go back to sleep!"

Xander wasn't in the kitchen for the lunch prep shift. He wasn't at lunch. He wasn't in Cullerne Garden as she took a long walk in the breezy afternoon. Nor in the nearby woods where they had had their midnight tryst.

Had she imagined the whole thing? Her body told her no. Her stomach had begun to knot up. Was she still in the same damned pattern she'd been in most of her life? Had she given herself, only to be immediately rejected?

She didn't even have his cell number. She couldn't even text him like the young people constantly text each other. Maybe that was a good thing. One less opportunity for misunderstanding.

She sat by the lotus pool, and began her deep breathing in preparation for meditation. Impermanence. Maybe it was meant to be a one-time exquisite encounter, not the beginning of something.

She pushed her thoughts aside and they pushed back. She remembered that she was supposed to cut through them, to dissolve them. That worked a bit better. For a nanosecond or two. She took another deep breath, and slowly slitted open her eyes, gazing into the water between the floating white water lilies.

A face floated in the reflection, above hers. She thought she was creating it, and attempted to let it dissolve, but it stayed. Finally she looked up, over her shoulder, to see Xander standing motionless behind her. Like a feather, he floated down next to her, his hands in prayer position, and sat cross-legged in meditation, his jeans-clad left knee touching her bare right knee.

She attempted to let go of her attachment, noticing the sensations in her body and heart and letting them course through her. She felt bliss in her secret chakra, felt the Kundalini rising, felt heat shimmering all through her body, light surrounding her and blending with Xander's light. She closed her eyes, simply letting it be. Their breaths were one, synchronized to perfection.

She didn't know how long it lasted, that sex without sex, union without conscious touch. Like the tide in Findhorn Bay, slowly the energy went out, and they were just two humans sitting in the grass by a lotus pond in the twilight.

"Sorry," he said softly.

"For what?"

"I was called away. Or didn't you notice?"

"I noticed."

"I was afraid you'd think…well, you know, the man makes love to the woman and then…Well, I'm not like that and I didn't want you to think that."

"No. I just…went about my day," she said breezily. "Came here to meditate."

"Did it work?"

She looked at him in surprise. "Yes, actually. I was okay. After a bit. I did…wonder."

He looked away, gazing at the white lilies. "I'm not very good at this. It's been a long time. Really since I first met Happiness."

"You haven't dated since she passed?"

"Dated. Bloody stupid word, dating."

"I agree. I just…well, you're a handsome man, spiritual, self-supporting."

"A real catch?"

"That's a good term."

"And a very busy man. After Happiness died, I threw myself into my work. Traveled even more. Joy was okay by then. She was almost out of university, and then went to India and met Dawa."

"I suppose you'll stay busy."

He cupped a hand under her chin and turned her face to his. "And I suppose you will as well."

"Well, we've both got our work, and it's part of our Dharma path."

"Tara."

"Yes?"

"We've got this time, these couple of days here."

"Yeah, I'm grateful. It's been so long."

"I know how to make a commitment."

"Clearly. You were married for years."

"And faithful. Don't doubt that for a moment."

"Oh, no, I don't. I just wonder…"

"If I'm ready to be close again?"

"Well, it crossed my mind."

"What about you?" he asked. "Oh woman of the world, dashing from conference to seminar to interview to assignment, with an occasional hiatus to attend Rinpoche's teachings. Are you ready to change your life?"

"God, I hadn't thought about it," she said truthfully. "All my life, it seems, I've been looking…I'm saying way too much way too soon, aren't I?"

He looked at her and brushed a strand of silver and black hair away from her face. "No, you're being very candid. Tara, this isn't a one-night stand. I've never done that in my life. It's not the way I was raised, and I'm just not capable of that."

"Me neither." She rolled her eyes and sighed. "I try to apply all my spiritual principles, to be non-attached. In theory, one can have non-attached passion, right?"

He laughed in delight. "In theory. You've described it beautifully."

She dared to look into his eyes, afraid of what she might see. She saw only love, the kind gaze of their Rinpoche, mixed with impish affection and the dark swirl of passion.

"Xander…you don't know my history."

"Is it so bad? Brothels? Nunneries? Serial online dating?"

She laughed. "None of above. I mean, I have had relationships, even lived with men. Well, for a few months, a couple of times. I've wanted commitment…oh shit, maybe I'm not supposed to say that at this stage."

"Yes, you are. You are supposed to say whatever is in your mind and heart. Or else what are we playing at?"

"Good point." She paused and took a breath. "Xander, I really don't know what's going on here. I'm trying to just be in the moment, do what you are supposed to do, let go, all that."

"Talk talk talk." He silenced further words with a kiss. "You'll find I'm rather different to anyone else you've ever met."

She made a soft sound of pleasure at the kiss, and lingered, feeling a lightning bolt of desire shoot down to her root chakra. "How so?"

"Just as you are. Two odd peas in a pod. Finally in the same pod. Let's not question it, let's just get on with it."

He took her shoulders and breathed a long, deep kiss that left her dizzy, soaring.

As she looked up into the soft white clouds streaking the blue sky, she thought she saw Rinpoche's face, for just a moment, winking.

She looked at Xander in the wake of their kiss. "Do you think Rinpoche...?"

His broad smile, so much like Rinpoche's, lit his face. "Wouldn't put it past him, dear Dakini."

"Thank you," she murmured, to Rinpoche, to her namesake Goddess, to Xander, to anyone who was listening.

Chapter
7

9 October, 2050

Stonehenge,
New Avalon

Two more days had passed, and nothing else dramatic, or even interesting, had happened.

Tara spent much time sitting in the circle, alternately weaving and dreaming, sometimes drifting off. She would meditate on the Triple Spiral, she would visualize, she would *will* something to happen, someone to appear. Nothing.

Georgie respectfully avoided actually touching the image in the grass, but said nothing.

"No feline wisdom?" she asked aloud.

The cat was silent. He stuck close to her except for feeding time and to answer the call of nature, alternately sleeping in her lap and sitting upright like an Egyptian cat statue as he stared with her at the pattern.

Leona, being young, had soon tired of the vigil. She and Janus would cast long, longing glances at each other, exchanging silent signals. Tara would pretend to ignore them, amused at how youth perennially forgot that the old had once been young. Leona would leave, and soon Janus would follow. They'd be gone for quite a while and return in a much better mood for another stint of meditating on the Spirals.

"Gran, what are we supposed to be doing?" Leona finally asked in frustration.

"If only I knew," said Tara, shrugging her shoulders. "It's strange though. I feel better since they appeared. Less tired. I didn't have too many aches and pains, but now they're *all* gone. I feel like I could walk to Avebury Encampment in a day."

"Should we go back, then?" asked Janus.

"Let's give it a day. Leona, what do you think?"

Leona looked startled, uncertain that her wise old Gran was actually asking her what she thought. She settled, looked inward for a moment.

"Fair enough. I guess if they come back, they can find us even if we leave. They followed me before."

"I don't know if they'll be back," said Tara, with a touch of sad curiosity. "I had hoped they'd come to help us. Finally. But maybe it was just a fluke, or a visit. Or maybe we just imagined it."

"No!"

Janus' voice, Leona's, and the cat-voice in her head, punctuated by a slap from Georgie, claws extended just enough to get her attention.

"Okay, okay. Let's just let it go. I'll sleep here in the Henge tonight. If nothing happens, we'll head back towards Avebury in the morning."

"I'm staying too," said Leona.

"Obviously I am as well," added Janus.

The fog closed in at midnight, and a fine mist began to fall on them. It was, Tara thought, rather like the old rains in the old days in the British Isles, the last years of the 20th century and into the 21st. Strange. Like so many other things, it reminded her of Xander.

It actually felt slightly cold, a nice change, so she pulled a reed blanket over her huddled body, making sure Georgie was covered too. He thanked her with a normal cat purr, no human words.

And then a bright light stunned her eyes. The cat's eyes contracted to tiny slits, and he shut his eyes, burying his face in the folds of Tara's skirt.

When her vision cleared, she saw the three ghostly figures she had seen before, shining a bluish-white. Leona and Janus clung to each other, but their energy was anticipatory rather than fearful.

The tall, Tibetan-looking man, the slim woman, and a stouter man whose skin glowed a darker blue than the others, stood on the Triple Spiral, one on each spiral.

Tara, Leona, and Janus all stood up and held out their hands, palms upward, in a gesture of welcome. Georgie drew himself up to his full height, then sat up on his hind legs to see better.

As one, the three figures stepped off the Triple Spiral.

"It worked!" said the tall man jubilantly. The three figures hugged each other, ignoring the humans and feline waiting in the stone circle. As Tara watched, they stopped glowing and became more…ordinary.

The tall, balding man was of uncertain age, but fit body. His features looked Tibetan, mixed with something else, and his black eyes shined. The slim woman was of a Nordic type, her light blond hair in a thick braid that hung down her right side, her blue eyes shining like stars. The other man settled into the figure of a stout, sturdy man of African descent, with kind brown eyes.

Finally the three finished congratulating each other and turned to Tara, Leona, Janus, and Georgie.

"I feel like I should have some kind of momentous words," the tall man began. "But to tell you the truth, I'm at a loss for words."

"You speak English," said Tara.

"After a fashion. We still do, in the future. It's changed of course, evolved, but I can match language to you. It's pretty exciting."

"Are you…" She stopped, uncertain. "Are you the ones who have been sent to help us? I think it might be too late." There was a hint of resentment in her voice.

"Help? Yes. Sent? It depends what you mean by sent."

"The Prophecies, all over the world, they talked of spiritual beings, or Star Beings of great knowledge who could come to help humanity in its most crucial hour."

The tall man appeared to muse for a moment. "Well, I don't know if we are the fulfillment of prophecies or not. But we're here to help. Not only you, but ourselves."

"How's that?"

"Please allow me to introduce myself, and the others. Do you shake hands in this time period?"

"Sure," said Tara, extending her hand.

"I am Yeshi," he said. As his warm hand enfolded hers, she felt a jolt, a recognition of she knew not what, perhaps just a profoundly loving intention.

"My female companion is Sitara, and my male companion is Jonah."

"Jonah?" Tara couldn't help but ask. It was such an unusual name.

"Got swallowed by a whale on Sirius once, so it seemed appropriate." He had a rich baritone voice, reminiscent of the old-time actor James Earl Jones.

"Pleased to meet you," said Sitara softly. She had a frank, welcoming look in her eyes. For a moment, Tara wondered what her relationship was to Yeshi, which seemed silly to wonder about under the circumstances.

"You are the Elder here?" asked Sitara gently.

"I'm probably the oldest person around here. That I know of," said Tara.

"I think we're supposed to say something like 'Take me to your leader,'" quipped Yeshi.

"Well I'm certainly not regarded as a leader. Respected, I guess, but not a leader. Oh, my name is Tara. This young one here is my great-granddaughter, by marriage, but truly a daughter of my heart, Leona."

"And I am Janus, named after the god of time." The young man stepped forward, uncharacteristically brave, perhaps protective of Leona, Tara thought, though she didn't feel a threat from any of the visitors.

"So who is your leader?" asked Yeshi.

Tara pondered.

"We don't really have a leader, as such," said Janus. "Auntie Tara is the oldest, and definitely the wisest, person among us. Leona here is the best shaman. But there's this bloke, Seamus, he sees himself as the head of the Weather Menders and as some kind of Druid priest or something."

"Weather Menders…" said Yeshi. "So climate change is part of the problem that is bleeding through."

"That's why *our* Timeline has become unstable," said Sitara primly. "We've successfully reached the alternate universe, the Timeline where humanity collectively didn't make the right choices. Climate breakdown is only part of it. There was extreme inequality, war, plagues, racism, male domination…"

"We get it, Sitara," said Jonah. "We've studied the alternate Timelines too. That's why we're here."

"But they don't get it, do they?" she asked, gesturing at the other three. She turned to them. "Do you have any idea who we really are?"

Tara remained silent, troubled, unable to wrap her mind around what was happening or being said.

"You're from the future," said Leona. "So you are the answer to our prayers and prophecies."

"As you must be the answer to ours," said Yeshi.

"Time Travelers?" Tara asked. "Seriously? How can that even be possible?"

"How can it not?" asked Yeshi. "We're here. And for whatever reason, so are you."

"Strange Karma," said Tara, musing aloud.

"What?" asked Yeshi sharply.

"Karma," she said. "An old word, Sanskrit."

"And still relevant in our time."

"Which is…when?"

"Approximately 300 years in your future," said Sitara. "Provided that we restore our Timeline. The one you're in now has somehow bled through into ours, and if we don't fix yours, then we, and our whole civilization of humans and other beings originating in the eco-system here on Earth, disappear. You've doubtless heard of the Sixth Extinction? We won't come into existence. The Timeline dissolves."

"Oh dear," sighed Tara. "I must be dreaming. I must be in the Bardo."

"You should be so lucky," chuckled Jonah. "No, baby, you are alive in the year…What year is it anyway?"

"2050," said Tara.

Jonah let out a soft whistle. "Okay, 2050 it is. Anyway, you're obviously who we were meant to find. We're not quite sure of the next step. All we know is that we have to go back to a certain time, which Sitara here is going to calculate for us, maybe more than one certain time, a Pivot Point they call it. It's some kind of mathematical thing that's her specialty, but it means that we go back to the Pivot Point, change a certain thing, and all is hunky-dory again. Humanity survives, all the animals and plants survive, and Earth goes on to join the brother and sisterhood of galaxies."

Tara frowned in concentration, trying to take it all in. "I've heard of theories like that," she said. "In the old days. When we had books, and computers, and Internet. You know we don't have anything like that now?"

"We don't quite have our formula down for when we arrive," said Yeshi apologetically. "So we weren't able to study up on all the details of your current customs and circumstances, though we do have a general idea. Time travel is not an exact science, though getting very close. Sitara is refining it at every moment."

"Is she AI?" asked Janus.

Sitara looked offended. "Artificial Intelligence? No," she said a trifle icily. "We didn't need to go that route. In our Timeline humans themselves developed sufficiently intellectually, and spiritually as well."

"Sorry," said Janus. "It was just something I remembered from the stories in the old books that we find here and there. Didn't mean to offend. Actually I'm glad you're not AI."

Leona elbowed him sharply in the ribs and he stopped talking.

"We can trust them," Leona announced.

"I feel it too," said Tara, "in my old heart in this old body."

"What next?" asked Yeshi. "Seriously, we should introduce ourselves to someone in a leadership position."

"That's kind of hard," said Tara. "I guess you don't know how our society is organized. Maybe you know some general things, I don't know how, but I assume you don't have books with the history of this particular Timeline. Things didn't work out so well in this Timeline, at least not so far. The Star Beings didn't come to help, the climate broke down, there were Three Plagues. We are what's left here, other than the Elite in the City."

"The ones with the rockets?" asked Yeshi. "We had to send one back. It wasn't helping our mission. But we were able to test mental repelling power, a form of telekinesis. Sitara has it strongly, and it worked."

"Thank you," Sitara said, smiling gently.

"I was an anthropologist by training," said Tara. "I traveled the world and saw it all break down, gradually at first, then more quickly. Finally it was exponential and couldn't be stopped." She hesitated. "We don't know what is happening in other parts of the planet. There is no communication anymore, unless the Elite have it. I don't know what happened to my family in North America. We don't know if anyone survived on other continents."

"Can you find out for Gran?" asked Leona. "Can you travel in space as well as time?"

"There are parameters we can set," said Sitara, not without compassion. "Maybe we can help. But we have a primary mission."

"Which is?" asked Tara.

"Restore your Timeline to harmony, so that it blends with ours," said Yeshi. "I'm optimistic that we can do it. Not everyone is. All we have to do is figure out the Pivot Point, or maybe two or even three, where it all went wrong, and go back in time to undo it. Then humanity survives, animals, plants, the whole eco-system survives."

"And what about us?" asked Tara.

"It depends on when the Pivot Points are, or were. If they were in the past, then you are still alive, but in much happier circumstances, and you probably won't remember this alternate reality you're living now. If they are in the future…well I suppose you live out your lives and then are reborn in the future. If we can fix it. But I'm sure we can."

"You don't sound very certain," said Leona.

Yeshi put his hand on the young woman's shoulder, soberly. "I hope we're right."

"Three meet three…" she said softly, her gaze shifting inwards. "There's a good chance."

"Come, eat," said Tara. "You do eat?"

"You bet," said Jonah. "All of us have great appetites. Our bodies are here and now. We just have to assess a few things about your lifestyle at this time period and this space. Yeshi here, he's trained as an anthropologist, just like you. So you've already got something in common. For example, we've got to match not only language, but clothing and accessories."

As Tara watched, Yeshi raised a hand and the three visitors transformed. Their starship-like suits wavered and became the loose, worn homespun cotton clothes that Tara, Leona, and Janus wore.

Janus' eyes got big. "Can I learn how to do that?"

"Later," said Yeshi. "First, we eat. We require nourishment."

"It's adequate," said Tara. "Not delicious. Don't expect much."

"Nourishment is all we require at present. Which way do we leave the circle?"

Tara gestured towards the eastern gate, and picked up Georgie, who scrambled onto to her shoulder.

Yeshi gestured to her to lead the way, touched the cat gently under the chin, and said, "Yes, little one, we do have cats in our Timeline. You have a part to play as well, just as in ancient Egypt."

Chapter
8

August, 2018

Edinburgh, Scotland

"Do you think she'll like me?" asked Tara nervously as Xander maneuvered his Prius into a tiny parking space in front of his mother's lovely Georgian home in a quiet, upscale neighborhood of Edinburgh.

"She'll love you. How could she not?"

"I could think of lots of reasons." Tara was uncharacteristically nervous, having found out that a part of Xander's somewhat unusual good looks came from the Afghan relatives on his mother's side of the family. How had a Scottish man married an Afghan woman back in the 50's? Xander had merely smiled and told her that no one could tell the story as well as his mother.

Xander let himself in, and called up the stairs. "*Madar Jaan!*"

"*Bal-e, bia, bia!*"

"We still speak Dari," he explained to Tara. "I never could quite get used to calling her Mum."

A stately woman with silvery hair in a bun, wearing a long, elegant black skirt and a pale aqua silk blouse greeted them at the top of the stairs. As Tara held out her hand, Bibi Amina dispensed with formality and put her hands on the younger woman's shoulders, kissing her three times on alternate cheeks.

"*Salaam aleikum*," Tara murmured. "*Chetour asti? Khoob asti?*"

"*Farsi mefahmi!*" said Bibi Amina. "My son did not tell me you spoke Farsi."

"I hadn't mentioned it. I'm out of practice," said Tara. "I learned a bit when I was working on an aid project in Kabul, back in the early 2000's."

Xander grinned, proud to have discovered something else about his new love.

Bibi Amina ushered them into her small but elegantly appointed front room. A bay window gave out onto the bright summer day. The older woman moved with grace and confidence. Tara hadn't asked Xander his mother's age, or many details of the story of his parents' meeting. She quickly calculated. If Xander was born in 1959, he's now 59 and so his mother must be, well at least 78, if she had married Xander's dad right out of high school. And she hardly looked much older than Tara herself.

Bibi Amina poured them delicately-scented Afghan tea. Cardamom wafted through the room. She proffered a plate of sugared almonds.

"*Noql*," she said. All the way from Afghanistan."

"I remember it well," said Tara. "*Ta shakor.*"

"Ach, it's getting hard to get now." Bibi Amina's accent floated somewhere between cultured British, Scottish, and a hint of Afghan. "Like so many things."

Xander sipped at his tea, watching his mother with great affection.

"So, he has never brought a woman to me, not since he first met Happiness. You must be special."

Tara burnt her lips on her tea, and quickly put the cup down. "He is special. You must be proud of him."

"Indeed," said Bibi Amina. "Indeed. I was only blessed with one child, and he is a fine one, much like his father."

Tara's gaze drifted around the room. A silver-framed, faded color photograph showed a tall Scotsman in a kilt standing beside a small, dark-haired, exotic woman dressed like an Eastern princess. In other photos, as the couple aged, they wore ordinary Western dress, changing with the decades from Carnaby Street to Hippy Chic to big 80's hair. The anthropologist in Tara was incredibly curious as to how the two had met. The woman-in-a-new-relationship part of her held her tongue, treading carefully, wanting so much to be liked without self-compromise.

"Xander tells me you met at the Dharma center," said Bibi Amina.

"Yes, the first time," said Tara. There were a few Buddhas around the room, and one exquisite *thanka* painting of White Tara, but Tara didn't want to make assumptions about Bibi Amina's spiritual beliefs.

"Mother goes to teachings upon occasion," said Xander. "Especially when Rinpoche is there. Perhaps you might have seen each other."

Tara did vaguely recall a handsome older woman sitting at the back, on a chair. It was unusual for an Afghan-born woman to explore other spiritual traditions, but something told Tara that Bibi Amina, like her son, was no ordinary anything.

"I come from a Sufi lineage," said Bibi Amina. "I don't have the same, oh I suppose one could call it hang-ups, that many people have about sticking to the religion of one's birth. I am a Muslim, and also a Christian, a Buddhist, a Hindu, a Jew, a Jain. I've loved and studied them all. I've been very fortunate in my life."

"Mother came from a branch of the royal family," said Xander.

"Ach, nothing to be proud of anymore. It was just Karma, but it led me to your father, so for that I am grateful."

"How did you meet?" asked Tara.

Xander settled back in his chair, no doubt having heard the story a multitude of times.

Bibi Amina looked for a moment like a young girl in love. Her hazel eyes drifted up and to the right, remembering.

"It was the late 1950's, a period of liberalization. We didn't have to even wear headscarves, let alone a stifling and awkward *chadari*, the ones like a big tent, unless we were out in the countryside. My father was very forward-thinking. My mother had died young, but she had asked him to make sure all of her daughters were educated, and he had promised that on her deathbed.

"All my life I had wanted to be a doctor. I'm not even sure where I got the idea. Maybe from films? And some of my father's friends were doctors. Most of them were only interested in high status, serving the upper class. But one, Dr. Abdullah, was very passionate about helping the poor, and used to go out into the countryside a lot. He always came back with so many stories, both harrowing and inspiring."

Bibi Amina leaned towards Tara as she continued. "It never occurred to me that women couldn't be doctors, so I studied all my subjects really hard. Dari of course, poetry, but also French, English, science, math, biology. I was one of only five women students admitted to the Medical Faculty at Kabul University."

Tara watched Bibi Amina in rapt attention, her tea growing cold.

"One day, there was a *tamasha*, a big commotion, and a party of *farangi* doctors, foreigners, walked into the hospital. The tallest was a Scotsman, Dr. Alexander MacFarlane. It was my turn to present a case. I was so nervous. There was a translator there, but I chose to speak in English, I don't know why.

"The whole time I was presenting, that Dr. MacFarlane had his blue eyes on me."

"So it was love at first sight?" asked Tara.

"Oh, nothing so simple as that. I was a very serious young woman. I had made it clear to my father that I was not interested in an arranged marriage, but I had no thoughts of a love match either, let alone with a foreigner. It just wasn't done in those days."

Tara sat on the edge of her chair, waiting for the rest of the story.

Bibi Amina waved a hand. "Oh, it was nothing so dramatic as eloping or escaping the country. Dr. MacFarlane was posted there for a time with the British Foreign Service. We moved in the same circles, and over time we came to know each other. It was the 1950's and it was Afghanistan, so as you can imagine it was very chaste.

"In the end it was not a big drama. Alex came to my father, probably the only time in his life he was terrified of anything, and asked for my hand. He promised to convert to Islam, and he did, in his fashion. As I said, we are from a Sufi lineage, and educated, so we were not as strict as most others.

"We had a quiet wedding, by Afghan standards. A great celebration, but really only immediate family. Conveniently, Alex received a posting in

Kenya right around the time of our marriage, and so off we went. That's where Xander was born."

"Did you work as a physician?"

"Oh yes, mostly with the Asian women there at first, the Indians and the newly minted Pakistanis. Muslims, Hindus, Christians, Sikhs. Later, the women of the Kenyan tribes as well. Kikuyu, Luo, Masai. They all loved having a woman doctor."

"And I loved growing up in Kenya," said Xander. "It was easier there, being a mixture. And I loved when we would go out into the Bush. I'd tag along helping Mother and Dad, or thinking I was helping. I wanted to do what they did, to help people, to make them well and teach them how to have healthier habits."

"And you still do," said Tara. "How many months a year are you working overseas?"

"It varies. But we'll make it work."

Bibi Amina looked at Tara appraisingly. Tara felt a warm flush rising to the roots of her hair. What was he really saying? She looked at this man she had already come to love. "Yes, we will."

They had a lot of figuring out to do. She still had a mother and a sister in New Mexico, and her sister had a daughter and grandchildren. She had a house in Albuquerque, and a housesitter taking care of two cats and a lot of plants.

She had no idea how they were going to figure out this long distance thing. They'd talked about volunteering together for assignments abroad with NGOs, but this was so new they hadn't gotten very far with making plans. And certainly no one had mentioned rings or engagements or marriage.

Bibi Amina looked pleased. A slow smile played around her lips. "In Afghanistan we would say, '*Naseeb, qismet*—fate, destiny.' I've somehow gotten to be an old woman, though I still work part-time mind you. There's such a shortage of doctors nowadays in the NHS.

"And look at this crazy mixture of a family of descendants I've got— Afghan, Scottish, Zulu, and now Tibetan mixed in. Tara *Jaan*, you will fit right in."

"I hope so."

"It's been a long time since Happiness died," Bibi Amina said, sighing. "And we all loved her so much. I've worried about my son, working so hard. I'm happy that he has found someone to share his life."

Tara felt momentarily dizzy. Something she'd wanted all her life was actually happening, faster than she could think or react. So she just took a breath and flowed with it.

"That went well," said Xander as he held the car door open for her.

"You think she likes me?"

"She practically called you daughter-in-law and asked when we were setting a date."

Tara got into the car and watched him go round to the driver's side. "Are we?" she asked when he got in. "I don't mean to be too forward."

He laughed as he started the car. "You're not. I just need to catch up."

As the car started, the radio came on, a news bulletin from the BBC. "Worldwide, shares have fallen drastically, in the biggest one-day slide since 2008. Governments are going into emergency meetings, and the public are being urged not to panic and precipitously attempt to withdraw funds."

Xander reached out a hand to Tara, and drew her hand up to his cheek. He sighed. "It was inevitable, wasn't it? Just a matter of when." He kissed her hand. "Well, there will always be work for doctors, I suppose."

"Not necessarily for anthropologists."

He eased the car forward out of the parking space. "Tara, we are now in this together. Whatever it is, it's begun."

Chapter
9

Night of 9 October, 2050

Stonehenge,
New Avalon

Tara marveled at how the three visitors all curled up on sleeping mats and were instantly asleep, just like Georgie.

Did time travel make one tired? Or were they just exceptionally adaptable? Was that why they were chosen for the "mission?" Or had they volunteered? Had there perhaps been a competition? An essay contest? "Tell us why you think you are uniquely suited to travel 300 years into the past to try to restore the Timeline and save the planet's eco-system from total destruction."

Leona and Janus had of course taken sleeping mats and disappeared into the misty night.

That left Tara awake alone, tossing and turning. The restlessness wasn't physical. She didn't have aches and pains. The bit of backache she had had, and the sore shoulders, probably from the cat riding on them, were all mysteriously gone.

The cat opened one eye to check on her and then settled back down to a long sleep. She was on her own.

She worried, as she hadn't in years. She was excited, hopeful, as she hadn't been in years.

The disasters and losses had just kept coming and coming. Family members, friends, weather disasters, extinctions, change more rapid and permanent than anyone had ever dreamed or feared. Thankfully, Xander had been among the last. Having survived the first two plagues, he had finally succumbed to the Third Plague, only nine years ago. Mercifully it had been the Sleeping Plague, the one that killed quickly, and without much suffering. He had drifted away in her arms at the ripe age of 82. His faculties had been intact, if not his optimism, and he had continued working till the day he fell ill.

Tara still missed him terribly, truth be told. She had done the Tibetan Buddhist *Phowa* for him, the Transference of Consciousness, as she'd been trained to do so long ago by Rinpoche, and felt certain that Xander's spirit had immediately passed into *Dewachen*, the Pure Land of Great Bliss, where he would complete his Enlightenment process. She smiled in spite of her sadness. She was pretty sure he was already quite far along on the Bodhisattva journey and would return as a helper to others, a world server. She only hoped she could catch up.

She sat up, leaning against a lodge pole to keep her spine straight. A sleepless night was always a particularly good time to meditate.

Tara cleared her mind. She'd been meditating for over 50 years and had been taught well. And she still struggled from time to time.

But tonight was not one of those times. Tonight she slipped into Samadhi, into the gap between thoughts. The memories of Xander dissolved, the precarious possibilities of the mission of the Time Travelers dissolved, all dissolved into light, into compassion.

When she finished her meditation and made a dedication wishing for the happiness of all sentient beings, she slipped easily into a dream that was more than a dream.

Tara was back in Alaska, much younger, in a fish camp not far from Barrow. She was taking notes in the long, light summer night. The tent flap moved. "Hi, Emmy," *she started to greet her Inupiat shaman friend.*

But it wasn't Emmy. A white snout, black nose, bright black eyes poked into the tent. Her heart stopped. Polar bears were extremely dangerous, especially these days, with the sea ice melting so quickly and so many of them starving because they couldn't hunt seals from the ice floes anymore.

A voice in her head. "Help us."

"I'm trying." *She spoke silently, mind-talk.*

"Are many humans trying?" *Sadness. There would be tears in a human.*

"I don't know. The ones I know care."

"My children don't have enough to eat. And *we* don't have so many children like humans have, on and on."

"Can I give you something?"

"It would not be enough. But I'll take it. I promise I won't eat you. You are not my natural prey, and I don't want to hurt you. Besides, you care."

Tara reached over to the portable propane freezer full of fish ready to be smoked. Emmy would not be happy, after all her hard work. But she had promised the bear. She pulled out a package of fish and handed it to the bear, who took it hungrily in her mouth.

"Remember to remove the plastic," *Tara thought.* "It might hurt you or your cubs."

"Thank you," *the bear whispered, then departed swiftly into the midnight sun.*

The scene shifted. She floated above the Arctic ice cap, up in space. The ice cap was growing, the Earth was turning. She could see its movement, and watched with fascination. Purple, green, and gold flames danced in a circle above the pole, like an enlightened master's crown chakra.

Floating, flying gracefully closer, she saw the white bears all along the ice shelf, strong, healthy. She saw walrus, whales, snowy owls, Arctic foxes, wolves and ptarmigan. Herds of caribou roamed the tundra a little bit south. The lights of the giant oil facilities at Prudhoe Bay were nowhere to be seen. The flames that usually lit the night sky had gone out. Yet human habitations, small and large, softly glowed.

Tara heard music, singing, instruments. Was it angels? she wondered. Dakinis, Dakas, deities?

Human laughter. Joy. She flew around the globe, saw and heard this soft gentleness. Murmured prayers. Quiet. The guns and bombs to which humans had become accustomed had gone silent. Rivers flowed, rain poured down gently, oceans moved ceaselessly, teeming with life. Birds flew in vast migrations, landing in lush wetlands. Small gardens had replaced the vast tracts of agri-business.

The Earth seemed happy. Tara felt happy. She knew that Xander wasn't here, wasn't with her, wasn't in incarnation. And she felt his presence in the Oneness.

She gradually circled down to Earth, like a feather, and rejoined her now sleeping body, curled up next to a gray cat, three Time Travelers, and a young couple in love.

Chapter
10

August, 2018

Edinburgh, Scotland

The news of the financial Crash was unsettling, but no one quite knew what it meant. CNN, SkyNews, and the BBC speculated endlessly. There would be a worldwide depression. Food would not get to market. It was a last ditch attempt by the fossil fuel companies, or the Arabs, or the Russians, or China, or the Iranians, to manipulate the economy. There would be terrorism. There would be civil unrest.

Tara and Xander didn't listen to most of it. As if by unspoken agreement, they stopped checking the Internet. They preferred to get the news a day old, in a morning newspaper, so they could digest it in bits over tea and granola.

"Should I keep the ticket I have and go back to New Mexico next week?" she asked one morning.

He looked up, peering over a pair of reading glasses. "The planes are still flying."

"You don't think I might get stuck over there? Or you stuck here?"

He breathed deeply. "We have to trust."

"Trust doesn't guarantee that bad things won't happen to good people. I'm scared, Xander."

He put down the newspaper and took her in his arms. "Me too."

"I don't want to leave you. But I've got to see my mother and sister and make sure they are all okay. And my cats."

He smiled and smoothed her hair. "Especially the cats," he teased. "The humans can take care of themselves."

"They're family," she protested. "We have a Karmic agreement."

"Bring them here, then. I've always loved cats, all animals really. Bring your whole family here."

She looked at him in exasperation. "You don't know them. They're not about to leave New Mexico. Besides, with what money? I had retirement savings, but with the Crash, and the low interest rates…"

"We have some family money. Well, we did. I suppose I should look into it."

"Xander, we've got some hard decisions to make really quickly."

He stood up resolutely. "I think we'd best get married as soon as possible."

The words she'd always wanted to hear from the right man. "Aren't people supposed to wait a year, a whole cycle of seasons?"

"Did your parents?"

"No. They were married in two months."

"Circumstances change what is considered wise. We don't know where this financial collapse is going. They might close borders. You'll have a far better chance of getting back here, or me coming over there, if we're married."

"That's not quite the way I'd imagined it."

He smiled at her, his eyes sparkling, and got down on one knee. "Let go of your schoolgirl fantasies, my Dakini. No white dress in a church, no bridesmaids in ugly dresses, no ostentatious reception with people you don't really much like."

"You always seem to be able to make me laugh."

"Well then, that's a good start. What else?"

"Okay, I give up all the fantasies. What do we do next?"

"Blood tests, paperwork, that sort of thing. We can probably download it from the Internet," Xander said.

"Are you sure you want to take a chance on marrying someone who is getting married for the first time at the age of almost 64?"

"Maybe you're right," he said solemnly. "What are your faults?"

"My faults? I thought you would have figured out a few of them by now. Well… I'm often told I think too much. I talk to myself aloud. I complain about corporations and stupid governments…"

"And when are you going to get to the faults?"

"I'm not a very good housekeeper," she said ruefully.

"So we'll have cat fur dust bunnies floating around?"

"I try. I just get busy."

"We'll manage. None of us know what is going to happen next, do we?"

"Uncertainty. We'd better get used to it….Xander, your knees must be getting sore. You've proved your point."

Still kneeling, he hugged her around the middle and rested his head in her lap, then looked up at her mischievously. "I will do one thing traditionally."

"What's that? I can't imagine."

He got up on one knee and pulled a small ring box out of the pocket of his dressing gown. He opened it to show her an elegant platinum and diamond ring that looked like it must have been made in the early part of the previous century.

"Xander?"

"Tara, will you marry me?"

"I think that's a foregone conclusion. But this must be a family heirloom."

"Yes. It was mother's mother's ring. My Afghan grandfather bought it on a trip to Europe in the 1920's. South African diamonds, long before blood diamonds, cut in Holland, and set in Italy."

"But this is a priceless heirloom…" Her face fell, uncertain again. "Did Happiness wear it?"

He shook his head impatiently. "No, and what of it if she had?"

"It's just…it would be strange to wear your wife's ring."

"Tara, Happiness is dead many years now. In *Dewachen*, I am certain. I thought of her constantly for many years. I'd be lying if I told you I don't think of her at least once every day. But she wanted me to be happy. When she was dying she told me to be open to marrying again. I never found the right woman. Till now. Till you. I'm certain. Are you?"

"Yes," she whispered. "It just feels right."

"I think Happiness had a hand in this, along with Rinpoche," he said thoughtfully. "I don't know what they can do over there, in Spirit, but I think she helped bring us together. So will you try it on?"

He slipped the ring onto her finger. It caught a little on her slightly enlarged knuckle, then slipped on, as if it belonged there. Its beauty was in its simplicity rather than ostentation. She watched the rays of morning sunlight coming in through the window play on the sparkling stones, casting rainbows around the room.

"It suits you," he said.

She looked at him, bemused. "I never thought I would have a diamond ring if I married."

"Why?"

"Well, mostly the blood diamond trade. But it just seemed so, I don't know, over the top."

"Well do you like it?"

"It's beautiful."

"The wedding ring matches. A simple platinum band, in a time when everyone else wanted gold. My grandfather saw the value in it. On the other side, the Scottish side, there were no heirlooms. My father was a farmer's son who went to university on scholarship and distinguished himself through intelligence and hard work. No diamonds on that side. My mother wore this ring at her wedding, and then she took it off. She said it was impractical for her, being a doctor and always needing to wash her hands."

"I like your mother."

"And you'll come to love her." He stood up. "Take a shower. We've got rather a lot to accomplish in the next few days. I've got to round up Mother, and Joy and the family, and some witnesses from the *sangha*."

Tara felt a shadow cross her face, and tried to hide it from this man who could see into her soul.

"What?" he asked.

She took a breath, repressing tears.

"I'll come as soon as I can to meet your mother and sister," he said gently, reading her mind. "Do they Skype? Maybe we can Skype the wedding."

Through her tears, she laughed. And that's the way it would always be between them.

Chapter
11

12 October, 2050

En route, Stonehenge to Avebury Encampment, New Avalon

The mugginess had set in again by the time Tara and her companions had nearly reached Avebury. The Encampment was as close to a capital city of as close to a government that things got these days, outside of the Elite. Who knew what hierarchy still existed there? There were rumors of elaborate flood-proof tunnels under Buckingham Palace and other former government buildings, and stories of dissenters either summarily executed or imprisoned in a modernized Tower of London, but it was impossible to know what was true and what was a storyteller's fancy embroidered by copious quantities of rice wine.

At least there was a slight chill to the air tonight, Tara thought with relief as she trudged behind Leona and Janus, her cat moving from shoulder to shoulder in rhythm to her tiredness.

The three Time Travelers spoke little during the journey, either to the inhabitants of the present Timeline, or to each other. They seemed a little nervous at first when they boarded a barge for the part of the journey that was simply less tedious on water than walking through the misty humidity.

Tara had negotiated their passage by trading some of the fine baskets she had woven. She was secretly proud of the minor reputation she had developed in the past few years as she had incorporated designs into her weaving from various cultures she had visited in her years of doing aid work. Most other weavers went for sheer functionality, but Tara's background as an anthropologist had conditioned her to crave both beauty and meaning.

The baskets were lightweight, and Janus never minded carrying them in his pack. Tara had an uncanny ability to assess the ethnic backgrounds of various people with whom she would trade, and pull out a basket in a design that would appeal to whatever genetic meme was most important to the person. Leona had caught on over the past three or four years, and was able to regale people with tantalizing phrases like, "Perfectly in harmony with your Masai ancestry," or "the heart of Bali is found in this ancient design."

Yeshi, Sitara, and Jonah had watched the haggling with some fascination, Sitara no doubt converting her observations instantly into mathematical formulae.

The "ferryman," as Tara had dubbed the old man—who was probably decades younger than she—in her mind, poled the barge quietly through the reeds of the overgrown canal. The old waterways were particularly difficult to keep free of weeds and reeds, and it was the duty of the young to clean them, much as it had been the province of the Acequia Societies in the New Mexico of her childhood, and even the days up until the droughts and plagues, to keep the irrigation ditches flowing freely.

"This is the nearest we get to Avebury," said the ferryman at last. He pulled off his turban and wiped sweat off his forehead and face, wringing out his long beard. "Thank you for the baskets." He looked curiously at the Time Travelers, but to all appearances they didn't look much different from the rest of the people who lived hereabouts. They'd matched their vibrations well to the people of the present day, thought Tara. And a day of slogging through mud before they reached the canal had made sure that their newly manifested clothing was as worn and dirty as everyone else's.

"Thank you," said Tara as she leapt into the springy grass at the side of the canal. "Blessings to you."

The ferryman watched curiously as they disappeared into the close fog.

Leona and Janus walked ahead, as they knew the paths well. Despite the continuing summer warmth, Tara felt energized and was easily able to keep up with their pace, even with the added burden of Georgie.

"Sorry I've gained a bit of weight," came the soft voice in her head.

"It's lucky I like your company," she answered in her mind. She felt extended claws reaching in momentary annoyance through the padding Janus had made for the cat's seat, and reached up to pet his head.

The fog began to lift a little as they got close to the ancient village of Avebury. Tara waved at people working in the rice paddies and fishing the canals. As the small procession passed, people momentarily stopped their work to gaze at the strangers. It had been a long time since strangers had come this way, and people couldn't help but view them with suspicion mixed with curiosity.

Leona and Janus stopped automatically at the gateway between two standing stones.

"What are we stopping for?" Yeshi asked Tara.

"I suppose you could call it tradition. An old way of honoring the ones who came before. We are entering the circle."

"Is there anything special we need to do? To fit in?"

Tara was tempted, for some reason, to tease her new friends and tell them they had to raise their hands and twirl three times. "No. Just pause. Honor the ancestors."

"How do we look?" asked Jonah. "Can we pass?"

"Well look at the three of us," said Tara. "There's quite the ethnic mixture amongst the survivors, so you'll fit right in. Some say that that's why some of us survived, that the genes of the mixed people were generally stronger than those whose ancestors had stayed in one place. I don't know."

"Come on," said Leona urgently. "I can feel Seamus waiting. Obviously the stories of strangers have already reached him."

Many eyes were upon the travelers as they entered the Longhouse. The day had begun to dim, the light fading as the sun set behind a bank of clouds. The rank scent of fish oil lamps enfolded them as they entered the Longhouse.

As the elder, Tara entered first. Seamus sat at the end of a long wooden table, a clay mug of, no doubt, rice wine before him. His stick of authority, the branch with the CD's and DVD discs tied to it, stood behind him. The rainbow colors of the discs glinted softly in the firelight.

"What's this?" he bellowed. "Visitors? We haven't had visitors for… months, maybe years. You don't bring plague, do you?"

Tara felt Sitara bristle. Yeshi put a gentle hand on Sitara's shoulder.

"Travelers," said Tara carefully.

"From where?" Seamus asked suspiciously. "Across the sea? Or are you spies from the City?"

"From across the sea," Tara said quickly. "You know Leona would recognize spies instantly, and she can read their hearts."

Seamus narrowed his slightly bloodshot eyes, and looked at the young woman. "What do you read?"

"Their hearts are pure," said Leona. "They are here to help."

"Help? What makes them think we need help?"

Tara looked around and sighed. Seamus was middle-aged, didn't remember all that much of the times before the devastations. "It's always good to accept offers of help, don't you agree, Seamus?" she asked sweetly. "Don't we always welcome help, from our fellows and from strangers?"

"Yes, yes, of course. We just haven't seen strangers in such a long time. I've forgotten my manners." He pushed a clay pitcher of rice wine towards them. "Here, grab a cup and help yourselves. Welcome."

Yeshi reached out for a mug. Tara noticed fleetingly that Sitara suddenly seemed to age before her eyes, her white-blond braid darkening to a dirty blond streaked with gray, her face lined and plain.

"France, you come from France, from the mainland?" asked Seamus. "It's not so far, but no one's come that way for quite a time now. So, *bien venew*," he said heartily, stumbling over the pronunciation. No one corrected him, least of all the Time Travelers.

"Let me introduce everyone to you, Seamus," said Tara. "This is Seamus, Chief of the Weather Menders." She tried not to let her tongue freeze with distaste at having to introduce this incompetent man in that way. "He says he is the descendant of the Druids," she added, envisioning Druids turning over in their graves.

"This gentleman is Mr. Yeshi," Tara said. "And this lady is Sitara, and this is Jonah."

One by one, the travelers held out their hands to Seamus, smiling politely. Jonah had a particularly firm grip and tried to be friendly, flashing a smile Tara thought was slightly goofy.

"Well, how do you think you can help us?" asked Seamus. "You all look strong enough. We can use some extra hands in the paddies, and it's nearly time for threshing. We don't have horses anymore, so strong humans are helpful. Or maybe you're good at fishery, coming from over there in France."

"I do have some facility with fishing," said Jonah. "I come from an aquatic area."

"Quatic?" asked Seamus.

Tara remembered the reference to having been swallowed by a whale on Sirius. She'd have to ask Jonah about that at some point soon. At least there'd be a good tale in it if nothing else.

"Water planet…uh, an area with lots of rivers, and oceans."

"We're not far from the edge of the sea anymore," said Seamus. "Gets closer every year it seems. But we should be fine here for a time. Kids," he said, turning to Leona and Janus, "bring some of the special stock of smoked fish for our guests. And some of the greens. We'll have a feast."

Yeshi was quiet throughout the meal. The copious quantity of rice wine he consumed seemed to have no effect on him whatsoever. Sitara merely observed. Tara, who sat next to Sitara, was certain that the strong scent of alcohol was being removed from Sitara's cup. In deference to Tara being the oldest person anyone knew, everyone knew she didn't drink wine. Sitara caught Tara looking at her cup and, with a slight smile, offered it to her to taste. It tasted like the sweetest, most refreshing water Tara had ever tasted, reminding her of the stream that flowed from the Blue Lake into Taos Pueblo.

Jonah, by contrast, seemed to be as drunk as Seamus and his buddies, a motley crew of young to middle-aged men and a few women. Tara could hardly blame people for getting drunk. Life wasn't exactly easy, and there'd been so much loss. As long as the necessary work for survival got done, what did it really matter if it got done a little more slowly than it could have? There were times she really wished she drank, that she could temporarily give in to oblivion as most others seemed to, but her body simply had no desire for alcohol or its effects.

Jonah was regaling Seamus with stories. Of France, and fishing. Tara marveled, wondering how Jonah could possibly have gotten the information. Had they studied a variety of possible Timelines before they transported here? Or was he just making it up?

When Seamus began to sink into a slumber, Tara remembered the old expression of "drinking someone under the table." He slumped in his big wooden chair, and would have fallen to the ground if Janus, aided by Leona, hadn't half-coaxed and half-manhandled him to his sleeping alcove.

Tara gestured to her friends to follow her to her hut on the edge of the village. Everyone else was drifting off to their own huts, no longer all that interested in the "Frenchmen." Jonah, who had seemed as drunk as anyone else, was suddenly and utterly alert, like a wild animal. As Tara saw Leona and Janus sidle off in the direction of the Young Huts, she gestured at them fiercely to come back.

Tara was glad that her tiny hut, which was going to house three others instead of just her and Georgie, was isolated, right at the edge of the Encampment, in the very shadow of one of the great stones.

"Fantastic!" Sitara said softly, sitting down on a mat stuffed with soft cotton and resuming her former shape as a young athletic blonde.

"What?" asked Tara.

"The mathematical vibrations of these stones! I can see how they were placed here."

"Really?" No one had ever figured it out, though there were speculations ranging from the mechanical to the metaphysical.

"So beautiful, so perfect. The people just matched their vibration to the stones and then sang them here."

Leona suddenly began a low growling sound in her throat, that proceeded from nearly subsonic to supersonic in seconds. Georgie's ears turned every which way. They looked out the open door of Tara's hut to see the great stone glowing with blue light, and seeming to lose substance.

Tara was frightened, about to cry, "That's enough!" when Leona stopped. The light faded, the night grew silent.

Sitara beamed at Leona in satisfaction. "Excellent. That may come in useful in our travels."

"Did anyone else hear?" asked Tara. "We don't want to draw too much attention."

Yeshi laughed. "I don't think we could possibly help drawing attention. We have to make it work in our favor."

"So when is the next stage of this…mission?" asked Tara. "Shouldn't we get on with it if every passing day your Timeline is decaying?"

"Yes, it is urgent," said Sitara. "But we have to gather the necessary data on many levels. This is also a portal to the past, and from it I can get information to help me calculate the Pivot Point, or Points. If we tried to leave too soon, not knowing our task for certain, well, it could be disastrous."

"Disastrous?"

Yeshi cleared his throat. "It's very delicate. If we miss the Pivot Point, or if we know when the Pivot Point is but we go to the wrong geographical area, or we miss the coordinates and end up in the right place at the wrong time, then not only would our mission fail, but…"

He sighed. "In a worst case scenario we could hasten the destruction of the biosphere. It could already be dead in this Timeline, in 2050, let alone in our own Timeline 300 years from now. So you understand why we have to move carefully, why each of our talents, and yours, are needed."

Tara looked at each of them, at the two young faces before her, and finally at the little gray cat looking up at her with enormous green eyes. "Right. What next?"

Yeshi took her hands gently in his, and smiled, reminding her of her beloved Rinpoche of long ago. He squeezed her hands. "Sleep. We will all sleep, even Sitara. Things happen in sleep, journeys happen, knowledge grows."

Tara felt her eyelids grow heavy. It felt natural to curl up, just like Georgie, on her sleeping mat. To the rhythmic purring of the cat and the soft breathing of her companions, she watched Yeshi's eyelids flutter in REM sleep, wondering.

Chapter
12

1 September, 2018

Edinburgh, Scotland

Tara watched Xander sleep as the gentle rays of a misty dawn shined golden through the east-facing window of his bedroom. *Their* bedroom, she reminded herself. About to be made official later today.

His lips puffed in a soft purr on the exhalations, and she smiled at the thought of her cats. His eyes moved beneath the lids in REM sleep, then popped open, alert and joyous as he took in the form of his beloved propped on one elbow, gazing lovingly at him.

"Good morning," she said.

"Good morning. A particularly good morning. Tara," he said softly, "I am so very happy that I am going to be married to you for the rest of my life."

He caressed her long hair, with its silver strands shining golden in the dawn.

"Me too," she said. "It's a miracle in my life."

"In both our lives."

"It's early," she said. "Too early to get up. The ceremony isn't till noon, and I think all the arrangements are in place."

"Well then," he said, leaning over to kiss her as she rolled over on her back. "How shall we pass the time?"

They arrived at the Registry Office early. Xander wore his clan MacFarlane tartan, the deep red plaid kilt she had seen him wear at the dance in Findhorn. Tara had chosen a simple dress of turquoise silk. Her dress was complemented by an eye-catching necklace and earring set, turquoise and sugilite set in silver, combining traditional Native American motifs with modern design.

Bibi Amina arrived a few minutes later with Joy and her family, all dressed with a touch of their primary ethnicity in their clothing. Two Scottish *sangha* members, Kate and Ian, a middle-aged couple who were longtime friends of Xander's and new friends of Tara's, were there as witnesses.

With Afghan, African, and Tibetan chic, they were easily the most colorful people in the crowd. A young, nervous Scottish couple looked to be barely out of their teens. Other couples were in their 30's and 40's, and some had their children with them. An Indian man quietly held the hand of a Scottish woman, gazing at her with an adoring heart. They had to be at least in their 70's, thought Tara with a fluttering heart. At least we aren't the oldest!

Xander touched her earring, then quickly caressed her left ear.

"Nervous?" he asked.

"Yes and no," she whispered. "Part of me thinks I must be crazy. And the other part just knows I am, and it's fine."

He laughed heartily, and everyone turned to look at him.

"Da's just happy," said Joy. "Happiest I've seen him since my Mum died. We're all thrilled."

Tara breathed a sigh of relief. She hadn't had much chance to get to know Joy, Dawa, and their little girl Dechen, it had all happened so quickly.

"Oh, before they call you, I forgot," said Joy. "You've got the something old, the ring that was Grandmother's, the something new is the dress, which is also the something blue, and so is your jewelry. But have you borrowed anything?"

"No," said Tara, smiling at the old rhyme. "I'm not much for…"

"But you have to have something borrowed," said Joy effusively. She took an agate wrist mala off her wrist and slipped it onto Tara's. "Rinpoche gave it to me when we were at Lapchi, so his energy will be in the ceremony."

"Thank you," said Tara, fingering the brown beads with swirls in them. "Is this a real *dzi* bead?"

"Knowing Rinopche, yes. That's why I'm only loaning it to you! Well of course I shouldn't be attached, so if you want to keep it…"

"MacFarlane and Garcia-O'Connor," called the official in charge, lifting his eyebrows slightly at Tara's hyphenated name. "Let's keep things moving if you will."

Tara kissed her beautiful…stepdaughter to be, she marveled. "I wouldn't dream of it, but thank you for offering." She pointed to her heart, and then to Joy's. "The blessings are right here, aren't they?"

The ceremony passed in a blur. Tara remembered only Xander's eyes, and his hand slipping the platinum band onto her finger as she slipped a thin golden band onto his. Then the kiss, of course, one of many on a continuum she hoped would stretch many years into the future. And the beeps, clicks, and flashes of cameras going off.

Their simple reception was at an elegant, upscale vegan restaurant, in deference to Joy's and their witnesses' dietary preferences. They enjoyed organic white wine from France with their delicious meal, and shared all the dishes around as they looked at photos on their phones and digital cameras.

There were few other diners, due to the recent economic crash. Tara thanked the staff and the chef warmly as they finished their chocolate-avocado pie dessert with the little figurines of a man in a kilt and a woman in traditional Native American buckskin dress.

"It was the best I could do at short notice," said Joy, who was an artist as well as a Tibetan translator. "I wasn't entirely sure what else to put to represent your various heritages, so I put the Zia symbol and the Triple Spiral on her necklace."

Tara looked at Joy, marveling at the light and the love in her dark eyes. "I can't believe how lucky I am to have married into such a wonderful family. Truly, I'm blessed."

She picked up the figurine of the woman, looking at the details of the clothing and jewelry. "I did wear buckskins like this, as a little girl. I'll treasure this always."

Joy got tears in her eyes. "Take good care of my dad," she said. "I know you will. It's just…well, he travels so much. I know you can't go everywhere with him. But I can't help worrying."

"Joy," Xander said, "think how I felt when you went running off to Tibet and India for all those years. Let your old man have his travels too. It's all for a good reason, just like yours."

"I know, Da."

They waited for taxis on the quiet street, saying good-bye and thanking their witnesses, Kate and Ian, who lived close enough to walk home. A light rain had begun to fall, and Tara shivered slightly in her thin dress, pulling her pashmina shawl around her shoulders.

They gave the first taxi to Joy's family, as Dechen was nodding off on her feet.

Tara and Bibi Amina shared the backseat of the taxi that pulled up immediately behind, while Xander joined the driver, a recent immigrant from Pakistan, in the front, conversing with him in Pashtu.

Bibi Amina smiled, and squeezed Tara's hand. "*Zindegi,*" said the old woman softly. "Life. It never quite turns out how we expected. As a little girl growing up like an Afghan princess, I never in millions of years thought I would grow up to marry a Scotsman and have a fine son who would be so lucky as to find two loves in his life." She hugged Tara close. "I am honored to have you in my family."

"The honor is all mine," said Tara. "Oh, Bibi Amina, maybe you can come with Xander to meet my mom and sister soon."

Bibi Amina sighed deeply. "Maybe. I will try. *Inshallah.*"

When they got home, Tara propped the wedding pie figurines up on Xander's altar, next to Sakyamuni Buddha, her namesake goddess Tara, and a picture of Rinpoche.

"Oh, I forgot to give Joy her wrist mala back!"

"No worries. It can bless our first married night together."

"Perfect."

Xander lit candles all around the room and in the bathroom. Tara's ring glinted in the flickering lights as they first bathed together, then enjoyed sacred union in the manner of Tibetan deities.

Chapter
13

15 October, 2050

Avebury Encampment,
New Avalon

In just a few days, the Time Travelers had learned to blend in well, and Tara was relieved. Jonah, with his immense physical strength and enthusiasm, led parties of young men and women in threshing rice, and proved a master at catching catfish in the canals.

Yeshi worked alongside Jonah's crew, and was soon accepted as the Quiet One.

Sitara had a surprising knack for basket-weaving, which allowed her ample time to sit with her back against the coolness of the massive dark stone in the Cove of the Moon. She had again altered her appearance, and though she didn't look quite Tara's age, she looked like an Elder who should command respect and brook no interference.

Leona, who normally would be a team with Janus whatever the young man was doing, had torn herself away from her lover in order to sit with Sitara. Leona's sudden enormous interest in basket-weaving, for which she proved to have quite an aptitude, kept the more controlling members of the community at bay. As long as she was doing something useful, no one was going to interfere.

Sitara's blue eyes dilated as she tracked the movements of the sun behind the clouds, and tuned in to the vibrations of the standing stones. Tara spent time with her and Leona, quietly weaving, not speaking. One time she looked up to see Sitara leaning back into the stone, which seemed to have melted around her. She drew in her breath sharply, and Leona looked up.

"Cool!" said Leona. "Can I learn to do that?"

Sitara momentarily came out of her trance. "Yes, no doubt, but you need the wisdom to only do such things when necessary," she admonished. "Otherwise…"

"Otherwise what?" asked Leona sassily.

"It uses a lot of energy. We have to save our energy for when it's needed."

"Why did you need to do it now, then?"

"To make sure it could be done in this Timeline. There are certain… skills I have, talents. All of us have them to some degree, but for some of us it's easier, and it makes sense to have everyone do what they do most easily. Especially on such a crucial mission."

"Do I have those skills?"

"Yes. I think so."

"So should I be practicing?"

"Not too much. You proved that you could do it, that night you sang. Just remember what you did. It might come in handy someday."

Georgie the cat sidled up through the grass and dropped a mouse at Tara's foot. She reached out absently to scratch his ears in praise.

"What are *my* skills?" asked Tara suddenly.

"Talking to me," came the soft voice of the cat. *"And others."*

Sitara laughed and petted the cat. "I think you know."

Leona looked a little resentful. She was used to being able to do things others couldn't, but she couldn't hear the cat.

Till now. *"If I shout a little louder in my mind, then you can hear,"* came the feline voice. Georgie stared at Leona. *"You're named after a big cat. You should be able to hear cats."*

"Oh!" said Leona aloud. Then in mind-talk, *"Thank you, Georgie. This is so cool."*

"Don't think you can hear me all the time. Sometimes I'm just going to talk to your Gran, privately. Right now I'm on a channel to talk to all who can hear, all three of you."

"I always thought maybe I was a little crazy," said Tara aloud. "You know, losing it with age."

Sitara looked at her strangely. "Have you looked at yourself lately?"

"No, we've grown accustomed to not having mirrors. And who cares what an old lady looks like?"

Tara looked down at her hands and stretched them. Oddly, they did look more youthful. Some dark sunspots had vanished.

Sitara pulled a shiny disc out of her blouse and handed it to Tara.

"A mirror? You travel with a mirror?"

"That's not really what it's for. It's more for what you used to call scrying, communication between Timelines is what we call it. But it will do. Look."

Tara looked at the shiny surface. She was astounded to see the face of a woman not in her 90's, but in late middle-age. Her silver-white hair now had black at the roots. Her eyes were clear, and the eyelids that had drooped and become puffy over the years had lifted and opened.

"Is this some kind of magic mirror?" she asked, handing it back to Sitara.

"The mirror of Avalon?" asked Sitara. "Maybe. Something similar."

"You know so much about our Timeline. And before."

Sitara shrugged. "We have access to much knowledge and I'm able to tap into more every day. Luckily. For we will need it on the journey to come."

Tara sighed. "I can't believe I'm having this conversation, that I've got Time Travelers staying in my hut, and I'm so calm about it."

Sitara looked at her deeply, and for a moment Tara saw the young woman as she liked to present herself. "You're an anthropologist, like Yeshi."

"So anthropology still exists 300 years in the future?"

"Not in all Timelines, but yes, in ours. Humans still exist, animals still exist, the great forests still exist."

"And glaciers? The ice cap?"

A shadow passed over Sitara's face. "Yes. Till recently. That's how we began to know something had gone wrong in one of the Timelines. There were decisions that were supposed to have been made, had been made. But something changed."

"How could that be?" How could any of this be? It contradicted the known laws of physics, even the new discoveries in advanced quantum physics that scientists had studied until the great devastations had made research impossible.

"Honestly, Tara, not everything is understood. We don't always know why things work, just that they work. Could you have explained your Internet, when you had one?"

"Not really. I was good at researching. I used it well."

"Precisely. So it is with Time Travel. For some reason, I was born with a facility for mathematics. Perhaps past lives, that sort of thing. I am *not* Artificial Intelligence, believe me. In our Timeline, history tells us that our ancestors made a very conscious decision not to go that route. And I wasn't genetically engineered for it either. That too was decided against. So the past life explanation is the best I can offer."

"I can understand that," said Tara. "So my Tibetan teachers taught."

"Mathematics is the service I offer to the world. To the universe, really. It is my special talent. As I read the stones, I feel the repository of vibrations of all that has happened here for the past, oh, 5,000 years or so."

"Just here?"

"And on the planet." Sitara suddenly grew sad, and looked like a very old woman, even older than Tara. "And I feel it. Every loss. Every species that has gone, animal and plant. And all that you have lost…"

For a moment, Tara felt her losses piercingly. Xander had at least had a good long life and had gone peacefully, but the rest of the family, Joy, Dawa, Dechen and her husband Kennedy…she couldn't bear to think of the suffering.

"I'm sorry," said Sitara softly. Tara felt a wave of comforting light, warm and cool at the same time, hold her aching heart and pass through her body. Georgie began to purr. Leona, who had been silent, listening, wiped away the tears that had begun to course down her beautiful young face.

"It's..." Tara didn't have the words. For a moment she saw the faces and forms of her most loved ones—Xander, her mother and her sister and her nieces, cats she had loved over decades, and Xander's family, all suffused with rainbow light.

"I think you called it the Rainbow Body in some traditions," said Sitara.

"Oooo, I miss my Mum and Dad, and that must be Granma and Granpa," wept Leona as she stared raptly into the distance in the same direction Tara was looking.

"But look, how beautiful..." said Tara, gathering her great-granddaughter into her arms. "Can you see them as I can?"

"Yes, the rainbows. I know they are happy. I just miss them." Leona sniffed, and wiped her face off with the back of her hand. "I wish I could be there with them."

Abruptly, the vision vanished.

"It's not your time," said Sitara, a little harshly. Then more gently, "Leona, in truth, there is no time. It's all going on at once, just in different dimensions and forms. That's why we found out that Time Travel is possible. You are not separate from them, just in a different state of being."

"If it's all going on at once, then why do we have to go back to the Pivot Points to change something?" asked Leona stubbornly. "Why can't we just change dimensions or something? Just jump to a different Timeline."

Tara had wondered the same thing.

Sitara finished off the edge of the basket she had been weaving. "Ah, if only it were that simple. Believe me, I wouldn't have volunteered for this mission that is anything but certain of success if there were another way."

"But why?" asked Leona. "Why isn't there another way?"

Sitara sighed and reached for Leona's hands. "If only we knew. Maybe together we can find this other way." She stroked the young woman's tightly braided hair and wiped the moisture off her brown cheeks.

"I don't know if we are the fulfillment of your many prophecies," said Sitara. "But we were all destined to meet, here, now, at this nexus in time."

Chapter
14

30 September, 2018

En Route to Taos Pueblo,
New Mexico

Tara wrinkled her nose, which felt parched and bloody. Smoke from two major wildfires burning in the Jemez choked the land. The air was strange, warm and heavy as Tara drove north from Albuquerque in the early morning, her heart breaking at the devastation to this land, still her land. She felt sad for the many homes lost, and also for the animals burnt and displaced, and the forests themselves.

But she was looking forward to seeing her mom, and her sister Christina and her family. San Geronimo Day was always a day of reunions, and she'd made an effort to come back to Taos for it nearly every year since she'd gotten over her youthful rebellion phase.

The drive was not nearly as beautiful as it used to be. She entered the tight curves of the road through the canyon where the Rio Grande ran, and was surprised at how low the river still was. Driving through Santa Fe, she had noticed that the aspen groves in the Sangre de Cristos, those that had survived the tent worm infestation of a few years before, remained stubbornly green, with not a hint of autumn's gold even in the high country.

There was surprisingly little traffic on the road, especially for a Feast Day that used to draw so many tourists. People seemed to be staying home, sitting tight to see what the economic fallout was going to be, and whether government actions in the U.S., Europe, Japan, China, India, and Brazil were going to be enough to stave off a descent into poverty and chaos.

She took a breath, clearing her mind. She missed Xander terribly. They texted a couple of times a day and Skyped nearly every day, but he had not been able to fly back with her to the States the week after their wedding after all. Now he didn't think he could get away till Christmas, what with the upcoming assignment for Doctors Without Borders in Sierra Leone. She bit down a taste of resentment. After all, Xander had volunteered for another stint there long before they had fallen in love, and he was a man of integrity. It was one of the things she loved most about him.

She had spent the first couple of weeks home formally applying to join him in the UK as a spouse, and had had to fly to Los Angeles to appear in person at the British Consulate. Xander had retained an immigration attorney to expedite her case, and much time had been spent sending paperwork back and forth, and trying to figure out the best way to get her two cats over to Scotland.

Tara came up over the ridge that opened up into the panoramic view of Taos, the blue mountains overlooking the vast valley rift by the dark, jagged scar of the Rio Grande Gorge. This view always lifted her heart, and did so today, even obscured by the strange haze of smoke and dust that blanketed the whole state.

Tara's world's tectonic plates had shifted with her commitment to Xander. They knew they wanted to be together as much as possible, and be based in the same place. Together they had decided on Scotland, but in light of the current economic situation, she felt queasy thinking of being so far away from her mom and her sister's family.

She wasn't all that thrilled about Xander going to Sierra Leone again, but she knew he was careful about the various exotic epidemics that had emerged, or perhaps mutated, after the vaccine for Ebola had been developed.

Uncertainty. Impermanence. She focused on the mountains in whose shadow she had grown up. They hadn't seemed so impermanent then, and the world had not seemed so uncertain. She sighed. Or perhaps it had. New Mexico was, after all, the birthplace of the atomic bomb, and she had experienced the same Cold War frenzy of fear that other children her age had. But the difference was that Nature was always nearby.

Her father, a well-known anthropologist specializing in the ancient cultures of the American Southwest, had taught her and her younger sister Christina a love of Nature and a healthy respect for its power. Her mother had always used the herbs she had learned about from her own mother, Tara's grandmother from the Pueblo, and had likewise been proud of her Hispanic heritage from her father's side. Tara's grandfather had been a particularly fine carver, and her mom's home was filled with *Abuelo's* furniture, as well as several of his Santos that were too special to sell.

This all had just been part of who she was—the mountains, the languages, the fiestas and the Pueblo feasts, the music, the art, the cycles of changing seasons. And later, when she was just a bit too young to run off and join them, the hippie communes north of town.

Her parents had insisted that she and Christina always come in first in their respective classes. Education was all that mattered, and in any areas where the public schools might have fallen short, her parents encouraged them to read books, from novels to science to metaphysics, to peruse art and photography books, and to learn the languages of their ancestors.

Tara slowed through the speed trap in Ranchos de Taos. So very little traffic, she thought again. She noticed that the hotel parking lots on Taos' main drag weren't very full. Maybe everyone was already at the Pueblo. But there usually weren't vacancy signs around San G. Day.

There wasn't much of a line of cars to get into the Pueblo parking lot. The young tribal policeman on duty didn't recognize Tara, so she told them what family she was from and her brother-in-law Tony's name.

"Welcome. You can go round to the right," he said.

"Thanks." She knew the way by heart. At least that hadn't changed. She pulled into Christina's and Tony's yard in the family home just outside the bounds of the Village, and was greeted by her niece Daphne, now a striking, graceful young woman in her 20's with two toddlers in tow.

"Hey! Aunt Tara! We were wondering when you'd get here. Everyone's over at your Grandma's old house in the Village."

Tara hugged Daphne and the kids, commenting on how much they'd grown. How long had it been? Surely not a whole year since she'd been up here? Had she been traveling that much?

Tara had never seen such a small turnout, but a few tourists and locals milled around the stands of crafts and jewelry, and the scent of oven bread baking in the mud *hornos* wafted temptingly through the air.

Tara pulled open the squeaky screen door to the old house, so familiar from her childhood. Her mom, Christina, and various cousins piled out of the little kitchen at the back of the house to hug her. Tara's mouth watered at the smells of chile and posole.

Tara's mom Flora pulled off her oven mitts and enfolded her much taller daughter in a big hug. Tara held her mom, thinking how thin she'd become.

"Well honey, I can't believe you finally got married," said her mom.

There was that slight hint of judgment folded up in the love. No, she hadn't married at a normal age like Christina had. She hadn't married a famous artist from the Pueblo. She hadn't had children and grandchildren, and wouldn't continue the maternal bloodline.

"I wish Xander could have come," said Flora.

"Believe me, so do I," said Tara.

"We won't be able to go over there and visit," said Flora. "Not with the way things are now. So I guess I'd better just enjoy having my daughter home."

"I'm happy to be home, Mom. Hey, what can I do to help?" Tara wasn't about to be treated like a guest, a stranger, in her own family.

Christina hugged her, keeping her floury hands away from Tara's velvet dress.

"Here. Let me get you an apron. We got stuff you can help with."

Tara settled into the old routine, the one she had known year after year, since she was a little girl. They cooked, they served. Family friends were invited in, to eat at the third or fourth or fifth house. A few slightly shy and startled strangers were invited in to enjoy the traditional foods, the red and green chile soaked up by warm oven bread, the spicy posole, the potato salad and sweets, and best of all, Tara's favorite food from childhood, *soupa*, the cinnamony bread pudding.

The adobe house heated up as the afternoon wore on, and finally everyone went outside to watch the Pole Climb. Tara had laughed with everyone else as the *koshares*, the "clowns" painted in black and white almost like skeletons, teased and occasionally slightly terrorized tribal members. Kids who weren't paying enough attention to school ran shrieking. A couple of sulky teen-aged boys cowered as two clowns yelled right in their faces. A handsome young man who was well-known to have a gambling problem was unceremoniously dunked in the river that ran through the Village.

What would Xander think? Tara wondered, as she watched the Pole Climb in the golden, smoky afternoon. He'd been all over the world, but she was pretty sure he'd never been here, the home of her heart, the place that had formed and informed her.

She held her breath as the first man climbed the slick pole, arm over arm, his painted legs holding tight. He nearly slipped at the top—though one could never tell if it was for effect—and there he stood, the first man who had tried, right on top of the slim, swaying pole.

Perhaps it was a good omen, thought Tara. Maybe things are somehow going to be okay, at least here. She knew that there was a strong movement towards locally-grown organic food, not only in the Pueblo, but throughout the Valley. Maybe this community would pull together and it would be okay.

With a pang, she realized that she didn't see herself staying here. She would miss them all terribly. Who knew when she would get back? And Mom looked so thin. Was there something that they weren't telling her?

For a moment she wondered, could Xander move here? Could they change their plans, be based in New Mexico at her house in Albuquerque? Joy and Dawa and Dechen seemed fine, and were often gone traveling with Rinpoche. But what about Bibi Amina?

Only a few months ago, it had seemed like they had endless choices. But with "the crisis," as people were calling it, choices seemed to narrow. They still had more choices than a lot of people, and more resources.

All she could do was wait, and spend as much time with her family as she could in between the reports she had to finish and the ongoing immigration paperwork. Surely she'd be able to come back with Xander and visit Taos, and they could afford to fly Mom over to the UK. Mom had traveled plenty overseas with Dad once they became empty-nesters, and Tara knew she had enjoyed it.

The scientist in Tara knew that the world was in serious trouble. It was a chicken and egg situation—had the environmental decline caused the economic collapse, or had the economy of inequality and greed that had prevailed since around 1980 caused the environmental collapse that was unfolding before all their eyes like a slow motion rocket crash gaining speed?

Daphne's little daughter, a bright-eyed three-year-old named Chloe, was pulling at Tara's midnight blue velvet skirt.

"Auntie, come and eat," said the little girl.

Tara scooped up the little girl, who was an armful. "Okay, let's go eat some more."

She savored every bite, every taste, with gratitude.

Chapter
15

17 October, 2050

Avebury Encampment,
New Avalon

Sitara was in a deep trance, her back melded to the great standing stone, her eyes closed. To Tara, she seemed to waver in and out of focus. One moment Sitara seemed to be engaged in methodically weaving a reed basket, the next she appeared to be enfolded by the rock itself, which flowed around her like liquid.

Tara blinked a few times.

"You're seeing first what she wants others to see," said Leona, "and then you shift and see what's really going on. She's gathering data. I think she'll have figured out the Pivot Point soon. And then we can go!"

"We?"

"I think we're all going."

"Who?"

"You, me, and Janus, along with the Time Travelers. Won't it be cool? To get out of here and see somewhere else? Didn't you want to travel when you were my age?"

Tara smiled. "I hardly remember." But she did, so very clearly. She had loved Taos, but she had so wanted to get out of Taos and "see the world." She had been so excited at that first trip to Europe with her family when she was 15, her mom and dad taking her and Christina to all the museums in Paris, Florence, Rome, London.

"Gran, your mind's wandering again."

She reached out and flipped Leona's braids. "It happens when you're as old as I am. Actually I think it's happened all my life."

"So you were like me when you were a kid?"

"No one could ever be quite like you, Leona. I keep forgetting that we are not actually blood related though. Your spirit reminds me of me at your age."

"We're all mixed up now anyway, aren't we?" said Leona thoughtfully. "But it's not about who married who or had what child. We're family now, by choice, right?"

"Right."

"Me too?" came a teasing male voice. Tara turned to see Yeshi approaching with two fishing poles.

"If you want," Tara said. She almost reached out to hug him, then stopped herself, feeling foolish. She didn't really know this stranger from another world and time, and besides, she was still an old woman and he was still…she wasn't sure what, or how old, but he looked like a man in the prime of his life, making him half her age or less.

"Come," he said, gesturing with the fishing poles. "Let's make ourselves useful. Sitara will be occupied for many hours to come, but I sense she is nearly finished. It may be today that she knows where we are to go."

Tara waved good-bye to Leona, and followed Yeshi along the path that led across the ditch and toward a nearby stream where they could fish in private.

"So you'll be leaving soon?" she asked carefully.

"*We* will, yes."

Had she heard a slight emphasis on the "we?" "I hope we have helped you."

"Yes. And you will continue to do so. You know you are meant to come with us."

She stopped on the path. "Oh, I *know*?"

He kept walking, and she hurried to catch up with him. "You three wouldn't have seen us and been waiting for us if you weren't meant to travel with us," he said matter-of-factly.

"Yeshi," she began, troubled. "I'm fine with going. I'm an old woman. If something goes wrong, I won't be missing much in life. I've seen a lot and lost the man I loved for decades. But Leona and Janus are kids. They…"

"Tara, you must understand. They won't *have* a life unless we succeed."

She stopped again, stunned at the truth. "You mean…?"

"This Timeline ends in a couple of years, at least for humans, unless we succeed in changing something at the most crucial Pivot Points."

"Oh."

"You know this. Scientifically you know it—the Sixth Great Extinction. And you know it from your lore, from your so-called myths and legends, your Prophecies of your own ancestors, and of so many indigenous tribes."

She took in a deep breath. The path opened up to where they could walk side by side. "And here we are, in 2050, fishing," Tara said.

"And here we are. Fishing, waiting."

"How much time do we have?"

"Enough. Well, we're pretty sure of it. Sitara may seem to be taking a lot of time, but we have to be sure we journey to the most crucial Pivot Point, the right place and time."

"How do we know what we have to change? Is it something big or something small?"

"It could be either. She will obtain that information from her reading and analysis of the data."

The two sat down on the bank of the stream, in the shade of a smallish standing stone. They cast their fishing lines into the waters, and waited.

"We're in trouble if it's something big," said Tara.

"Not necessarily."

She looked at him questioningly.

"Some small action may be enough to change some large outcome."

"Isn't that supposed to be dangerous? Messing with the time-space continuum and all that? At least in theory? Couldn't a tiny change mean that everything changes? Maybe that I don't exist in this Timeline anymore? That I was never born? Or never met Xander?"

"Slow down. We have allowed for many of those possibilities. Don't underestimate Sitara. She has had training not only in the Sirian worlds, but in Alcyon."

"I can't believe I'm having this conversation. I read all that stuff, the channeled stuff at the turn of the century and around 2012, and of course I've sat with many indigenous elders for years before and after that. It's just hard to believe. So, Yeshi, what I don't get entirely is whether you are from another time, in the future, or another planet, or both?"

"Yes, all of above."

She looked at him in annoyance, waiting for him to continue.

"That is to say, we are from approximately 300 years in the future. Sitara can tell you exactly, if you care to know. We are from Earth. And we travel to other planets, and other dimensions. Not in space ships. That would be quite primitive and time-consuming, and also consuming of physical resources."

"So you go through portals, or wormholes?"

"Even that would be limiting. In our Timeline, we have known for some time, not very long after this year 2050 actually, that the real physics of the universe far transcend not only Newtonian physics, but everything that you knew about quantum physics, string theory, and non-locality before everything was lost in the disasters in this Timeline."

"I think I have a bite," she said suddenly. She began reeling in the fish, automatically saying the "*Om Mane Padme Hum*" mantra, honoring the life she was about to take so that she and her friends could eat.

"Non-locality was the closest," he said thoughtfully.

"What about what the mystics all over the planet said? What about the Tibetan Rinpoches, like my own teacher, and people like the great yogis? They could bi-locate, they could dissolve and walk through walls, they could attain the Rainbow Body when they died. Is that the same thing?"

Yeshi nodded his head. "Right. Very similar. And you know why it worked?"

"Why?"

"Just like in your mystic teachings. You know how you needed to have kindness and love as the basis, or it was just sorcery?"

"Yes."

"We learned that. In *our* Timeline, we learned it in time. Humans evolved and stopped relying on machines. We didn't need Artificial Intelligence, we didn't need supercomputers or space ships or huge generators. We learned to do what the cetaceans were doing all along. And the felines. Where is that cat, anyway?"

The grasses rustled, and Georgie suddenly, mysteriously showed up, his gray whiskers and nose twitching at the prospect of fresh fish. Tara petted his smooth head and listened to him purr. "Yes, you can have some even though you didn't help us catch it."

"How do you know I didn't?" came the feline voice in her head.

"Right."

"We do know a thing or two about directing prey, just like your ancient human hunters with their songs and paintings."

She chucked the cat under the chin. "Great. I'm being lectured by a cat. Now I know I'm senile."

Yeshi laughed hard. "Tara, it's all a dream. And it's all reality. As long as you can hold that paradox, you'll be fine."

She let out a breath, deciding to say nothing. For awhile, the two humans and the cat sat in companionable silence. Yeshi caught two fish, and Tara caught another.

"Where did you meet him?" Yeshi asked, as they settled back against the stone, most of the afternoon gone.

She smiled at the memory, knowing he meant Xander. "Scotland. North of here. In 2017 first, then we met again in 2018 and got together."

"The year Scotland became independent."

She shook her head in surprise. "No. It didn't. Did it in another Timeline?"

"Sorry. I forgot. In this Timeline it didn't. Yes, in several Timelines it did."

"Several? How many are there?" Suddenly she felt very weary.

"In any one moment, really an infinite number. But about nine main ones. We are constantly making choices."

"Oh Yeshi, how are we ever going to make the right choice without making things worse?"

He smoothed her hair tenderly, and she felt a strange moment of almost-attraction, which of course made no sense at all.

"Remember your spiritual training. At some point we just have to use our intuition, and trust."

"Even after all that data that Sitara is gathering?"

He nodded once and looked off into the distance, where the mists had begun to lift in the direction of the sunset. "Intuition is a big part of the success of our Timeline, of our Earth-based human culture in that Timeline, working along with felines, cetaceans, and pretty much all of your favorite animals and plants." He took her hands in his, and his eyes shined. "Tara, we learned how to do it right! We learned how to live in such harmony with Earth that we graduated, we connected with first the solar system, then the galaxy, then the whole universe."

"Then why are you here?" she asked in astonishment. "What went wrong?"

"It was a bleedthrough," Yeshi said sadly. "The negativity of this particular Timeline, your Timeline, became so strong that it started to seep through into other Timelines, including ours. Something had to be done. We three, the ones you know as Yeshi, Sitara, and Jonah, were in a unique position to change it. We knew we had to come through the Stone Circle portal, and that there we would find wise beings alive in this time who were meant to help us. We have great confidence in the success of our mission."

Yeshi looked into Tara's eyes kindly, reassuringly. Tara trusted him. The universe, less so.

Chapter
16

Albuquerque,
New Mexico

She was grateful, grateful, grateful. She and Xander embraced and kissed with abandon the minute he came through the heavy revolving doors at the Albuquerque Sunport.

"Careful of that attachment thing," he said to her, his hazel eyes twinkling.

"What attachment thing?" She finally let him go and they started off towards baggage claim.

"You know. Desire-attachment being the root of all suffering."

"Oh, *that* attachment thing." They reached baggage claim, and she smiled at a memory. "Right there, that's where I first met Rinpoche, at the bottom of the escalator. I was running late and he was already down in baggage. I'd never seen him in my life, at least this life, and ran to offer my *kata*. He hugged me and greeted me like I was his long lost heart-daughter, and gave me the first of those Third Eye blessings that he gives."

Xander laughed heartily. "You *are* his long lost heart-daughter. I've lost track—where is he now?"

"On retreat in Crestone. But he'll be out after the beginning of the year. Maybe we can go to see him before you go back, or I go back, or...what is happening anyway?"

Xander hauled a large suitcase off the carousel. The airport was eerily deserted, much as it had been in the weeks after the September 11th attacks.

"We'll talk."

He grabbed another large suitcase. "So much for the simple life and traveling light," he said, rolling his eyes. "One whole suitcase is gifts for your mom, Christina, and the whole family, mostly from Bibi Amina."

She kissed him lightly, dragging one of the suitcases down the corridor towards the parking lot. "I'm glad you dressed warm. It's actually cold outside, like it should be."

A few snow flurries dusted the roads as Tara drove them through the night to her adobe house just north of Central. "This snow is a surprise," she said. "It wasn't predicted."

"Maybe Rinpoche blew the conch shell."

"Maybe. It's like a miracle. It's been years since we've had snow on Solstice."

She pulled into her circular graveled drive. Multi-colored solar Christmas lights twinkled softly in the snow as the branches of a tall pinon tree swayed in the breeze.

"I can't believe you're really here," she said, hugging him fiercely once they got into the hallway and closed the front door.

"All well, and safely out of quarantine."

"Quarantine?"

"I didn't want to worry you. Just routine, actually, and voluntary. More or less. Never mind. I'm starving. Shall we go out to eat?"

"I've got a better idea. Why don't you make a fire? I'll go see if what I cooked us stayed warm."

Xander was a bit out of his element with the kiva style fireplace, perplexed that there wasn't a grate. Tara found him Googling "how to start fire in kiva fireplace" on his phone when she came back into the room bearing a steaming casserole dish. She couldn't help laughing at his momentary embarrassment.

"That's resourceful," she said. "I forgot, you wouldn't have seen one before. Would your male pride be offended if I showed you how to make a fire?"

"No, dear Dakini. I humbly defer to your superior knowledge."

"It won't take but a minute." Tara expertly stacked three logs in a vertical tee-pee shape, shoved some egg cartons and kindling under them, and lit the fire. As they sat down on the floor by the coffee table to eat, the fire roared to life, its golden light dancing on their faces.

"What's…" he started to ask. "My God, *qabli pilau*! Where did you ever learn?"

"I hope I did it right. Bibi Amina was so sweet to Skype with me as she was making it."

"And *nan*? Did you make the *nan*?"

"No, that's from an Indian restaurant."

They tucked in to the savory rice dish. Tara's two cats, Daka and Dorjee, finally showed up, their noses crinkling at the scent of chicken. A lightning paw almost succeeded in stealing a morsel off of Xander's fork.

"No!" admonished Tara. "I already gave you your special treat. And spices aren't good for cats."

"It's just like Mother used to make," said Xander. "Thank you. It was my childhood favorite dish."

The two humans quietly ate the blend of rice, raisins, pistachios, and carmelized carrots. The two cats sat on the back of the couch, purring madly.

Tara felt like a giddy girl. She enjoyed the food, and was thrilled that Xander so appreciated it. But she couldn't wait to finish their meal and get on with their reunion.

Xander did not disappoint. As soon as he had set his fork down from his last bite, he cupped her chin in his hand and gave her a long, slow kiss. The cats withdrew discreetly into another room as the two humans melted into each other in front of the fire.

It was not yet midnight when Tara awakened. The fire had died down, and she was shivering a little. Xander, jet-lagged, snored softly, then opened his eyes and was wide awake.

Tara threw on her discarded sweater as Xander moved to add fresh wood to the fire.

"I must say I never thought of becoming a nun, even though I was celibate for…oh, I won't even count how many years."

He laughed. "No, the consort route always appealed more to me as well. Though I learned a lot in meditating during all the years I was celibate as well."

"I'm glad," she said. "I did miss this aspect of life."

He leaned over her, kissing her forehead. "Well it's a very nice aspect, isn't it?"

She looked at the clock on the wall. "It's still Solstice."

"Longest night of the year. A very long night in Edinburgh."

"Shall we set some intentions and put them in the fire? It's really the New Year, according to most indigenous traditions of the Northern Hemisphere."

"My dear anthropologist, what do you propose?"

Tara put her hand on a stack of rice paper and gave him a few sheets and a pen. "How about…what do you want to let go of? Then what do you want to bring into your life? And then…what are you offering to the world, for the sake of all sentient beings?"

"Marvelous. I'd like to let go of economic inequality and climate change, I already have what I really want in my life, excluding world peace, and…" he sighed, "I offer everything of myself, every skill I have, to help end suffering."

"Be serious," she said.

"I am. I have you. I'll ask for world peace as well." He wrote as he spoke. "And you?"

She suddenly felt shy. "For so many years I prayed to meet my Twin Flame…and now I have. I hardly know what to ask for on a personal level. So, how about…I let go of imbalance, in the world and in my life. I give thanks that I have you in my life. Oh, and I pray for your safety…"

"You're cheating. Adding extra things."

"It's just a ritual. My ritual. I made it up, so I get to change it."

"Go on then."

Her face became serious. "I want safety for the world. I want species to be saved. I want all suffering to end. I want the Sixth Great Extinction to be stopped just in the nick of time."

"Ah, it's like all those birthday cake wishes for world peace."

"Well…maybe it is, but why not wish big, dream big, pray big?"

"So what are you offering?"

"Same as you. Everything I am, everything I know, every skill I have, my writing, my photography, my scientific training. May we be guided to do good in the world. In the universe. For the sake of all sentient beings."

Together they threw their intentions on the fire and watched the flaming tendrils of rice paper go up through the chimney. They held hands and nestled their heads together. As one, they made their way to the bedroom, as two slightly annoyed cats exited and took over the space on the couch by the fire.

They drove up to Taos on Christmas Eve, a pot full of chile in the back seat. The snow had not yet melted, and the mesas were iced with white sugar. More snow threatened, so they left early, eager to reach their destination.

"Shall I drive?" he asked as snow began to fall north of Santa Fe.

"You're used to the other side of the road." She concentrated, peering through the swirling snow.

"I've driven in many countries. I'm probably more used to snow than you are."

She found herself getting slightly annoyed. "I know this road like the back of my hand. I've driven it since I was 16."

"I'm only trying to be helpful, and keep us safe."

"Are you implying that I'm not driving safely?" Why was she bristling? Why was this minor issue suddenly a feminist defense against the last bastions of male chauvinism?

"Not at all," he said.

She glanced at him and saw that he was smiling. And she decided to pull over. "What are you doing?" he asked.

"Letting go of my stubborn position and ego-attachment. I forgot, you've lived in a lot of countries and you do know how to drive in difficult conditions. I'm just not used to having anyone take care of me."

They got out of the car in the flurrying snow and changed positions. Xander put the car in gear and confidently pulled out onto the road.

"Thank you," she said.

"Pleasure. I'll go carefully."

"No, for more than driving. For helping me see where I'm attached."

"Ditto," he said.

It took a long time to reach Taos, snaking carefully along the icy roads in the canyon, then through the town to the Pueblo. The snow had settled in thickly by the time they reached Christina's house in the late afternoon.

Xander was clearly relieved to pull safely into the yard through several inches of accumulated snow.

Christina and her husband Tony came running out to greet them and help them take in their luggage and the all-important pot of chile.

They stomped the snow off their boots before taking them off and leaving them by the front door in a wooden tray.

"Where's Mom?" asked Tara.

"In the kitchen. Where else?"

Flora emerged from the kitchen, sizing up the tall son-in-law she had not yet met. She looked at him appraisingly before extending a hand.

"Mom, this is Alexander. Xander. This is my Mom, Flora."

"Delighted to meet you, Mrs. Garcia-O'Connor," said Xander, squeezing Flora's hand warmly.

Flora dropped her serious expression. "You don't have to be so formal. In fact, please don't be. Just call me Flora. It's good to meet you after hearing on and on about you for the last few months."

He grinned. "Thank you. I think."

"So what did my daughter tell you about me?"

"How much she loves you. Honestly."

Flora looked skeptical. "So that's why she's moving halfway across the world? Well, this girl always did travel. I suppose it's partly my fault."

Tara sighed. The old family trance starting its play, on this night of all nights. Well, she wasn't going to play the old role.

And Xander wasn't going to be a new cast member. "We haven't decided," he said.

"What?" Tara asked, confused.

"Well, we haven't, not really. We just need for you to have legal residency in the UK. That doesn't tie us to living there permanently."

Flora's face cheered up a bit. "Well, Merry Christmas. We're glad to have you here, Xander. Has this girl of mine cooked you any of our food yet?"

"Oh yes, Mrs....sorry, Flora. Being a good cook is among many of Tara's fine attributes."

"Xander too," said Tara. "We love to cook together. We actually met, well, met the second time, doing food prep in the kitchen at Findhorn."

"I'd be happy to help you, Flora," said Xander disarmingly.

"Tonight you can help by eating," said Flora. "But that's later. It's just getting dark, so they're going to light the bonfires. Get on your warm things and let's go out."

Unlike most Christmas Eves Tara remembered, almost all of the crowd were locals, people from the Pueblo and people from town. And unlike the last 10 or 15 Christmas Eves, the snow fell thickly, flakes sizzling to death in the pitch black smoke and sun-like flames of the huge bonfires. Children played and danced in the snow, slipping and sliding, as the statue of the Virgin was brought out of the church for the procession.

Xander watched with curiosity and respect, and Tara wondered what he was thinking. All of this was so familiar to her. Was it alien to him? She wanted him to love it, as she did. Part of her wanted him to really consider moving here, or at least being based here part of the time. She reveled in the snow, letting the thick flakes catch in her long black hair, adding to the silver streaks that had appeared in recent years.

She smiled as her niece Daphne took pictures of her and Xander together, her and her mom, her sister, the kids, the fire. They drank hot chocolate and coffee out of the same blue enamel mugs they had used for decades, and stamped their feet to keep warm.

"It's been years since it's done this on Christmas Eve," said Christina's husband Tony. "I don't think I've seen it like this since I was a little boy, have you?" he asked Tara and Christina.

"It's like old times," said Tara. "Maybe it's a good omen."

But she thought, maybe it's the last time we'll ever see it like this. Maybe this is some throwback, before it gets worse, and all the snow disappears. Or maybe the prayers of the Pueblo have changed something, balanced something, at least locally and maybe for the region. But how long could they hold balance against the widening gyre?

The words of the old Yeats poem came to her, unbidden. "The center cannot hold…"

She frowned. What was the rest? Something creepy, something "slouching towards Bethlehem to be born." An image of the anti-Christ? She didn't believe in the anti-Christ, and had been trying to transcend duality for the past two decades since she met Rinpoche and received her first teachings and initiations into Tibetan Buddhist mysticism.

She shook her head like a wet cat, and the snow flew around her into the faces of Daphne's laughing children.

She would remember. She felt deep gratitude in the knowing, the experience. She would remember what snow was like, what it felt like to be cold, what it felt like to catch tiny, absolutely unique snow crystals on your tongue. She would remember the smoke of the fire and its blazing warmth on a cold night. She would remember all the faces of all her loved ones, celebrating the birth of light, a birth of hope and compassion that may or may not have been historical. And did it matter if the stories were literally true?

Rinpoche would say no. Rinpoche would say, "Jesus is Chenrezig, the Bodhisattva of Compassion. Mary is Tara. All one."

Tara felt a deep peace as she shivered in the snow, her feet like blocks of ice despite her high-tech faux shearling boots, her hands cold even in her warm gloves. Xander caught her eye, and then her hands, and drew them inside his coat to keep them warm.

The holiday was joyous. The children made snow angels and snowmen and women. The food was as delicious as it had ever been. Bibi Amina's presents were received with enthusiasm and gratitude. The children loved the toys, and the adults kept stroking the warm tartan-patterned shawls and scarves.

On Christmas morning, which dawned with an azure sky and a golden sun, they watched the sacred Deer Dance. Xander was transfixed, listening to the snow-muffled sounds of the jingles and shells on the dancers' feet. In an ancient re-enactment of gratitude for what Mother Earth provides, the dancers slowly, rhythmically moved as herds of deer, the actual heads of deer as transforming masks over their heads, and one dancer becoming the Mountain Lion with whom the People would share the hunt.

The drums, the feet, the deep singing, the colors of the brightly-striped traditional blankets of the people gathered on rooftops against the brilliant blue sky. Tara closed her eyes, burning the scene into her retinas, knowing that she would never have a photograph to remind her, as the sacred, ephemeral nature of the dance forbade it. And at the same time, made it unnecessary. It was part of an ancient cycle, repeated for over a thousand years in this place.

When it was over, Tara looked at Xander. She wanted to ask, "What did you think?" But she didn't. He looked at her, and she knew, she felt his awed reverence, and they both felt their connection with Mother Earth, for now relieved of her fever.

Chapter
17

17 October, 2050

Avebury Encampment,
New Avalon

Noisy heli-shuttles buzzed overhead, black streaks across the misty sky. Tara shuddered slightly. Yeshi looked up impassively as they walked back towards the encampment, several catfish in a basket strapped to Tara's back. Georgie rode on Yeshi's shoulder, purring worriedly into his ear.

Yeshi looked at her questioningly.

She shrugged. "They come sometimes. They haven't landed, that we know of. I suppose they are keeping track of us."

"I wonder how many there are?"

"Sorry, we don't have spies in London. We just refer to them as 'the Elite' and who knows how they refer to us?"

"How did there come to be such a separation?"

She laughed, adjusting the basket as she walked ahead of Yeshi. "It was growing for a long time, since the late years of the 20th century in our timeline. After each plague and natural disaster it got worse. Some people left London and the other cities and came to the countryside, for peace, or because they felt guided. Other people desperately tried to get into the cities, thinking they'd be safe there."

"Were they?"

She looked at the lingering contrails in the sky where the heli-shuttles had been. "We don't hear much. They didn't come back. At least I've never known anyone who did, or anyone who knew anyone who did. Maybe they were accepted. Rumor has it that the people there live in sort of bubbles, or that parts of the old Underground were converted. Obviously they still have technology."

"Are there other cities still functioning?"

She sighed. "Aren't you supposed to know this kind of thing? Isn't this what Sitara is supposed to be reading?"

He smiled tolerantly, which emphasized the Tibetan aspect of his features. "In theory, yes. But she's concentrating on finding the Pivot Points. That's what is crucial. So I'm just asking."

She looked at him archly, almost flirtatiously. "I have no idea. Given what we know of the way the climate has broken down, I doubt there are many cities left in the tropics, or even in the temperate regions." Her heart contracted at the memory of her sister and the rest of her family. Were some of them still alive? Maybe the plagues had not been as bad in the Southwest, as it was somewhat isolated. If not Christina, then maybe her daughter Daphne and her husband, or their children, might still be alive.

"We could find out, you know."

"No," she said sharply. "It wouldn't do any good. I can't go there."

"Actually, you could."

She stopped, and put a hand over his mouth. Georgie batted at her hand.

"No. I think I understand," Tara said emphatically. "Sitara has to spend her energy figuring out something very big, not checking in to see if my family is alive."

"Maybe after we accomplish our mission…"

She laughed. "And if we do, then it's all changed, right? Maybe I just teleport on over."

They were interrupted by Leona's excited shouts. "Gran! Gran!"

The young woman raced up the path, mud splattering behind her onto Janus, who ran with long, loping strides behind her.

"Is everything okay?" asked Tara.

"More than okay," said Leona. "She's done it. She's figured it out."

"What?"

"The Pivot Points," said Janus. "Come on, man, hurry up. She won't tell us anything till we're all together."

Tara and Yeshi quickened their pace, following Leona and Janus back to Tara's hut. Smoke rose from the smokehole of the Longhouse, lit from inside by oil lamps and from outside by a suddenly golden sunset. In the dusk, some people played games in teams, kicking a skin ball around, and some people sang, while others drank. The rest of the Encampment seemed quite oblivious to Tara and her visitors.

Outside of Tara's hut, Sitara was stretching her arms towards the stars that were starting to appear in the night sky as the mists, oddly, began to clear in spots. Tara blinked, thinking her eyes were deceiving her as she saw a light shine from Sitara's brow. As the Time Traveler raised her arms, Tara saw her as a priestess of Old Avalon in indigo robes, parting the mists with her intention.

Sitara turned and smiled at Tara as she lowered her arms, again the young Nordic woman wearing homespun, just like all the inhabitants of New Avalon.

Sitara went into Tara's hut, where she sat down in lotus position. Jonah and Yeshi sat beside her, creating a triangle.

Outside, Janus roasted the catfish over a small fire as Georgie patiently groomed himself. Tara impatiently poked her head into her hut, but the Time Travelers did not look up.

"She's processing," Leona hissed from behind Tara.

"How long is that going to take?"

Leona shrugged. "In the scheme of things, not long I suppose. She's downloading the data into Yeshi and Jonah."

"How do you know all this?"

"I don't know."

Leona walked over to Janus and put her arms around him from behind, affectionately and seductively. He turned around and gave her a kiss.

Tara smiled, hoping desperately that they could create a true future for these young ones.

"Leona, why is she downloading the data into Yeshi and Jonah?" asked Tara.

Leona looked down. "Um, in case something goes wrong, I guess."

"Great. They're really not as sure as they seem, are they?"

"Oh Gran, can't you just get into it? It's so exciting. And it's our best hope."

"That it is." Suddenly, she felt weary, not sleepy, just tired in her soul. "What were the heli-shuttles doing?"

"Not sure," said Janus. "We think they landed though. Not here, but a ways away."

"Do you think they talked to anyone?"

"No telling. I wonder about Seamus. He was out of the camp for a long time today. Unusual for him. You know how he likes to be the center of attention."

"I wonder if we should be worried," said Tara thoughtfully.

"I'll ask the other cats," said Georgie from his place near the fire.

"Do they talk too?" asked Tara in surprise.

Leona rolled her eyes. "At least to each other. They always have. I thought everyone knew that."

Tara looked chagrined. "Not everyone. Leona, I knew you were different and had abilities, but I never suspected the extent of them."

"I'm better at all of it since they arrived," said Leona proudly.

"The fish is burning," said Tara. "Janus, quick, don't waste food."

Yeshi emerged from Tara's hut as Janus was rescuing the fish. "It's time," Yeshi said. "While we share food, she will tell us."

Leona could hardly contain herself as she served clay plates of fish, rice, and cress to everyone. Sitara picked delicately at her fish, smiling like an ancient statue of Quon Yin, Tara thought.

"I will share when we have finished our feast," said Sitara. "It is our custom, not to rush."

Tara had traveled and lived in enough indigenous cultures not to argue, so she took a deep breath and simply enjoyed her meal.

"Leona, bring out the real tea," she said when they were nearly done.

Leona put the crushed, aromatic leaves into six clay cups and poured boiling water over them.

"Tea?" asked Yeshi. "Real tea? Like we have in the future?"

"Oh, good," said Tara. "It's nice to know that real tea survived into at least one Timeline."

"Coffee too," said Jonah. "And chocolate."

"What's chocolate?" asked Leona.

Tara sipped at her hot tea, from the plantations far away in the Highlands of Scotland, a luxury she had traded some of her finest baskets for. "Oh, my darling, I hope that by some miracle we get to go to a place where you can taste chocolate. It was something rich, dark, and sweet…"

"Like Leona," teased Janus.

"Yes, like Leona," said Tara. "It was a treat, not completely a luxury. Something special. Lovers gave it to each other. It just…made people feel good. It gave us energy and it did something to the brain that made you feel like you were in love."

"And what if you already were in love?" asked Leona.

"Then it made you feel even more so."

"Okay," said Sitara, smiling. "Enough of the remembering. We are going to a place and time where they will have all those things, and more, some memories for Tara and surprises for Leona and Janus."

Tara looked at her expectantly, scenes flashing through her mind, and tastes of Mexican chocolate, Indian tea, Kenyan coffee. "Where are we going?"

"Where we are going first is right here on this island. London, 1978."

"What happened in London in 1978 that could change the Timeline?" asked Tara, puzzled. "I was in London then, getting my Master's degree, but I don't remember anything all that significant."

"It's what didn't happen that is so important," said Sitara. "We have to go that year so that Margaret Thatcher is not elected Prime Minister in 1979."

"Who was Margaret Thatcher?" asked Janus. "And what was a Prime Minister?"

"Head of the government, silly," said Leona. "But I don't know who she was."

"They called her the Iron Lady," said Tara. "My friends all intensely disliked her and feared what she would do to the country. And they were right. The UK had problems, of course, but when she was elected, it was as if the ones we now call the Elite suddenly had all the power. She broke the unions—groups of workers that came together for better working conditions and wages. She took away regulations on big banks and big corporations. It's hard to explain, since those things don't exist anymore, not for us."

"Banks were where people kept money," said Leona. "Instead of trading and bartering what they needed. Some people had a lot of money, much more than they needed, and they tried to keep it away. Some people were hungry and had no place to live."

"Some people admired Mrs. Thatcher," said Tara thoughtfully. "She was the first woman Prime Minister. But she was more male than the men. And very much against Scottish independence. Xander never much got mad at anything, but he would go off if you mentioned her, even decades later."

"So what did she do that was so important to fucking things up for us?" asked Janus.

"Not a single thing, many things," said Sitara. "Not just her, she was a symbol, a representative. Really a perversion of the feminine energy. In *our* Timeline, the Divine Feminine energy was reclaimed, beginning right about that time. In your Timeline, the dualistic, patriarchal domination model prevailed for decades, and here you are."

"So what are we supposed to do?" demanded Leona.

"We just have to make sure she was never elected," said Sitara.

Tara was dumbfounded. "Something simple."

"What's an election?" asked Janus.

"You know, like when we vote who is on the council. But it was millions of people, more than we've ever seen," said Leona.

"But why did they elect her if she was so bad?" Janus' face was puzzled.

Tara smiled. "It's complicated. And I have no idea how we can prevent it."

"We'll find a way," said Yeshi. "Sitara has calculated the date and place that will lead to the most favorable combinations of synchronicities. We just have to arrive there, then use our intuition."

"Wait a minute, we need some details here," said Tara. "First of all, who all is going?"

"All of you," said Yeshi. "Well, except I don't think Georgie can come…"

There was a yowl inside their heads. *"Whyyyyyy not?"*

Yeshi spoke aloud. "Georgie, we don't know if Time Travel is safe for cats. You're so much smaller than we are."

"I am made of the same molecular matter and share 90% of your DNA."

"Still, we don't want to risk it."

The cat got up and stalked angrily out of the hut, scratching at the threshold as if he was scratching cat litter, Tara thought. She felt bad for him, but was secretly relieved. One less precious thing to lose.

"When do we go?" asked Tara.

"We should leave in the morning," said Yeshi. "Time in this Timeline is growing short, so we should not delay."

Tara could not sleep, so she stood outside, breathing in the night air. She supposed it didn't matter whether she slept or not. It was just a matter of having enough physical energy to journey to the Henge over the next couple of days. She wondered if her appearance would revert to the age she had been in 1978, twenty-three going on twenty-four. What if she ran into herself? What if she saw herself on the Tube on the way to a tutorial at the university? Would that be dangerous?

The night was clear, and the stars burned overhead. Maybe Sitara really had parted the mists. Tara felt an unaccustomed longing for tobacco. She'd never been a recreational smoker, but had made tobacco offerings many times, and had smoked the Sacred Pipe in Lakota sweatlodge. There was nothing like it now, unless the Elite still had it in the City.

So much lost, and yet the lives of the survivors were not unpleasant. For now. Was it, as Yeshi had implied, just going to keep getting worse, until in a few decades it was so hot and there was so little oxygen that no organized life at all was possible on the Earth? How much farther north could humans, and their sources of food, migrate? Would some of the Elite survive in underground cities? Even if they did, would they just kill each other off in competition for scarce resources?

Tara was aware of a figure standing beside her. Yeshi took her hand, almost like a lover. Tears sprang to her eyes, but she held on for comfort.

"Tara," he said softly, "there is so much more than you have ever dreamed of, than your poets and scientists have ever speculated."

"'There are more things in heaven and on earth, Horatio, than are dreamt of in your philosophy,'" quoted Tara.

"Shakespeare. Hamlet," said Yeshi.

Tara looked at him, startled, and held his hand between hers, close to her heart. "Shakespeare is still known 300 years in the future?"

"In our Timeline. As long as we can preserve our culture through this mission."

"You're not sure if we can do it."

"No one can ever be sure. That is the nature of life. But the calculated probabilities are high. We have to try."

"'We have to try' could be my epitaph. I wonder if I will die in this Timeline, or some other? What if I die in another Timeline?"

He cleared his throat. "We are pretty sure that can be prevented. A quick move aside, just before a death occurs, seconds before. It's better to die in your own Timeline, at your own time."

"Hmm."

"Tara, I have something for you."

"What?"

"It's possible to bring objects through time, and space."

"I've heard of that. They were called 'apports' in the Spiritualist tradition. And I once heard one of our early astronauts, Edgar Mitchell, speak of someone bringing back a cuff link, a piece of jewelry, he had lost years before. Suddenly it was in the man's hand."

"Like this?" Yeshi opened his hand. Starlight glittered on the diamonds of the engagement ring Xander had given Tara, so many decades ago.

She shook her head to dispel the illusion. "Thank you. A sweet hallucination."

"No." He pressed it into her hand. "I asked to bring you something you want, and need."

She looked at it as if it were an alien thing, not the familiar ring she had worn, and eventually lost during the travels and the plagues. She had loved it because Xander gave it to her, but she had truly not been attached to it, at least not by the time it was lost, when diamonds and platinum no longer had any worth.

"I loved it. But I loved him more, and him you can't bring back. Unless you take me to that time when he was alive."

"That is not where we are needed," he said gently. "I don't know why you might need this, or even if you really will."

She closed her hand around it, weighed it, felt its edges, the hardness of the diamonds, the smoothness of the platinum circle. "It seems real enough," she marveled. "But what good could it do me here? Or us? Or is it useful in another time? Will it come with us?"

"It can, if you need it to. Or it might remain here. It's just molecules, really, just a pattern of meaning."

"That humans started wars over. Blood diamonds."

"Humans started wars over just about everything, until we learned not to."

"Thank you, Yeshi." She pecked him on the cheek, chastely. "It's a wonderful memory of my Xander. I know his spirit is well, somewhere. I just miss him."

She took the ring and slipped it into the deerskin medicine pouch she wore around her neck. No tobacco, but a diamond ring joining the lock of Xander's hair that she still carried with her next to her heart.

Chapter
18

3 January, 2019

Drolma Ling Dharma Center,
Crestone, Colorado

Tara held a pinch of tobacco up towards the golden sun that rose over the majestic white peak. Xander watched her offer to Mother Earth, Father Sky, and the four directions, taking shreds of tobacco out of the worn leather pouch she always wore around her neck along with a brocade Buddhist amulet from Rinpoche.

Her words seemed to form into frost and steam as they came from her lips. Just as she finished her prayers, the sun's rays spilled over the sacred mountain.

Xander was respectful, and for this Tara was grateful. Rinpoche taught that all religions and spirit ways were to be respected as pathways to non-duality, but she knew that not all his students understood and embraced that part of the teachings.

When she was finished with her offerings, Xander rubbed her cold, bare hands between his to warm them. Her only ornament was the thin engraved platinum band on her left ring finger. He looked at her questioningly.

She understood immediately and tapped her Medicine bag. "It's in here."

"I was just wondering why you've stopped wearing it?"

"My hands are freezing here, and it was loose. I don't want to lose it."

He felt the leather pouch, shiny with wear, and was reassured by the shape of the ring.

"Maybe we should put it in a bank vault," he suggested.

"But then I could never wear it. Are you a wee bit attached to it?" she asked, teasingly. By his pained expression, she was suddenly aware that she had hit a tender spot.

"Well…it's just that it was my mother's, and my grandmother's before that. It's not the money of course," he said hurriedly. "Though it is worth rather a lot, and we are in difficult times."

She took the ring out and slipped it back on her finger. The heavy diamonds caused it to slip to one side. "See what I mean?"

"Yes, by all means…it's just. Well, never mind, I suppose I am attached to you wearing it. It shows that you are part of the family."

She tucked the ring securely back into her pouch, and looked at his earnest eyes. "Xander, I have to be honest with you. I love it, of course. But I do feel so funny wearing it. It's so…I don't know, I hate to use the word ostentatious, because you're not, and your family's not. But especially in these times…I don't want to draw attention."

He pursed his lips. "You've got me. I'm more than a wee bit attached to it. We have so little left of that side of the family, and things only keep getting worse in Afghanistan. But we can hardly leave it in a vault in this country, if we might be going back to Scotland soon."

"True. It's just…well it's just not me to wear something so…shiny. So valuable. I tend to rush around and I'm a bit clumsy. What if I lost it, or a diamond fell out?"

Just then she felt a presence behind her, and the two turned to see Rinpoche walking from his retreat hut, his open-toed sandals leaving prints in the fresh snow. He had a grin on his face, as if he had heard and understood every word of their conversation.

Rinpoche stilled his prayer wheel and impishly grabbed at her pouch, feeling what was inside. He made a dramatic face of exaggerated curiosity, then looked at both of them in turn and shrugged.

Tara wasn't sure what he was getting at, so pulled the ring out to show him. She was sure he had seen it before, and didn't understand what he was asking.

Rinpoche made a face of wonder as the diamonds dazzled in the bright morning sun. He held out his hand, palm flat. Tara placed the ring in his palm. To her and Xander's shock, he suddenly threw the ring as far as he could in the direction of the sacred mountain. She watched as it arced like a shooting star, and sank in a distant mound of snow. She felt Xander start towards the mound, then restrain himself. She felt her husband's growing anger, and her own upset and shock. How could she be angry at her beloved Lama? But why would he do such a thing?

She wasn't as non-attached to the ring as she thought. She watched her beloved Xander's set jaw as he struggled to contain his reaction and frame some kind of appropriate response.

Xander looked around, and cleared his throat. "I wonder where Joy is?" he asked. "Rinpoche, Joy *kaba yurey*?"

Rinpoche looked up at the tall man innocently, and shrugged. "Coming later," he said in nonchalant English.

Tara saw Xander's keen eyes make note of the exact mound where the ring had embedded itself, pretending he wasn't doing so. She could feel the struggle between attachment and the teachings of non-attachment he knew he "should" follow, and felt the echo of a similar struggle within herself. This was a harsh lesson, and she dared to name what she felt about the situation, and even her teacher, "resentment."

Rinpoche ingenuously opened his palm to reveal the ring, and made a clown face of delighted surprise, his glittering black eyes wide and his lips a small "o" shape. He placed it on Tara's ring finger and patted her hand, then hugged Xander, drawing the tall man's forehead down to his level and placing his Third Eye upon Xander's.

Tara watched a tear slip down Xander's face. Rinpoche placed a hand tenderly on Xander's cheek. He took Tara's hand and fingered the ring, then emphatically exhaled the syllable "*Phet!*" that was meant to cut through attachment and break it.

Tears streamed down Tara's face as her emotions tumbled about in her heart, ranging from shame to attachment to compassion to simple devotion.

Xander clutched her hands, similar tears in his eyes. "Tara," he whispered, "may I give it to Rinpoche to sell to support the center? It's yours now. I won't do it without your permission."

"Of course," she said gently, slipping the ring off her finger and putting it in her husband's palm.

Xander cupped the ring in lotus-hand palms, and proffered it to Rinpoche as an offering. Rinpoche looked surprised.

"For you," said Xander. "For Drolma Ling. You sell it. It will get a good price."

Rinpoche smiled, looked at the ring closely as if inspecting it, then brought Xander's and Tara's hands together around it, shaking his head. He spoke in Tibetan.

"He says that you may need it someday, now that you're not attached to it anymore," said Joy's voice from nearby.

Joy and her daughter Dechen had just left the Lama House and were shivering a little in the cold air.

"*Tashi Delek*, Rinpoche," she greeted their teacher with a gentle bow. Then "Good morning, Da, Tara. Do you need me to translate?"

"I think he just gave us quite the teaching," said Xander. "But yes, later, for our interview, whenever it works for Rinpoche and for you."

Rinpoche set his prayer wheel to spinning and headed up the path to the Tara stupa, seemingly oblivious to the Karmic shock he had caused.

"Will do," said Joy. "After breakfast then. Rinpoche has to do his circumambulations."

Joy and Dechen headed off to the dining hall, while Xander and Tara followed Rinpoche to the stupa. Tara looked at the ring thoughtfully. It seemed to shine with even more rainbows than usual in the resplendent light of the mountain morning.

Xander's mouth murmured the Tara mantra, his lips curling in a joyous smile. His eyes crinkled as he looked down at his wife.

"'Through Kuntuzangpo's prayer, may all you desirous and lustful beings who have attachments, neither reject longing desires...'" Xander intoned.

Tara's voice joined him in the prayer aloud, "'nor accept attachment to desires. Let your consciousness relax in its natural state…'"

The two grinned at each other as they stepped out of the snow and onto the flagstone under the stupa's overhang.

"So wear it or not wear it," said Xander. "Keep it in your Medicine bag, or wear it on your hand, or put it in a vault, or throw it in the trash…well, I must admit, I rather hope not. *Madar jaan* would be upset, even if we wouldn't be. And that would be a trip to the hell realm!"

The sky had clouded up again while they engaged in their Karmic drama, and flurries began to fling thick heavy flakes of snow all around them. A storm swirled around the three as they joyously circled the sacred structure whose central pillar housed treasured relics of the Buddha, which Rinpoche had brought from Tibet after he was released from the Chinese labor camp in which he had attained a high degree of spontaneous and natural enlightenment.

A few hours later, as the snowstorm settled in, the two sat formally in front of Rinpoche on the rich burgundy lotus flower-patterned rugs on the floor of the stupa. Xander and Tara had made their offerings, and Rinpoche sat beaming at them as they waited for Joy to arrive.

The young woman entered breathlessly, a shawl of snowflakes trailing after her. She was laughing with delight. "We haven't seen anything like this in years," she said. "Not at the center, nor in Scotland, have we Dad?"

Xander shook his head.

"I hope…" began Tara, then shook her head as well. "I'm afraid to hope. I guess we are supposed to be beyond hope and fear, but it's hard when so many humans, not to mention other species, are involved."

Rinpoche looked questioningly at Joy, who began to translate for him. Then he spoke in Tibetan, looking back and forth between Tara and Xander.

"Rinpoche says it is not hopeless. He says that the Earth warming is excess of the fire element, which is anger and hatred. Reducing the anger and hatred in your own hearts will help reduce it in the world."

Tara looked at Rinpoche, troubled. "But how?" She spread her hands helplessly.

"*Om mani padme hung,*" said the Rinpoche firmly.

"I know there have been many studies of the effect of meditation on the world around us," said Xander. "Joy, you've read them. For example the TM study on violence going down when just 1% of the people in a given area practiced TM regularly."

Joy translated, and Rinpoche cocked his head to listen carefully, then spoke.

"That is part of it," Joy translated. "That is an explanation of how it works from a scientific point of view, and that is good. But the important thing is to feel it in your heart. Rinpoche says that perhaps this snowy weather, which is what we used to regard as normal, but which we haven't seen for many years, reflects the balancing in the hearts of the devoted disciples, like yourselves."

"Does he think that we have successfully rebalanced?" asked Tara eagerly. "Will this lead to actions being taken in the world on a large scale, politically and economically, in time to permanently restore the balance?"

Tara waited with baited breath while Joy translated her questions to Rinpoche, and watched as Joy and Rinpoche spoke back and forth in Tibetan.

"Probably not," said Joy wryly. "He says it will be hard for me, because I have a little one, but we have to forget our individual lives and families and keep doing our mantras and meditations. He says we shouldn't meditate just to change the external circumstances, but if our motivation is truly Bodhicitta, the benefit of all beings of all species, then our efforts will not be in vain. It's just that he can't predict the time scale. For example, he can't just say, 'Meditate ten million mantras before Losar and then there will be successful climate conferences and laws passed and new technologies and all the problems will go away and things will be normal again.' For one thing, he says, it is not linear. There are many different possibilities."

"What about the possibility of large scale organic farming and Regenerative Agriculture sequestering carbon?" asked Xander. "Joy, is that something you can explain?"

Joy looked at her father with a tolerant smirk. "Of course, Da. Rinpoche is aware of all of those things, and we have discussed them before, so I know the words."

"It could work," she finally translated. "But you can't count on it. There are many complicated and interacting Karmas involved. He says just to do your best, that both of you have studied with him for a long time, and you both know the things he always says, to cultivate Bodhicitta always, and to at the same same time rest in Nature of Mind. He says you both understand non-duality very well, and you are both altruistic."

Rinpoche began to speak, and pulled an agate mala out of his capacious robes.

"Now he says to ask your personal question," said Joy. "He said you have a request for a *mo*."

Tara looked at Xander. They had tried to frame the words of their divination request carefully.

"So, Rinpoche, we are wondering where it is best to live, to be based."

Joy translated the simple question. Tara watched as Rinpoche held the rosary of swirling brown agate in his hands, blew on it gently a few times, and then looked at it, dividing the beads as he stared at it, and began to speak.

"There will be separation no matter what you choose," translated Joy carefully. Tara could see the effort the young woman was making to keep her own feelings out of the conversation.

"If you live in Scotland, Tara may not see her family for a very long time, or very often. If you live here, then Xander will worry for Bibi Amina as she gets older." She laughed a moment with Rinpoche. "He says Bibi Amina will not be easy if you are not there for her."

Rinpoche divided the beads one last time, and spoke.

"So it is up to you to choose," continued Joy. "Any choice you make will be right. He knows this is not the answer you want, that you were hoping he could give you a yes or a no. But the answer is that the two of you have to make your own decision. There will be some separation no matter what you choose, but also some happiness in either course of action. You cannot escape your Karma, and the two of you have a destiny. Remember that you have taken the Bodhisattva vow, so you are coming back anyway, even after you attain enlightenment in *Dewachen*."

Rinpoche leaned forward, and again blessed them, first on Tara's forehead, then on Xander's.

After a moment, Joy continued. "There will come a time when Rinpoche is not here in this body, and that is not too far away. But he says that you both know how to call him, and he will be there, in a body or not in a body, whenever you need him. He trusts you to make the right decision, and says that your choices may constantly change as a river changes course, as the winds change. But your constancy is the sun still rising and setting, and the moon, which changes its position in the sky and its phases, still rising and setting. He says that the two of you have a Karmic destiny together, but not to be attached to the importance of your destiny. Keep your humility."

"Rinpoche is the most perfect example of that," said Tara.

Rinpoche winked at the two of them, and gave them a thumbs-up sign.

Chapter
19

18 October, 2050

**Avebury Encampment,
New Avalon**

The churning sound of numerous heli-shuttles woke them up just past dawn. Tara's heart sank into her stomach. This was definitely not normal.

Tara poked her head out of her hut, squinting into the rising sun beneath the bank of clouds. There were at least eight of them, black like locusts, flying in a formation. This time they actually landed, not far from the Encampment.

Leona and Janus came running from the nearby hut they had built for themselves in recent weeks, her long braids and his dreads streaming out behind them.

Yeshi, Sitara, and Jonah were instantly awake. They stood by Tara, shading their eyes against the sun.

"Should we start for the Henge immediately?" asked Tara. "Maybe they have nothing to do with us."

"Oh, they do," said Leona softly. "Damn Seamus. He's such a weakling. He'll tell anyone anything, true or not, for a jug of anything alcoholic."

Tara did not correct her great-granddaughter's language or analysis of the situation.

Yeshi stood behind her and put his hands on her shoulders. She allowed herself to lean back into him for comfort for a moment. He gently turned her to face him.

"We should start, though I have the feeling we will be stopped. Don't be surprised at anything that happens."

"What do you mean?"

"We, the three of us from our Timeline, might just need to disappear, and then come back later."

"Can you do that? I thought you had to be at a portal?"

"Sitara is pretty sure the three of us don't need a portal. But she's also pretty sure the three of you from this Timeline do." He sighed deeply. "I guess we'll see. Let's start out as planned."

Tara hoisted the conical hemp basket that she had packed onto her back. It felt heavier than she remembered, but she hadn't slept well, and she was 96, she reminded herself yet again. She hoped she could keep up.

Leona and Janus hoisted their own baskets, as they all looked anxiously towards the marshland where the heli-shuttles had landed. People in what looked like old-fashioned SWAT team gear had emerged and could be seen surrounding the Longhouse, their black-shielded uniforms like carapaces of insects.

"Georgie," called Tara softly, looking inside her hut. The place where Georgie normally slept on her pallet was warm, but only gray cat hair remained. "Oh, Georgie, I'll miss you. I just wanted to say good-bye. You know it's not safe for you to come anyway."

The voice she had recently grown accustomed to hearing was as silent as the absence of his physical purr. Her heart sank. But she knew it was for the best. He was probably off in a cat-sulk somewhere. She knew he'd be all right, live out a cat's lifespan, hopefully find another human to be close to. Somehow she didn't think she was ever coming back here.

The party of six started off down the well-trodden path between the rice paddies. They didn't get very far before they were surrounded by the insect-like SWAT team, which blocked their way.

One of them took off his shiny black helmet. Tara wondered if this was supposed to put them at ease. She didn't feel easy.

"Morning to you," said a male voice in a London working-class accent.

"Good morning?" said Tara uncertainly. Leona and Janus remained silent, sullen.

"You off to the Henge?" He sounded like he was trying to make pleasant conversation.

"Um…" Tara yawned, trying to stall for time. "We were just out to do a little gathering…me and my granddaughter, and her mate."

"Just the three of you? I thought there were supposed to be six."

Tara looked around and realized that there indeed were only three of them standing on the footpath. She felt glad and abandoned at the same time. She hadn't seen them go, and hoped that the insect-man hadn't either.

"Yes, the three of us. I'm an old woman, see, and my only living relative is my granddaughter, actually she's my great-granddaughter. Her mate's a good boy, and they both help me gather and fish, and weave some baskets."

A man in, of all things, an early 21st century-style dress suit and shiny leather shoes, walked up the path from the parked heli-shuttles.

"That'll do," he said. "Where are the others?"

"Back at the Longhouse, I'd suppose," said Janus, yawning boredly. "No one else ever wants to help Gran," he grumbled.

"I coulda sworn there were six of 'em," said the helmetless insect-man.

"So their leader says. The visitors from 'France.' Well, have some of your men keep looking. We'll take these in for questioning. They'll get some good meals, and it will keep them out of mischief."

Tara moved protectively towards Leona, who just kept looking down. "Don't," Tara warned the girl in a low voice.

"But Sitara taught me…" Leona whispered.

"Not now. Please. We might need it more later."

Leona sighed, a tad resentfully.

"This way, then, children," said the man who had doffed his helmet. "Be good girls and boy, and let's get on to the shuttles. We're taking you off on a little trip."

Although the insect-men did not appear to be obviously armed, Tara saw no choice but to follow.

"Leave the baskets," said the suited man. "You won't be needing them. We have plenty of food where you'll be…visiting for a little bit."

"How long?" asked Leona angrily. "You have no right to just come in here and interfere with our lives. We're just fine."

"Oh, we have every right," said the suited man in his posh accent. "We are the government of this country."

Tara pinched Leona's arm. "We'll come back soon and finish our gathering," Tara said. "No need to be encumbered."

As she put her heavy basket down and turned to follow the insect-men, she thought she saw a flash of gray out of the corner of her eye.

Automatically, she clutched at her Medicine bag, feeling the unaccustomed hardness of the longlost ring. Shit. They would take it all away from her. Might as well let it go now. Surreptitiously, she worked at the hard leather around the knot at the back of her neck, pretending to fiddle with the straw hat she was wearing. As she walked, she felt her precious Medicine bag slip away, down the front of her clothing and into the weeds. She hoped it would not get disrespectfully trampled, and hoped even more that none of the erstwhile soldiers would pick it up. Again she thought she saw a flash of gray, but they had almost reached the heli-shuttles and she couldn't turn around to look.

Leona, who had never seen such a terrifying machine except at a great distance away in the sky, balked at entering. Tara could tell Janus was scared too, but he had a calm and phlegmatic demeanor, and comforted his love as they clattered up the metal steps together.

Tara let her mind move into a state of curiosity. She had ridden in many air vehicles in her 96 years, starting with passenger planes in the late '60s, and ranging from jets to single-engine bush planes to helicopters under fire in war zones.

These craft were less noisy than the gunships that had threatened from above in several wars, or the transports she had ridden in. The anthropologist in her came out as she looked at the cockpit. Full of gadgets and lights, but really it didn't look all that much more space-age than the dashboard of the Prius that she and Xander had driven when they were newlyweds. Physical, material technology hadn't really progressed all that much since the Three

Plagues, she supposed. The Elite weren't so much progressing as preserving a certain way of life, and death.

Leona and Janus clutched at each other as they flew. Neither of them would look out the tiny porthole windows. No one bothered Tara once they were prisoners on the heli-shuttle—no one even suggested that they strap themselves in—so she sat on the hard metal bench and looked out, curious what the landscape looked like now.

Everywhere was water, reflecting dead pewter light from the leaden sky. It was interesting to be between the layer of clouds that seemed to persist most days, whether it dropped more rain and mist or not, and the sodden land. The rice paddies were bright green, ready for harvest soon.

Tara sighed. It was so strange to see this landscape, which she remembered as an organic hodge-podge of irregularly shaped cropland, green and golden, now looking more like the fields of Southeast Asia. She wondered, for the millionth time, if humans were still able to inhabit those regions, or if the combination of temperature and humidity had become so high that human and mammal life could no longer exist there. She wondered if these soldiers who lived among the Elite knew, or if the suited man who sat in the co-pilot's seat knew. Or if they even cared to know.

London was surprisingly intact, though it was weird to see the streets completely void of traffic and even pedestrians, and many streets near the river had become virtual canals. She saw that tall dykes had been built along the part of the Thames that snaked through the City—the old financial district—and the water level was disconcertingly far higher than the streets.

The heli-shuttle put down smoothly in front of St. Paul's Cathedral. Tara's heart sank as she realized how close they were to the Tower Bridge, and had a sneaking suspicion where they were being taken.

Leona and Janus disembarked looking slightly queasy, with shaky legs. Tara cautiously made her way down the metal steps, feeling more spiritually disoriented than physically ill. She hadn't been around so much metal in years.

The air was stifling and humid. It was much hotter in London that it had been at Avebury. She remembered the urban heat island effect.

There was not a shred of green anywhere, in a city that had had numerous parks and trees. Everything was, and felt, dead.

"Can you walk, Mrs. MacFarlane?" asked the suited man pleasantly.

Tara felt jarred. No one had called her by that name in decades. "Yes, and since you know my name, what is yours?" she asked in equally pleasant and false tones.

"Clive Baker, at your service."

I doubt it, thought Tara. "Mr. Baker, I can't honestly say I'm pleased to meet you under the circumstances…"

"Clive, please. You're free to go, of course," he interrupted her. "We just need to make some inquiries."

"Of course. Clive. Let me introduce my great-granddaughter, Leona. And her mate, Janus."

The two young people looked warily at Clive. Janus smiled with fake politeness. Leona refashioned her glare into something resembling friendliness.

Clive smiled quickly and politely and looked away towards a group of insect-men approaching from the direction of the Tower.

"Our bodyguards," he said.

"Guarding us from what?" asked Tara, looking around at the deserted city.

"Anti-social elements. Dissidents."

That would be us, she thought.

Tara was amazed at the high-tech environment inside the old Tower of London. The ancient prison, long a tourist attraction, had been converted into a modern…prison. Not that they called it that.

Tara, Leona, and Janus were led into a shiny, clean, very white two-bedroom "flat." The bedrooms each had double beds, looking much like beds had in the early part of the 21st century, except that they were covered with a silvery micro-fiber instead of bedclothes. Tara wondered if the fabric was meant to keep one's body at a comfortable temperature, or if it was some kind of tracking or surveillance technology, or both. She wondered if it was still manufactured, or if it was left over from the times before the Third Plague.

"Healing fabric," said Clive.

I'll bet, thought Tara. It probably contains drugs to make one placid.

"Once we re-establish government throughout the rural areas, everyone will have these, and other advantages."

"We're doing perfectly fine, thank you, on our own," said Leona.

Tara shot her a warning look.

"Well we are. We have everything we need. We grow or catch enough food, we have shelter from the rains, we get outdoors and play games, we're healthy. What else is there?"

"Oh, there is so much more to life," said Clive pleasantly. "Civilization. Order. You can live with so much more certainty."

"I thought life was inherently uncertain," said Janus.

Tara was surprised. The young man had become a philosopher overnight. Then again, he'd had some pretty unusual experiences in the past few weeks.

"But we can control so much," said Clive blandly. "Improve lives of those who have survived such harrowing times."

"You'd improve my life right now if you just let us go home," said Leona fiercely.

"In time. I'm sure you won't mind assisting us with some inquiries. Well, I must go. Someone will be along in a little while. Help yourselves to whatever you need."

Tara had immediately started looking around for avenues of escape, out of habit. She'd never actually been imprisoned, just detained from time to time in various parts of the world, and her instinct impelled her to look for both physical means of escape, as well as whatever passed for legal means in a particular society.

There wasn't much to go on here, but she stilled her breath and sat in meditation on one of the beds, from which she had removed the metallic-looking bedspread. The sheets beneath seemed harmless enough, she hoped. Leona and Janus were in the other room, comforting each other.

"I'm sure there are cameras everywhere on us," Tara called to them. "Just so you know."

"Then we'll give them something fun to look at," said Janus. Leona giggled.

Tara went into meditation, leaning her back against the straight, cold white wall. She actually managed to attain moments of Samadhi, due to long decades of practice.

"*I'm coming,*" said the soft, familiar feline voice. "*I can find you.*"

"*Georgie!*" her mind thought. "*So you're all right.*"

"*I saw everything. I was in your basket, ready to go with you. I won't abandon you. There are still a lot of cats to help me find my way, and I can make my way to you.*"

Tara opened her eyes and looked around the room.

"*It's not like it used to be,*" she thought to Georgie. "*It's all white walls.*"

Her eyes lingered where the walls met the ceiling. There was wavering. The white parted, showing the old stones beneath. And a vent with a grating. She restrained the surprised expression on her face. "*A hologram,*" she thought.

"*A what?*"

Could cats even see holograms? This would be a test. "*Not sure, Georgie. It's an illusion. When I meditate enough I can see through it. I don't know what you will see, but there's a grating, a vent. I think you could get through it. But how will you ever get to London?*"

"*You leave that to me,*" said the cat's voice. "*Bye for now. I'm walking, and I've got to save my energy for that.*"

Tara wondered if she had made up the conversation with Georgie in her head. Prisoners did such things, she had read. And then there was her age. If one really started losing it, did one know, or did one just think one's thoughts were normal? She had been taught that ultimately everything is an illusion, even our agreed-upon reality. So did it matter? Could the little gray cat actually help get them out of here?

Having finished her meditation, Tara allowed herself to worry. Could the Time Travelers go to 1978 on their own? Is that where they were now? Or had they had to abort the mission? Were she and Leona and Janus somehow a necessary part of it?

More importantly, if they were, was time running out? If there were too long a delay, would they miss some kind of window? Would the Timeline borders crumble and the negative Timeline they were in now merge with the one Yeshi, Sitara, and Jonah had come from, bleed into it and change it? What if the Time Travelers were never even born, or the spiritual technology of Time Travel was never discovered?

Tara felt guilty, even though there wasn't anything she could have done to have prevented their arrest. Detainment, she corrected herself. Right. Leona hadn't foreseen it, and neither had she, nor even Sitara. They could have left the night before…but probably could have been spotted from the air anyway, on their way to the Henge.

She fervently hoped that the Time Travelers could accomplish the mission without the three beings from 2050. She wished she'd asked more questions.

Suddenly, Sitara was there right in front of her, in her classic Nordic goddess guise, her blue eyes shining in the artificial holographic light.

"The cameras…" Tara murmured.

"No worries. I've suspended them. There won't even be a blip in the footage."

"So we can talk?"

"Yes."

Sitara touched Tara's shoulder, and a warmth passed through her. Her neck, shoulders, and back released a tension she hadn't been fully aware she had been carrying.

"Thank you."

The two women faced each other, sitting cross-legged on the bed. Leona and Janus were asleep, judging from the soft sounds of breathing coming from the other room.

"Should I wake them up?" asked Tara. "While you have the camera stopped?"

"No. Let them sleep. They'll know what they need to know in a dream. With Leona it's easy. Janus is learning more, and will get it from her, a download so to speak."

Tara took Sitara's hands. "Can't you three go to 1978 and see what you can change without us?"

"We've been," said Sitara shortly. "Your presence is required to increase the probabilities."

"Which are?"

"With only the three of us from the 24th century, we have a 65% chance of success."

"I'd like to have a 65% chance of winning the lottery."

Sitara looked at her skeptically. "Lottery?"

"A game of chance. The odds were rather high against winning."

"Oh. With the six of us, the odds of success increase to 92%."

"Oh! That's quite a difference. How do you calculate?"

Sitara shook her head impatiently. "Too complicated to explain in 21st century terms, even to you. Just trust me."

"What about the delay of us being stuck here?"

"So far, it's okay. We have some more days."

"And if it goes on?"

Sitara looked troubled. "It starts to fluctuate. The odds go up and down."

"How much time before the fluctuation?"

"Three to four days, a week at most."

"Oh. We'd better start figuring out how to get out of here then."

"Maybe we can help. I'm not sure how yet."

"Shut off the hologram?"

"You're still in a prison, by any name."

"Shut off the cameras? That will be necessary in any case."

"When the time comes."

"Can't you just port us out of here? How did you get here?"

"We're not sure yet. This was an experiment. We have to be sure that we can get all three of you out at the same time, while the cameras are suspended. That will buy us time."

"My Tibetan teacher was in prison for 20 years. He told us a story of one of his teachers remaining voluntarily in prison to teach the others. Then one day when he was done he just dissolved the walls and walked through them into freedom. He was seen far away, in other parts of Tibet. The thing is, he could have done that at any time, but he stayed and suffered with the others to teach them. I wish I had that skill. Not to mention that degree of compassion."

"Maybe you do," said Sitara. "Maybe we all do. Sometimes, when it's for a higher purpose, the odds of success increase exponentially. I must go now. We don't want to test the limits of our ability to suspend the cameras."

The two women hugged each other fervently, and then Sitara was gone. Tara could hear Leona and Janus yawning and stirring in the next room. For the benefit of the cameras, she stood up, as if she had just now finished her meditation, stretched, and did some qi gong exercises, wondering where exactly the cameras were.

Chapter
20

20 March, 2019

Kabul, Afghanistan

Xander's first cousin Fauzia had insisted on meeting them at the airport herself, despite the danger. Civilians were banned from the airport, but Fauzia still had connections.

Tara watched the flurry of kisses and greetings, punctuated by tears, as Fauzia greeted her aunt Bibi Amina and her cousin Xander, whose name she pronounced in the Afghan way, Sikunder.

Tara felt something of an outsider, empathizing but unable to fully understand what 40 years of war had done to her new extended family and their countrymen. She had watched Bibi Amina sympathetically as Xander held his mother's hand on the plane. Tears had streamed silently down Bibi Amina's dignified face ever since the plane had begun circling Kabul before diving steeply down towards the airport as the rising sun peaked over the eastern horizon.

Xander and Tara were both on a mission, on three-month assignments for UNICEF that they had managed to secure together as a husband-wife team. Xander was to advise on public health issues, with Tara running a team of eager young Afghans commissioned to do a survey on maternal-child health care needs. Originally they were to have covered a large area of the northern villages, but the worsening violence had curtailed their activities to the capital city.

Still, it enabled them to accomplish their second mission, bringing Bibi Amina home for her first visit in 15 years. With Bibi Amina's health fragile after a bout with colon cancer, they all knew it could be her last visit to the land where she was born.

Tara had no idea if they'd be able to accomplish Xander's third mission. He was determined to bring his recently widowed cousin—a longtime women's rights activist and an on and off member of the Afghan Parliament—back to Scotland and hopefully out of the danger that had claimed the life of her husband, a prominent human rights activist assassinated by the Taliban. Neither Fauzia nor Bibi Amina knew anything about his plan.

Well, they had three months to accomplish it. Tara joined in the enthusiastic Dari greetings as Fauzia's attention turned to her.

"*Khosh shudam az didan-e-shoma,*" began Tara formally, truly pleased to meet her cousin by marriage in person at last.

"*Man khosh shudam az didan-e-tu,*" answered Fauzia. Tara recognized that Fauzia had immediately embraced her into the family by addressing her in the familiar.

Fauzia rushed them into a private armored vehicle, talking all the while, mixing Dari and English.

Fauzia's two trucks' worth of bodyguards fell in ahead and behind their vehicle. "So so sorry for all the trouble," said the beautiful middle-aged woman. "But we want to ensure your safety."

Similar actions had not ensured the safety of Fauzia's late husband Jamil, but Tara refrained from pointing that out as the small convoy speeded through the unseasonably warm morning.

"So, *Nawroz Mubarak, Khala Jaan,* Sikunder *Jaan,* Tara *Jaan.* Happy New Year. Well, each year just seems to get more difficult, but we are still hopeful every new year."

They bounced along on the rutted roads. Public works had not been maintained for years, and the only shiny new buildings were either NGO compounds, fortified embassy compounds, or the villas of wealthy Afghans. Barbed wire and colorful, lethal glass shards topped the walls of the compounds, some made of cement, others of traditional mudbrick.

Bibi Amina had finally let go and was sobbing. "Kabul *Jaan*, my home, what has happened to you? I should not have come. I should have remembered it the way it was till my dying day."

It was not the way Tara remembered it either, and she hadn't seen it in the good days, just the slightly better ones. In the very early years of the 21st century, just after the fall of the Taliban's regime, in a time of optimism, goodwill, and creativity, she had served a yearlong stint working with a Swedish NGO. Much of the city had been destroyed in the relentless civil war between the Taliban and the Northern Alliance, and who knew what other parties? But at the time Tara was there, rebuilding was going on at a fevered pace, women and girls were back in school, young people were forming peace groups, and the Internet was just catching on.

They had reached the metal gates of a relatively modest home in Shahr-e-nau, which was still regarded as a desirable district, said to have the best security. As if by magic, the gates opened, but Tara realized that the driver had phoned ahead with precision. Their car roared into the gates, which were shut behind them as quickly as possible. The two pickup trucks full of bodyguards remained outside. Tara tensed, hoping not to hear automatic weapons fire or an explosion.

Fauzia's house, though spacious, lacked the ostentation of most of the other houses in the neighborhood. The rooms were clean and white, and several hummed with air conditioning on this already warm day.

Tara was grateful that her and Xander's room was air-conditioned. Bibi Amina's was just down the hallway. The older woman retired to her room almost immediately, claiming the need for rest and meditation, only she called it *namaz*, as the five daily Muslim prayers are called.

"Is your mom reclaiming her Muslim identity?" asked Tara as they unpacked their duffles.

"What is left to reclaim?" asked Xander with a touch of uncharacteristic bitterness. "What is left of Islam? We've always been Sufis anyway, but the Taliban has been busy killing them too. I don't think Bibi Amina wants to

126

stick out. She's not going to say, 'I'm a Sufi, as my family always was, and I do Buddhist meditation.'"

Tara put a stack of sweaters in the wooden cupboard. The clothes she had brought were way too warm if it was already this hot. She'd be going with Fauzia to visit a tailor and to a *chadar* shop to get a couple of shawls to cover her head as soon as the bazar reopened after the New Year festivities—such as they were. She was glad that at least she had brought one light cotton Pakistani-style *shalwar kameez*. She carefully laid the tunic and trousers out on the bed, to put on after her shower.

"Do you want the first shower?" she asked Xander solicitously.

"No, you go ahead." He kissed the top of her head. "I'm now beginning to be sorry that I dragged you into this."

"You didn't. I'm a big girl. I might have applied for this job even if I'd never met you."

"Really?"

"Well, no, probably not."

"Go take your shower."

"Join me?"

"That's probably illegal here, even for married people."

It turned out that Tara, Xander, and Bibi Amina were not invited to accompany Fauzia to the public Nawroz celebrations. Fauzia looked at them as if they had left their minds behind in the UK, and the idea occasioned some heated discussion in Dari that was beyond Tara's ability to follow.

"Absolutely not!" Fauzia finally said in English, just below a shout.

"I am elder to you," said Bibi Amina quietly. "I am Afghan, though I married a *farangi*, and I shall sit beside you and take my chances. However, I agree, I will not allow my son to go, and certainly not Tara."

"I'm told that I look Afghan if I wear Afghan dress," Tara protested.

"You think they are not killing Afghans? Or women?" asked Bibi Amina. "The Taliban are now even saying that our ancient tradition of Nawroz is 'unislamic' and celebration of a pagan holiday is prohibited."

Xander brooded, looking at Fauzia's family pictures on the white marble mantel above the fireplace, including her late husband Jamil.

"Most likely we would all survive," said Fauzia. "You know, *naseeb, qismet*, if it is your time it is your time. *Khala jaan*, if you insist then I must defer to you as an elder, but Sikunder and his wife would only be targets."

Xander started once again to protest, but Bibi Amina silenced him. "Do you want to draw fire on your own family?" she said. "It's bad enough that we are troubling Fauzia by staying here. We are putting her in even more danger than she is already in. So please, stay away today, I beg you. Then we shall see if we even should stay here."

That occasioned another round of argument, ending with Fauzia saying in English, "You are family, you can't go elsewhere. You will be safe here, safer than in some NGO compound. If you do as I say, you won't be noticed. I should not have gone myself to the airport, as it could have put you in danger. From now on, you will not come and go with me, so you will not be a target.

"Now I must go. *Khala jaan* can come with me. Happy New Year."

"Happy New Year," answered Tara mechanically, ironically, watching her mother-in-law and cousin-in-law wrapping black *chadars* around their heads and upper bodies, and donning huge, out-of-style dark glasses that covered most of their faces.

"We will be back before dark. *Inshallah*," said Fauzia. "I have cooked the meal myself, and we will enjoy it then."

Tara spent most of the afternoon alternating between napping and meditation. She always loved it when she and Xander meditated together. But this time she could feel his restlessness, his unusual difficulty in settling. She refocused her mind, again and again mentally saying the Tibetan "*Phet!*" syllable to cut through her worried thoughts.

It grew dark, and Fauzia and Bibi Amina were not yet back. Tara and Xander flinched at the sound of explosions, relieved to see the light of colorful fireworks shining through the window.

"God knows why they still like fireworks after all these years of war," muttered Xander.

A moment later they heard the gate opening and the roar of the engine as the car returned. Xander visibly relaxed.

"We've made it through our first day, family intact and alive," he remarked. "Come, let's join the feast."

In the old days, except for the very darkest days of the Soviet war and the days of the Taliban oppression, there would have been a huge party of family and friends. "People are afraid now," said Fauzia. "Since Jamil was killed, they all think I am next. So to save them embarrassment, I no longer invite them, and I politely decline their invitations. They always look so relieved. But they try not to show it of course."

Tara was familiar with the story, which was all too common amongst human rights activists, educated Afghans going about their business, and Afghans working with NGOs. It didn't matter that the overwhelming majority of Afghans held the Taliban and its so-called "values" in contempt, viewing the Saudi-inspired Wahabist philosophy as a dangerous and alien foreign influence. The tiny minority were well-armed, apparently well-funded, and ruthless in their persecution of all who did not toe their archaic line.

Tara wondered if she could bear three months of this. But she was committed. Perhaps once they began their work, they would fall into a daily routine…oh, that's right, they had been warned not to fall into a daily routine, but to vary their times of coming and going.

How were they ever going to be of service to the Afghan people under these circumstances? The recruiters had been delighted that they wanted to sign up. Tara suspected that they didn't get very many volunteers. And in the continuing world economic crisis, it was the best way, well really the only way, of funding a trip for them and Bibi Amina.

Tara tried to lay her fears and doubts aside and simply enjoy the delicious food, but she could not fully allay her sadness. Even Fauzia's children and their families could not safely celebrate the New Year with their mother. She had forbidden it as too dangerous, and told them to stay home with their families.

After dinner, they retired to an interior media room, Fauzia's sole luxury.

"No one can hear us from outside," Fauzia explained. "It's better this way. We can watch movies, we can listen to music. There is even room to dance."

Fauzia put on old traditional Afghan music from the '70s, from before the series of wars that had never ended. She grabbed her aunt's hand and pulled her onto the dance floor.

Tara was amazed to see how Bibi Amina could still move in the steps of the Afghan traditional dances, and how graceful her hand movements were. One would never dream she was in her 80's, thought Tara.

Bibi Amina grabbed her son's hand as the voice of the late pop singer Ahmad Zaher, killed by the Soviets in the 1980's, sang of beloved Kabul: "*Kabul jaan, Kabul jaan, Kabul jaaaaaan, Kabul jaan.*" She pulled him up onto the dance floor, and he in turn pulled Tara to join him. In a circle, the four danced, losing themselves in shameless emotions of love and longing for the return of a more joyous time.

Chapter
21

20 October, 2050

Tower of London,
London, United Corporations of Northern Europe

"Where are the companions that you were hosting?" asked Clive once again. He poured Tara another glass of lemon water.

She had made the mistake of sipping at the delicious, now lost beverage. It was only her meditative discipline on the subject of non-attachment that enabled her to dissolve the illusion of attachment and just enjoy the drink in the moment, knowing that she would probably never have it again in what was left of her life. Unless the Time Travel mission succeeded.

"Oh, you mean the people from France?" she asked sweetly.

"France. Is that what they gave about?" commented Clive with a slight smirk of disbelief.

Tara shrugged, hunching down like an old woman, trying to remember the body language of advanced age, which her body seemed to be progressively forgetting. She even tried to look a little addled.

"No one's come over from there for a long time, so why should we doubt them? It's what they said."

"Mrs. MacFarlane. Tara. May I call you Tara?"

She shrugged.

"Tara." He sat down, straddling a chair in a most ungentlemanly way, facing her. The chair, like the table, like the walls, was unrelievedly, unimaginatively, white. "We know your history. You were, are, an anthropologist. You've been all over the world, in what, 70 countries?"

"So I counted once. That seems familiar."

"And you wouldn't know the difference between a French person, and… what?"

She shrugged and stared into space, trying to look disinterested. "I'm 96, or thereabouts. Memory does not serve me well. It gets all tangled now."

Clive sighed deeply. "Your friend Seamus told us that these visitors came very…abruptly. As abruptly as they seem to have left us the day we landed to invite you to help us with our inquiries. He rambled on, something about Time Travelers."

Tara guffawed, or at least made an attempt to. "That's rich. Surely you don't believe in Time Travelers, a gentleman like yourself, an officer of the Corporation."

His gray eyes, hard and flat as steel, looked at her grimly. "I'm not saying there are Time Travelers," he said icily. "Just that there are people who say they are. People who say they are what they are not are dangerous. They lead to delusion and discontentment. Look at those two children of yours. They could be model citizens, but now they are discontented dreamers."

Tara felt a chill at the mention of Leona and Janus. Leona had a hot temper, but she was strong and probably had the ability to confuse this man's mind. Of Janus she was less sure. He had no real training, and might be a weak link, but he did have a natural cleverness about him.

She looked at Clive blandly. "I was trained as a scientist. Why would I believe something like Time Travel?"

"You were a Buddhist," he said thoughtfully.

"Once. Before the Plagues. Before my husband died."

"You meditate now. We see you on vid…uh, some of the guards have seen you."

"Habit. It's useful, being a prisoner."

"Madam, you are not a prisoner."

"I'm free to go, whenever I wish, with Leona and Janus."

"Yes. Just as soon as we are finished with our inquiries."

"In other words, we are not free to go."

"Yes, you are," he insisted. "Just a few more days of inquiries."

She looked as vague as she could. "A few more days. Right."

She was grateful that they hadn't tortured her, or worse, hurt Leona and Janus. And she was almost 100% sure that they hadn't given her any truth drugs. She wondered if they still had them. She didn't know if, even with all her training over many decades, her mind could resist the truth drugs that had been developed in the early years of the century.

Clive sighed in frustration and got up out of his chair, carefully replacing the white chair under the white table.

"Madam, enjoy your dinner. We'll speak again tomorrow."

Madam. No longer Tara, or even Mrs. MacFarlane. "Thank you. You have some delicious foods that we can't get at home, in Avebury."

"For you they are a memory. For the children, they are new. We could provide them to you, to your whole Encampment, on a regular basis if you could only help us with our inquiries."

"Clive, I'm doing the best I can. It's just that you keep asking the same questions over and over again, and I get so confused by that. I tell you what I know, what I believe to be true, and then you ask me again like you don't believe me, or like I've forgotten the question." She patted his hand. "You shouldn't treat an old lady that way."

Exasperated, he withdrew his hand.

"Good day, Madam. Perhaps tomorrow you can help us more."

Tara sat back, slumped in the white chair. She moved over to the bed, peeling back the silvery bedspread, and bounced a few times for the sake of the cameras, then settled down into meditation.

Her mind became instantly clear. Because of the cameras, she'd been unable to speak aloud to Leona and Janus about anything at all meaningful.

But she knew that they'd received the transmission, as Sitara had promised. Leona had started to say, "Gran, I just had the strangest dream…" when Tara cut her off.

"Always dreaming, useless child!" she had shouted at her. She didn't know where the cameras were, or how many, so she couldn't be sure of looking away from them. She just looked down and THOUGHT with all her might to Leona.

"We can't speak aloud. Only this way."

"Oh, I get it, Gran. Yes, I had that dream. It wasn't a dream, was it? Sitara was here and suspended the cameras."

"Yes."

"She's figuring out how to get us out of here. And we have to do it soon."

"Yes."

Tara fiddled with her toes and then started swaying around the room, like a crazy old lady.

"Gran?" Leona spoke aloud. "Are you okay? What are you doing?"

"Dancing. Remembering dancing with your great-grandfather Xander."

"Oh, Gran…"

"Great idea," whispered Leona's mind-voice. *"Make them think you are dotty."*

"I'm doing my best."

"When is Sitara coming back?"

"I only wish I knew. Hopefully soon enough."

"Poor Gran, you're losing it, going dotty," said Leona aloud.

"Does Janus know? Can he hear the Mind Voices?" asked Tara in silence.

"Yes!" came his triumphant thought-voice.

"Must have come from making love to me so much," thought Leona saucily.

"Might be," answered Janus' thought voice. *"In that case a win/win."*

At that moment all three of them heard a familiar whining meow, and scratching above their heads. The electricity in the room went out, and with it the hologram, and presumably the cameras.

In the thin gray light of an autumn afternoon, Tara, Leona, and Janus could see that they were really in a stone cell with gratings high overhead. And that the form of a gray cat cast a shadow on them as Georgie squeezed himself through the bars. He dropped to the ground and with satisfaction dropped an object at Tara's feet.

Long conditioned to the ways of cats, she automatically cringed, wondering what dead present he had brought her.

"*Ingrate!*" came the cat's voice in their heads. "*Look at it. I've carried this all the way from Avebury. I had to put it down when I was hunting, and then go back and find it. I had to ask directions from other cats, and I got wet and muddy. My paws hurt from walking on stones and cement, and I even had to swim across canals. And you think I've brought you a dead mouse?*"

"*Sorry,*" she thought to her beloved Georgie, bending down to pet him and scratch his ears. He was purring, despite his mental tirade.

She picked up the object he had dropped. It was her Medicine bag. Inside she could feel the diamond ring that had been lost and found so many times in her life.

"*Well, put it on under your clothes before they get the hologram and the lights back on,*" hissed the cat's thought-voice. "*Be quick about it.*"

Tara uncurled the leather cord, put it over her head, and tucked the bag well under her upper undergarments.

"*Thank you,*" she said silently.

"*I thought you'd want it back. Thought maybe it would come in handy. Humans still like these things. I saw those shiny things in some of the shop fronts on the way here. Maybe you can use it to buy your way out of here.*"

The lights flickered, but then dimmed again.

"*We might not have a lot of time,*" Georgie said.

"*How did you arrange this?*"

"*I made friends with the mice. Really. Showed them where those delicious wires were, and they chewed them good.*"

"*Can you do it again?*"

"*There are many mice, and many wires. They'll try to poison the mice, but I'll tell them what not to eat. Mice have lived here for centuries.*"

The lights flickered again, and the hologram started forming. Georgie dashed under the bed. "*They won't see me here.*"

"*But the cameras...*"

"*I'll only come out at night.*"

"*They have night vision, most probably. Or infrared.*"

"*I'll become invisible.*"

"*Can you do that?*"

"*I'm a cat. I came into incarnation as a cat for various reasons. Invisibility is one. I won't grin, so my teeth can't be seen, like the one in the story. Or maybe that's just superstition. They are not expecting to see a cat, so they won't see a cat. But just in case, I'll be under the bed.*"

The lights came on, and the hologram flickered back into being, whiteness and steel gray. No cat could be seen.

That night, Tara cried, clutching the ring beneath her bedclothes, stroking the lump that was a purring Georgie. Whoever, whatever, he was, he was loyal in a way few humans were.

Tomorrow she would offer the ring to Clive. She pegged him for a greedy man, and if such things still had value, then the diamonds and platinum in this ring surely did. She had no doubt that he could hack the cameras, erase any vestige of her bribery if he so wished, if it benefited him. He was loyal to the Corporation only because it had served him well, she thought.

Suddenly, several things happened at once, and afterwards she couldn't quite sort out what happened when, or in what order.

Georgie's purring became so loud that the walls began to shake. Leona, in the next room, began a moan that at first Tara thought was extremely loud and passionate love-making, but then the walls began to break down, not only the hologram, but the walls themselves.

The white hologram disappeared, the grates at the top of the walls, near the ceilings, actually fell to the ground with a clatter, and Tara had to dodge them. Leona and Janus came into the shaking room. Janus held onto Leona's shoulders from behind while her voice rose in a wail that started in the lowest registers and was proceeding up several scales to beyond human hearing.

Georgie's ears were moving back and forth like semaphores, but he just kept purring, and Tara covered his furry body, suddenly so small and delicate, with her own to shelter him from falling objects.

And at some point Sitara, Yeshi, and Jonah all flashed into the room. Each of the Time Travellers grabbed a 21st century human and squeezed tight. Georgie hung onto Tara with all his might, and all his claws. It was painful, and she was sure he was drawing blood, but she gritted her teeth against the pain. Wherever she was going, she wanted her strange little loyal telepathic cat to go.

All she remembered after that was intense shaking, a sense of tilting, a disorientation, the pain of the frightened cat's claws, and then a sweet blackness, the sound of water running, the taste of chocolate, the smell of grass.

Chapter 22

5 May, 2019

Kabul, Afghanistan

Xander had thus far failed to convince his cousin Fauzia to leave Afghanistan and come live in the relative safety of Scotland, even for a time. It was eating at him, and Tara felt his pain and anger. She cultivated equanimity when he snapped at her, and tried not to take it personally.

The extreme heat was not helping at all. In early May, it was already like a summer night during the worst heat waves of the previous century. Tara was grateful for the air-conditioned rooms in Fauzia's house. That is, when the electricity was on, which luckily was most of the time. When it was off for long periods, there was a solar generator, but it could only run one small air conditioning unit, so on those nights Tara and Xander slept on the floor of the salon in Fauzia's house, and the few servants she had left were welcome to join them.

Tara's work was not going well, through no fault of her own. She wondered if she could get her surveys done in the time frame allotted. Nearly every day there was some major delay. The driver did not show up, or her translator was unable to make it through traffic or police blockades. It seemed that every day there was a terrorist attack somewhere in the city, fostering fear and despair.

Yet Tara loved the Afghan people, Xander's people, Bibi Amina's people, Fauzia's people. Sometimes when her translator Rabia did not show up, Bibi Amina came with Tara to translate so that she wouldn't lose another day.

The ongoing worldwide depression had steadily eroded what progress had been made in maternal and child health care, reducing infant mortality, and encouraging family planning. Girls were going to school and university still, but more and more, in fear of the Taliban, had started to cover their heads or even wear the all-enveloping tent-like billowing *chadari* in the stifling heat.

Tara, Xander, and Bibi Amina did their daily meditation sessions together, and Bibi Amina had taken to reciting the five sessions of Muslim *namaz* familiar from her youth. Fauzia was assiduous in doing them, and appreciated having someone to share the prayer sessions with. Afterwards, they would engage in as long a quiet contemplation as time would permit.

Xander's role had become one of teaching and mentoring, much like his father had done in the 1950's. He not only taught the courses in public health that the UN had hired him to teach at Kabul University Medical School, but supervised rounds and freely dispensed his knowledge and experience of decades in both modern Western settings and resource-deprived developing nations.

After a particularly dramatic argument between Xander and Fauzia on the question of her coming to Scotland for a spell, the subject was dropped. Xander had even stopped strategizing with Tara at night before they fell asleep. They both were so exhausted that they fell asleep in the middle of listening to each other's sentences anyway.

Then one awful morning it all fell apart. Explosions in the night had kept them all awake. Cell phones stopped working, and there was only sporadic communication on Xander's UN sat-phone. A journalist friend was able to tell him that an attempted coup was in process.

Which was apparently successful. They came for Fauzia on the morning of May 5th, in a burst of automatic rifle fire that killed or wounded all of her bodyguards stationed outside the house, and a few of the Taliban. When Fauzia realized what was happening, she gave herself up, hoping to save the lives of the remaining bodyguards, and fearing for Bibi Amina, Xander, and Tara.

Tara was in shock, though she'd felt a sense of foreboding for days, even weeks. Xander had become so distraught that he had begun to seem like a stranger to her. He spoke less and less English, engaging in long, intense conversations in Dari with Fauzia and his mother, which Tara could only partially follow. She was forever asking, "*Chi shud*?"—"What happened?"—and often being ignored.

The morning they came for Fauzia, Xander, who had not shot a gun in decades, grabbed one of the AK-47's from the hall closet, determined to defend his cousin.

Fauzia rounded on him. "Put it down!" Tara heard her say in Dari. "Fool! They're not here for you. I don't want you killed."

"How do you know?" asked Xander. "They don't mind who they kill, and they've targeted Brits and Americans."

She put her hand on the barrel of his gun. "Put it down, or they have every excuse to kill you, your mother, and your wife. Maybe they won't. You're a doctor. Maybe some of my men are only wounded. Try to save them."

In a few moments, it was over. The black-turbanned men took Fauzia away, roughly throwing a dirty green *chadari* over her and shoving her into the back seat of a pick-up truck. They sped off, leaving the dead and dying bodyguards.

Xander ran out after them, cursing in Dari, Pashtu, and English. Tara watched in horror as one of the men in the truck casually turned around and fired at Xander. He was either a bad shot, or just trying to intimidate, as luckily the bullets missed Xander and smashed into the pock-marked adobe wall behind him.

Tara rushed out as the truck disappeared round a corner.

"Xander! Are you all right?"

He looked at her helplessly for a moment, then went into action. "I'm fine. Tara, run and get my medical bag. Ask Bibi Amina to tear up some sheets and the servants to boil some water. Perhaps we can save a few of the men."

In the end, they did save three out of the eight bodyguards. Xander reached the Red Crescent Society on his sat-phone, and went with the wounded men in the ambulance to the hospital.

Tara ran out after him with his passport. "Xander, wait! You need this."

He took a minute to caress her cheek. "Take care of my mother. And yourself. I will be back later, *inshallah*, and then we can see if we can help Fauzia. It's a good sign that they didn't assassinate her outright. Perhaps they will negotiate. Call the office on the sat-phone and see what's happening, if they know."

The Taliban let them know what was happening. The electricity was still off in the city, and the feeble air conditioner was working on the solar generator. Tara wondered when it would be stolen, or simply destroyed for the sake of destruction. In the absence of electricity, the Taliban sent trucks through the streets with megaphones announcing with triumphant "*Allahu akbars*" their takeover of the heathen government.

Tara held Bibi Amina's hand, and gave her cold cloths to soothe her tear-streaked face and cool her puffy eyes. They didn't talk much. There wasn't much to say until Xander came back.

They waited all day and into the night. The cook made them tea on a gas ring, and they all picked at cold, leftover rice.

Bibi Amina had fallen asleep, and Tara was in meditation when she heard a motor, and the creak of the gate.

An exhausted, blood-stained Xander entered the house. Tara had never seen her husband shed more than a few tears, but he broke down in her arms and sobbed. She just let him cry and held him tenderly, mentally invoking the strength and compassion of their Rinpoche.

Xander finally looked at his mother and his wife. "We'll have to leave. But first I must try to get Fauzia released. I have some contacts among the Taliban. I'll go to Pul-e-Charkhi prison."

"But what can you do?" asked Tara.

"She's a prominent prisoner. She's won human rights awards. It's a good sign that they didn't just kill her outright."

"How much *bakshish* are they going to want?" asked Bibi Amina. "We have money, but we don't have access to our funds at home here."

Tara remembered the diamond ring that she wore in the Medicine bag next to her heart, and pulled it out.

"Take this," she said urgently. She glanced at Bibi Amina, remembering that it had been hers. "With your permission."

Bibi Amina nodded. "It might buy a life."

Bibi Amina searched for a nondescript but clean piece of cloth to tie the ring in. She picked up a scrap of makeshift bandage that she had torn from a sheet that morning.

"I'll go now," Xander said.

"Bathe first," said Bibi Amina. "Don't present yourself that way."

"It's what they caused," said Xander bitterly, looking down at the bloodstains on his clothing.

"Wear a clean *shalwar kameez*. Borrow a turban from the servants. You can't grow a beard in a moment, so they'll know you aren't one of them. But still, let them think you are showing respect." Bibi Amina spat out the final word with contempt.

"Shall I come with you?" asked Tara.

He looked her in the eye, for the first time in ages it seemed, and put his hand tenderly on her cheek. "Dearest Dakini, it would only be harmful. Do your prayers, do your meditation. They are powerful."

Xander returned at dawn, looking defeated, the ring still wrapped in its makeshift package.

He shook his head in answer to his mother's and wife's silent queries. "What's the world coming to when the Taliban won't accept a valuable bribe?" he asked ironically. "They must have something else in mind for her."

"Did you get to see her?" asked Tara.

"Only for a moment. We touched through the bars of her cell. They have not harmed her. Yet."

"What's our next step?"

"The UN wants us to evacuate. First thing in the morning."

It was another sleepless night. Tara packed for both of them, and helped Bibi Amina pack. Tara regretfully left behind almost all the lovely gifts that her colleagues had given her. They wouldn't be taking the Afghan rugs back to Scotland, or having them shipped as they'd planned. She kept a pair of gold earrings that a new friend had given her, and a lapis and silver bracelet that her sweet translator, Rabia, had given to her.

What was life going to be like for the women she had worked with? If the Taliban regime of the '90s was any indication, this, a generation later, was going to be even worse for women, the men who loved them, and their children.

At dawn they headed for the airport, Xander driving. They were stopped again and again at Taliban checkpoints, where Xander had to produce their diplomatic passports.

The airport was a scene of chaos. Diesel-spewing vehicles and UN-marked jeeps choked the road and the air. It was not an orderly evacuation.

"Should we try again tomorrow?" asked Bibi Amina.

None of them saw any planes taking off. The airport was ringed with tanks with Afghan government insignia, but they were manned by Taliban in their signature black turbans and flowing beards.

Xander pulled out of the lane of traffic and made a U turn, just as an explosion engulfed the departure terminal behind them.

He drove like a madman, ahead of the fleeing crowd.

"Shit!" he cried. "I wish I could help. But I've got to get you to safety first."

"Where are we going?" shouted Tara. "We can't go back to the house!"

He glanced behind his shoulder, into the back seat where Tara and Bibi Amina sat in their blue shrouds. "Pull down the face covering," he said grimly.

"Just in case we didn't get out today, I've arranged something that can be a chance for us."

Tara hated the crocheted grill of the *chadari* with a passion, as most Afghan women did. The world was broken up, fragmented, and she could hardly breathe as they streaked through the deserted streets of the city. Most of the checkpoints had been abandoned as Taliban had hurried to the airport, or who knew where, or who had done what? Some of them did man emergency vehicles, fire trucks and ambulances. Tara knew that every single one of them wasn't evil. Some of them truly cared, in their own way, for their fellow Afghans.

Tara and Bibi Amina were jostled around in the back as Xander took corners at speed. At last he pulled into a courtyard in the old part of the city. As the gate slammed behind them, Tara saw Fauzia's son and daughter and their families sitting under the shade of a verandah.

"It's all arranged," said Xander shortly. "We have to cram in. It's our best chance."

Tara had a million questions, but knew better than to ask. Later, if there was a later for them, they would sort it out. He would tell her the story of the intricate connections and synchronicities that had saved their lives.

Afterwards, Tara remembered few details of the harrowing journey. She was crammed in tightly with several adults and children in the stultifying heat. Even the babies were silent. The only conversation she remembered was Xander turning to Fauzia's son and saying, "This was the same route your mother and father took as young people, when you were a baby in their arms."

Tara remembered dust and bumps and jostles. Her lips were dry with the heat, and sometimes she dozed and dreamed of home, of her mother and sister in Taos, of the stream through the village. And sometimes she wasn't sure if she had passed out into unconsciousness. Someone would pass around a metal bottle of lukewarm water, and they would each take a sip, just enough to keep going.

Somewhere, on some obscure dirt road, they crossed the unmarked Pakistani border into safety. Relative safety, she reminded herself. It was all relative, wasn't it?

Chapter
23

21 October, 2050

Stonehenge,
New Avalon

Tara's head was buzzing. Something both soft and hard was knocking against her forehead and her cheek. Slowly, she came to. She became aware, by degrees, that she was lying on her back in green grass. It was daylight, but a shadow kept moving in front of her eyes, in front of the watery white sun.

The buzzing turned to purring, and the shadow resolved into the face of her beloved cat friend Georgie. His long canine teeth kept scratching the tender skin on her face as he head-butted her.

She tried to sit up, but had to fight down nausea as her head spun.

"Yeshi, she's awake."

A female voice, familiar. S…Sitara. Tara began remembering everything that had happened in the past few weeks. She had rather hoped it was all a bad dream that she had awakened from. But no, it was life before the Time Travelers' arrival in their Timeline that had been an ongoing bad dream, about to get worse. Now they had the chance to change the dream.

She sat up too quickly and had a moment of dry heaves. Sitara's strong arms surrounded her and held her as she tried to throw up.

"Here, drink some water," said Sitara. The young woman held a clay jug to Tara's parched lips. "Not too much, not too fast."

Tara sputtered slightly. The water did make her feel better. "Leona," she said weakly. "Is Leona okay? And Janus?"

"They're fine," said Sitara. "They woke up a little before you, but just as dizzy. They're okay now."

"Where are we?" Tara's eyes came into focus. The imposing stones of the Henge reared against the misty sky in her field of vision. "Was this...did we just Time Travel?"

"No, that was just place to place in the same time frame. Simple teleportation."

"Oh yes, simple." She still felt like throwing up. "Is that why I'm feeling so sick?"

"You get over that," said Sitara matter-of-factly. "Actually it's good that we got to practice simple teleportation before doing actual Time Travel together. That hadn't been part of the plan, but it's worked out really well."

"For whom?"

"It's usually only the first time that Travelers get so disoriented and so sick. Now you've had your initiation. When we go back to 1978 it should be much easier."

Tara groaned. Her head hurt. She didn't really want to go anywhere at the moment, not even to save the future of the eco-system.

"*We've proven that cats can Travel*," said Georgie's mind-voice. His purr quickened in speed and intensity.

"Simple teleportation, Georgie," corrected Sitara. "Not Time Travel. We still don't know if it's safe for you."

Tara examined the long scratches down her arms from the cat's claws.

"*Sorry*," he said softly. "*I had to hold on. You didn't have my pillow with you.*"

Tara scratched his ears. "I know you didn't do it on purpose," she reassured him.

Georgie let her scratch his ears and under his chin, and then moved his head so she'd get both sides. *"I still think it proves a lot,"* his mind-voice said. *"And it's a lot better, and quicker, than walking. Remember that someone walked for days to find you in the Tower Prison, I'm willing to risk the Time Travel. After all, I'm just a cat, right?"*

"You're not just a cat," said Tara. "Clearly. Georgie, I don't want to lose you. It's not fair to risk your life."

"Well, one of nine, right?"

"But for what? For humans?"

The cat got up in a huff and stalked off, stretching, grumbling. *"You think I don't know what is at stake? Do you think I'm some lower life form?"*

"Hardly. I am just following the advice of those who know more about these things than you and I. We've only recently started conversing this way."

"Not for lack of trying," the cat grumbled. *"You weren't the quickest learner."*

"I'm sorry." Tara was at a loss. She couldn't believe she was arguing with a cat. But so many things had happened recently to change her conceptions and perceptions.

Yeshi sat down next to her in the grass, carrying something. "Feeling better?" he asked. "The first time is hard for everyone, so it's just as well that it was simple teleportation. Had we had more time, we would have practiced more, but we kind of got forced into it anyway."

"What have you got there?" asked Tara, shading her eyes against the sun.

"Georgie's pillow."

"Is this something else you molecularly manifested?"

"No. I found it on the ground when we checked back in after you'd been taken. I thought you and Georgie might want it again."

Tara felt the well-used pad that fit over her shoulders. "Thank you." The cat had walked some distance away and was now furiously grooming himself. "I don't know if we'll get the chance to use it much. He's still insisting on coming, but if you don't think it's safe, I don't think it's fair to take him."

"Fair, there's nothing fair about any of this," grumbled the cat's mind-voice loudly, still following their conversation. *"What are you going to do, tie me up somewhere? Put me in a basket-carrier?"*

Tara got up and stretched, finally feeling normal again, or close to it. "How long do we have?"

Yeshi looked at her, his face open and transparent. "We should go as soon as you feel able. You can rest in the other time frame, but we need to leave this one as soon as possible so we don't miss the window."

"Here, help me," she said to Yeshi as she put Georgie's carrying pillow on her shoulders. "Help fasten it."

Yeshi helped settle the cushion on Tara's shoulders.

"Georgie," she called aloud. "Let's go for a walk. Just us two."

The cat looked up at her, hurt showing in his face. *"You're going to try and ditch me."*

"No! I just want some time together. Frankly," she said, addressing Yeshi, "I don't know why you want me Time Traveling anyway. I'm an old woman."

"You don't look it. I don't know why you are changing, but you are."

"Perhaps an old meditator's trick," she said. "Rinpoche looked maybe 60 years old, and he was in his 80's when he left his body."

"Tara, you have to come with us. It increases the probabilities."

Tara was nearly knocked over by Georgie leaping onto her shoulders, but he landed cleanly and didn't scratch her.

"What are the probabilities if the cat comes along?" asked his mind-voice.

"I'll ask Sitara to calculate," said Yeshi.

But they didn't have time. Like everything lately, time from Tara's perception seemed to suddenly speed up and multiple events seemed to happen all at once.

Leona shouted something and then started that strange warbling that she had learned to do. The stones of the Henge lit up and glowed. Streaks of light came from the east, the direction of London, and resolved into a veritable flotilla of heli-shuttles. Some landed in the nearby marshland, and the rest remained hovering.

"Can you run?" asked Yeshi.

Tara was surprised at the strength that she found deep inside. Cat on her shoulders, clinging for dear life, she ran ahead of Yeshi into the center of the great stone circle, meeting Sitara, Jonah, Janus, and Leona, who still warbled. Leona's voice was creating a protective force field around the stones as the six humans and one cat on a shoulder-pad stepped into the Triple Spiral time portal in the tall grass at the center of the circle.

Lasers from the helicopters pointed at the stones, but were, so far, deflected by the force field created by Leona's voice.

"They're firing at us," shouted Tara. "Can they destroy the Henge?"

Yeshi held onto her firmly, and she felt the Earth fall away from her feet.

She was dimly aware that Sitara was holding Leona, and Jonah was holding Janus, and that they were all touching, including Georgie, whose head pressed against hers.

From above, she saw the pattern the lasers made as they were deflected from the ancient stones.

"Hold on, hold on," Yeshi was saying, or his mind was saying, she wasn't sure.

"But they are trying to destroy five thousand years of history!" she mind-spoke indignantly.

"That's because they now know what we are capable of. We may change them out of existence."

"What if they destroy our portal?"

"We come back before they do. If we do this right, it will all have changed."

Tara gave herself over to the sensation of Time Traveling. Yeshi was right. It was much easier, much clearer than her first experience of simple teleportation. She felt like she was being stretched, but it wasn't painful at all. She felt like she was floating, like a feather. She felt serenity, like a meditation.

Chapter
24

June, 2019

Edinburgh, Scotland

With the news of Fauzia's execution, which became a human rights cause célèbre throughout the world, Bibi Amina's health began to decline. Despite the warm weather of the Scottish summer, she developed a persistent cough and found it difficult to go up and down stairs.

Fauzia's children's families had found temporary quarters while they awaited a decision on their reluctantly applied for asylum applications. Bibi Amina tried to remain the strong matriarch, but Tara knew, with an aching heart, that her mother-in-law was fading.

"We have room," she said to Xander one morning at breakfast.

He had become distant and distracted since their experience in Afghanistan, and sometimes she wondered if he still loved her, or had time and energy to love anyone.

"Hello?" she said, "Earth to Xander."

He looked at her directly, for the first time in what seemed like ages. "Sorry?"

"Have you thought of Bibi Amina living here, with us?"

"Yes, I've thought of it," he said a trifle crossly. "I don't know if she'll leave the house. I didn't want to ask you until I was sure."

Tara took her husband's hand and squeezed it. "Xander, we married late. I'm here for the duration. You can't get rid of me that easily."

He squeezed her hand back, like a patient coming out of a coma. "I hope you're not thinking I want to get rid of you! Have I been that distracted?"

"Well…it's all happened so fast. We haven't even had a first anniversary."

"Ah, my Dakini Tara, I wish I'd never dragged you into this."

"I know I can't be what Happiness was to you…"

"It's not about that," he said emphatically. "You don't need to play that card to make me feel guilty for my behavior."

She was a bit stunned. "I wasn't. I was being perfectly sincere."

He put down his coffee cup. "I'm going. I have a lot to do today. I'll do the washing up later, if you don't mind."

"I don't mind doing it."

"Ach, Tara, your perfection makes me feel guilty."

Now she was stung, and tears started to burn in her eyes. "Perfection? Hardly."

Xander put his hands to his head and rubbed his temples. "Sorry. I'm not fit for human companionship. I'm out for a walk. I need to clear my head. Let's talk later."

Tara felt lonely. Joy and her family were off traveling with Rinpoche in Australia, and she hadn't become close with any of the *sangha* members here yet. She had no idea how to comfort Fauzia's children, in deep mourning for their mother, their father, and their country, and Bibi Amina seemed to fade farther away with every day.

She cleared the table and did the washing up, all the while concentrating on her mantras, which seemed to help a bit.

She was startled when the phone rang. They didn't get many calls on the landline.

It was her sister Christina. "Tara! Mom had a heart attack."

Her heart fell down past her feet. Not now. Not ever, but especially not now. "Is she okay?"

Christina started to cry. "She's conscious, on and off, but I think it's bad. You'd better come."

She took a deep breath to calm herself. "I'll get there. I'll let you know."

"Come as soon as you can."

Only 10 a.m. and it was shaping up to be a bad day. She rang Xander's cell phone, but he didn't pick up. She sent him a text, but he didn't answer that either. So she went online and booked the most expensive air fare she had ever booked in her life, Edinburgh to New York to Albuquerque, leaving tomorrow, for herself only. She felt fortunate to have some savings accessible for emergencies like this. So few did anymore.

She phoned Bibi Amina, but Xander wasn't there either. Bibi Amina was kind, and said she'd pray for Tara's mother and family, and would tell Xander to call her immediately if she heard from him first.

What should she do next? She started packing, for a hot summer. She had no idea how long she'd be staying. She could always buy clothes there if she had to, if it ended up being a long time.

She put their regular cat-sitter, a woman from the *sangha*, on alert, in case Xander could come after all. Her two cats, Daka and Dorjee, looked at her reproachfully as she pulled out the suitcase. She'd been gone far too much and too long since she'd managed to bring them over from the States. She sat on the bed and petted both of them. They purred comfortingly and butted their heads against her on either side.

"Sorry, babies, I've got to go again," she said aloud. She didn't know if they could understand her, but they looked at her with liquid eyes full of intelligence. "I don't know for how many sleeps I'll be gone. My mother, your kitty-grandmother, is very ill and…" She started to cry, and big hot drops fell down on their fur.

She didn't hear words in return, but felt a sense of comfort wash over her, and the purring grew louder.

"I don't know if Daddy is coming with me or not. Auntie Kate will stay with you if he comes."

The cats seemed to be assuring her that they would be all right.

Tara continued to pack, doing mantras, feeling abandoned. Where the hell was Xander? He hadn't abandoned her in Afghanistan. He had done everything possible to get her out safely. But where was he now? Off sulking somewhere when she needed him, when his family needed him. Pure self-indulgence, when she was willing to give up her own privacy so Bibi Amina could live more comfortably and be safe.

He was so angry all the time lately. Not without reason. The news of Fauzia's execution had hit them all hard, and the manner had been brutal, public, and publicized. Because Fauzia had been forced to wear a *chadari* when she was shot to death in the stadium in front of a howling crowd of men, they had held out hope for a few days that it was a fake, that some poor hapless woman had been forced to stand in for her.

But a few days ago the Home Office had confirmed Fauzia's death. Reporters had briefly besieged Bibi Amina's home, until Xander had read out a statement from the family honoring Fauzia's and her late husband's human rights work for their country, and asking forgiveness for the deluded beings who had killed her and were killing all hope in Afghanistan.

How could all this be happening at once? Tara wanted to be there for her husband's family, for Xander, but now she needed to go to be with her own.

It was getting hot, especially with her moving around packing in a frenzy, so she flipped on the air conditioner in the bedroom. Above the noise, she didn't hear Xander come in the front door, and didn't know he was there until he stood in the doorway to their bedroom, staring at her suitcase on the bed.

"Don't you ever look at your mobile?" she snapped at him.

"No, I left it. Well, I see it's all too much for you. I tried to be there for you, but I don't blame you for leaving."

"What? You dear idiot, you thought I was leaving you?"

"Well, I come in and you've got a suitcase half-packed on the bed," he said testily.

"Xander, no! Something terrible has happened. Christina called, in the middle of the night her time, and said Mom had a bad heart attack. It doesn't look good." Her voice started to dissolve into tears. "I couldn't reach you for hours, so I made a reservation."

"Then I'd better start packing."

"Oh, I'm so glad you'll come. I'll see if I can get you a reservation on the same flight."

"You only made a booking for yourself? It didn't occur to you that your husband might want to be there to support you?"

"I couldn't reach you," she said lamely. "And you have responsibilities here."

"Bibi Amina is not dying."

"I don't know how long I will have to stay there. And it cost a bundle, thousands."

"We have the money. I can't believe you wouldn't have booked a flight for both of us." His eyes looked wounded.

"I didn't know if you'd be able to come, and I have to go as soon as possible. I don't even know if I'll get there on time."

He sat down on the bed and petted the two cats. "How is she then?"

"Christina said she is in and out of consciousness, so maybe I'll get to talk to her if I get there quickly. Xander, she's had a great long life, but I wasn't expecting this, not now. This is the worst time, what with Fauzia, and your mother being unwell. I just wanted to suggest that Bibi Amina might want to live with us, that it might be good for her, and you jumped down my throat."

"Has it ever occurred to you that maybe I might have a touch of PTSD too?" he asked, looking up at her.

She realized it hadn't. Even as she had dealt with her own trauma, through meditation, yoga, and a couple of trauma release healing sessions with *sangha* members who were therapists, she had assumed that Xander was strong and resilient. Her own trauma had blinded her to her husband's.

She hugged him. "No, you're right. It hadn't. I see you as so strong. You got us out of Afghanistan. I see you meditating, sitting like a rock. I thought you were so much more advanced than me."

"That I was fully enlightened?" he asked ironically. "Like Rinpoche? Give me a few more incarnations."

Tara hugged her husband close. They had not made love for…it had to be months. Not since they'd come back from Afghanistan, and not during the many weeks of hard work, tension, and worry when they were in Afghanistan.

She felt his heart beating against her temple and she rested her head on his chest. He stroked her hair tenderly, but did not seem inclined towards lovemaking. She thought of touching him to arouse him, but conditioned by years of rejection in past relationships, she wanted him to make the first move, and he just wasn't ready.

He kissed her on top of her head, a trifle absently she thought. "Tell me your dates. I'll go online and see if I can book. And what about the boys?" he asked, gesturing towards the cats.

"I called Kate, in case you were coming. I'll just call the airline and see if we can get another seat." She paused, as their eyes met and held each other's gaze.

"Xander."

"What?"

"Thank you. I understand, if I have to stay longer, you may need to come back."

"We can discuss it later," he said. "Let's see how it unfolds. Tara, you need to understand, marriage is a 'we,' not a 'you' or 'I.' We help each other face the challenges in life. Being together is not an afterthought."

"I just…" She stopped. "I'm overwhelmed. I didn't think so much would happen all at once and we'd have to choose."

"I'm afraid it's called triage in my profession. And we have to make decisions very quickly sometimes. One thing I've learned is that life, and death, are seldom convenient."

Tara leaned against him, again wishing he would just make love to her. The cool air of the air conditioner, something they had only begun to need this year on and off during the summer, soothed her skin.

He read her thoughts. He pressed his forehead to hers, kissed her lightly but juicily, and sighed. "Yes, I still want you, dear Dakini. Yes, I still desire you. Let's work together today, let's get it all done, and *inshallah* we will leave tomorrow, together."

And that hot, sultry night in Scotland, Tara got her wish. Tender passion again bound them together, and they awoke in the early summer dawn, ready to face the waves of Karma together.

Chapter
25

21 June, 1978

Stonehenge, England

In the center of the great stone circle, crowds of mostly young people surged around, swaying to the rhythmic beat of drums, raising their voices in ancient chants.

Tara and the Time Travelers had arrived uneventfully. No flash of bright light, no dizzying descent, no falling to the ground in nauseated unconsciousness. They were clearly in Stonehenge, and at a different time, but what time? She wondered if Sitara's calculations had worked. How would they find out?

Tara looked down at herself. To her slight disappointment, she wasn't in her 20's as she had been during the 1970's. But she didn't have gray hair either, so she certainly hadn't manifested as 96. The best she could tell, she was in early middle age, older than most of the people here, but not out of the realm of appropriate participation. Perhaps an old Beat Era poet in her flowing purple peasant dress?

As they swayed with the crowds to the chants of the robed Druids, she oriented herself in space, if not time, simply enjoying the cool, pre-dawn breeze and gentler air than that of 2050.

Tara observed that Yeshi still looked Tibetan, especially in the loose, flowing, richly-colored Nepali cotton jacket that he wore over his jeans. Sitara looked like a gentle young flower child, her blond hair straight and full, her head crowned by a glittery pink scarf that matched her flowing Afghan dress.

Jonah looked...great. A bit like Jimi Hendrix. Embroidered vest over jeans, an Afro, a little beard on his face, mature enough to pass as Leona's father.

Leona and Janus had come through looking much as they had in 2050. Her braids and his long dreads fit right in. Tara suppressed a smile as she saw Leona looking down delightedly at her new clothes, a frilly babydoll top over tight bell-bottom jeans with embroidery of a lion at the bottom. Janus looked fine indeed in torn jeans and a white poet shirt that set off his dark skin.

Tara wondered how the calculations could determine exactly what was needed to fit into a new time period. It was amazing, down to the details. She didn't see anything that was an anachronism—except for the Travelers themselves.

Georgie perched on his shoulder-cushion, looking exactly the same, purring distractedly.

"*You okay, Georgie?*" she mind-spoke, scratching him on the side of the face.

"*Fine. It worked, as I said it would. And I can still mind-talk with you.*"

Tara's companions looked at her and Georgie and smiled. Obviously they could hear him too, which might come in handy.

A great cheer went up as the sun rose, a golden ball of light precisely above the Heel Stone. The sacred chanting intensified, and those in Druid robes began to dance, joined by the hippies who thronged the circle.

It wasn't as big a crowd as Tara had expected, but then it was only 1978 and Stonehenge wasn't as popular as it would later become. Nor was it fenced, as it had been in later years, for many years. Those stones had seen much in millennia, she thought. They vibrated with the chants and with the light of the sun.

She shivered slightly in the pleasant coolness of the dawn. June 21st and it was actually cool. She smiled, remembering the complaints of her fellow students at university about the often cool English summers of the period. Careful what you ask for.

In 1978, the concept of global warming was known, but not discussed much. It was thought to be centuries in the future, if humans didn't wise up and stop consuming fossil fuels, which surely they would. There were already solar panels on Jimmy Carter's White House, a gas crisis caused by OPEC, and lots of people imagining a world powered by renewable energy.

It had been a heady time, the late flowering of the hippie era, wedged in between the evacuation of Americans from Vietnam off the Embassy rooftop and the takeover of the neocons and their corporate sponsors.

The gathering was beginning to break up, though the Druids would go on all day with their celebration.

Leona was spitting out a chunk of a chocolate brownie that someone had offered her and she had eagerly tried. "Ew, what's that?"

A tall Englishman with a blond ponytail looked at her in shock, picked the chunk of brownie off the grass and popped it in his mouth. "Man, such an ingrate. That's made with Afghan hash oil."

Leona and Janus just stared at the man, who shook his head and walked away muttering.

"It's a strong drug," explained Tara.

"But what's that dark stuff it was in?" asked Leona. "That's what I didn't like."

"Chocolate?" asked Tara in surprise. She'd forgotten. Chocolate, along with coffee, honey, vanilla, cinnamon and a host of other delectables, had disappeared before Leona had been born. "People loved it. Give it another chance. Without the drug."

"How do I know...?"

"You don't. I'll watch out for you. You need to keep your head clear."

Janus was coughing as he sucked on a joint someone had passed to him.

"Is this your first time, man?" asked a West Indian man with dreads like Janus'. "I thought for sure you were a Rastaman."

Janus didn't say anything, just tried to look cool as the mild high came over him. He grinned at Leona. "Lungs," he said. "Just me lungs are a bit sensitive is all."

The crowd was friendly, and all manner of food, drink, and drugs were being passed around. Pretty women were approaching Yeshi with obvious come-ons, and Tara found herself unaccountably jealous. Jealous? What was she thinking? He did look good, and so did Jonah.

Yeshi was making his way towards her as a young woman with long blond tresses asked him in a posh English accent, "Are you a real Tibetan?"

"Yes, I'm a refugee. And this is my wife, Tara."

Tara fought down a flinch at the word "wife." It had been so long since she'd lost Xander, the only man she had been wife to in this incarnation.

"Oh. Pleased to meet you," said the woman in a clipped accent.

"Likewise," replied Tara.

"Oh, American?"

"Born in Taos."

"Oooo, a real Indian then?"

"Partly. Also Hispanic and Anglo…"

"Anglo?"

"Well, mostly Irish."

Yeshi put a hand on her back and led her away from the curious woman, smiling in such a charming way that the woman wasn't offended. "Buddha's blessings be upon you," he said in parting. "*Om mani padme hum.*"

"Buddha's blessings?" asked Tara.

"Something she can understand. Perhaps we've changed her life with that."

"Perhaps."

A tall young man with light skin, bright green eyes, and a mass of long black curls came up to Tara.

"What a cool cat, and a cool way to carry him. Her?"

"Him. This is Georgie."

The man reached out to let Georgie sniff his hand. "May I?" he asked.

"Sure," said Tara, hearing Georgie's mind-voice echoing the same word. She was glad that her cat-friend liked the young man.

"Hi, Georgie, I'm Dermot," said the young man in an Irish accent. "Do ya like music?"

"I think he does," said Tara, as she heard Georgie say, *"depends on what kind."*

"What kind of music do you play?" she asked.

Dermot shrugged. "Rock, with a Celtic twist of course."

"I'm Tara," she said, trying to remember if men and women shook hands, or hugged, or just acknowledged each other in this time and culture.

"Cool."

"I'm her husband, Yeshi," said Yeshi, holding out a hand and flawlessly doing a street shake from the era. "I was born in Tibet, but, you know, we had to leave, so I got asylum here after losing all my family in the Chinese invasion."

"So sorry, man. I'm Irish, so I understand. But I don't hate the English. I have an English girlfriend. And my mate here, Harry. He plays guitar too. We're writin' music together."

A handsome young man with blue eyes, pinkish cheeks, and very long golden curls came up and politely shook their hands as they made introductions. He was dressed like everyone else in the combination of practical jeans and elaborately embroidered exotic vest and shirt, and wore amber love beads that Tara thought must be from East Africa.

"He's a public school boy," said Dermot, "and his dad's a government minister of some kind, but he's all right."

Harry looked embarrassed. "I'm just like everyone else, man. I can't help my background. I'm just trying to create peace through music."

"Cool," said Yeshi.

"You guys have a place to stay?" asked Dermot.

"We're just traveling around," said Yeshi.

"Well come home with us. We've got a squat in London, in Notting Hill. Lots of good weed, good tea, and music."

"It sounds lovely," said Tara. "But we've got…friends. We're traveling together."

She beckoned Sitara, Jonah, Leona, and Janus.

"We've got plenty of room," said Dermot. "And we can all fit into our caravan. Most of our mates are staying here or gone to Glastonbury, so we're heading on home and we've got plenty of room, and a huge space where you can all squat."

"Sounds good," said Yeshi.

"Man, you guys are cool, being American and Tibetan, and being your age and all. You must be almost as old as my parents," said Harry. "Are these your kids?"

"Leona's my daughter," said Jonah, a tad possessively. "And her boyfriend Janus is traveling with us."

"Wow, man, you are way open-minded," said Harry. "My dad would have a shitfit if I brought a girlfriend home."

"Peace, man," said Jonah, high-fiving Harry. "Let's make some music together."

"You play?" asked Harry.

"A little sax," said Jonah. "Cool jazz."

"Come and jam with us," said Dermot. "Where's your stuff?"

To Tara's surprise, Sitara had somehow manifested appropriately worn-looking backpacks for each of them. A saxophone in a worn leather case was an awfully nice touch. Tara appreciated her friend from the future's attention to detail.

Dermot chucked Georgie under the chin. "We've got cat food at the squat too. We don't have our own cat right now, but we feed the outdoor moggies. You can be our house moggy."

Georgie looked slightly offended, but Tara was pretty sure she was the only one who could see it.

"*Moggy?*" came Georgie's voice.

"*It's just a slang term for a cat. Like an alley cat.*"

"*What's an alley?*"

"*You'll see. But hopefully not too closely. Don't worry, Georgie, I won't let anything happen to you in the big city. You saved me out of the big city in the future, and I'll keep you safe.*"

"*I hope so,*" the cat grumbled, but it came out as a purr.

Chapter
26

Northern New Mexico

"Christ be with you," said the priest to the congregation.

"And also with you," Tara replied along with the assembly. Xander stood next to her in the front pew of the Santuario at Chimayo, reading with her from the prayer book.

Tara was still dazed from her mother's passing, though it had not been unexpected, and she had gotten to spend quite a bit of time with her mother when she was still lucid.

She was grateful that the priest, an old family friend, had been able to fit in a Mass in memory of her mother while she and Xander were still in New Mexico. Her Catholicism felt creaky after years of practicing Buddhism, the Tao, Sufi dancing, Hindu meditation, and Lakota Sweat Lodge, but she felt the beauty in it, the sincerity.

Mom had loved the Santuario, a place of healing and pilgrimage. Years ago, she said she had been healed of a painful case of arthritis by the Holy Dirt, and who were they to dispute her belief in her own miracle? Mom had been healthy and pain-free until a month before she died.

"In memory of Flora Concha Garcia-O'Connor," said the priest.

On Tara's left side, Christina began to sniff and cry softly, holding on to her husband Tony. Tara took her other hand and squeezed it. She was trying to be strong for her little sister, but she could hardly breathe, her heart hurt so much. She couldn't imagine what life was going to be like without her mom to talk about things with.

The sharp smell of frankincense swirled through the church, cutting through her thoughts. Rinpoche would always say, "Jesus is Chenrezig," referring to the Bodhisattva of compassion, "and Mary is Tara. All one."

Tara glossed over the parts of the mass that mentioned sin. The Church was slow to change, and even Pope Francis, for all his enlightenment, hadn't been able to change everything that many devout Catholics thought he wanted to change. Tara let her mind wander. She just didn't get all that emphasis on sin, but then she had heard Lakota people pray with similar words of unworthiness.

It helped her to look at all religions with the detachment of an anthropologist. That way she could take what she liked and let go of the rest. She only wished others could do the same.

It was hot and close inside the church, even this early in the morning. Adobe interiors usually stayed cooler than other materials, but once the heat got in, it was there to stay, for weeks and months, especially in a building with so little cross-ventilation. She fanned herself with the parish newsletter, as sweat beaded on her temples and poured down her back.

She was glad that the Catholic Church now allowed cremation, as it's what Mom had wanted. A free spirit at heart, Mom had always insisted, long before the Church agreed, that it was ridiculous to take up more land by crowding up cemeteries. If God was truly all-powerful, he'd have no trouble resurrecting her body from the scattered molecules of ashes in the mountains. It's not like there would be much of a buried person left by that time anyway.

Tara smiled slightly, and Christina looked at her curiously. "Cremation," she mouthed, and Christina's lips curled into a small smile as well. Both of them were glad that they didn't have to look at a waxy body in an open casket, just to be traditional, or to please their mom.

Tara followed Christina up for the Communion. Even though she hadn't been a practicing Catholic for decades, she felt right with God, and wanted to experience the Communion of Spirit. Xander wasn't sure of the rules, having been raised some combination of Church of Scotland and Muslim, so shook his head at her when she looked at him questioningly as she got up.

When the Mass was over, they filed outside into the little courtyard, where well-wishers gathered around Tara and her sister. Their mother had been well-loved and respected in the community, and Tara listened patiently to people telling her of healings that her mother's herbs had given them, and how she had listened to the troubles of others, and of course what a cook she had been.

She and Christina had been too exhausted to cook for the expected crowd, and had agreed to have the wake in a well-loved restaurant just a short drive away. Though the food was delicious, Tara hardly ate, and the day passed in a blur.

"What will you do now?" asked Christina later, as they sat in their mom's room, looking at all her collections, of photos and feathers, herbs and books.

"Can I stay and help you sort through things? Xander needs to get back. His mother isn't well, and the asylum cases for his niece's and nephew's families are coming up."

Christina put down a framed Guadalupe image. "Sure. The way things are going, you never know, it could be our last time together as sisters. At least for a long time."

"What do you mean?"

Christina sighed deeply. "Taracita, you know I love you. But we have different destinies. You live so far away."

"Chris, you can have anything you want of Mom's. I hope you don't think I'm staying because I want something."

"No. You just…weren't here much in recent years. Or ever."

Tara stared at her. "You're bringing this up now? Mom was doing great. It's not like you had to take care of her by yourself in her old age. She was still driving until the heart attack and had tons of friends."

"I just wish you hadn't lived so far away nearly all your life. You left for college and then you never really came back."

"Christina, I just lived in Albuquerque. I came up for all the feasts and birthdays for years, and I was there at your daughter's birth."

"I know. You did your best. It just wasn't like the other girls whose sisters didn't move away. I guess I'm saying I really missed you, and I do miss you."

"What do you want? Do you want me to talk Xander into moving here? He's got his own problems, and I've got to go help him with his family."

"No, Tara, I'd never ask you to do that. Like I said, I just know we have different destinies. I have Tony's family, and his sisters have always treated me like a sister, so I've never felt unsupported."

Tara looked around the dark adobe room, overwhelmed by their mom's possessions. Was there anything she really wanted, or needed? Eerily, she had a sense that a time might be coming when possessions would be more of a burden than an asset. But she didn't want to say that to Christina, who had a daughter and grandchildren. They hadn't talked much about the way the world was going, the economy and the climate. Christina and Tony had been able to keep a garden going by carefully using their allotment from the acequia, and they had a few chickens for eggs and goats for milk and cheese. As the sales of Tony's artwork had slacked off, they were able to make do with their own and local produce. Luckily they had paid off their house before the Crash, when Tony was at the height of his financial success.

"Don't worry about us," said Christina, reading her thoughts. "We're in a much better position than most people, at least as long as we have water. And the monsoons are due. We haven't had a good one for a few years, but we always get something, and we collect it in the cistern."

"I'm more worried about you living up there in that big city in Scotland, and all the traveling you guys do to dangerous places."

Tara hugged her sister. "You're right, Chrissy, that's probably not going to stop. Not as long as Xander can still get assignments. But right now we've got to get his mom situated. Then we'll see. Maybe we can come back for Christmas, or at least I can. Xander and I aren't joined at the hip."

Tara was surprised that Christina's face was wet with tears. "I know. I just get so scared. I have to stay strong, for Tony, for Daphne and her kids. I don't have to stay strong for you, and maybe that's why I miss you so much and sometimes I'm so pissed at you for living so far away."

"I don't blame you," said Tara. "Look, I'll stay for at least two more weeks. And I'll try to come back at Christmas, with or without Xander. And we can Skype more often."

"Yeah, it's all good. Thanks." Christina looked around the room. "So if you could have anything of Mom's you wanted, what would you pick?"

Tara sighed. "Same thing as you. Mom still being alive and living years more in great health."

Christina laughed. "She's laughing at us. But seriously, what would you pick?"

Tara's heart ached as she looked around the room. "Um, if someday you have time to scan the photos, I'd just love to have them on digital."

"I can't promise when, but we'll do that, of course."

Tara went to their mother's jewelry box, a sturdy wooden box carved by their mother's grandfather early in the last century. She set it on the bed.

"You want the box?" asked Christina.

Tara thought she heard a hint of disappointment in her sister's voice. "I love it," Tara said. "But it's yours. Just let me…I'm just looking for one thing." She fished out a silver barrette in the shape of a dragonfly, inlaid with turquoise and coral. "I've always loved this. She used to wear it a lot when we were kids."

"I remember."

"So would you mind? It's the only thing. But if you want it…"

Christina laughed. "You're the one who still has long hair," she said, running her hand through her short, stylish, thick hair. "Mom would want you to have it. Here."

Christina took her sister's silver-streaked hair and piled it on top of her head, fastening it with the dragonfly barrette.

Tara looked at herself in the mirror, thinking how much she looked like her mother when her mother was about the age she was now.

"Look!" said Christina, holding up a smaller version of the dragonfly. "I never knew there was a pin that went with it. Take this too."

Tara folded her sister's hand around the pin. "No. We'll always be connected, big sister dragonfly and little sister dragonfly. No matter what happens."

"No matter what happens," Christina echoed.

Tara fastened the pin onto Christina's blouse, and the two hugged for a very long time.

Chapter
27

22 June, 1978

London, England

"Mmmmm." Tara savored the taste of Earl Grey tea with milk and honey. Yeshi looked on with amusement. "What? You have honey in the future too?" she asked, laughing.

"In our Timeline, yes. The bees never disappeared."

"So we'd better get it right and keep it that way. Any ideas?"

Yeshi took a sip of tea, clearly enjoying it as much as she did. "Nothing definite yet. We're still learning."

Tara heard stifled yawns and a giggle from the adjoining room where Leona and Janus slept on a waterbed on the floor.

"Might as well let the young ones have some fun," said Tara. "They couldn't believe that people slept on waterbeds."

Leona walked through the door yawning, a quilt around her like a cloak. "Gran, I'm freezing," she complained. "I've never been this cold in my life."

"You're right," said Tara. "It's been decades since it was this cold, especially in the summer months. But this is the way I remember it. Come and have a hot cup of tea."

"Janus is taking a shower. I think I'll go in with him while it's still hot."

The squat was spacious, and had all the utilities needed to make life comfortable. This one was organized rather informally, though the regular inhabitants met once a week to come to consensus on various issues, including the ever-changing roster of guests.

Sitara and Jonah were already out exploring, whatever that consisted of. Tara guessed that it went far beyond picking up groceries and listening to the local buskers.

Georgie stretched, purred, and mewed plaintively. He drew himself up in a stretch and rubbed up against Tara's ankles.

"Yes, Georgie, you don't even have to say anything. We saved you the cream at the top of the milk bottle." She poured the cream into a chipped saucer. "Here, enjoy what your ancestors got as a special treat."

The cat lapped eagerly at the cream, a white moustache appearing on his gray lips and whiskers.

By the time Leona and Janus were out of the shower and dressed in their cool new hippie clothes that they found in the backpacks that Sitara had manifested, Tara had made toast with butter and jam. All of which were new to the young ones. She had almost bought bacon and sausage with the money of the time period that Sitara had so graciously and accurately molecularly manifested, but Yeshi had held her back.

"I think we are supposed to be living really simply in a squat. They may even be vegetarian. Let's not call attention to ourselves."

She had settled on eggs and toast. Real eggs, from the era before force-feeding and antibiotics and factory farming. Farm eggs from not far out of London, no doubt. With Irish butter and whole wheat toast, though the healthy bread had been harder to find in today's London, where anemic white bread was still the norm.

Leona had quite an appetite, but Janus ate quietly, steadily. Tara wondered if at some point the poor boy had been starving, before he had found Avebury Encampment.

"What do you like best so far?" Tara asked him.

"Mmm, the butter I think. And the milk. I see Georgie likes the cream. These are all from cows, right?"

"Yes. Though some people drank goat and sheep milk also."

"My Gran, she used to talk about cows," said Janus. "Said they were smaller than water buffalo. Not that the likes of us get water buffalo milk all that much at home."

"Are you sure we can't just stay here in 1978?" asked Leona.

"It wasn't a bad time," admitted Tara, crunching down on her crisp toast with delight, using the rest to soak up the golden egg yolk and butter.

"You'll have all those things, and more," said Yeshi. "In the future…" He paused. "I'm sorry, I forgot, you're not coming back to my Time, but to your own, when this is all over."

"Why not?" asked Leona. "Why can't we go forward into your Time? It sounds like it's a lot better than ours."

"Because that would be disturbing the Timeline too much," said Yeshi. "We can't risk it. Besides, if all goes well, then your Time is going to be a great place too."

"Well I hope so," said Leona. "Because right now I don't *ever* want to go back to what we came from. It was okay so long as I didn't know any better, but this is amazing. All this food, all these people, these different kinds of music."

"All the blokes," said Janus sourly.

"And the cute girls," Leona teased him. "So much more choice," she said thoughtfully, sipping her hot cup of tea.

"We have an agreement," said Sitara sharply as she came in the room, dropping string bags full of groceries. "We didn't bring you here to save you or give you a better life personally, but to change the Timeline. Perhaps you're simply too young to know what's at stake. I thought better of you."

Leona was stung by the rebuke, which was uncharacteristically harsh. Then she rolled her eyes and gave Janus a look.

"Leona," said Tara, "may I have a word? As soon as you're finished with breakfast."

Leona wolfed down the rest of her toast and egg and said with her mouth full, "Sure. Where?"

Tara led her great-granddaughter into the room Leona shared with Janus. The two sat on the jiggly waterbed. Leona kept pressing on it, causing waves, and laughing.

"Have you been smoking something?" asked Tara.

"Um...maybe, just a few...tokes."

Tara suppressed a smile. "Was it good?"

"Gran, I've never felt anything like it. Did you used to smoke it?"

"Sure. But not that much, not like some people. I tried it. I got a little high, a little hungry, and then I found meditation. I decided about, oh, 70 or 75 years ago that I didn't need it."

"Well it's so cool to try something new. We've got nothing in our Time except for the hodgepodge drink that Seamus and them make."

"Better than that, I agree." Tara stroked the girl's braids and rubbed her forehead as Leona lay on the bed. "Leona, you're here for a reason. I've never heard Sitara so harsh. I was shocked. We need to ask her if she found out something that upset her."

"Gran? I was only kidding about wanting to stay here. It's great, but I know my responsibilities."

"Good. How is Janus feeling?"

"A little jealous, I think. At home there's no one to be jealous of. But here there are all these good-looking blokes, such a variety. I think Janus thinks I'm going to go off with one of them."

"Harry does seem quite smitten with you. Even I noticed."

"And he's cute. But he's not Janus."

"Well you'd better tell Janus that...Oh, God..."

"What?"

"I hadn't even thought of the possibility of you getting pregnant here, or Janus impregnating someone."

Leona screwed up her face into concentration. "Oh..." she said worriedly.

"I don't know what the implications would be if you brought a fetus back into your Time, or Janus left his genes back here."

"I wonder if it happens more than we think," said Leona thoughtfully. "These can't be the first Time Travelers to ever come through. What if they've been coming from the future all along, to keep things straight, back to ancient Egypt and Rome, to the Second World War?"

"Then they haven't done a very good job of keeping things straight," said Tara ruefully. "Unless, of course, it could have been a lot worse if they hadn't come."

"Let's ask Sitara what she thinks. Maybe she's calculated all these possibilities."

Tara and Leona found Sitara moodily munching on a piece of toast. Egg spattered the corners of her mouth. She and Yeshi were deep in conversation, while Jonah strummed on someone's guitar. He was a natural, Tara thought. Had he already picked up "Mr. Tambourine Man"?

Tara's mouth watered at the smell of brewing coffee. What an unimaginable luxury. Sitara must have broken down and bought something that would have been a luxury for a band of hippies living in a squat.

"What's that smell?" asked Leona suspiciously.

"You are about to taste one of the great delights of the 20th century, that will have disappeared by the time of your birth," said Sitara. "Roast Kenyan coffee blended with Hawaiian and Indonesian. With cream and real cane sugar."

They were interrupted by the sound of Harry tripping over a guitar as he entered the room. His face lit up at the sight of Leona.

"Hey man. Wow, what's that wonderful smell?"

Dermot was not far behind. "Public school boy, raised with coffee and going on Caribbean cruises," he teased, not unkindly.

"There's plenty," said Tara. "A bit of a luxury. Mom sent some money from home," she improvised. "We've got enough for everyone to share."

Harry gave her a strange look as she poured him coffee in a chipped mug with a picture of Queen Elizabeth on it.

Tara almost made a remark about Charles and Diana, but stopped herself just in time. So many things hadn't happened yet. Would these things happen, if they succeeded? How would they know what things would happen and what wouldn't? Was Leona right that Time Travelers might have changed history before?

So far 1978 was just as she remembered it.

"You've never had coffee before?" Harry asked Leona.

"Course I have."

"I heard you say you hadn't."

"Well you heard wrong then. And what were you doing lurking around listening to us?"

Harry blushed crimson. "I wasn't."

"Eavesdropping. A survival skill in public school," said Dermot.

"Was not eavesdropping."

"Oh well, it's a small place," said Tara brightly. "We can't help overhearing one another. The kids aren't used to so many people."

"Where are you from then, that you're not used to crowds?" asked Dermot curiously.

"An island," said Jonah as he walked into the room. "A very small island. My wild child lost her mother young, and I did the best I could to raise her, till my music took me out of the island and landed us here. Want to play some music?"

Pretty soon the whole squat rocked to the jam of two electric guitars and Jonah's saxophone. Yeshi got into the act, playing percussion on pots and pans. They started improvising, then moved on to songs Tara knew well. Tara started singing with them, in the full voice of her youth. Janis Joplin's blues version of "Summertime". To her surprise, Sitara joined in with her in harmony. The woman never ceased to amaze her.

The only one of the Travelers who didn't enjoy the music was Georgie, whose sensitive feline ears hurt. *"I'm off to find a patch of dirt,"* said the cat's mind-voice loudly, to get Tara's attention. *"Since no one has thought to provide for my needs."*

"You didn't have a litter pan in 2050," Tara pointed out in mind-talk. *"And no one's ignoring you. Everyone here loves you. How do you even know what a litter pan is?"*

"*I talk to other cats,*" he sniffed. "*I have regaled them with stories of the future, and heard their memories of now.*"

Great. A Time-Traveling cat bragging to other cats. Could that too jeopardize their mission? "*Have a good time. And don't get lost, whatever you do. I love you.*"

"*I love you too.*" He fled the room at the wail of Dermot's guitar solo.

Chapter 28

September, 2019

Edinburgh, Scotland

Bibi Amina just couldn't be dying, please, not so soon after Tara's mother. But a few weeks ago Tara had returned to a mother-in-law who had suddenly become frail, and a husband who seemed in a perpetual, albeit politely suppressed, rage.

Tara had been in constant contact with Xander while she was in New Mexico, so she was not surprised to find Bibi Amina living in one of their ground floor bedrooms. But what she was not prepared for was Bibi Amina's listlessness and despair.

Tara couldn't help resenting Xander's seeming indifference to her own recent loss. She had to use all of her spiritual training to constantly "cut through" her feelings and dissolve their illusion, and try not to take anything personally. She loved Bibi Amina, and she did her very best to prepare delicious meals, which her mother-in-law barely picked at.

To make matters worse, they were experiencing a cash flow problem. The UN was still investigating the circumstances that had prevented both of them from completing their missions in Afghanistan. All of the data had been lost, and with the Taliban takeover, it had suddenly been made irrelevant. The Taliban were not known for their concern for women's and children's health, or even for general public health. But until the red tape was cleared up, Tara and Xander could not know how much, or if, they would be paid.

Xander had originally planned to suggest to Bibi Amina that she sell the splendid Georgian house that she and his father had bought at just the right time. Oddly, the market was still good. As in the long recession of the first decade of the 21st century, the truly wealthy were not hurting at all, and to the contrary, had prospered even more as the middle and working class suffered.

But Bibi Amina displayed little interest in clearing out her house, in designating what precious things should go to whom, what could be sold, and what she would like to keep for the rest of her life. She had come to Xander's and Tara's house with two suitcases, and wore the same simple black clothes every day. She petted Tara's cats, and consequently her dark clothes were always covered with fur, but that didn't seem to bother her much either.

In the interim, Fauzia's son's and daughter's families had moved into the rambling Georgian, which seemed a reasonable solution while their asylum cases were in process. The wheels of immigration ground slowly, Tara had learned long ago when she had sponsored Tibetan and Afghan refugees to come to the U.S., and tried to help some of her Mexican-born, U.S.-raised students avoid deportation. One just had to be patient, and hope.

"Tara!" Bibi Amina called out one morning when they were the only two in the house. "Come here, Tara *jaan*."

Tara set down the dish towel and rushed into Bibi Amina's room. "Is everything all right?"

"I fell asleep. I had a dream."

"Do you want some tea?" asked Tara solicitiously.

"No. I want to remember it. Here, sit down beside me." The old woman patted her freshly made bed, which she had meticulously made herself.

Tara obliged Bibi Amina. She was in no hurry, had nowhere to be and nothing specific to do.

"Acchhh…it started out as a terror, like what we went through leaving Afghanistan," began Bibi Amina haltingly. "We were in that stifling hot jeep and we bounced on and on, and there were explosions all around us. But then it changed. I was in Africa with Xander's father. I saw Xander as a little boy, but it wasn't happy. There were giant insects. I kept calling them tsetse flies, but these were much bigger, like small birds. They were attacking children. Children were dying in pools of blood, just collapsing and turning into pools of blood."

Tara frowned, listening in concentration, not interrupting her.

"Then it switched again. We were here, in Edinburgh, but it was burning hot. People were out in the parks in shorts, enjoying the heat at first. Then there was rain, but it was like a monsoon rain, hard and blinding, and wouldn't stop. The roads were flooded, cars were floating, and houses were sliding away. There was no food. The crops had all been ruined."

Tara said nothing. What could she say? This was all what was now being predicted on a regular basis, though it was said that it was still fifty to a hundred years in the future. She wanted to reassure Bibi Amina, but she couldn't, so she just listened.

"These strange creatures appeared, out of light in the sky. ETs, I suppose you would call them, the silvery-gray ones with the big black almond eyes?"

"Like the ones from Roswell," Tara said.

"They stopped everything, like a frozen motion in a film, and made an announcement. They said that humans had not used wisdom, and had overbred and ruined a good planet. They didn't want to destroy us, but to teach us a lesson, before it was too late.

"So first they were going to destroy all things metal. I saw my rings, my gold earrings, my watch all just melt away. I thought, strangely, of all those people who were always saying to buy gold in case of an economic collapse. They'd have nothing now.

"I thought that was enough, but then the ETs said, 'Now we are going to take away everything made of petroleum, for you should not have raped the earth and continued to do so when you knew the consequences.'

"And there went nearly everything else. All the plastic, all the computers, all the communication, and a lot of our clothing.

"No plastic, no metal. I wondered what we were to live on. Then this old man came, with long flowing white hair and brown skin. I didn't know if he was a dervish, or an old Native American man, from your people. He held out a simple stick with a pointed end, and several ears of corn. He smiled and said, 'Plant.'

"'Where are we going to get water?' I asked him.

"'Enough will come. But not extra, not for a long time.'

"So I took the stick and I started to plant, grain by grain, in a hole, thinking how primitive it was, how we were back in the Stone Age. I wondered how I was even going to sharpen the stick, with no metal, only stones I suppose."

Bibi Amina sighed deeply, and stared out the window into the bright, white-blue sky with its tracers of crossing contrails. It had been a dry summer, and the leaves were withering, but not turning autumn colors yet.

"Was that the end?" asked Tara.

"No. It went on. I watched those corn plants grow, and grow, and they grew up so tall that they touched the sky. The sky was blue, the way it used to be when I was a child. And the sun was golden, gentle, and warm, not harsh and white like it is now.

"In the distance I saw a village. Not a big city, but a village. It looked like an Afghan village in the 1950s or '60s. Poor and simple, but very clean. There was corn, maize we called it, and all kinds of vegetables. It just seemed a peaceful way of life," she said plaintively.

"That was it. Logically, I know that those times were not perfect. Far from it. People got all kinds of diseases and died young. There were droughts, floods, hailstorms, and freezing winters. Worst of all, there was war. When the Taliban pulled up the fruit trees and the beautiful nut trees, they destroyed our land for generations to come.

"But Tara *jaan*, what do you think of my dream?"

Tara hesitated. "Many are having such dreams," she said cautiously.

"You?"

She nodded her head. "Similar. Over and over, since I was a small child. For a while, when I was young and traveling and finishing my degrees, things seemed good. We seemed to be heading in a good direction as a planet. All those scary prophecies and dreams seemed overblown.

"Then in the '90s I met Grandfather Thomas in Hopiland. I suppose he agreed to talk to me because I am also part Native. One night over coffee he told me the prophecies. He said it was the Time of Purification. He said there were still choices we could make collectively as humans, but not for much longer.

"He talked to me of Prophecy Rock, and took me there the next day. It was still a secret then, but it was soon written of, with permission, in a published book, because the Elders felt it was time to warn people.

"He said that humans had a choice, basically either to live in harmony with Mother Earth, which was represented by the digging stick and the corn, or to go off on the jagged line, which represented technology. He didn't think all technology was bad. He said it was over-reliance on technology, at the expense of respecting the Earth from which we came."

Bibi Amina looked sadly out the window. "I won't be here long," she said. "I'm dying of a broken heart. It's possible, you know."

Tara squeezed Bibi Amina's hand and looked into the older woman's eyes, pleading. "Please don't go. I don't know if Xander can bear it."

"He'll be all right," she said. "He has you now. I was worried about him for years after he lost Happiness, but he had Joy, and then she married Dawa and they had Dechen. And then he found you, and started all over again. I can truly say to you that he is as happy now as he was when he first married Happiness and they had the baby, and times were good for them. Please take care of him, for me, as only a woman can do.

"I know he has been harsh of late, but he loves you, and he will take care of you until the day one of you dies.

"Hard times are coming, Tara *Jaan*. I won't live to see the worst of them, and I'm not inclined to try. Maybe some of us are meant to help, from a much less encumbered position, without bodies and breaking hearts."

Tara looked dismayed, and tears leaked from the sides of her dark eyes. Bibi Amina patted her on the hand. "Oh, don't worry, Tara *jaan*, I'm not dying right this moment. But I am under no illusion that I am going to be here a very long time. I keep hearing, 'soon, soon,' like a rhythmic bell, but I can't tell when it will be. I'll be seeing your mother soon, *jaan*, and our dear Fauzia and Jamil. I think there must be more Afghans in heaven than almost anyone else, after these decades of war, so I shall be comfortable and I shall have my *qabli pilau* and *noql* and *chai*."

Tara sat on the floor of the living room, cross-legged on her meditation cushion, a cat on either side of her. Bibi Amina had lost consciousness, and Xander was with her in her room, holding her hand and doing the Prayer to be Reborn in *Dewachen*. Tara visualized Amitabha, the Buddha of Infinite Light, and practiced the *Phowa*, the transference of consciousness, as Rinpoche had taught. Just as she had done with her own mother, Tara visualized the hole at the top of the crown, and mentally instructed Bibi Amina to leave that way, to seek the very brightest light.

Then she practiced her own *Phowa*, in support of Bibi Amina, practicing raising her consciousness through the top of her crown, practicing freedom from Karmic winds. Tara visualized the brightest of bright lights, so bright as to be unbearable, almost frightening, and let herself be engulfed in it. She knew that Xander, in the room next door holding his mother's hand, was doing the same.

The moment of death was uncertain, by definition, unknowable. Weeks had gone by since that conversation with Bibi Amina, since the vivid dream she had shared with Tara. Xander had bowed to the inevitable, getting his mother's affairs in order, ascertaining her wishes, getting her signature on the necessary papers. She said to do whatever he wished with all her things, as she didn't need them where she was going.

Xander and Tara had discussed the matter. There were only a few things that he particularly treasured. The rest of the household possessions would be divided up between Fauzia's son's and daughter's families, as they had left everything in Afghanistan. Some familiar things of beauty would comfort them and ease their transition into a life of exile.

The house would be put on the market as soon as suitable accommodation could be found for the families. The proceeds would give them all something to live on. They couldn't be attached to the elegant Georgian home. Bibi Amina wasn't.

Tara continued to focus on the *Phowa*. She felt a strong sense of disorientation, a sense of lifting out of her body, the most vivid and physical experience she had ever had with the *Phowa*. Then she knew why. She heard a sob, a sharp breath from Xander in the next room.

She quickly dedicated her practice for the benefit of all sentient beings. Should she go to him?

"Tara!" he called out, and she had her answer even as she was already in motion towards Bibi Amina's room.

Bibi Amina had the most beautiful smile on her face, and radiance seemed to dance around her head.

"Can you see it?" asked Tara in awe. "Mom was the same way."

He squeezed her hand tight, and gently closed his mother's eyes with his other hand.

"So strange, the way the body looks when the spirit has vacated it," he remarked. "So empty."

"The 'guesthouse of the consciousness,' as in the 37 Bodhisattva Practices."

"I will miss that particular consciousness sorely," he said. "As I know you miss your mother."

"I'm glad you got to meet Mom," said Tara. "And so happy that I got to know Bibi Amina, that we had this precious time together."

"And one day it will be either me saying goodbye to you, or you doing the *Phowa* for me," he reflected. "Unless we should go at the same time of something or other."

"I only hope I'll be ready." She breathed out the words slowly, measuredly. "However it goes. Whenever it happens. I hope we have a while together. I'm weary of loss."

Chapter
29

July, 1978

London, England

A chauffeured black Jaguar pulled up in front of the squat. Tara and Leona leaned out the window, watching as the uniformed chauffeur went round to the back door and opened it for a tall, good-looking middle-aged man in a pinstripe suit.

"You'd better hide your black face," said Dermot cheerfully from behind them.

Tara glared at him, and Leona looked at him in astonishment. "Black?" Leona asked.

"And me my Irish arse," said Dermot. "Seriously, make yourselves scarce."

"Is it the landlord?" Tara wondered.

"Worse. Harry's Dad, the government minister, come to try to persuade Harry to give up his life as a wastrel and take up his place at Oxford."

Mr. Beaton politely knocked on the door with the doorknocker, first at a normal volume, then more loudly and firmly. He looked around uncomfortably, straightening his tie. Clearly this was a man who rarely found himself at a loss, thought Tara.

She could hear Harry's reluctant tread on the stairs, as he dragged himself heavily down into the bowels of the house.

Outside, Mr. Beaton peered up and met Tara's even gaze. She wondered what he thought, or even saw. Did she look like a middle-aged hippie, about his own age but on a different path? Or a young girl? Or the old woman that she was chronologically in her own time?

She held his gaze, impassively, praying to open his heart towards his son.

She heard Harry's voice as he opened the door. "Hello, Dad," he said. "Would you like to come in? I can offer you a coffee. But I'm not changing my plans."

"We'll see about that," said Mr. Beaton. "But yes, thanks for the coffee. You have coffee, in a squat?"

Tara stifled a giggle, and slid back off the windowsill and into the room.

"What did he mean, 'hide my black face?'" demanded Leona.

"At least he didn't say 'arse,'" said Tara. "1978 has a lot going for it, but lack of racism isn't on the list."

"Racism?"

"Prejudice against one group or another. Quite honestly, mostly against darker skinned people by lighter skinned people."

"Hunh? That's stupid, isn't it? Don't we all need each other to get along? And anyway everybody is so mixed, everybody has their own skin tones, and the darker ones get less sunburned."

Tara couldn't help laughing. "True. I hadn't thought of it, but we are a lot less racist in 2050. I guess partly because so few people survived the Three Plagues, and generally the mixed people did the best, maybe had a stronger immune system because of the mixture. Though plenty of mixed people died too," she said quietly, thinking of how it hadn't helped either Joy or Leona's mother, Dechen.

"So should I have come through to this Time looking like Sitara?" Leona asked testily. "Should I ask Sitara to change me now, to lighten me, or try to do it myself? And what about Jonah? Why does he stay black if people are so prejudiced?"

"I can't speak for Jonah, but no, dearest, please don't try to lighten your skin! There is a reason we've come through to this Time looking as we do, even if we don't yet know what it is. People have been trying to lighten their skin all over the world for centuries, to no avail. It doesn't really work. I remember people in India used to use a paste of turmeric in yogurt to try to lighten their faces and arms, and all it did was get yellow color all over the place."

"What's turmeric?"

"Another lost medicinal spice. It was a root that was dried and ground into a yellow powder, for spice. It was still available at the time of the Second Plague, and helped a lot of people survive. That may have been partly why Xander lived through that one, when he was constantly exposed to it because he couldn't stop helping people."

"What happened to it? Why did so much get lost before I was even born?"

Tara sighed. The squat didn't have television, and this was before personal computers, but it did have radio, which fascinated Leona and Janus. They'd also found some copies of *National Geographic* and had eagerly devoured the stories and stared at the pictures, talking about them and speculating, asking Tara how it had all changed so quickly, and why no one had done anything to stop it.

"Things got lost by degrees," Tara remembered. "We didn't even know they were going away, most of the time. The world got hotter, and crops failed. The Plagues happened, and everyone was just preoccupied with trying to survive, or help their loved ones get better. When the population was so reduced, trade nearly stopped. The ships and planes weren't going anymore. We hadn't realized how much we depended on things from other places.

"Suddenly we were in something like Medieval times. We ate what we could grow around us, or nearby, like we do in 2050. Oh, Leona, you can't fully imagine what this land, England, and the lands of your various ancestors were like."

"It looked so different, driving in to London in a caravan," said the young girl. "The land now is so green, but there's no rice, and so much less water everywhere."

"We couldn't believe it would change so quickly. No one did. It was a matter of years, maybe a decade at most at the end. It was too hot for a lot of animals, and a lot of plants. Clever people had seeds of crops that would grow better in the hot, wet, tropical climate that we became. That's why we have food."

"Life is simpler in 2050," said Leona thoughtfully. "Quieter and more peaceful, but more boring, not as exciting. Except when that Clive bloke came with all the insect-army men and took us into London to the Tower."

Tara said nothing, leaving Leona to draw her own conclusions.

"We don't have much variety of food at home, but it's all good, and nutritious and pure, isn't it?" observed Leona.

"That it is."

"And we don't have that...racism you called it."

"That change too came about so gradually that I hardly realized it had happened. It was one of the few good things that came out of the decimation."

"So were you ever prejudiced against?" Leona asked Tara. "You're dark. Did you ever have people be racist against you?"

It seemed so very long ago. "Oh, yes," she said. "I was called all kinds of names over the years. Not so much as a child in Taos, where a lot of people were mixed and we had three major communities. There were the Native Taos Pueblo people, the Hispanics who were descendants of Spanish, also mostly mixed with Native stock from Mexico, and the Anglos, who were white Americans who might be English, Irish like we were, Slavic, Italian, German, whatever."

"So is Dermot racist against me?"

"Oh no, he just thought he was making a joke. The English were often as prejudiced against the Irish as they were against immigrants. Not all English, of course, not the people I chose as friends. I didn't realize it until around this time period, when I came back late from a film and found one of my housemates, an Irishman, all beaten up by Skinheads."

"Skinheads?"

"Ah, Leona, I wish this Time Travel business came with a primer and you automatically knew everything you needed to know. Maybe Sitara does. Actually I hope she does. Where *is* Sitara?"

"Out with Jonah, Yeshi, and Janus, reconnoiter...um, exploring I guess. Trying to suss out what we need to do next. We need a council," said the young woman seriously. "This is fun, but we've got to get a move on with changing things. What are Skinheads?"

"Uh, they were gangs of mostly young working class white men who shaved their heads, hence the name, and beat up people who weren't white Englishmen."

Leona pursed her lips. "Is that something we can change?"

"I hope that if we prevent Thatcher's election, a lot of things will change, and that we'll keep the good things we have in *our* 2050. I guess the alternative is that the planet becomes uninhabitable before you get anywhere near my age."

"Right. We'd better have a council soon."

The two looked out as the front door opened, and watched as Mr. Beaton stood for a moment on the front stoop, looking back at his son. His voice drifted up to them. "Thank you for the coffee, Harry. I suggest that you think very carefully about everything I have said. Think about whether you can really survive as a writer, with no education. You can't live off the dole, you know."

"But Dad, it's better than ending up like you and Mum."

"Thank you, Harry. Someday perhaps you'll see what I have tried to sacrifice for the good of the majority of people in this country."

"No, I don't mean that. You're a good person, Mum's a good person. But the bloody Labour Party is really no different than the Tories."

"Goodbye, Harry. I'll drop by again. This conversation is over for now, but it's far from over."

"Bye, Dad." The muttered words, "I love you anyway," sailed quietly up the hall after Harry had closed the door.

Tara was watching when Sitara, Jonah, Yeshi, and Janus walked up the steps just as Mr. Beaton was being shown into his vehicle. The proper gentleman looked faintly askance at them. Sitara turned a piercing, calculating blue gaze on Mr. Beaton and held his eyes for a moment. Tara saw something change imperceptibly, and wondered what it was.

This time the shopping expedition had produced cocoa powder and lots of delicious vegetables to be cooked in olive oil. Out of respect for Dermot's and Harry's vegetarian convictions, no one suggested any meat or even fish products.

In an aside, Yeshi had remarked that in his Timeline humans had long since abandoned eating other animals, and that they thoroughly enjoyed gourmet meals that tasted like steak or chicken or fish, but were constituted completely on a molecular level so that no life was harmed.

Tara used much of the day's milk delivery to make hot cocoa for everyone. Leona and Janus hadn't tasted it yet, though it was familiar to the three Time Travelers. Her mouth literally watered as she smelled the sweet aroma.

"So, chocolate was another thing that was lost along the way," said Tara to Leona and Janus. "Remember I told you about chocolate. It started to get very expensive when Ebola mutated and the Blood Plague epidemics couldn't be suppressed anymore.

"Then around the time of the Second Plague..."

"What are you talking about?" asked Dermot from the doorway. Harry was behind him, standing a head above him, listening intently.

"Yeah, maybe my dad's right," said Harry. "I'm with a bunch of nutters. But you seem so nice, and sincere otherwise."

"Ebola's only just been discovered, a couple of years ago," said Dermot. "I may look like a dumb musician, but I follow developments in immunology. You're talking like it became a pandemic, but it's barely known."

"It becomes a problem later," said Tara carefully. "A big problem. Would you like some hot cocoa?"

"Sure," said Dermot, and Harry followed him into the room.

"How's your dad?" asked Tara.

"I think you heard the whole thing," answered Harry, snickering.

"Including you telling him you love him, once the door was closed."

"Yeah, well."

"What's the deal between you two?" she asked, expertly pouring out hot cocoa for the newcomers.

"I just feel he's such a hypocrite," said Harry angrily. "I mean, when I was growing up, up till a couple of years ago, he called himself a socialist. And now it's like he's afraid to say the word. He's got a posh house and a posh office and car, and he's got the ear of the Prime Minister, and he's forgotten his roots and his beliefs."

Tara looked at him thoughtfully. She had noticed Sitara's eyes narrow and Yeshi's large ears prick up like a cat's. Jonah looked at the young man thoughtfully. Even Georgie, who had come into the room at the scent of milk, looked at Harry appraisingly as he groomed his right hand, chewing on the claws noisily.

"Well that's all well and good," said Harry in response to their silence. "And thanks for your sympathy, and for listening. But really, who are you? Are you so high that you don't know what time you're living in or something?"

"We'd better tell them," said Sitara, her eyes sweeping over the group. "I think it's meant to be, it's part of the plan."

"Whose plan?" asked Tara. She hadn't been aware that there was actually a plan.

"Not a particular person's or even a particular Higher Being's," said Sitara primly. "Part of Karma, or destiny if you will."

"Tell us what?" asked Dermot. "I'm tired of being kept in the bloody dark about bloody everything."

"Shall I?" said Sitara.

"Let Tara," said Yeshi. "She's closer to their time period. Remember? She lived here, in London, during that time. They could have been her friends."

"Wait, wait, wait," said Harry. "Look, you're no old lady, but you're hardly a contemporary of ours. You're way beyond a mature student."

Tara laughed. "Do you read science fiction?"

"Oh yeah," said Harry. "I love it. My Dad used to read it to me as bedtime stories when I was a little boy. I've taken a stab at writing some short stories myself, but haven't gotten anything published yet."

"Sure," said Dermot. "Though my main gig is music, I like to read, and I've read a lot of Harry's favorite books, and the stories he's written too."

"What do you know about Time Travel?"

"Oh, like Ray Bradbury? Or Dr. Who? Or Star Trek?"

"They all had a piece of it," said Tara. "Look, I didn't believe in it either, until…gosh, a few weeks ago."

"A few weeks?" asked Harry suspiciously. "Around the time we all met at Stonehenge?"

"A few weeks in my Timeline, I mean."

"Which is when?"

"2050."

Dermot whistled. "I'll be dead by then. Especially the way I'm going with the drink and drugs."

"Maybe not," said Tara, smiling. "But the way things went, which is what we are hoping to change, is that human population doubled what it is now by about 2015. Then there were three major plagues between 2022 and 2041, and I'd say 80 to 90% of the population died. Many people I loved died." She stopped, suppressing tears, aware of the gravity of the moment. For some reason it was crucial that these two young men understand the reality of Time Travel, and the task that they somehow had to be involved in.

Harry and Dermot were listening raptly, she'd give them that.

"What about you?" said Harry to Leona. "Are you from the future too? Is that why you've never heard of chocolate and never tasted coffee and never smoked weed?"

Leona nodded her head. "From 2050. She's my Gran. She's 96."

"Right," said Harry. "And I'm 103. Come on, you taking the piss out of me or what?"

"Not hardly," retorted Leona. "You know, Harry, you are a real prig. I really kinda liked you, not loved you, Janus is the one I love and I want you to know that. But you are really an arsehole sometimes."

"Thanks a lot. Because I don't believe some made up story about Time Travel? Why would Time Travelers come back here then?"

"The rest of us are from about 300 years after 2050," said Yeshi quietly. "I'm not a Tibetan refugee from 1959, though I am partially of Tibetan descent genetically."

"And why would you come from, what 2350, back to 2050 and then back to 1978?" asked Dermot.

"It's a Pivot Point," said Leona. "Sitara, tell them about Pivot Points."

Sitara took a delicate sip of her cocoa and licked her lips. "Pivot Points are points in time where crucial nexuses come together. You might have heard of the term bifurcation point in evolution?"

"Of course we have," said Harry. "We both got into Oxford and if we so choose, both of us can take our seats there in October."

"Pivot Points are rather like bifurcation points in time, but they relate to collective choices, and thus to political, social, and economic events."

"Supposing, and just supposing, anything at all you say is true," said Harry, "what's so important about 1978? I can't think of anything terribly significant going on right now."

"Margaret Thatcher," said Tara.

"Thatcher?!" Harry burst into laughter. "That old witch? Look, Labour's got its problems, but no way people in this country are ever going to vote Conservative. And the country's not ready for a woman Prime Minister, but when we are, I'm sure she'll be Labour, in a few years or a decade or so."

"No. Margaret Thatcher won the election in May, 1979, in what they called a landslide. Prime Minister Callahan didn't handle disputes with organized labor well, there was a miserable winter, and people thought they wanted change. What they got was extreme economic policies, a course towards endless war, beginning with the Falklands…"

"Where are the bloody Falklands?" asked Dermot.

"Off Argentina. No one cares about them," said Harry.

"She will be called the Iron Lady, and stir up nationalism when she leads a war against Argentina to win back the Falklands."

"You've got to be bloody joking," said Harry.

"Worse, she'll become good friends with Ronald Reagan, who will become president of the United States in 1981. They'll dance at fancy balls, make sure the laws are rewritten to benefit their rich cronies, start even more wars, lower taxes on the super wealthy, and bankrupt the middle classes."

"Who's Ronald Reagan?" asked Dermot.

191

"Um, I think he's some B movie actor who used to be governor of California. A nobody," said Harry.

"Greed will become good. The 1980's will be the Me Decade, and selfishness will be its core value."

"This is unbelievable," said Harry. "It's like some nightmare story my dad would tell me to make me go to university. Only you can prevent that, etcetera etcetera."

"Except it's true," said Tara, meeting his gaze levelly.

He didn't look away. "This is deadly serious," she said.

Harry got up and paced. "I'm clean and sober today," he said. "I'd gotten Dad's note in the post that he planned to drop by today. Besides, I ran out of money for weed, which is just as well, as it's rather a temptation. If I were high, maybe I'd believe all this. But I'm stone cold sober, and I find it hard to swallow." He looked one by one at the six Time Travelers, and then at the cat.

"And what's with the cat? Is he a Time Traveler too? I must admit it seems uncanny the way he just seems to know what you're thinking."

Georgie stared at Harry, and then at Dermot.

"*Don't think of it,*" said Tara quickly in mind-talk.

"*I have no idea of what you are speaking,*" answered Georgie.

"*Just don't mess with their minds. Let them accept us, and then you can try talking to them.*"

The cat heaved a great sigh.

"Yes," said Tara. "As a matter of fact, the cat is a Time Traveler too."

"From hundreds of years in the future, or just 2050?"

"He somehow attached himself to me in 2050. He's lovely, really."

"That he is," said Dermot, reaching out to stroke Georgie.

Jonah hadn't spoken before. "So what these kids are wanting is proof, right? Why should they believe us without any proof? They're obviously bright young men, not gullible freaks."

"Thank you, Jonah," said Harry.

"So, Sitara, can we take them up to 2050, or to somewhere else, and show them that it's all true? Is it safe?"

Sitara looked at the young men thoughtfully. "I've got a better idea," she said. "We can briefly bring 2050 here, into this room. We really should check on things, see if things are still stable. Our being here might already have helped. Or not."

Tara was continually amazed by her friend from the future, even a little jealous. Sitara had Siddhi powers the equal of any Tibetan adept she had ever heard of.

"Wait," said Sitara. "I can project 2050 into the center of the room, as a hologram. I'll make it large enough to be seen, so the young men know it is real, but not large enough to frighten anyone or to get lost in."

Sitara closed her eyes and went into a sort of trance. A beam of light shot down from the ceiling and projected out her Third Eye into the center of the room. There, about the size of a puppet theater, was an image of Stonehenge. Black armored vehicles and heli-shuttles were still throwing red lasers at it. A blue force field around it was wavering, and there was damage to some of the stones.

"Wow, way cool," said Harry. He reached out his hand, which passed through the hologram. "Do these really exist?"

"In the future," said Tara. "Just like this is going on in the future."

"I've never seen anything like it."

"No one in 1978 has."

Dermot approached and looked at it more carefully. "Shit, there's palm trees growing around Stonehenge. And rice paddies in the distance. What the fuck?"

"Climate breakdown," said Tara. "Thatcher and Reagan are against renewable energy, clean energy like solar and wind. So that technology is never funded. The world keeps using fossil fuels for decades. There are wars over oil where hundreds of thousands, even millions, die. And then the climate breaks down in a series of runaway feedback loops. It's not over in 2050. That's why we're here."

Janus spoke up. "Man, it's serious. They're serious. If we don't change it now, back in our past, then it just gets worse, and Leona and I never get to have a family, or if we do, our child won't even survive, and we'll probably die young, of starvation or heat stroke."

Harry and Dermot looked at the hologram in fascination. They passed their hands through it, half-expecting it to disappear, half-expecting to get burnt by the tiny lasers.

Tara could see that Sitara was getting exhausted by sustaining the projection. No more was to be gained.

"Sitara, let it go. You're tired," Tara said solicitously.

All at once the hologram vanished.

"All right, I'm in," said Harry.

"Me too," said Dermot.

"What can we do?" asked Harry in wonder.

"That's what we're here to figure out," said Tara. "Let's talk a little more."

Chapter
30

February, 2020

Kathmandu, Nepal

Now they were going to lose Rinpoche too. As much as Tara was still grieving the loss of her mother and Bibi Amina in less than a year, she couldn't imagine how much worse it would be if she didn't have her meditation training. This, of course, was why it was called practice.

Sangha members from all over the world had been called to Boudhanath, the Tibetan complex around the great stupa just outside the city of Kathmandu. Everyone who could possibly make his or her way there was urged to come.

It wasn't that Rinpoche was ill and suffering. It was more like he had decided that the time had come for him to leave his body. He didn't need the support of his disciples to do so, but there was a profound teaching in the process for them, a teaching of letting go of their most precious connection.

The recent sale of Bibi Amina's house had provided Xander and Tara with the extra money to take time off from looking for work assignments and devote themselves entirely to Rinpoche's last days in this incarnation. Joy had given them a heads-up a few weeks before the announcement went out to the international *sangha*.

Although Rinpoche had tens of thousands of disciples around the world, only a few hundred had managed to make the trek to Kathmandu. It was enough to crowd the small guesthouses and hotels that dotted the area around the great stupa. There were more foreigners in Boudha than there had been for years, between the earthquake in 2015, the economic crash, and the effective Chinese takeover of the Nepali government. Tibetans were not allowed to gather publicly except within the confines of a temple or monastery. Sullen police with *lathi* sticks prodded any Tibetans who even chanced to run into friends in a gathering of more than three people.

Tara wondered why Rinpoche had chosen Kathmandu to be the place from which he departed the Earth plane. She supposed that Tibet was more problematic. On his several trips there over the past 20 years, she and other *sangha* members had felt that perhaps his destiny was to leave his body among his beloved people in the land of his birth. Joy had confided in Tara and Xander that Rinpoche had indeed considered dying in Tibet, but felt it would be too difficult for his international disciples to get to the high altitude village with little infrastructure, and also too painful for the villagers to see him fading away.

Why not Crestone? Tara wondered. Or Edinburgh, or Malaysia, or Australia, or any number of places where he had centers? Couldn't people get to any of these places as easily as to Kathmandu?

"There's a reason," Joy had said. "I'm not holding it back from you. I would tell you if there was something I couldn't tell you. I don't know what it is. Rinpoche hasn't told me. I just feel there's a reason."

The days were warm in a way they never used to be when Tara had done fieldwork here in the '80s and '90s. The sun burned their skin as it burned off the daily morning fog of pollution. The nights were chill and dim, starlight hidden behind the haze. The snow peaks of the Himalayas were barely visible through the smog, and when they did come out only the very tops were now covered with snow, even though it was technically winter.

All this Tara and Xander tried not to ignore but rather to observe and transcend. They tried to feel both honest grief and non-attachment at the same time. Tara realized that she was grieving every loss in her life, every death resonating with the deaths of all the loved ones before.

Since Bibi Amina's death, Xander had again become both more tender and more amorous. The bitter brittleness that had clung to him since their escape from Afghanistan and Fauzia's subsequent death had begun to melt away, leaving the tender, vulnerable shoots of a renewed heart beneath. Tara was careful not to be too demanding of her husband, and to treat his heart with mindfulness at all times.

They began each morning with circumambulations of the great stupa, walking in measured rhythms while they said their mantras. On some days, Rinpoche walked with the *sangha*, but Tara saw that each day he walked more slowly and his body seemed less present.

They joined in the Amitabha *drupchen* at the temple, where mantras were chanted 24 hours a day for several days in honor of the Buddha of Infinite Light. Dutifully, they did their part in the middle of the night shifts and the pre-dawn shifts.

In the afternoons, Xander would be called upon to offer medical care to *sangha* members and to locals who couldn't afford it. Tara was kept busy going to pharmacies in the main part of Kathmandu to buy a selection of medicines and medical supplies that Xander might need.

So the days passed, melting into each other like beeswax in the sun. Tara only knew how long they'd been there if she saw a newspaper or checked her e-mail or looked at her phone, which she didn't do every day. Actually she preferred the timelessness.

Somehow, eight days went by in this fashion.

"Da! Tara!" There was an urgent tapping on the door of their room.

Xander leapt out of bed and rushed to open the door. Joy was standing there, tears spilling down her face.

Tara was immediately behind Xander, ushering Joy inside their tiny room.

"It's soon," said Joy. "You'd better come right now."

Tara and Xander threw on yesterday's clothes and followed Joy, walking swiftly through the relieving chill of the pre-dawn. Hardly anyone was stirring except for the dawn birds that were beginning to utter tentative calls.

Tara clutched her mala as she quickened her pace to keep up with the young woman. There was something unusual about the morning itself. Finally she realized, as she walked briskly, that the air was clear. The sky above the Himalayas was actually blue, and the mountains were cloaked in snow. The first rays of the golden sun tinted the range from the side.

Tara blinked her eyes as rainbows began to dance around the peaks. "Xander! Joy!"

Joy turned back to her, not slowing her pace. Her tear-streaked face was nonetheless radiant. "*Ja-lu,*" she said. "It's a sign of the Rainbow Body."

When they entered the dim hall, there was a glow from the front. Tara thought at first that there was some kind of portable LED light, but the glow emanated from Rinpoche himself. He sat, as they had seen him a thousand times, deep in meditation, upright, eyes closed.

Tara took a place among the *sangha* as Joy took Xander's hands and pulled him through the crowd of Tibetans and people of many nations, all of them raptly gazing at Rinpoche. Many had tears on their faces, and the expressions ranged from grief to joy and some combination of the two. Their beloved teacher was leaving them; their beloved teacher was attaining enlightenment, and teaching them as he left his body.

Tara kept doing her Amitabha mantras. Her heart contracted, and then expanded. Another loss, another transcendence. She remembered a thousand fragments of time with Rinpoche, from the first moment she had seen him in this life until now, like the thousand arms of the Bodhisattva Chenrezig, with the thousand eyes in his palms that let him see a thousand sufferings.

She could not tell the moment of Rinpoche's physical death, for unlike a normal person, his body did not slump. The light did not leave him, but increased, dancing around first his meditating figure, and then the whole room.

She saw Xander reach reverently to one side of Rinpoche's neck. Rinpoche's physical body's neck, she corrected herself, fairly certain that he had already left it, that he was the rainbow light that played around the *sangha* and the butterlamp-lit temple.

Xander's face remained impassive. He conferred with the Tibetan *amchi* who Tara knew was Rinpoche's personal doctor of Tibetan medicine. The two nodded at each other somberly, with reverence.

Rinpoche's chief attendant monk spoke, first in Tibetan, then in English. The great Lama had completed this incarnation.

There were sobs, mostly muffled. A few older Tibetan women threw themselves on the ground in grief, no doubt remembering other losses.

Tara herself felt a deep peace, deeper than the relieved peace she had felt when her own mother had crossed, and when Bibi Amina had left the body. Rinpoche was truly free of the bonds of samsara.

She knew he'd be back. But when? How? Would they recognize him? Would it be in Tibet, still brutally occupied by China, or elsewhere?

And then the years when the spirit of Rinpoche would be a child, perhaps wise for his—or her—age, but a child nonetheless. Who would they learn from, who would help keep them strong?

The last time she had seen Rinpoche, he had said, through Joy, that he had taught her, and most of his students, all he knew. He had looked at her steadily with his deep black eyes and said, "You know everything you need to become enlightened." She had heard the English words clearly, in her mind, before Joy had spoken the translation.

It was a heavy responsibility, knowing that one knew how to get enlightened, even if one didn't consciously know all the steps. What excuse did she have for not being enlightened in this very lifetime?

Xander joined her in the throng, his job done. *Sangha* members surged forward, offering white silk *kata* scarves, until the body that had been Rinpoche's was covered in white silk.

After they made their offerings, Xander took her hand and led her out of the incense-filled temple and into unexpectedly crisp, clear mountain air. It was as if all the cement factories of Kathmandu had shut down overnight, and all the vehicles had disappeared.

Prayer flags in the five elemental colors fluttered in a fresh breeze. A rainbow arced over the Himalayas, impossibly. There had been no rain, and no rainbow could encompass the whole mighty range.

She simply accepted what her eyes and other senses told her. It was an unusual and auspicious morning, the first of the Tibetan New Year, Losar.

Quietly, crowds were gathering in the lanes of Boudha, and around the stupa itself, watching the display in the sky. The sun, too, was ringed by a bright circular rainbow. The Nepali soldiers charged with maintaining order were also staring at the sky, talking among themselves. Some brought their hands together in *Anjali* mudra, the offering mudra, and raised them towards the sky, towards the rainbows, towards the spirit of compassion that had departed a body and now floated free, still influencing the Earth and its people.

There were days of ceremonies still ahead. The body of the departed Rinpoche remained upright and did not decay. Xander was the representative of Western medicine chosen to certify this. The body shrank, day by day, but remained otherwise intact.

It was a time of miracles, and they were much needed to maintain hope and strength for the times that lie ahead. The prophecies of this illusory world were of grim times ahead, indeed.

Chapter
31

July, 1978

London, England

"So how do we prevent the Conservatives from winning and Margaret Thatcher from becoming Prime Minister?" asked Harry. "It sounds like she suddenly became immensely popular, and then did a lot of damage."

"We could just throw her under a bus," said Dermot. "Without getting caught of course," he added, as everyone turned to look at him.

Harry clipped him on the back. "Arsehole. We're supposed to be doing this non-violently, like Gandhi, or else it's going to backfire."

"Just kidding, man. You know I was just kidding, right?"

The adults in the room looked at him balefully. "I knew you were just kidding," said Janus. "I might have said the same thing if I'd thought of it first."

"This is distinctly not helpful," said Sitara icily. "Ideas?"

"A lot of historians thought that if Callahan had called the elections for the autumn of 1978, that's this autumn coming up, then Callahan would have, should, win handily, or at least with a coalition," said Tara.

"But how do we bring that about?" asked Yeshi thoughtfully. He looked at Harry.

"What?" asked the young man, surprised and uncomfortable in Yeshi's intense, dark gaze.

"What exactly does your father do?" asked Yeshi.

"He's an advisor to the Home Minister."

"A close advisor?"

"Yeah, I guess so. I sorta stopped paying attention. I was busy with my A Levels, and then I was just pissed off."

"Does the Home Minister seem to listen to him?"

"How should I know? I suppose so. I gather he's quite well-respected. A behind the scenes sort of man though."

"That's it!" said Sitara triumphantly. "All we have to do is to get Harry's father to understand the importance of convincing Mr. Callahan to call the elections early. That should be enough."

"And how on Earth do you expect us to do that?" asked Harry. "I can't even get him to stop ragging me about going to Oxford in October. I mean, for what I want to do, what's the use of reading English at Oxford?"

"You'd be surprised," said Tara.

"Well I have absolutely no influence on my dad whatsoever."

"He does love you though," said Dermot. "He wants the best for you."

"Which isn't hanging around a squat with an Irishman and what he thinks are a bunch of aging hippies—sorry—and a couple of mixed-race kids."

"You've got a bargaining chip," said Jonah.

"Hunh? Oh, no, no way. I hope you're not suggesting what I'm thinking."

"Would that be the worst thing?" asked Jonah. "For both of you to go to Oxford?"

"If you had any idea how expensive university is going to become, especially in America, but even in the UK, also due at least in part to Thatcher's policies, you'd jump at the chance," said Tara.

"Please, not another 'appreciate the privileges and opportunities you've been born with' speech," sulked Harry.

"Well maybe you should, for once," said Leona. "Really, I think you're really handsome and smart and nice, and if I wasn't with Janus I might have wanted to go out with you…"

"What?" Harry looked at Leona's flashing eyes in surprise.

"Really. I'm not, I mean, I'm with Janus and all. But you know why else I wouldn't? You are just so full of yourself. You're not thinking about the world or how you can help, just about getting high and sleeping till noon and playing a little music, writing a few words of a book you never finish, and maybe someday getting laid."

Harry stared at her. Her dark skin concealed her blush, but she looked uncomfortable and embarrassed.

"Don't worry, Janus," she said, turning to her boyfriend, "I'm not offering."

"Not even to save the world?" asked Dermot. "What if it was the only way to talk Harry into trying to talk to his dad?"

"Not funny, Dermot," said Sitara severely. "Women are not to be used that way."

"Dumb ass remark, Dermot," said Jonah. Jonah clapped him on the back to soften the blow of his words. "Made quite a few of them myself over the years, so I can be in your shoes."

Leona looked exasperated, then softened. "Aww, Harry, like I said, you've got so much going for you. You get yourself to Oxford and you'll have beautiful and smart young women falling all over you. I'm from a different time, I'm not as educated as you are, for one thing."

"But I don't want to go to Oxford just because my father did."

"Oh, quit rebelling for the sake of rebellion, man," said Janus. "I'd love to stay in this Time and just hang out with you guys and go to Oxford and learn stuff, party a little, get high a little, sit up late nights talking about history, making music, and reading to each other. It ain't gonna happen. So do it for me."

"Show some discipline," said Leona.

"Now you all sound like my father," said Harry sourly.

Dermot strummed a chord on his guitar. Tara had noticed that he always seemed to be able to think better if he had a musical instrument in his hands. "That's not all bad," said Dermot. "I don't have a dad to please or displease. Just me mum and meself. Actually I've been thinking I might take up my place at Oxford after all."

"We had a pact, man," said Harry.

"Reading what subject?" asked Tara.

"Biology. I love it. But I'm afraid I'll never do my music if I go into science."

"Times are changing," said Tara. "Well, even more so if we are successful."

"All right," said Harry decisively. "All right. I'll give it a go. I'll write to Dad and ask him to come by for coffee again, and tell him I'm considering going to Oxford. But you've got to help me with what to say, and then we've got to figure out how to convince him that getting Callahan to call the elections is important."

"We've got our work cut out for us," said Yeshi.

"Anyone want to go out busking?" asked Dermot wistfully. "Our days at being street musicians seem to be numbered."

"I'm in," said Jonah.

Harry sighed. "I'm not as good as you, man. I never will be. But I'm not as bad as some people either. Can I come?"

"I sing pretty well, don't I?" asked Leona. "I don't know all the new...well, old, songs, but I'm learning pretty quickly. Tara knows them all."

"I do remember them," she said wistfully.

"I'm pretty good on percussion," said Janus. "Can I take one of those dumbek drums?"

"And I, on the other hand, have no musical talent whatsoever in this incarnation," said Yeshi. "So I can act like the poor Tibetan refugee and pass the hat."

"We hardly need money," said Sitara primly. "Should we be drawing attention to ourselves?"

"It's just for a lark," said Leona. "Just some fun until we finish what we're doing here. As soon as Harry meets with his dad and convinces him to get the Prime Minister to call the elections early, we're outta here, right? Please can we have some fun?"

"I have to say that busking was always a secret fantasy of mine," said Tara with a wicked smile. "But don't you have to have some kind of license?"

"No one bothers with that," said Dermot breezily, loading his guitar into its case. "The day is yet young. If we leave now, we can catch the evening rush hour."

So that was how Tara, at age 96 and looking about 40, found herself living out her youthful fantasy of busking in Covent Garden.

All went well, at first. They quickly unloaded the van, and Harry even found a legal parking space only a couple of blocks away. They set up, Dermot and Harry on guitars with portable amps, Janus playing the dumbek, and Jonah on sax. Sitara kept her distance at first, but once Tara and Leona started singing Dylan, Joan Baez, Judy Collins, and other classics, she joined in with gusto. Yeshi played his part, pulling a Tibetan hat off his head and working the crowds of market-goers and commuters on their way home. Georgie stretched out in a guitar case, looking sweet, and got even more donations.

And then the cops came. Tara had always thought of the London bobbies as rather benign, especially compared to American police with their boots and motorcycles and big guns. And these police were indeed unarmed, except for their billie clubs. But there were a lot of them, and they descended en masse on the little group of illegal buskers. Three police cars pinned them in, lights blazing, and a fracas ensued.

Tara had no idea how Sitara had so quickly manipulated molecules to produce the needed ID's, from American passports with valid work visas for her, Jonah, and Leona to a refugee status for Yeshi, and British ID's for Sitara and Janus.

"We're going to make an example of you," Tara heard one policeman say viciously as he grabbed Dermot by the hair and smashed his precious guitar. "Not only drugs, but hard drugs you're carrying."

"I don't have any kind of drugs!" shouted Dermot. "You think I'm stupid, to lose my place at Oxford?!"

"Oh, an Irishman going to Oxford, is it? I don't think so, as I'm arresting you."

Harry started to protest, and was arrested too. Harry and Dermot were led away in handcuffs, and when Janus started to protest, they took him too. The three of them looked helplessly back at their Time Traveler friends, who couldn't seem to do a damned thing to help them.

"Well that was unexpected," said Yeshi a little bit later. He sipped on a sweet coffee. He was as nervous as Tara had ever seen him.

"How long do they keep people in this time period?" asked Jonah.

"It depends," said Tara doubtfully. "I suspect Harry's dad can bail him out pretty quickly. Unless he wants to teach Harry a lesson. This isn't going to help his case."

"Will it prevent the boys from going to Oxford?" asked Yeshi. "That's our bargaining chip with Harry's dad."

"Not a good thing," said Tara grimly. She could hardly taste the coffee that she had so treasured mere days ago.

"What about poor Dermot?" asked Jonah. "Who's gonna bail him out? He told me he's on scholarship and his mom's in Ireland."

"We are," said Sitara grimly. "Tara and I. Money is not a problem, of course. We'll just need a subtle alteration of appearance."

"What about the charges that are brought against them?" asked Tara. "Harry's dad is going to be really pissed off. It's only July now. If they're convicted, though we know they are innocent—aren't they? They didn't have any hard drugs, like the police said. At least I'm pretty sure they didn't."

"Absolutely not!" said Leona, seething. "What an unfair time. This is just as bad as that Clive bloke taking us off to the Tower. And now Janus has gone and gotten arrested too." The young woman started to sob.

Tara put a hand on her and hugged her close, as she had when Leona had been a small orphan.

"Oh, Gran...." Leona wailed.

"Shhh, shhh. We'll think of something."

"You couldn't save my mum and dad."

Tara said nothing. Nor could she save Xander in the last Plague.

Gradually, Leona's sobs subsided.

"We'd better go," said Sitara.

Sitara closed her eyes, and instantly she and Tara were both dressed in respectable linen suits in a fashionable cut of the day. They wore practical, low-heeled pumps and had matching bags slung over their shoulders, full of the necessary cash. Tara's skin was a few shades lighter than normal. Simple gold earrings and conservative pendants completed their ensembles. All that was left was for each of them to put her long hair up in a tidy bun.

"Right, where do we go?" asked Sitara.

Tara realized she had no idea. And they had no friends in this time period to ask. So they would ask strangers.

Tara went to the pay phone in the hall and looked at the dog-earred, almost shredded phone book attached at the bottom. She found the number for the local constabulary and dialed.

"Hello? I'm so sorry to trouble you…" Her voice had a perfectly posh English accent, more so than it ever had after years of living in the UK. "My son's gotten himself into terrible trouble. My husband is abroad on business, and it's left to me to sort it out. I'd like to inquire as to the procedure for bail."

Tara and Sitara phoned for a taxi, which took them to the jail where Harry, Dermot, and Janus were being held. The police saw a proper Englishwoman, with ID that proved her to be Janus' presumably adoptive mother, and a well-dressed Irishwoman with ID proving her to be Dermot's mother.

When the boys were remanded to their custody, they were shocked to see the way Tara and Sitara were dressed. Dermot started to say something, but Janus jabbed him in the ribs.

"What about Harry?" asked Dermot loyally as they walked down the stairs out of the police station, breathing free air.

Sitara sighed a deeper sigh than Tara had ever heard her friend sigh before. "His father needs to bail him out. It seems to be a wrench in our plan, but I'd prefer to think of it as a complexity to work with, as part of the new and evolving plan. Perhaps it's necessary for Harry's father to bail him out."

"But we're being accused of things we didn't do," protested Janus. "I know I could just get out of here—couldn't I?—but what about Dermot and Harry? Are their lives ruined now? Will they still be able to go to Oxford?"

"They're trying to frame us," said Dermot darkly. "Harry might get off, with his dad's help. But what about me? His dad doesn't bear any special love for me."

"I've heard of such things, now that I think of it," said Tara. "It happened to friends of friends, around this same time period."

Leona ran out to the big London cab as soon as it pulled up in front of the squat. She clung to Janus, trying to comfort him, trying to comfort herself. It fell to Georgie to comfort Dermot, the cat-lover. He sat on Dermot's lap, kneading his claws through the thick jeans, purring and purring until the young man was distracted from his worry by petting the cat and scratching his ears.

"It seems there are a number of separate issues," said Yeshi thoughtfully. "The most important, which we must not lose focus on, is the need for Harry to convince his father to use his influence to get the elections called earlier than they were in the original Timeline.

"Then there is the need to clear the young men's records of this injustice, so they can be off to Oxford. I have the feeling there is something important about both of them going to Oxford, other than Harry's bargaining chip with his dad."

"What if they've blown it?" said Tara glumly. "And what if Harry's dad won't even speak to him if he's blown it?"

"Couldn't we just go back in Time again?" suggested Leona. "Just go back to before this afternoon, and we never went out busking at all?"

Sitara sighed. "It doesn't work quite that way, Leona. A little later, we could. But there are time ripples, like when you throw a stone in a still pond. Until the time ripples subside, you can't go back."

"How long does it take the time ripples to subside?" asked Leona.

"I'm not exactly sure," admitted Sitara, a tad guiltily. "This is still a little bit of an experimental process, even in our Time. Not fully tested. We can't risk this mission by over-reaching."

"So we have to work with what we're given," said Yeshi. "We'll figure out something. We have a number of great minds here, and we can all work synergistically."

"And don't forget about the cat," came a feline mind-voice.

"What can the cat do?" asked Dermot.

Everyone else in the room stared at him.

"What?" said Dermot.

"You heard?" asked Tara

"Heard what?"

"The cat. Georgie."

"Wasn't that one of you?"

They all shook their heads in unison. Georgie stared up at his friend Dermot with liquid green eyes.

"We'll think of something," said Georgie.

Chapter
32

October, 2022

Eshowe, Kwazulu Natal,
South Africa

Xander pounded his fist on the scarred wooden desk, cursing as the tenuous video connection with Joy's in-laws in Kathmandu went out the moment it was established. Tara drew in her breath, but kept silent. For a moment she thought her husband was going to hurl the laptop across the cramped, stifling room. Xander took a deep breath, repeated the "*Om Mani Padme Hum*" mantra several times, and clicked on "reconnect" for what must be the tenth or fifteenth time.

Xander had been frantic for days, in a way Tara hadn't seen him since the time in Afghanistan, ever since the news had come that the mutated Ebola pandemic, later to be known as the First Plague or the Blood Plague, had reached Nepal and Tibet. All they knew was that Joy and Dawa had gone on pilgrimage to Mt. Kailash, a long-held aspiration of theirs, about a month ago, and had left their daughter Dechen with Dawa's family in Kathmandu.

Tara and Xander had been working on a public health assignment for months in this remote corner of Zululand, where his late wife Happiness' family was from, when the pandemic began to spread quickly around the world. International communication was erratic at best, especially from the hot zone they were in, and they had been trying to get ahold of Dawa's family for more than a week.

At last the video picture crackled to life. As Dawa's father Nyima's drawn face came into focus, Tara knew immediately that something was very wrong, and clutched at Xander's shoulders from behind the creaky chair.

Tara watched as Nyima shook his head, his expression that of a man who has witnessed great sorrow in the course of his life, and can hardly bear more.

"I am so so very sorry to tell you," said the gray-haired man, looking far older than he had when they had last seen him in Kathmandu two years ago.

"What?" cried Xander. "Just, please, tell me. How are they?" Xander's voice broke.

Nyima shook his head again. "We…they…I'm so so sorry. We are in quarantine, but we are safe. Dechen is safe with us."

"Joy? Dawa?"

Tears began to slowly roll down Nyima's face. "We just got news, two days ago. They had finished the *kora* and were on their way home. They came to a camp of Chinese workers, a big camp of people trying to get to Nepal, but many were very sick. Some people told us that they stayed to help the sick people. My son, your daughter, both expired there."

Tara bowed her head and squeezed her eyes shut against the tears, trying not to imagine what their last days had been like. It had been too much to hope that they would be safe on their pilgrimage in an isolated area. She hardly heard Nyima's words about the traditional "sky burial" that was done for Joy and Dawa, giving their bodies back to creatures of earth and sky, but felt Xander wince as she held him.

"It was a very holy death, please understand," said Nyima, regaining some of his composure. "They had just completed the *kora* around Mt. Kailash."

Tara could feel Xander struggle between faith and grief, as she simultaneously felt the two emotions rend her own heart in two.

"I know, but…" Xander had no words to continue.

"Dechen is well. We are all well." Nyima turned away and then Dechen's sad, wide-eyed face filled the screen.

Xander wiped away his tears quickly, wanting to appear strong for his granddaughter. Tara leaned in, her head on his right shoulder, her fingers kneading the tight muscles in his neck and shoulders.

Dechen's face was solemn. At this moment she looked much older than her ten years. "Gran-da, I'm okay. We went to the Lamas, before the quarantine, and they prayed for Mummy and Daddy. They said it was a holy death, helping others, and all the Rinpoches have done the *Phowa* for them."

Dechen was trying to be brave, but suddenly she looked like a young orphaned child as she blinked back her overflowing tears.

"We will do the *Phowa* for them too, darling," Tara said in a husky voice.

Xander cleared his throat. "Dechen, you poor wee thing, are you being well cared for? Do you feel safe?"

Dechen nodded her head. "None of us are sick, and we have food and water. We can't go anywhere, and the electricity is out most of the time. But, please, don't worry about me."

"We'll come and get you as soon as we can," promised Xander. "We can't leave now, because of the travel bans. Let me see, maybe I can get the UN to help us. There are still aid flights coming and going. And once the epidemic is over…" He stopped and cleared his throat. "Something like a normal schedule should resume."

Dechen lifted up her chin and pressed her lips together. "Gran-Da, don't do anything that could hurt you or Granma Tara. I'm safe here, and I can wait. I love you." Dechen started to say something else, but the connection terminated as the electricity went out in Eshowe.

Xander slammed his fists down on the wooden desk. "Fucking hell!"

Tara breathed deeply. "Come here."

She led him to the rickety double bed. As he threw himself down and sobbed, she massaged his aching back, his shoulders, his neck, until, like a child, he fell into much-needed sleep.

She stayed awake in the oppressive spring night, listening to the distant and beautiful sound of Zulu polyphonic singing, punctuated by the dissonance of agonized wailing and ululations. Another funeral. The decimation of AIDS had been bad enough, but in this epidemic the dead had to be buried quickly, many in mass graves, to prevent contamination of the living. People were not supposed to gather in groups, but they did anyway. Pretty soon she heard the rise and fall of sirens. That would be the police breaking up the groups of mourners.

She had never had a calling to be a nurse, but in these extraordinary circumstances, she had learned to assist Xander. The safe-suits were generations better than they had been only a few years ago, but still hot and cumbersome. Thankfully it was only spring here in South Africa, and though it was much warmer than it used to be, the weather was not as unbearable as the tropics had become. Perhaps that had helped to slow the spread of the disease here compared to many other places in the world.

Their trip had begun as a routine, even pleasant assignment. Xander had used his longtime connections with Doctors Without Borders to secure a position in public health in the Zulu cultural center of Eshowe, where his late wife Happiness still had many relatives. Tara had updated her filmmaking skills, learning the latest cameras and editing apps so she could document Xander's public health work on preventing the spread of epidemics, knowledge that would be useful in an increasingly dangerous world.

When they had first arrived in South Africa in the autumn, only six months ago, before the epidemic had spread like wildfire south from the Sub Saharan region of the continent, they had enjoyed a driving safari in Kruger National Park. Both of them had been before, but never together. It was almost like the honeymoon they had never had time to take. Wildlife, while not exactly flourishing, was still hanging on. Tara delighted in the antics of baby elephants. She wakened early to the chorus of birds at dawn, and lay beside Xander in the deep star-studded night listening to lions roaring and chuffing not too far away. Though lions were now considered endangered, a few of these magnificent beings still lived in a wild state in their increasingly circumscribed world.

The trip had been spoiled when their Land Rover happened upon a killing field of hornless rhinos, the carcasses of parents and baby fly-blown and rotting in the harsh sun.

"Why are they still doing this?" asked Tara in outrage, choking back a gag against the stench.

Xander closed his eyes and sighed. "There's a rumor that rhino horn confers immunity against the new plagues. Poor things, dying for naught. "Xander put the Land Rover into gear. "Nothing we can do but call in the GPS coordinates," he said resignedly.

The day after they received the shocking news about Joy and Dawa, Tara watched Xander sleep, his breathing regular, deceptively peaceful. Unable to sleep herself, she had tried to meditate, but ended up mostly thinking over the past six months. Within a few months of their arrival, the country had seemed to be collapsing about them, but then so did every country these days. Riots were a common occurrence, and the crime rate was off the charts. Scotland would have been safer, despite the general unrest, but Xander and Tara shared both a need to be useful, and an international perspective. With Joy, Dawa, and Dechen safely living under the protection of their late Rinpoche's lineage in Nepal, and Joy's secure job as a translator for the international Dharma center there, they really didn't have strong reasons to stay in Scotland.

Tara felt guilty sometimes about her sister Christina and her niece Daphne's family growing up without Tara's presence. She hadn't made it back to Taos the Christmas after Mom died, nor the next one. Now years had gone by, and travel was more difficult than it had been in decades. As far as she knew, everyone was still all right, but communication had been sporadic. How long had it been?

A knock on the door startled her. Xander stirred slightly. She knew she shouldn't answer the door, not with crime the way it was and the pandemic still going strong. The rambling old colonial hotel and its once-stately garden was supposed to be a secure zone against both, so she peered through the peephole before beginning the laborious process of unbolting four systems of chains and bolts.

Her dear friend Victoria, who was both a *sangoma*—a traditional healer—and a Western doctor, waited outside the door. Tara had known Victoria for a long time, as the formidable Zulu woman had been a key informant from the days decades ago when Tara was doing her dissertation on traditional healers. Strangely, as they had discovered upon their arrival in Eshowe six months before, Victoria was also a close cousin of Xander's late wife, and he had met her several times on their visits to South Africa.

What could she possibly want at this hour? Victoria startled Tara by pressing her eye to the peephole from outside.

Xander awoke as Tara struggled to remember the order of unlocking bolts and chains.

"What's going on?" he asked urgently.

"It's Victoria."

He came instantly fully awake, a trait he had always possessed but which had eluded Tara. In perfect order, he untangled the chains and locks and let their old friend in.

Victoria's usually ageless ebony face looked tired and old as she sat on the faded upholstery of the one chair in the tiny, musty room. Tara lit a gas ring to boil water for *rooibos* tea.

"I'm so sorry to disturb you so late," said Victoria. "And so sorry to hear of your sad news."

Xander closed his eyes and ran his hands through his silvering hair. "Thank you. Lots of sad news about, I expect. How is your family?"

"Most of them better than one would expect, if they listen to me. That's why I've come."

Victoria accepted the mug of steaming hot tea from Tara's hands, and cupped her hands around it, sniffing it before she drank it.

"There is something. Something I will share with you. *Muti*, a medicine that works."

"I knew there had to be something," said Xander. "Some kind of herb?"

Victoria nodded slowly, the white beads in her hundreds of thin braids bobbing. "Yes. This is not a new disease, you know, anymore than the HIV was."

"What is this herb? Can we grow it fast enough?"

"Indeed it is common. Right here in Kwazulu Natal."

She beckoned the two of them to lean forward, and whispered the English name, and the Latin name, of the plant into their ears.

"That grows everywhere!" said Tara. "I remember it from when I was doing my fieldwork with you."

"How much will it grow when the pharmacy giants come to steal it from the land?" asked Victoria bitterly.

"But if we know it works, we can't ethically keep it away from people," said Xander.

Victoria looked at him severely. "It is my secret. Our secret. The Zulu people's, your late wife's people's."

"But…"

She held up a hand. "I only told you for your own sake. I can provide enough for you to keep yourselves safe. And we, our village cooperative, can provide enough to keep the people here safe, the ones who still trust the old ways."

Xander looked at her doubtfully. "But shouldn't you tell the authorities? It could save many lives if it could be synthesized."

She snorted. "We've consulted the spirits. It would be stolen, misused. We have been shown that clearly." Victoria grabbed Tara's hand. "Tara, believe me, if there were any way we could share it with the world, we would. It's not only my ancestors. We gathered together all the most respected *sangomas* and had them, one by one, talk to their ancestors. All received the same answer."

"Let me take some seed," said Xander urgently. "Let us try to grow it in other places. We won't say what it is, or how we got it, just that it may work."

"They will track you down," said Victoria. "They will know where you have been, and who you have spoken to."

"But don't we have a moral duty…"

"I am a physician, an MD, as you are. I know about the moral duty. But I also know about triage. Think of this as triage."

"What would Rinpoche say?" wondered Tara aloud. "We don't have him to ask anymore."

"He'd want us to help as many people as possible," said Xander stubbornly.

Victoria took Xander's hands in her own, and stared intently into his eyes. "Yes, as many people as possible. And it's only possible to help some, not all. You have to stay alive, you two. If *you* stay alive, you can help many to stay alive. So take the *Muti* I am giving you."

Victoria gave them each a muslin bag filled with herbs. Tara wrinkled her nose at the smell, pungent and not particularly pleasant. "Only a pinch is needed, in your tea. Three times a day, for three weeks. You can then have your immunity tested, and see if we are right."

"Thank you," said Tara. "Why us? What about the other doctors?"

Victoria waved a hand around the compound. "Their safe-suits are cumbersome, but they work. The ancestors have chosen the two of you to have this extra protection. Why? Tara, because you are my old friend, my adopted sister, and you are trained in our ways. Alexander, because you are cousin to me through your late wife. Both of you are family."

The three of them held hands on each other's knees in the close quarters, sealing their pact.

Victoria got up to go, hesitated, and then drew one more packet out of the bag hidden by the crossed snakeskins that she wore over her chest. "Here are the seeds," she said in resignation. "Test this herb, then take the seeds to someone trustworthy, and try to grow it. The ancestors say that the pandemic will be over before this is needed, but it is knowledge that perhaps will be useful to you for future. It cures many things, many viruses and bacteria, because it does not work to kill those things specifically, but rather to stimulate the immune system to kill those things."

Tara and Xander watched out the window as Victoria wearily made her way across the floodlit courtyard of the secure compound that the hotel had been turned into. Bravely, the Elder walked out the gates of safety, back into the city of lamentation.

Chapter
33

August, 1978

London, England

Harry's father had indeed bailed him out, that very night—on the condition that Harry move back home.

It took a couple of days for Harry to get away to visit his old squat, and that only for the purpose of "collecting his things."

"Shit, man, I wish we'd never gone out busking," said a very shaken Harry. "That'll cure me of music forever."

"I hope not, man," said Dermot. "That may be all we can do if we lose our places at Oxford. And besides which, we were framed. How could we know that would happen?"

Harry looked at Dermot and his friends from the future apologetically. "I fucked up, man. Not only have I fucked up my own life, but apparently the whole future of the world. Now bloody Margaret Thatcher will get elected, and it all goes to hell."

"Don't flatter yourself," said Dermot resentfully.

"And anyway, don't give up hope yet," said Yeshi. "I've had some of my own problems with my dad."

"You did?" asked Tara. "Three hundred years from now?"

"About this Time Travel business. He didn't approve of my volunteering."

"There's a story in this," said Harry, perking up a little.

"For another time," said Sitara sharply. "Let's keep on task. This is an important Pivot Point, and we have to figure out how to change it. Every one of us. Including the cat. So let's put our heads together."

"Invite your father over to meet us," said Tara.

She was shouted down, but kept going. "Seriously. Go home with your things, tell your dad that you've stopped smoking weed—you have, haven't you?—and tell him you are completely innocent."

"He doesn't believe me."

"Well keep telling him. And we will too. We can make ourselves presentable and cook a wonderful meal for him."

"Tell him your buddy Jonah is a famous American jazz musician," suggested Jonah.

Harry looked up. "Dad does love jazz."

"Tell him that I've been doing my best to get you clean and sober, and your buddy Dermot too. Tell him that I've asked Dermot to play in my band, but only during summer holidays until he gets his degree. After that we'll see, depending on if he's going on for higher degrees."

"I only wish it were true," said Dermot, laughing.

"If we change the future, lots of cool things can be true, Dermot. You've got a lot of capabilities to make your own future, it's not all stacked against you. But that's a topic for another day."

"It might work," said Harry doubtfully.

"Here's proof. Take this home and put it on the record player." Sitara handed Harry an LP that hadn't been there a few moments ago, with Jonah on the cover, a major internationally-known American record label, and liner notes with praise from the likes of Miles Davis.

"Can I listen to it now?" asked Harry.

"Let it be a surprise," said Jonah. "Like it's a surprise to me," he added, winking at Sitara.

Harry tucked the album under his arm, and hoisted his duffel. "Okay, wish me luck."

Two days later, Tara and Sitara were busy cooking a delicious dinner with Leona's and Janus' help. Sitara had suggested that she simply molecularly manifest a gourmet dinner, but Tara had insisted on actual cooking. She had forgotten how much she had enjoyed cooking a proper meal on a proper gas stove out of real and varied ingredients.

They had chosen to prepare a vegetable curry, as Indian food was just taking off in popularity in London, being infinitely preferable to most British cuisine of the time.

Tara's mouth was watering as she sautéed the garlic, onion, and spices. The rich aromas of turmeric, coriander, and cumin soon wafted through the hallways of the squat. An electric fire, enhanced by Sitara's intention, warmed the sitting room. Yeshi and Jonah had scrounged up a decent table and chairs through more normal means, in Portobello Road Market.

All in all, they were creating a warm welcome for Harry's gentleman father. His mother was away helping Harry's sister get settled in Australia, so she wouldn't be a problem, upset as she was about her son's troubles.

Dermot went as far as tying his hair back in a neat ponytail, though he refused to cut it.

When they answered the door, they were momentarily surprised to see Harry's new short haircut, his long blond curls shorn into a neat cut suitable for an Oxford man.

This was the first time they had actually been introduced to Harry's dad. Mr. Beaton was impeccably polite, though he seemed a little confused by the large party and their relationship to each other.

Georgie sat on the red velvet chair, in quite good condition till he had shed on it, that they had picked up for Mr. Beaton in Portobello Market.

"What a sweet moggy," cooed Mr. Beaton unexpectedly. "Just like my Mr. Grey from when I was a boy."

Harry winked at everyone. There was a chink in his dad's armor.

Georgie lazily opened one shimmering green eye, and then the other, and gave a loving look to Mr. Beaton, his eyes half-closed in a cat kiss.

Mr. Beaton was captivated. He scratched the cat's ears, and took another chair. "Oh, I don't want to disturb the cat. What's his name?"

"Georgie," said Tara.

"Score one for the cat," everyone in the room heard, except Mr. Beaton.

By the time the curry meal was finished and they were on to the port, Mr. Beaton was quite relaxed and was friendly even to Dermot, whom he had blamed for his son's corruption. He was enjoying his conversation with the "famous American jazz musician Jonah" and his pretty young wife Sitara. He was impressed by the American anthropologist Tara, who had married the Tibetan refugee Yeshi and was helping him in his cause to free Tibet. And that young couple, Jonah's daughter Leona and her fiancé Janus, were seriously talking about wanting to continue their studies.

It was Dermot who finally broached the subject of their legal troubles. "Sir, I want to apologize for any trouble I've caused Harry. Harry's like a brother to me. Ever since, I've given up marijuana, and all but a little drink. I want to make my mother back in Ireland proud, and take my place in Oxford to read Biology. I want to go to medical school and become an immunologist."

"Very impressive, Dermot," said Mr. Beaton pensively. "But you've got legal troubles to sort out first."

"Dad, I swear to you that neither one of us had what they say we did. They're saying heroin, for God's sake. I'd never touch that sh…stuff in a million years. I hope you know me better than that."

Mr. Beaton sighed. "I thought I did, son. I can't say I'm not disappointed. I don't know what to believe. I suppose the police might make mistakes, but I can't believe that they'd actually frame anyone. This is a free country. Why would they do that?"

It was Yeshi, the "refugee," who spoke. "Mr. Beaton, I am so grateful to be here in the UK, and to have asylum in America, both beautiful and free countries. But I have seen much injustice, as you can imagine. And I have to say, after being in India for many years, I know the look of heroin, and I can testify that neither your son nor his friend Dermot would ever have touched that stuff. I saw the police pull those bags out of their own pockets, and I am willing to swear an affidavit to that effect."

Mr. Beaton looked shocked. "You saw it?"

"I've learned to observe closely."

Georgie chose that particular moment to crawl onto Mr. Beaton's lap and start purring and kneading his claws into his black suit. Mr. Beaton seemed oddly comforted by the cat's attention, and it made him thoughtful.

"Do you boys both swear to me that you did not have heroin on you?"

Both of them held up their hands. "I swear on my father's grave," said Dermot.

"I swear on anything you wish me to swear on," said Harry sincerely.

"Well then. I believe you both." He heaved a troubled sigh. "Dermot, I'll pay for your defense. I've got the best lawyer for Harry already. But this changes everything. We've got to show police corruption. Do you suppose..." He paused. "Do you suppose they went after you to get at me, because of my position?"

"Stranger things have happened," said Jonah darkly.

"We've got to get this cleared up. Obviously, you've both got to be able to take your places at Oxford in October. But there's more that you don't know about. The Prime Minister is thinking of calling elections in October."

"Exactly," said Tara. "It's crucial that he do so."

"It will keep Margaret Thatcher from being elected," chimed in Harry.

"What do you know about Mrs. Thatcher?" asked Mr. Beaton. "She's no real threat to us. And Mrs..."

"Just call me Tara," she said quickly.

"Tara, how does an American come to be so interested in British politics?"

"I did my Master's at LSE," she said smoothly.

"We'd better just tell him," said Sitara.

"Tell me what?" asked Mr. Beaton, looking at each of them in turn.

The Time Travelers looked at each other. No one wanted to be the first to say, "We're all Time Travelers from the future come here, to this time, to make sure that your grandchildren actually have a future."

"Dad, my friends are on a sort of mission," began Harry. "To make sure that Mrs. Thatcher never gets elected."

His father burst out laughing. "There's little enough chance of that. Though I suppose the more Mr. Callahan delays, I could see how it could play into the hands of the Conservatives. But the public would get their fill soon enough, and Labour would be back in power."

"No," said Tara. "Begging your pardon, Sir, that's not the way it will go."

"Indeed, I do beg your pardon. I don't see…"

Suddenly a hologram appeared in the center of the table, as Sitara stared with her physical eyes and Third Eye.

"What the…" Mr. Beaton frowned, and blinked his eyes hard. "I must be dreaming. I just hope this legal business is all a dream too."

The hologram got bigger. In it, Mrs. Thatcher was addressing Parliament. A newspaper headline read, "PM Thatcher breaks Miners Strike."

"What on Earth is this?" asked Mr. Beaton incredulously, sputtering slightly. "Is this some new kind of TV receiver?"

"Dad, you're not going to believe this," said Harry. "My friends, all these people, well it's going to sound ridiculous, but they are Time Travelers from the future, and this is part of their technology."

Mr. Beaton slammed his glass of port down on the worn coffee table, startling Georgie awake. "You're right, son. I don't believe it."

"Believe your eyes, sir," said Yeshi gently.

"Believe me," said the cat quietly.

Mr. Beaton looked down at the cat in his lap who, now thoroughly awake, was staring at him with intense green eyes. "Did the bloody cat just speak? Is he in on this too?"

"Please, sir, do not refer to me that way," said Georgie. His dignity injured, he jumped off Mr. Beaton's lap and groomed furiously on the floor nearby.

"I'm sorry," said Mr. Beaton to the cat. "Oh dear, I'm afraid I'm losing my mind. Have you spiked the port?"

The faces starting at him were deadly serious.

The 3-D hologram moved on relentlessly. Images of war in the Falklands, images of prosperous bankers juxtaposed with decaying social services, invasions of Middle Eastern countries, and was that an older Tony Blair urging his countrymen to war in Iraq? The sequence ended with an image of Stonehenge overshadowed by palm trees and surrounded by rice paddies, the Stonehenge of 2050 that the Time Travelers had left.

"Bloody hell!" swore Mr. Beaton angrily. "I don't know what this is, or how you're doing it, or what you're playing at. This is like…" He struggled for an analogy. "The Ghost of Christmas Future. Is it some kind of warning?"

"Much as I dislike the Conservatives and strenuously disagree with their policies, I can't believe that Mrs. Thatcher could have to power to cause all this havoc. And really, Stonehenge with palm trees? Of course, scientists are concerned about the Greenhouse Effect and carbon emissions, but England tropical? That would be hundreds of years in the future, if it would ever occur at all."

"No, 2050, the year that Leona, Janus, and I came from," said Tara sadly. "It's already changed—and it's considered irreversible."

Mr. Beaton looked at her incredulously.

"Mr. Beaton, you are in a unique position to change this," Tara said fervently. "We hope we're right. We think that if you can use your influence to convince Mr. Callahan to call elections in October, rather than waiting till May of next year, Mr. Callahan will win the election and so much harm can be avoided."

"Well I've had a strong feeling that that would be the best way to go," mused Mr. Beaton thoughtfully. "And he does seem to be leaning that way. But there are a lot of forces going against me."

"Dad," said Harry. "I know you can do this. You may not go down in history, but you'll be doing a great service to history."

"I've always been a bit of a behind the scenes man," said Mr. Beaton. "I prefer it that way." He picked up the glass of port and toyed with it absently, spinning the glass nervously in his hands. "I do believe I can prevail upon Mr. Callahan to listen to me," he said at last. "We've already been in discussion on the matter. Of course, I can't promise anything. But you've convinced me, the old skeptic. That thingamajiggy is most impressive. I promise, I'll do my best, now that I know what's truly at stake."

Mr. Beaton downed the rest of his port in a single gulp. "And is there any way I can get one of those receiver things?"

The hologram swirled in the air, contracted to a point, and was gone.

Chapter
34

November, 2033

**Eshowe, Kwazulu Natal,
South Africa**

Victoria had been right. The pandemic had been brought under control, but not until the world had lost about 20% of its population. Tara and Xander had taken the herb she had given them, and blood tests had indeed shown an increased immune response. Xander had taken the precious seeds to a colleague in Doctors Without Borders whom he felt he could trust, and that friend had shared them with WHO.

But in the 11 years that had passed, nothing had come of it. Certainly many physicians and scientists had pushed for more of the herb to be cultivated, or for the active compounds to be synthesized. But they were thwarted by the giant pharmaceutical companies, which somehow had survived the chaos and did not see sufficient opportunity for profit in keeping mostly poor people alive to "justify" the expense of synthesizing and producing a life-saving, immune-boosting drug.

"Short-sighted bastards," Xander had called them.

"Do they think it's cheaper to let the population die off and the economy continue to collapse?" asked Tara. "Isn't not having enough consumers cutting into their bottom line?"

"That would be both far too logical and far too compassionate," Xander had replied.

Tara never thought they would spend so many years in South Africa, but as the planet proceeded on a downward spiral, it seemed that it didn't really matter where you were, as long as you were with people you loved.

Air travel had gradually resumed, and she'd been able to visit Christina and the family twice. Miraculously, no one in her immediate family had died in the Plague. The virus had lost much of its punch by the time it reached North America in a big way, and most people who fell ill recovered, especially in more isolated rural areas.

Xander had never wanted to hear the details of Joy's and Dawa's deaths, and Tara was glad that there wasn't even a possibility of ever knowing. The Plague had killed unpleasantly, with people's organs essentially dissolving into mush and blood. Fortunately, once a person was ill enough to be dying, the fear was gone, and the process was not too painful.

Two months after Joy's and Dawa's deaths, when the worst of the pandemic had abated, Xander had gone alone to Kathmandu to fetch Dechen, traveling a circuitous route from Johannesburg to Cairo to Dubai to Delhi and finally to Kathmandu. It had been a harrowing time for Tara, left alone in the secure compound. Phone and Internet communication had been sporadic during the weeks he was gone, and she'd thrown herself into both meditation and work, dutifully donning her safe-suit to aid the doctors. There was comfort in knowing that they were saving at least some lives, and alleviating at least some suffering.

Finally she'd gotten a call from Xander that he was on his way back with Dechen. Tara was pretty sure that she had the right date and flight number, but there was no way to check. She was relieved and grateful that Victoria offered to accompany her to Johannesburg. The Plague had crashed South Africa's already fragile economy and left crops unharvested, drying maize stalks rotting in the fields. Hungry, desperate, ragged survivors roamed, looking for the more fortunate to beg from or steal from. The presence of an elder *sangoma* would not only be a comfort but, Tara hoped, a protection. In her unmistakable *sangoma* hairstyle of hundreds of thin braids strung with red and white beads, Victoria exuded an aura of strength and invulnerability.

Procedures at the airport had broken down, and the two women didn't know what to expect. They had heard that some days there was extreme security, and one couldn't get near the place. Other days the soldiers simply didn't show up, perhaps off at the funeral of family or friends.

Today was one of the latter. The *bakkie* driver drove Tara and Victoria right up to the stairway wheeled up to the recently arrived aircraft.

Tara waited as bedraggled passengers stumbled down the stairway, wondering if any of them were sick, wondering if Xander and Dechen had been exposed to any pathogens on their series of flights.

They were last off, Dechen looking like a little girl half her ten years as she tiredly clomped down the metal stairs, half held up by her grandfather.

Tara raced to embrace and comfort her, and Dechen held tightly to her, finally letting herself cry.

In their 60's, Tara and Xander suddenly found themselves raising a child.

They'd done pretty well, she reflected now, 11 years later. Dechen, like her grandfather, had married into the Zulu nation. She'd met Kennedy in her Regenerative Agriculture classes at the university in Durban. As the country had rebuilt after the decimation, the new government had encouraged agrarian and environmental studies. Permaculture was an important part of the curriculum. On a local scale, these practices were successfully creating a kinder microclimate, less extreme and arid than the climate had become in most of the region.

No one really knew much about what was happening in the rest of the world. Snippets of data would come through: Brazil's drought was worsening, but there was enough water because of the population decline; northern Europe was able to grow oranges and grapes, but people had had to adapt to extremely hot summers and mild, snowless winters; much of India's coastline was regularly flooded, and the greatly reduced but still large population had begun to move inland.

There were bright spots, at least from some points of view. Due to the Plague and the resultant chaos, the Chinese central government had collapsed, leaving minorities, including the Tibetans, to run their own regional governments. Many of the Han Chinese settlers who had survived the Plague due to their remote location were heading back to what was left of their families on the coast, glad to get away from the hardships of altitude.

The Tibetans, including most of Dawa's family, had returned to a much-changed, much warmer Lhasa. Water was a problem, as the glaciers had all but disappeared. But Dawa's father Nyima, in sporadic contact with Dechen, spoke optimistically of drilling bore holes, since the aquifer had never been tapped out. Barley, long a staple, was getting harder to grow, but naturally hybridized varieties of wheat adapted to altitude and high-UV light were starting to thrive, and careful cultivation of greens in greenhouses sheltered from the harsh UV light was yielding nutritious staples.

Yaks were not doing well in Tibet. They had already retreated to the very highest altitudes, with nowhere to go if the climate kept getting warmer.

And the Dalai Lama, alas, had not lived in that incarnation to return to a free Tibet. For decades, he had specifically stated that he was the last of the Dalai Lamas, and that no one should look for a future incarnation.

Tara had wondered at times if the compassionate energy of the Bodhisattva Chenrezig, said to be embodied in the Dalai Lamas, had gone utterly from this world when His Holiness left his body. But she realized that she saw it every single day in so many ways, and doubled her resolve to live her own life with boundless compassion.

Xander had continued his work as a doctor. Tara had learned quite a bit about medicine, and helped whenever he asked, but her true passion, like Dechen's, had become growing things. Together she and her granddaughter worked in the large community gardens of Eshowe, alongside the villagers— by turns stoic, full of laughter, and deeply passionate—who had embraced them as family. They grew tropical fruits that would not have grown in the green hills ten years before, bred chickens and cattle for heat-resistance, tended medicinal herbs, and constantly took soil measurements and air samples.

They were proud that this region had been one of the first to mitigate some of the effects of the overly-carbonized atmosphere, succeeding on a local level in sequestering enough carbon to lower the proportion of carbon in the air. This success gave Tara hope. Of course it would have to be done worldwide, but perhaps others were in that process now. Perhaps there would be some breathing space, literally, some time to stabilize adaptations and then start reversing the effects. So much of the world was already unlivable, and so many people had died either of the Plague or from the natural disasters around the planet—droughts, floods, earthquakes, tsunamis, and resultant famines.

She knew that they were among the most fortunate. At nearly 80, she had as much energy as many women half her age, and Xander was a healthy, robust 74. Life was surprisingly good for all they had gone through, and each day both meditated on gratitude.

"Grandpa, Grandma Tara, we have news," said Dechen at dinner one November night. The beautiful, willowy woman reached out for her husband Kennedy's hand.

"We're pregnant," the two of them said together, beaming.

Both Tara and Xander took a moment to react. Tara knew they were disappointing the young couple, but it was hard to muster excitement for bringing a child into a world that would probably only get worse.

"Well," said Xander. "Congratulations are of course in order. But have you thought this through? Do you think this is a good time?"

"This was not unplanned," said Kennedy. "We've talked of this on and off since our marriage, and have been, uh, working at it for several months."

"How far along are you?" asked Tara, stalling her emotions for time.

"Not quite three months," said Dechen.

They could still…Tara stopped her thought.

"We thought you'd be happy," said Dechen defensively.

"Oh, of course I'm happy," said Xander, but he didn't sound happy. "It's only…well, you know all the risks."

"The population is down considerably," said Kennedy. "And we did discuss adoption as well. If we want more children, we will happily adopt."

"We are showing our hope in the future," said Dechen. "We believe there is going to be a future. Look at how much has been accomplished here."

"The medical care is better in Scotland," said Xander.

"What, Grandad, are you expecting problems?" asked Dechen in surprise. "The medical care is fine here. And you're here."

Tara looked at Xander. They hadn't discussed going back to Scotland, and she was rather annoyed with him at the moment. She liked her life here.

"The climate is more stable, I hear," he said. "The population is less, and they need people with agrarian knowledge."

"But my knowledge is specific to South Africa, and to this region," said Dechen. "What would I do in Scotland?"

"I'm in contact with people there. It's far north. The Highlands have quite a temperate climate. The Findhorn folks have expanded their methods throughout Scotland and into northern England. The government seems to be stable."

Tara stared at him, putting down her fork and leaving the rest of her dinner untouched.

"Sorry, Tara, I had been thinking of this for a while," he said, glancing at her.

She controlled herself in front of Dechen and Kennedy. "When were you going to discuss this?" she asked evenly. "Don't we always make our decisions together?"

"Well I was waiting for the right moment. Then the kids made their announcement, and well, it just seemed the time."

"Thank you."

"Just be happy for us," said Dechen forcefully. "Whatever you decide to do."

Kennedy put a reassuring hand on his wife's and squeezed it. "We can discuss your idea of moving later," he said to Xander. "I have my family here, and I am inclined to stay here. But I am also inclined towards adventure. And we have to think what is best for our child. Victoria thinks it will be a girl."

"Victoria knew before we did?" asked Tara, feeling a bit betrayed.

"She helped us conceive with some herbs," said Dechen. "We agreed not to say anything until we knew for sure."

"I promise you, we will consider all your arguments carefully," said Kennedy.

"Well I'm off to meditate," said Xander. "It seems the best course of action under the circumstances."

"Good night then," said Dechen. She and Kennedy got up from the table and headed for their room.

Tara was left alone at the table, her dinner, even the sweet mangos for afters, no longer appealing. She cleaned up on her own, automatically starting mantras to calm herself, remembering to use the "*Phet!*" syllable to cut through yet another illusion.

A pride of White Lions lived free on the veldt. Tara and Victoria stood on a small koppie, watching them rest in the late afternoon sun, languidly stretching like all the wonderful cats Tara had had in her long life. It was nearly sunset,

and the pride was getting restless. The lionesses were stirring, getting up and stretching. They cuffed the cubs that were particularly annoying.

The magnificently maned male at last got up, stretched, and roared.

The night fell swiftly, and the air cooled to a pleasant temperature. Victoria signaled to Tara to simply sit with her there on the hilltop in the cool breeze. They would make no fire, shine no light, only watch.

Tara fell asleep staring up at the bright stars, which shone like beacon fires in an indigo ocean. Orion, the autumn constellation…only it wasn't autumn now, here, in Africa. It was spring, November.

Victoria was no longer with her. She sat up on the hilltop, and saw her friend waving good-bye from a distance, from a beach below. A beach?

She was lucid now, aware that she was dreaming. Was she to change anything?

The lions, visible like ghosts of the past or future in the night, played with the cubs, blissfully unaware of human activities that threatened their lives, and changes in the atmosphere that threatened all lives.

Tara became aware that she was in a huge stone circle, a henge, the henge of henges, Stonehenge. The male lion approached from the east, his mate from the west, as two stars, morning star and evening star, drew together in the sky above, forming a bright light, like a comet.

She lay still, aware that these great animals could dispose of her with their giant paws, could easily shake her to death with one strong shake of their heads. She didn't want to offend them. After all, it was humans who were the interlopers here.

The two lions met in the middle of the circle, and then turned to her as one, staring, and…purring?

She hadn't noticed that the female had something in her mouth, but she dropped a tiny cub into Tara's lap. The parents sat like house cats, waiting for Tara to do something, until she comforted the mewling cub, which Tara somehow knew was female. The cub surprised Tara by burping contentedly and yawning.

As Tara looked at the two adult lions, she saw that their faces were etched with glowing light symbols, hierogylphics, the ankh, the Triple Spiral, petroglyphs from the Southwest, an Om.

Stars blazed through the foreheads of the two lions as they faded into the mist.

Tara awoke, startled, in the warm African night, in the room where they had lived for over a decade. Xander snored softly beside her. She looked down, expecting to see a White Lion cub in her lap, and for a moment thought she did.

She looked at Xander. She shook slightly, reaching out for the shreds of her dream. A cub. A child. At Stonehenge. Not Scotland, but on the same island of Brittania.

Perhaps Xander was right. She put her hand on his forehead, and stroked his silvery hair. They would talk, in the morning, and see what the children had to say.

Chapter
35

July-October, 1978

London, England

"*That went well*," said Georgie with great satisfaction, after everyone had said good-bye to Mr. Beaton. Harry had remained behind with his friends, after an unusually affectionate and demonstrative parting from his somewhat shaken dad.

"I think it did," said Tara aloud. She turned to Sitara. "How are we going to know for sure if it worked?"

Sitara mused, tapping her fingers on a coffee mug. "It's not like we've done this before," she said, somewhat evasively Tara thought.

Tara put down the pan she was washing. Even the mundane chores of the day seemed pleasurable to her, familiar, after all that had changed in the past 70-odd years.

"So are we done?" Tara asked. "Is it all fixed?"

"There are a couple of ways we can do this," said Yeshi. "We, or one of us, could pop back home to 300 years in the future and see if the Timelines are still bleeding. But that entails some risk."

"What kind of risk?"

235

"On the simplest level, the one who goes might not be able to get back. In a worst case scenario, if what we did here didn't succeed, the portal could close, either temporarily or permanently."

"Meaning?"

"We could fail."

Tara slammed the heavy cast iron pan down on the counter, liking the sound it made and enjoying the release of energy.

"I thought you guys had this down."

"Relax. We have a very high probability of succeeding."

"I hate it when people tell me to relax, calm down, stop getting so upset and raising my voice," said Tara, raising her voice. "I'll raise my voice if I want to."

"I didn't tell you to lower your voice," said Yeshi.

"Well, you know what I mean. Look, it doesn't matter for me so much. I will die soon, in my Timeline, or this one, or any one. It's the nature of things, and it doesn't particularly scare me after all the deaths I've seen. Except for Leona, and now Janus, and Georgie of course, all my loved ones have preceded me. Except for you three, whom I've grown quite fond of, but apparently you live way after me."

"And we might incarnate at the same Time, sometime in the future," said Yeshi. "Have you thought of that?"

"You mean I might be alive already in your Time, and we haven't yet met?"

He spread his large, expressive hands. "It's a big universe. In our Time there is inter-galactic travel. But those who are meant to meet, meet."

She narrowed her eyes. "Do you know something I don't know?"

He shrugged and looked at her with open palms and eyes.

"Or are you just trying to distract me from the worry at hand?" she countered.

Sitara had been sitting quietly against a wall, in meditation. "I think we just need to do a short jump," she said. "I think it's the safest way."

"Who? To where?"

"All of us. Three months into the future, to early October, to see if the elections were called and if so, who won."

"Us too?" asked Dermot. "Can Harry and I come?"

"Absolutely not," said Sitara. "There are enough variables as it is. It's nothing personal," she added. "Just trying to lower the complexity."

"Three months from now," mused Harry. "I guess by then we'll know if the charges against us were dropped, and if we made it to Oxford. Either of us, or both of us."

Dermot strummed chords on his guitar, trying to act like he didn't care. "I reckon your dad can get you off."

"Stop it, man, we're in this together now. You heard what Dad said."

"And you trust him now?"

"After tonight, yeah I do. I think he was pretty impressed. How could you not be changed by knowing that there's Time Travel? It changed us."

"That it did," said Dermot.

"What's your proposal?" Sitara asked Yeshi.

"We do a short jump, the six of us, and of course Georgie. We meet the boys there, and they can fill us in."

"Then we can go home and see what happened to 2050?" asked Leona eagerly. "Maybe my Mum and Dad are still alive if we've changed the Timeline."

"Mine too," said Janus. "Wouldn't that be amazing?"

"One thing at a time," said Sitara. "But I hope you're not attached to anything here…No, Jonah, you can't take your saxophone or your LP. I'll make you another one back home, or you can make your own."

"So what should we do?" asked Harry.

"Just keep living your lives, one day at a time," said Yeshi. "We'll meet you in a few months. You'll have something to look forward to."

"We won't just forget you as soon as you go poof?" asked Dermot.

"Could you?" asked Jonah. "I don't think your dad will forget this either. He's got quite a secret to keep."

"Don't waste time on fond good-byes," said Sitara. "If all goes well, and I certainly expect it to, then we'll see you two in three months. For us, it will just seem like a moment."

"Where should we expect you?" asked Harry.

"How about the Oxford Student Union?" said Sitara. "I'm optimistic." She looked at Dermot. "And I fully expect to see both of you there."

"How do we do this?" said Tara. "Do we have to be touching? Do we need a portal?"

"Just come close," said Sitara.

Georgie, recognizing that the moment had arrived, leapt onto Tara's shoulders as soon as she put his shoulder pad on.

"Am I going to have to be in a carrier?" he asked nervously.

She smiled. "I think Oxford in 1978 might be just eccentric enough that you won't. Perhaps a lead?"

The six Time Travelers crowded in close, touching each other. Tara kept a hand on Georgie, just in case.

All that Dermot and Harry saw was a swirl of rainbow light, and their friends were gone. Most of their stuff disappeared with them, but Jonah's saxophone remained in its case, leaning against the wall.

Dermot picked out a complicated tune on his guitar and sighed. "It's gonna get pretty lonely here without them, and without you," he said to Harry.

"Come stay with us till term starts. I'm sure Dad won't mind," said Harry. "In fact, it might make him feel less crazy if we're both there."

6 October, 1978

Oxford, England

They materialized, gently, on a gray day, in a quiet lane not far from the university. Tara looked down, curious what she would be wearing.

She didn't mind the rather conservatively cut forest green wool suit, and rather liked the silk scarf that went with it. Practical knee boots fit perfectly, protecting her from the rainy streets. Georgie, on an elegant lead, was not so protected, and kept shaking his paws and glaring. Finally she picked him up and carried him in her arms. He started to purr as he sucked at his wet, bedraggled paws.

Jonah, Yeshi, and Sitara all looked like they could pass as Oxford professors, while Leona and Janus looked like new students finding their way around.

They made their way to the university canteen, all the while looking around for Harry and Dermot. Tara noticed that people were standing around in little knots, looking at newspapers, discussing something. The most conservatively dressed students looked quite down in the mouth. She hoped that was a good sign.

There were a few groups dressed more daringly, in neat versions of non-conformist garb. These young men and women had smiles on their faces. Tara was trying to get a look at the newspaper headline they were looking at when Leona ran over to a group of students shouting, "Harry! Dermot! How great to see you!"

A few older people, clearly professors, looked askance at Leona's public display. So much for not calling attention to themselves in public places in other Times.

Harry and Dermot were greeting Leona and Janus with very un-British enthusiasm, giving them effusive hugs. The two young men looked up as the other four approached, and flashed thumbs-up signs.

Tara couldn't wait for details. They all walked to a student pub in the rain, the young people splashing jubilantly in the puddles. They settled into a red leather-lined booth in a relatively quiet corner of the pub, drinking Guinness and cider, as they pleased.

"Dad did it," said Harry. "First he got the coppers to admit that they'd set us up, and all charges were dropped and our names cleared. We got rather a lot of press, but he used it to advantage. He got them to investigate why the police had nabbed *us*, and no one else that day, and proved that it was to embarrass him.

"Obviously he got Mr. Callahan to call the elections in October, and obviously Labour won." Harry raised his glass. "A toast to my dad, and to Prime Minister Callahan."

"Well it's hard to be that enthusiastic about Callahan," said Dermot, "but all right. Given the alternative that we just avoided, which no one seems to realize, let's toast."

They all raised their glasses.

"Quite a few people here not happy," said Harry. "Actually I'm not all that sure how well Dermot and I are going to fit in, but we're mates. We'll support each other through this, and make the best of it."

"I think you'll find there are far more people here who think like you than you realize," said Tara, smiling. "A lot of my friends went to Oxford during this time period, and they were hardly stuffed shirt types."

"Good! Bring it on," said Dermot.

"But did it work the way it was supposed to?" asked Harry. "Did everything change?"

"We don't know yet," said Sitara.

"Well what do we have to do to find out?" asked Harry impatiently.

"I can hardly manifest a hologram right here in the middle of the pub," she said primly. "Where are your digs?"

They crowded into the tiny room with the two single beds and desks. "You had a lot more room at the squat," said Janus.

"It's expensive here," grumbled Dermot. "My grant doesn't go that far, and Harry's dad has him on a strict allowance. Says it builds character."

"Yep, I remember those days," said Tara. "I was living in London working on my Master's Degree this year."

"Let's get down to business," said Sitara, sitting down on one of the beds.

"Do you need a table or anything?" asked Harry.

She merely shook her head, and concentrated, staring into the middle of the room. The hologram formed. Stonehenge was there, intact, no more red lasers damaging it. There were no tanks or heli-shuttles visible.

Tara let out a sigh of relieved held breath. They peered more closely as the image came fully into focus.

"Are you sure you're at the right time frame?" asked Yeshi anxiously.

"Certain," said Sitara. "The one we jumped from. We weren't followed, we weren't attacked. They didn't try to stop us. So something changed."

"Damn," said Tara. "The palm trees are still there, and the rice paddies."

"Looks like home to me," said Leona, not understanding Tara's disappointment.

Tara put an arm around her. "Yes. But that means that not enough changed. The climate didn't go back to normal."

Harry and Dermot were glum. "Dad's going to be so disappointed," said Harry.

"Not all is lost," said Yeshi. "We did accomplish something, we're just not sure what. I guess we need to go to Plan B." He looked at Sitara expectantly.

"I was prepared for this," she said confidently. "But don't think of it as Plan B. Think of it as…how about plan A, part 2?"

"You didn't mention it to us, did you?" asked Tara.

Sitara shrugged. "It was always part of the calculations, but I hoped it wouldn't become necessary. It may be that if we hadn't met Harry and Dermot and Harry's father, and hadn't been able to change the outcome of this election, then Part 2 would still be impossible to change."

"Okay," said Tara resignedly. "What's part 2?"

"Paris, October, 1980. We have to prevent Ronald Reagan's election. The data shows that if the Republicans hadn't made a secret deal with the Iranian revolutionaries to delay the release of the American embassy hostages, President Jimmy Carter would have been re-elected for having successfully negotiated their release.

"The easiest way to make sure that Carter wins, and the most moral way, by the way, is simply to prevent the meeting between the Republican operatives and the Iranians."

"And just how are we going to do that?" asked Tara.

"We'll figure it out," was Sitara's predictable reply. It was the only thing about the woman, or this whole mission, that was predictable, Tara thought.

"Oh, please, can we come?" asked Harry.

"No, you'll have to wait till 1980 in your Timeline. But that's only two years from now," said Sitara. "You both have a lot of learning and growing to do. It will be nice to see how you change. You are most welcome to meet us in Paris. It's a weekend, so you can easily come over. Harry, when it gets close to the time, remember, bring your Dad. He could be of great help to us."

"Where are we meeting then?" asked Harry. "And when?"

"Saturday, October 18th, 1980 at 8 a.m. Tara, where do you think?"

Tara formed the Paris of that time in her mind's eye, and thought of places she had loved. "In the Jardin des Tulleries," she said. "How about right by the Rodin sculpture, 'The Kiss'? It's near the Ritz Hotel where the Republicans and Iranians secretly met, and it's easy to find."

"See ya soon," said Janus to his friends as the six human Time Travelers and one feline vanished in a swirl of light.

Chapter
36

2034-2035

Edinburgh, Scotland

When Leona was born, Tara was sure they had all done the right thing by coming back to Scotland.

Although they had found Edinburgh much changed after their long absence, it still felt good to be there. Everything seemed on a smaller, more personal scale. Many survivors of the Plague had moved out of the cities, back to family and friends who lived in the countryside. Nearly every farm was organic, partly by default since the once-touted fertilizers and pesticides had become very expensive and nearly unavailable.

Different crops were being grown, through trial and error. Tara enjoyed working side by side with Dechen and Kennedy in the community gardens in Xander's neighborhood. They had all moved in to his old Victorian house, sharing with some *sangha* members who had been caretaking and paying a nominal rent for a number of years. There was plenty of room for everyone.

As Tara aged, she found herself more tolerant. She was glad it hadn't gone the other way, as she'd seen with some older people. But she was blessed with excellent health and had no aches or pains to speak of, unless she strained herself gardening. Things just didn't seem to bother her as much as they had in youth and middle age.

The climate, of course, was unpredictable and was much warmer than it had been when she and Xander had first married. But cool breezes still came off the sea, and they were able to take occasional trips to the Highlands and to visit Findhorn, where there were now experimental tea plantations. The electric grid was holding, so they were able to live comfortably and even to use the electric car that Xander had purchased for the occasions when there was a need to travel a long distance or carry a number of people.

They had left South Africa when Dechen was four months pregnant, and her pregnancy had proceeded practically by the book. It was as if she was born to be pregnant. Tara watched her granddaughter take on the proverbial glow, and Kennedy seemed to glow right along with her.

Kennedy was working at the university in hybridization of crops that could thrive in the ever-changing new climate zones. Bananas were doing well just outside Edinburgh, and much of Yorkshire had been given over to citrus. The climate was much like that of Southern California when Tara had been a child, mild from season to season with enough rain for agriculture to thrive.

Communication with South Africa, and with Dechen's father's side of the family in Tibet, had become slow and problematic. Under UN auspices, a new International Postal Agreement had been established, and a veritable army of letter carriers were being employed to once again take physical letters and packages from place to place, within the country or around the globe. The art of penmanship had been revived, and people began to think carefully about what they wanted to say to their loved ones.

Dechen went into labor one May day in 2034 when she was working in the community garden next to Tara. Tara heard Dechen gasp, then laugh, and saw that Dechen's loose cotton pants were wet.

"You know what this means!" said Dechen excitedly, before doubling over for a moment.

"Are you scared?" asked Tara.

"No, not at all. We've been practicing."

"It could come quickly. Let's get you to the birthing center and call Kennedy."

"She."

Tara looked at her questioningly. Dechen hadn't had the old-fashioned ultrasounds, now rare and costly, that let parents know the baby's gender.

"Victoria said it is a girl."

Tara took her by the arm and led her carefully through the small fields of the garden. "Well I don't argue with Victoria."

They didn't have cell phones any more, so Tara sent one of the teenagers to go find Kennedy and bring him to the birthing center. Once she got Dechen settled in, she went to look for Xander at his office at the nearby medical center.

So all three were in attendance of Dechen, along with her midwife, when Leona came into the world, a strong, squirming, reddish-brown baby who already had hair.

It wasn't a long labor, but the last part was intense, and Dechen had had to use all of her breathing techniques, everything she had been taught by Joy and by Rinpoche when she was a child. Tara held one hand and rubbed it, Xander rubbed her feet, and Kennedy held the other hand, softly coaching his wife.

The midwife cut the cord and laid Leona on her mother's belly, while everyone admired the tiny baby with huge dark eyes and, impossibly, the hint of a smile.

There were no cameras, no video, just a peaceful birth shared with family, and soon to be shared with Dechen's and Kennedy's many new friends.

Kennedy, who was quite an artist, drew pictures of his baby daughter, to send in the post to his parents in Zululand, and to Dechen's grandparents and extended family in their ancestral homeland in Lhasa.

Tara and Xander stood with their arms around each other, and kissed softly.

"Well done," he said.

"I didn't do anything. Deche   work, and Kennedy helped her."
"Well done for all of us," he   glad that we came back here."

A year later, just after Leona's first birthday, Dechen couldn't stop coughing. Leona cried in her crib, reaching out for her mother, whether to comfort her mom or comfort herself by suckling, Tara didn't know.

Tara took Leona out of her crib and bounced her and stroked her back. The baby began to quiet down, but another paroxysm of coughing from her mother sent her into fits of sobs, and she reached out desperately for her mother.

Please, please don't let it be this strange new disease going around, prayed Tara.

Their house was placed under quarantine by the government. Red pieces of cloth made an X on their front door, which could easily be seen from the street. Safe-suited government health workers interviewed them through the door, asking in muffled tones what provisions they might need. There was no medicine for this highly contagious disease, thought to be a form of bubonic plague that had quickly mutated into a communicable pneumonic form. The vector was surmised to be the same as it had been in the Middle Ages, infected fleas from the rats and mice that had thrived in the warming climate.

Tara and Xander nursed Dechen, and then Kennedy, who had fallen ill the next day. Tara kept waiting for Xander or herself to start coughing, kept thinking she felt a tickle or a soreness in her throat, but for some reason neither one of them felt the slightest bit ill. Perhaps the herb that Victoria had given them over a decade ago had kept their immune systems strong.

The baby also stayed well, but Leona could not nurse from her sick mother, so Tara held the baby close and fed her goat's milk from a glass bottle and a silicon nipple that had to be constantly sterilized. Tara was thankful they still had running water, even hot water most of the time, as lots of people didn't. Kennedy's jerry-rigged solar system had continued to serve them well.

They had none of the herb left. It hadn't transplanted to Scotland, despite Kennedy's best efforts, and the pharma-giants had never synthesized it.

Tara used up the very last of their carefully hoarded honey making soothing teas for Dechen and Kennedy. She put hot water in the last of the large glass jars of honey they had bought three years ago, when the bees began to disappear in earnest, and carefully scraped the sides of the jars to get every last bit. The smell reminded her of fields of sage in Taos, of fruit orchards in Velarde, of bees buzzing everywhere in wildflowers in so many countries she'd traveled in. In those days, no one would ever have thought that bees would disappear. Even when the dire warnings and online petitions had begun to go around, no one really believed that they would be gone in mere decades.

The honey-laced tea, mixed with precious turmeric, soothed Dechen's throat and put her to sleep. Kennedy managed a weak "thank you" as he gratefully sipped the tea. They were alone in the house. Their housemates had been caught out of town when they were quarantined, so it was only Tara and Xander who were there to take care of the sick young people, and the feisty toddler.

Tara and Xander slept together on a mattress on the floor near Dechen's and Kennedy's sickbeds, so they could hear if they were needed in the night. Leona, finally exhausted from reaching for her mother and father, fell asleep between them.

No one knew how to keep the baby from getting sick, but to their relief, she simply didn't.

One day, Dechen seemed better. She tentatively sat up in bed and had a little broth. Xander let her hold Leona for awhile, and even suckle the child. Dechen's milk had nearly evaporated with the high fever she'd come through, but Leona greedily sucked at first one breast, then the other, content to be in her mother's arms at last.

Dechen smiled, and handed the sleeping baby to Tara. "I'm going to sleep for awhile," she whispered. She never woke up.

Tara and Xander both woke at dawn to the wail of the baby screaming desperately for her mother, whose cold body lay on the bed. Kennedy's hand clutched Dechen's, but he was gone as well.

Tara wanted to scream, to cry, to curse every deity she could think of. Xander simply crumpled over his granddaughter and her husband. Suddenly he seemed like a very, very old man.

"Why not me?" he gasped, sobbing.

Tara shook her head. "Why not this old woman? Why can't I die instead of the young ones?"

Xander raised his tear-streaked face. "Darling, my Dakini, we have to have the strength. We have no choice now. We have to find our faith and have the strength to go on as long as we can. It's not natural for us to raise a baby, a great-grandchild, but these are not natural times."

Leona was inconsolable for hours. They were supposed to put out black streamers to show that someone in the house had died, and the authorities were supposed to come in safe-suits and take the bodies away.

But they couldn't do it, not yet.

Leona quieted down and watched with solemn eyes as Tara and Xander put their hands on the tops of both her parents' heads, and then sat in meditation position and murmured prayers.

This is so wrong, Tara thought, and then wrenched her thoughts back into discipline, into assisting Dechen, who had been trained from childhood, and Kennedy, who had been trained in the ways of his own people, to leave their bodies behind for another realm.

Tara would never forget Leona's intense, dark eyes, like burning coals of thought, staring at the scene of bereavement, then looking up, following the spirits of her parents, the tiny toddler waving at them as they rose and floated towards a vast, bright light.

Chapter 37

18 October, 1980

Paris, France

Tara looked up admiringly at the beautiful erotic sculpture. Rodin's "The Kiss." She had loved it since she had first seen it in an art book as a teenager, and had spent periods of time in contemplation in this very garden, at the gates to Le Musée de L'Orangerie and across from the Jeu de Paume, her father's favorite museum.

This materialization had been easy, seamless. They were getting better at this. She looked down curiously at her body and found herself rather elegantly dressed in a lightweight red wool coat, appropriate for an autumn morning in 1980. She was wearing one of those "little black dresses" that she had owned throughout much of her life, and pantyhose, which she would never have chosen. She did rather like the fashionable black leather platform shoes she was wearing.

She held a red patent leather leash, to which was attached her beloved familiar, Georgie, who wore a matching snazzy red patent leather harness, which contrasted nicely with his smoky gray fur.

On her left hand flashed the diamond engagement ring given to her by Xander. Her heart fluttered for a moment. He was alive in this time period, though they hadn't met until 2017 in her Timeline. Might they meet now?

She wondered how old she looked, and pulled a compact out of her delicate designer shoulder bag.

"*You look stunning,*" came a soft feline voice.

She looked down at Georgie, who was staring up at her intently in between fastidiously grooming his face. "*I hope I look as good.*"

"*You do,*" she assured him. Interesting, she thought. She truly looked a woman *d'un certaine âge*, as the French would say. Hardly an ingénue, but certainly not the old woman her years in 2050 would suggest. Sitara was a true artist in her attention to period details. "*Where are they anyway?*" she asked the cat.

She could have sworn he shrugged. Could cats shrug? "*They'll be along. Just enjoy the sights.*"

"*Is that them?*" she almost asked aloud.

A small crowd had gathered around a juggler who looked suspiciously like Jonah. He was throwing flaming torches into the air. Yeshi, in Tibetan hat and shirt, banged on a drum to accompany the show.

"*Ah, bonjour, mon amie,*" said a lilting voice. Tara turned to see Sitara attired elegantly in a coat not unlike her own, probably by the same designer, a sky blue to match her eyes.

"*Bonjour. Ça va?*" said Tara, kissing her friend on both cheeks in the French fashion. The whole French language seemed to be flowing back into her brain and cells.

"Where are Leona and Janus?" she asked quietly in English. She was pretty sure they were out of earshot of the few people out this early on a Saturday morning. "God knows they can't miss us."

"We decided to stagger the arrival, to avoid calling attention to ourselves."

"I think the red and blue coats and the cat on the fancy lead may already have done that."

Sitara looked around. "*Vraiment?* I don't see anyone staring at us. We look like two elegant women friends meeting in the park. We will need to look prosperous to get into the Ritz. Yes, you look a little eccentric with the cat, but this is Paris."

Tara saw three familiar figures entering the park from the west. Mr. Beaton strode towards them with Harry and Dermot. The two young men looked slightly older and infinitely more confident as they walked towards the Rodin statue with Mr. Beaton. Tara thought she detected an eagerness in Harry's and Dermot's body language, a desire to break into a run, but she saw them deliberately match their pace to Mr. Beaton's. They looked around the park as they walked, shading their eyes against the morning sun, no doubt wondering where Leona and Janus were.

Tara wondered the same thing. "Sitara, they can't be lost in between Timelines, can they?" she asked in a low voice.

Sitara smiled at her with twinkling blue eyes, like starlight. "It was designed this way. We are getting more subtle in our methods. Ah, there they are."

A young West African couple dressed in *kitenge* prints strode up to meet them. As they grew closer, Tara saw that they were unmistakably Leona and Janus, though a few shades darker than she was accustomed to seeing them.

"Could you possibly take our photo?" asked Janus in slightly African-accented French.

Tara took the Nikon, a model she remembered owning, and shot a few pictures of the happy tourists. "Where on Earth did you pick up French?" she asked Janus in English as she handed the camera back to him.

"Am I speaking French?" he asked in French.

Sitara smiled. "I told you we are getting better at this."

"Okay, so we're all here as scheduled. The Ritz is over that way," she gestured with her leash-free left hand. "What is our plan? Do we know whether they've met yet?"

Sitara hooked her arm through Tara's. "Darling, you and I will do a reconnaissance, along with Georgie. Then we will meet and discuss."

As the two women walked in the direction of the Rue de Rivoli, the city noise began to intrude. However it was a lovely autumn morning, free of the stinging haze of pollution that would mark the city by the closing years of the 20th century. Most of the trees had already lost their leaves, and there was a rich, moist smell to the earth. The air seemed unseasonably mild to Tara, but in retrospect this was the baseline year in which the climate had begun to precipitously change, so perhaps she should not be surprised.

They waited for the lights to change on Rue St. Honoré and crossed towards Place Vendôme. A few drivers honked and waved. Tara wasn't sure if they were flirting with her and Sitara, who looked like day and night, or commenting on the somewhat unusual sight of a cat walking on a lead.

Behind them, at a distance, walked Leona and Janus in their guise of prosperous West African newlyweds taking in the sights of the great city. At a discreet distance followed Mr. Beaton, Harry, and Dermot. Mr. Beaton was carrying a Michelin guidebook, looking the part of a British tourist.

They entered the Place Vendôme and crossed to the huge column in the center of the square. Jonah the juggler and his Tibetan drummer cohort were entering from the opposite direction. Soon they were joined by the others. All looked up at the column against the blue sky, pretending not to have met before.

"Do we actually have a plan?" asked Tara as they read the inscription at the bottom of the monument.

Sitara gave what Tara could only describe as a Gaelic shrug. "We have a mission, and we've made it this far. Let's see what develops."

They stared at the main entrance to the hotel, where a line of black limos were pulling up. Several swarthy men in well-cut suits got out and hurried into the front entrance, and the limos pulled away.

"Mossad, if I'm not mistaken," said Mr. Beaton grimly. "What are they doing here?"

"You'll see many strange things from now on," said Tara. "This phase of history was not well known, but I had read about it. It was called the October Surprise. Republican operatives from the Reagan-Bush campaign met secretly with the Iranian revolutionaries to make sure the American hostages in Iran didn't get released before the election. They wanted to make sure Carter didn't get the credit."

"Poor Mr. Carter," said Mr. Beaton.

"He's not a bad sort," chimed in Harry. "He's got solar panels on the White House and he wants to get the world off of OPEC oil."

"And the first thing that Reagan did when he got elected president in our Timeline was to take the solar panels off the White House roof," said Tara. "In our Timeline people were mad at Carter and humiliated by Iran holding our hostages. That's all they could see. So Reagan won the election."

"What about the hostages?" asked Leona. "Did they ever get released?"

"The moment Reagan took the oath of office," said Tara, remembering her bitterness at what seemed the ignorance of so many American people. "My friends and I all thought it was rather obvious, even then, not knowing yet what came out later. But everyone else seemed to be celebrating. They'd drunk the Kool-aid."

"What's Kool-aid?" asked Janus curiously.

"Oh…it's an expression. It was a powdered sweet drink that a cult put poison into so that hundreds of people would drink it and commit suicide, thinking they were going to some paradise."

Janus and Leona both made a face. "That's stupid," said Leona. "Did that really happen?"

"Yes…"

"Let's not get off track with the history lesson," said Sitara brusquely. "You all understand enough to know the danger we are trying to avert. We've got to either stop the Iranian delegation from meeting the Republicans, or at least prevent the deal from being agreed upon. It MUST not happen. This is the most crucial Pivot Point, according to the data. It can change everything, or not."

As they watched, a stretch limo pulled up in front of the elegant classical façade of the hotel. A tall, lanky man got out and was whisked into the hotel. Tara felt in a daze as she recognized the man. She was dimly aware of Janus taking pictures.

"George Bush," Tara said for those who did not know. "Daddy Bush."

Mr. Beaton was irate. "It can't be. He's running for vice president! But I'm seeing it with my own eyes. Are you certain? Is he really here to meet with the Iranians? Are they here yet?"

"According to history, other meetings have already taken place," said Tara. "This is the one that finalizes the deal, so I suppose that's why we were sent to this Pivot Point. In return for not releasing the hostages, the Mullahs ruling Iran get arms through Israel. The angry American public elects Reagan, and the Mullahs consolidate their hold on Iranian politics. Radicals win in both countries, the arms merchants get rich, and the oil keeps flowing even though plenty of experts knew even then that it was eventually going to cause catastrophic climate breakdown."

"We have to stop them," said Leona with focused determination. "There has to be a way." She looked into the faces of each of her friends. "Gran, don't you have any ideas? Sitara? You know everything with your data calculations."

"Not everything," said Sitara gently. "This is so crucial, such an important Pivot Point that…well I can only say that some of it is blocked from me, which is very unusual."

Yeshi and Jonah had sauntered up to them, unnoticed by the small knot of supposed tourists in the middle of the square.

"I've never seen her blocked," Yeshi said quietly. "We seem to be largely on our own. Not that we don't have a lot of information to work with. Just not as much as we usually do."

"What are the probabilities?" asked Tara, afraid of the answer.

Sitara took a breath. "Fifty-fifty."

Tara didn't like the odds. It felt so easy to make a mistake and cause the whole world to come crashing down in a mere 70 years. "I suppose if the lottery had those odds, I'd play it," she muttered. "Anyway, we don't have much choice."

Sitara stared at the entrance, as if she were looking deep within the hotel. "Tara, you speak some Farsi, don't you?"

"A little. But I was never fluent, and it's been years."

"That's enough data for me to go on," said Sitara. "You're an Afghan refugee, a relative of the royal family, on your way to Rome to visit the king. Um, let's call you Bibi Naheed. Your husband is in prison in Kabul and you are waiting here, not knowing if you are a widow. You are of course wealthy, so you can afford to stay here. I am your Swedish friend, distantly related to the Swedish royal family."

"I can't pull that off," protested Tara.

"Oh, but you can. With a little help. I know you can."

Tara felt something subtle shift inside her, and in her body. Some of Bibi Amina's story was suddenly inside her, except that instead of marrying Xander's Scottish father, she had married an Afghan man of her own class and had lived the life of a wealthy socialite.

"*Allons-y*," said Sitara.

The two women, Tara leading Georgie, who was taking the role of royal cat quite seriously, crossed the street and confidently entered the revolving doors of the posh hotel, as if they knew where they were going. And Sitara somehow seemed to. Tara imagined that she must have consulted a plan of the hotel in her data sets.

"I don't quite understand how being a refugee member of the Afghan royal family is going to get us any information," Tara whispered to her friend as they were being seated in the café.

"You'll see. I hope. I must go and powder my nose for a few minutes."

As Sitara left the room, an Iranian man entered, his eyes raking the room and settling on Tara with pleasure.

"*Salaam Aleikum*," he began, "*b'bakhshin. Shoma Iranistin?*" Are you Iranian?

Tara had to think fast, and really trust Sitara's alterations, to pull this one off.

"*Neh, Afghan hastam.*" No, I am Afghan, not Iranian.

And then it was as if she really was Afghan, really did have a tragic and uncertain history, really was flirting in some understated, highly ritualized cultural fashion that her core self had not a clue about.

The handsome middle-aged man introduced himself as Mehdi Karrubi, an esteemed emissary of the Islamic Republic of Iran. He expressed his sorrow for the invasion of her country by the brutal, atheistic Soviet Communists, and his support for the Mujahedeen fighting against them, and their hope to establish a sister Islamic Republic.

Some part of Tara's oversoul knew that it was all bullshit, but she kept up the glamour that Sitara had laid on her, and was rewarded.

An American man who looked vaguely familiar entered the café and came up to shake hands with Karrubi.

"Ah, Monsieur Casey," said Karrubi in near-perfect British-accented English. "A pleasure to see you again." Tara saw him wink conspiratorially, as if he was in a B movie. "Haven't seen you since summer in Madrid."

The American man laughed, a smirk on his face as if he was getting away with something. "I have no idea what you are alluding to, my friend. But I'll see you around, I'm sure."

William Casey, who would become director of the CIA, and was presently the campaign director for Reagan-Bush. So it was all true. She hid her shock elegantly. She noticed that Georgie's ears were flattened against his head in instinctive dislike.

"*I wouldn't take tuna from these people,*" said the feline mind-voice angrily. "*Can we get on with this and change the past already so we can go home?*"

"*I'm with you. We know the players. We've got to figure out how to keep them from meeting and agreeing.*"

"*Khanum?*" Karrubi was saying, addressing her with polite formality. "Are you all right?"

"I'm sorry," she said in Farsi, shaking her head. "I was distracted."

"As well you might be, in your situation. I must go now, but I will pray for the safety of your husband, and for your country to become an Islamic Republic just like ours."

"*Merci,*" she said, using the French word of thanks that had been appropriated by upper class Iranians, as she proffered her hand with gentility. She fought the urge to snatch her hand away, or to wipe it on her napkin after he had touched it.

Tara watched Karrubi walk away, her eyes following his progress in the direction in which Casey had gone. Casey, Bush, who else? Did it matter? The point was to prevent them from agreeing upon anything. They hadn't arrived in time to prevent their initial meeting. But tomorrow seemed to be the crucial day. Doomsday for the planet, or not. Could one meeting, one decision, really make so much difference?

"*So it was said in the ancient days in Egypt,*" said the cat. "*But you may or may not remember. Every life, even that of a cat, can make a difference to all others, given the right circumstances.*"

Sitara sat down across from her and lifted her café au lait to her lips primly. "So?"

Tara sipped at her own hot beverage, barely able to taste the delicious flavor she had long forgotten and even stopped longing for. "Well it's all true. But if they are all already here, how do we stop them from making a deal?" She clinked her cup down too hard, and a little coffee spilled into the china saucer.

Sitara narrowed her eyes. "This is the Pivot Point. We will find a way. We have our observers outside, watching them come and go. Come, don't be so glum."

Tara blinked away the start of tears. She didn't know whether the mascara she wore was waterproof or not. "Sure. One misstep and life goes extinct on Earth in a few years from 2050. Nothing to be glum about."

"And one right step, *the* right step, and the climate is rebalanced, the world economy and political systems become egalitarian, and plagues, overpopulation, and overconsumption are all prevented. It's worth a try, *mon amie*, or we wouldn't be here."

Georgie purred loudly at Tara's feet, and got up on his hind legs, asking to get into her lap. "*Many great minds working together overcome darkness*," he purred.

Chapter
38

21 June, 2041

Edinburgh, Scotland

Xander. No, please, not Xander too.

Tara watched her beloved sleep on this sweltering night, the Summer Solstice, wondering if he was going to awaken, or if, like so many, this was his passage gently into endless night, then light.

She stroked his forehead and watched his chest rise and fall. Still breathing. Still sleeping. He looked so deceptively peaceful, not exhausted at all, not near death. But none of this Plague's victims looked as if they were near death. They simply went to sleep and didn't awaken.

They called it the Sleeping Plague. No one knew where it originated, or even how it spread. Quarantine didn't seem to make a difference. It took young, old, and in between.

The scientific equipment to analyze epidemics was long gone, as were the computers on which to calculate and communicate. As the population had dwindled, and manufacturing had ground to a near halt, equipment could not be replaced. The giant water-cooled Internet servers in Iceland had long gone silent.

They had been left with intuition and compassion. As usual, even at the age of 82, Xander had tended the sick. A few, improbably, mysteriously, had gotten well. Most had not. But they did not suffer in their transitions, and for this everyone was glad.

Husbands and wives, mothers, fathers, siblings, children, friends, waited while their loved ones fell into long sleeps. A merely exhausted sleep was often assumed to be the path to death, until, joyously, the loved one awakened and started another day.

Tara had always had more trouble sleeping than her beloved, so all too often she had sat vigil as she did tonight, watching him breathe in and out, watching his eyelids flicker in the rapid eye movement of dream sleep. So far, he had always awakened.

They slept close, no matter how hot it was, wondering whether each or neither would awaken.

At first they had attempted to isolate their great-granddaughter Leona, now seven, but the girl would have none of it. Once Xander realized that it was an utter mystery who would catch the Sleeping Plague, and of those, who would die of it, they gave up their attempts to keep Leona away from them. The three of them together went to tend the sick, and so far, none of them had fallen ill.

Xander's eyelids flickered, and Tara's heart fluttered in answer. Outside a few once-tropical birds sang the morning into being. She took a deep breath as her husband, her Twin Flame, her long-awaited, awakened to another day.

25 June, 2041

Edinburgh, Scotland

Xander seemed unusually tired tonight, thought Tara. But she said nothing. A constant flurry of worried questions destroyed the peace of home and heart. Leona had shown off her bright spirit at dinner, reading from *The Chronicles of Narnia* and talking all about Aslan, the lion, and acting out parts. Tara and Xander had laughed like young parents a third of their actual age, rather than tired great-grandparents in their 80's.

Tara snuck a concerned look at Xander as he got up from the table and stretched and yawned. Usually he helped wash the dishes, pouring the heavy can of solar-heated water into the sink, since the public water system no longer worked. Tonight he smiled and kissed her tenderly as she stood at the sink.

"Dearest, I hope you don't mind if I beg off tonight. Long day and all that. You coming to bed soon? I'll wait up."

She ran her wet hands through his silver hair to cool him a little, and to check for fever. None. But then fever didn't seem to be part of this Plague.

She kissed him back. These days they appreciated every moment, every gesture, no matter how ordinary, every kiss. Perhaps it had always been that way with couples in their 80's, knowing that either one might not wake up the next day.

Leona seemed so full of life, so vital, that Tara didn't worry about her succumbing to the Sleeping Plague, even though many of Leona's tender age were dying. Leona helped her dry the dishes and put them away, dancing in place and pretending to be a lion. Tara kissed her goodnight and tucked her in under the light cotton sheet, beneath the improvised mosquito netting. The child was almost instantly, peacefully, asleep.

Xander was still awake when she got into bed next to him. Due to the heat that prevailed for most of the year nowadays, they slept naked under a thin cotton sheet. She spooned him, and they lay on their right sides, not speaking. They had done the *Phowa*, the transference of consciousness taught so long ago by their Tibetan teacher, for themselves and for each other. Each was confident that they both knew the way to bypass the Bardo, and if they were not the first to go, to help the other along the way. Ritually, each touched the crown of the other's head before falling asleep.

Tonight, despite the heat, Tara fell into a peaceful sleep. She dreamed, the old dream of the White Lions at Stonehenge that she had first dreamed in South Africa years ago, before they had returned to Scotland. When she was handed the burping cub, it now turned into a tiny, orphaned Leona, who had after all been named the lioness. Now in the dreams she played with Leona in the stone circle, and watched the child dance and laugh and grow before her eyes. And she felt peaceful.

Tara awoke to Xander's stillness. He was not breathing. She waited, expecting the expulsion of breath, the intake of another. She held her own breath for a long time, waiting, and moved her hands to his heart.

The heart that had beat entrained with hers for decades was still.

Tears coursed down her face as she sat up and gently laid him on his back. His eyes were closed, the light of the hazel gaze of compassion forever dimmed. She touched his crown among the still thick silvery hair. There was a soft depression, like the fontanel of a newborn. She knew the crown was open, and in the darkness she saw dancing silver light, a gentle spiral, rising and flowing out the window to join the starlight. Rainbows danced in her eyes, though she didn't know if they were reflections in her tears.

Scenes flashed before her eyes, as if at her own death, and for a moment she wondered if she was accompanying him, and longed with all her heart to do so. Then she remembered the sleeping child in the next room, and willed herself to return fully to her body, to her life. She was nearly 87, and had to stay alive as long as possible, at least until she found someone trustworthy to bring up Leona as their own if she were to depart, or to become too feeble.

She saw Xander as she first had at the Dharma teachings in Edinburgh. Not a young man. They hadn't known each other as young people in this lifetime. But a handsome man of worldly experience and great compassion, struggling like all of them to become a better meditation practitioner and draw that knowledge into daily life.

Then a tumble of images: Findhorn, carrots, fairies, full moon, ecstasy. Bibi Amina, snow in Taos, the Christmas bonfire, her mother and sister hugging Xander. Rinpoche's passing from his body in Nepal, Xander nurturing many, many patients, and his beloved daughter Joy. Tending patients and gardens in Zululand. A momentary memory of their wedding, a lovely day to be sure, but oddly, not the most important memory, not what floated first to the surface. Again, that first night of making love in the woods of Findhorn, surrounded by dancing lights and laughing voices. The utter, certain, familiar recognition of souls, of the twinness of their flames.

261

And now Xander's flame had gone out. No, she corrected herself, merely transformed to another form, gone beyond the veil, into another dimension, still mysterious despite her decades of study and practice of the mystical arts.

Into the Great Mystery that was the Oneness.

Leaving her behind, momentarily, in this world of sorrows and loss.

She looked up to see Leona standing silently in the doorway, looking up at the stars, starlight reflected in the tears on her tiny dark cheeks.

"Grandpa is gone, beyond," she said simply. She came to Tara and crawled into bed next to her great-grandfather and put one hand on the place where his heart had beaten millions of beats. "Nothing to do till morning. He's happy now. Gran, let's go to sleep now."

1 July, 2041

Edinburgh, Scotland

Xander had been cremated. Tara and Leona had lit the pyre together, as people had in India for millennia. There were no authorities left to stop them, no one to supervise disposal of the shells of the dead.

The city was silent, sleeping. A few people burned the corpses of their loved ones, in hushed reverence, or shock, depending on the person.

Not for the first time, Tara was struck by how quickly a human body disintegrated back into its basic elements. She thought of the word. Disintegrated. Integration of earth, water, fire, air, and spirit created a living, breathing being. When those elements were no longer integrated, life in this form no longer existed.

Xander's ashes cooled, and she gathered them reverently into a vintage biscuit tin. Danish Butter Cookies. Hers, she thought absently, had always been better than the store bought ones, but the tin was useful and closed well. His ashes fit perfectly.

What to do? She sat in meditation, Leona beside her. How had the child learned meditation? They hadn't tried to teach her yet, just shown her a few yoga positions. It was amazing what could be learned by example.

"*Go north, then south,*" came a voice that was both inner and not hers.

Her monkey mind leaped. "How will I travel with a child? How will we eat?"

"*There is still plenty. Take his ashes to your place of greatest joy, and then walk south till you come to the stones.*"

Tara felt like her spirit had clunked back down into her body, but she was invigorated. She wondered, as she would many times in the years to come, why she was alive and even well and strong. But she was grateful.

Leona was staring at her. "You heard?" Tara asked.

"Yes."

"Then let's pack. Let's go now."

It would be several days' walk to Findhorn, especially for an old woman and a small child. They wouldn't need much in the way of clothing, since it was so hot, and they could sleep away the hottest hours. No medicines or herbs were known to be helpful against the Sleeping Plague, so they wouldn't take any. Just cups to drink from, bowls to eat from, a set of camping utensils for each, an old Swiss army knife, some clean underwear and a change or two of clothes, and a sleeping sheet.

The backpacks were superlight design, some of the last ever made before the manufacturing collapse, so it was easy for Leona to carry her own, and she insisted. They set off, along largely silent streets, cobblestone roads, motorways, railway tracks that had not seen trains in years.

They drank water from streams and wells. Those who were still alive quietly shared what food they had. With so many gone, there was an abundance of food. Gardens had to be harvested, food had to be eaten or it would spoil. Shops were left unshuttered, for what was the point of locking up or exchanging useless money? There was a cornucopia of tinned goods for those who were still alive to eat them.

People did not ask many questions, but were friendly, silently compassionate to each other. There was no point in telling the stories. They were all virtually the same now. Tears fell when they fell, and eyes were dry when they were dry.

After many days of walking, Tara and Leona reached Findhorn Bay. The water was much higher than she had remembered from her last visit, but that had been a few years ago. The waters now lapped at the edge of the woods, and the trees closest to the water had brown needles.

Were the fairies still there? She wondered if she could even find the little clearing by the lily pond where she and Xander had first made love. Everything looked different. But some internal map led her effortlessly to the very place. It was on a rise, and the waters had not yet reached here.

Tara looked down at her hands as she scooped a handful of ashes from the biscuit tin. Her engagement ring, truly from another time in the history of the planet, sparkled with bright rainbows in the white sunlight as she formed Xander's ashes into the shape of a heart on the water. Leona took her own handfuls and followed the pattern as the ashes began slowly to spread, to disperse amongst the pure white water lilies.

1 August, 2041

Stonehenge, New Avalon

Tara was never sure where she had lost the ring. Had it slipped off her too-thin finger when she spread Xander's ashes on the lily pond? Or somewhere along the way? The last she consciously remembered seeing it was that day, sunlight on the diamonds as she spread the ashes of her beloved.

Leona was no help at all, seemingly disinterested in the loss of a valuable family heirloom.

Tara had noticed the loss a few days later, on their way walking south. They had decided, on the basis of shared dreams, and the recurring dream she had had since Africa, that their destination was Stonehenge. And anyway it was as good as any.

She felt a sinking feeling in the pit of her stomach as she suddenly realized the ring was gone. "Leona, wait!" she had cried. She had dumped out the meager contents of first her backpack, then Leona's. She had searched every pocket again and again. Nothing.

She had cried for a few moments, then taken a deep breath. It wasn't about the ring. Diamonds had no value in a cashless society, she realized. And the ring was not her connection to her beloved, now surely in *Dewachen*, the land of great bliss and Bodhisattvahood. It was, after all, only a thing, though a very pretty thing with much beautiful loving energy.

Perhaps the fairies would find it and it would give some delight in their world. She had definitely felt their presence still in that forest, in that lily pond. For a moment, she had seen a fairy stretch her legs out from under the white skirt of a lily, and dance upon the water.

Repacking their backpacks, they had simply gone on. Wherever they went, food was shared. The Sleeping Plague, people said, seemed to be abating. Fewer and fewer people were dying. They were invited many times to stay on, people charmed by Leona's bright smile and probably quite unaware of Tara's advanced age. She was clearly an old woman, but she had been blessed to never look her age, and she hoped she could pass as perhaps twenty years younger, in her late 60's raising a grandchild. People seemed friendly enough now, but if things got worse, if things got scarce, if she couldn't do something to contribute, would they turn out the aged into the fields and forests?

They had reached the rice paddies and palm trees of Somerset the day before, and had stopped at Avebury Encampment. Seamus, who claimed Druid descent and seemed to be regarded as a leader, seemed to be a practical man, if a bit of a drunk and a blowhard. One could forgive a lot these days, thought Tara. He had organized a commune, organized fishing, gathering of greens, and tilling of rice paddies and hemp fields. A breezy Longhouse had been built of hemp and reeds, and the village library still existed in an old stone building, which seemed relatively cool.

It seemed as good a place as any to raise a child, and Leona agreed. The only book she had carried with her all this way was *The Chronicles of Narnia*, which she reverently placed on the wooden library shelf, as she withdrew *The Lord of the Rings*.

So Tara and Leona had accepted the invitation to stay at Avebury Encampment and make themselves useful members of the community. The small community had voted unanimously to accept them, and had held a feast in their honor.

But, for some reason, the two felt that their journey had to end at Stonehenge. They both dreamed of it every night. Tara had been there, of course, a number of times, first in her youth as a student in London, before it was fenced, and then a few times to join in ceremonies at dawn with like-minded people, singing in the Mayan Day out of Time.

The fences had long fallen, and the mists lifted a little as they approached the silent stones, ancient and welcoming.

But it seemed an anti-climax. Tara spread the last of Xander's ashes on the grass in the center of the Henge, making a small heart that rain would soon wash away. The old woman and the little girl meditated, back to back. It was pleasant, but nothing dramatic happened.

Tara was just coming out of meditation, dedicating her practice as always to the happiness of all sentient beings everywhere in all the universes when an energetic ball of gray fur jumped into her lap and started purring.

She'd always been a sucker for cats, so she petted the wee thing, chucking him under the chin, scratching his ears. He looked just old enough to be weaned and to start hunting on his own. She slipped him a sliver of dried tuna from her pack, and won his heart forever.

Leona was delighted. "What shall we call him?" she asked.

Tara had once had a cat named Dorjee, a Tibetan name. "Dorjee?"

"Georgie," said Leona, mishearing, unfamiliar with the Tibetan word.

The sleek gray kitten looked up at the name, training his green eyes first on Tara, then on Leona, purring loud enough to waken the stones.

Chapter
39

18 October, 1980

Paris, France

Fifty-fifty chance, thought Tara, as she sat on a bench looking up at the graceful flying buttresses of Notre Dame, where they had all agreed to meet. Not the odds she wanted for reversing the Sixth Great Extinction, but better than the odds were by 2050.

"*My paws are sore,*" grumbled Georgie. "*And these city pavements are dirty.*" He licked one paw and looked up at her, then got up on his hind legs and put his front paws in her lap. "*May I?*"

"*Sure,*" she thought back to him, caressing his soft ears as he jumped into her lap.

Thankfully, her now-gray coat blended in with the crowds better, and was less likely to attract attention than the scarlet number she had worn earlier. Not to mention less likely to show gray cat hair.

As evening fell, the city lights began to glow softly, reflecting on the Seine. A city of history, of so many significant moments, unaware that this was the most significant of all, little noted by history books or by the Internet, and certainly forgotten by her time in 2050.

Sitara seemed to float towards her, now wearing a black coat, joining her on the bench. Mr. Beaton strolled up, guidebook in hand, Harry and Dermot close behind, craning their necks at the imposing cathedral. Yeshi and Jonah sauntered up, dressed as businessmen, while Leona and Janus remained *kitenge*-clad young African tourists.

Paris was cosmopolitan enough that no one noted the diverse gathering. Sitara cast a mist of glamour around them so that they would be barely noticeable to strangers. And it's not like the Republicans, the CIA, Mossad, French intelligence services, or the Iranian delegation had any idea that anyone even knew about their plans, let alone were plotting to thwart them.

"Let's go to a café," said Sitara. "I can hold the illusion while we talk. We have to stay in this Timeline and see it through. We don't have the energy to jump around."

"I'm just wondering what I'm doing here at all," said Mr. Beaton, sounding discouraged. "I thought I'd done my part in making sure the elections were called when they were, so Mrs. Thatcher never came to power. Then Harry absolutely insisted that I come along on this jaunt, and now I feel utterly useless."

"All of us do," said Leona, pouting. "We've been spending the day seeing tourist sights when the fate of the future world is hanging in the balance."

Yeshi appeared to be in deep meditation, and Jonah just stared at the lights reflecting in the river.

"Let's go," said Sitara. "There's a café nearby."

No one noticed what would have been an unlikely group of friends. The waiters simply took their varied orders and brought coffees, drinks, and aperitifs. At first, no one spoke much, each seemingly lost in his or her own thoughts. Georgie sat on Tara's lap, purring softly, not saying anything either, but clearly listening.

"Well? Any inspiration?" asked Tara finally.

"Perhaps we could create a distraction," began Mr. Beaton tentatively.

"Good idea," said Yeshi. "Have you ever met any of the players?"

"No, but they don't know that. I'm with Her Majesty's Government. I certainly know what Mr. Casey, and Mr. Bush, look like. I can greet them effusively, draw attention to them, the last thing they want I'm sure."

"What about us, Dad?" asked Harry.

"We can be students getting obnoxiously drunk and get ourselves thrown out of the bar," said Dermot. "That's easy enough. Or was. But we can fake it, remembering our old bad habits."

"Not bad," mused Yeshi. "I can be a waiter. A clumsy waiter."

"I need to be Janus' father," spoke up Jonah. "I will be a puffed-up minor African potentate furious at my son for eloping with a commoner. Sorry, Leona."

Leona's eyes twinkled. "Oh, I can play the part."

"Me too," said Janus. "Anything for love and all that."

"And when are we supposed to do all this?" asked Tara.

"No time like the present," said Sitara. "We've got the highest probability of creating the necessary change up till midnight tonight. We've got to stop that agreement from happening tomorrow."

"If only they would leave the hotel," said Mr. Beaton. "We're talking about creating a distraction, but is that enough?"

"Chaos theory," said Dermot, eyes twinkling. "It's a new thing in science. We're purposely creating entropy so that a new order can come out of it."

"Where do Sitara and I fit in?" asked Tara.

"*And me?*" asked Georgie. "*Don't forget about me just because I'm a cat.*"

"We all have a role to play," said Sitara thoughtfully, focusing inwards. She looked at Tara appraisingly.

"Oh no," said Tara. "No, no, no. I know what you're thinking. I don't think I could have carried that off even when I was young."

"You just have to flirt with Mr. Karrubi. Get him to take the poor possibly widowed Afghan refugee from the royal family out for a drink. Of course he can't be seen to be drinking in public, so you'll be in a limo with black windows."

"I thought we had progressed beyond using women's sexuality for manipulation," said Tara sourly.

"Not by 1980," said Yeshi, as if he remembered.

"You don't have to sleep with him," said Sitara primly.

"Well I should hope not."

"You don't even have to kiss him."

"Ugh. He has slimy energy."

"*I'll stay in between you,*" said Georgie.

Tara laughed in spite of herself, and scratched his ears.

"So where do we find all these people?" asked Tara practically. "Won't they be in their rooms calling room service? I'm not about to go knocking on Mr. Karrubi's door."

Sitara transformed herself into a young chambermaid in the Ritz hotel uniform, right in front of their eyes, then instantly back to the elegant Swedish woman. "You don't have to. I'll be delivering messages to their rooms that will lure them downstairs into the bars. Then it's up to all of you to cause your assigned distractions. Play it to the hilt," she said, with a wicked gleam in her eyes. "If all goes well, which I expect it to, the utter chaos should get them out of the hotel and into the street. The data sets indicate that the probabilities of stopping tomorrow's agreement are much higher if we get them off the premises."

"Right, then let's get on with it," said Mr. Beaton determinedly.

Sitara's blue eyes twinkled like stars. "This can actually be fun. It's Zero Hour. And if this all works out, then it really is. A new Timeline is born."

They paid for their drinks and meals and tipped generously. Each walked the few blocks to the Ritz Hotel, no longer intimidated by its aura of grand history and exclusivity.

Mr. Beaton ensconced himself in the dark-paneled, noisy Hemingway Bar, waiting for Casey and Bush to appear. Harry and Dermot proceeded to get roaring drunk in a leather-upholstered corner booth.

Tara, looking a shade younger and sadder than she had that afternoon, sat alone in a booth, nursing a drink and, improbably to her, smoking a

St. Moritz cigarette. Georgie perched delicately on the leather bench of the booth, head nestled into her knee.

Afterwards, neither Tara nor any of them could have told in what order events unfolded, because everything seemed to happen at once.

"Oh, I say, Mr. Casey, Mr. Bush," called out Mr. Beaton loudly to the two men entering the dark bar. "Over here! I haven't seen you since, when? The last IMF conference? Do join me for a drink."

Casey and Bush were clearly not happy to have their names shouted out across a crowded bar, and quickly moved to contain the situation, joining the representative of Her Majesty's Government in a private booth.

And then the Asian waiter tripped and spilled cocktails all over them, just as two British students were shouting raucously, breaking glasses, stumbling all over, and being asked to leave the bar…

But Jonah in his disguise as an African potentate was blocking the way out, shouting at his son in some foreign language, mixed with English and French. "How dare you dishonor this family by marrying a commoner!"

"I love her!" Janus shouted back in English. "You'll not stop me!"

"I'll disinherit you!" screamed Jonah in a deep voice, really getting into his role.

"No! I'll annul the marriage," cried Leona dramatically. "I love him that much."

Mr. Karrubi slipped into the booth opposite Tara and Georgie. "What a *tamasha*!" he said in Farsi. "Shall we perhaps go elsewhere? I would enjoy talking to you more about the Islamic Revolution."

Tara split her attention, half paying attention to Mr. Karrubi and half watching Mr. Beaton usher a flustered Casey and Bush, who had very wet laps, out of the bar. "I know a much more peaceful place," the whole room heard Mr. Beaton say. "I have a limo waiting outside."

Two limos were pulled up to the front entrance as Karrubi propelled Tara by the elbow out into the street. Was that strange, unearthly sound Georgie growling? Things were moving so fast, Tara felt dizzy, her consciousness splitting and following several different events at once. How had Sitara manifested the limos without even being there? But how did Sitara know to do any of the things she had been doing?

Tara got into the back of the first limo with a slight shudder, suddenly remembering that Princess Diana's last meal had been here at the Ritz. Later, in 1997, she would get into the death limousine with Dodi Fayed, perhaps right on this very spot. Or would she? If they changed the Timeline, did that accident have to happen? Or would Diana ever marry Charles, or divorce him if she did?

Tara was pulled back to the here and now of 1980 by Mr. Karrubi's predatory presence on the other side of the car, and the sickly mixture of overly-scented aftershave with the reek of alcohol. Georgie, as promised, ensconced himself between Tara and Karrubi, leaning hard into Tara's thigh.

And time seemed to slow. Tara was conversing in fluent Farsi in her role as the wealthy Afghan refugee. She wasn't very good at flirting, in any role, so she confined herself to imploring Karrubi to somehow use his influence, which he claimed he didn't have, to find out the whereabouts and well-being of her husband in Pul-e-Charkhi prison in Kabul.

They moved slowly in the heavy Paris traffic, and had only gone a few blocks. Though it was off-season for tourism, it still was a Saturday night in the center of Paris. Horns honked, drivers shouted and cursed.

The limo carrying Casey, Bush, and Mr. Beaton started dodging in and out of traffic. So much for not attracting attention, Tara thought.

Karrubi was becoming more and more agitated as it became evident that his attempted seduction was going nowhere. He was a bad drunk, thought Tara as she watched him, as if from outside her own body, gesticulate at the other limo and shout at their driver to keep up with those bastards from the Great Satan. Tara acted offended by his language, turning away from him and pressing herself against the car door, which made him even more angry.

The two limos entered the Champs Élysées neck and neck. The drivers gunned their engines and glared at each other. Part of Tara was fascinated by this display of what reminded her of rutting stags, and part was terrified. Sitara could get them out of this just before they were killed in an accident, couldn't she?

Or did Sitara even know where she was?

Or did it matter? Tara was, after all, 96 in her own Timeline, and wouldn't have all that much time left there even under the best of circumstances.

Perhaps this was the necessary sacrifice. She smiled ruefully. Was it a necessary sacrifice of a Princess, as had later happened to Diana? Did Diana's death change a Timeline—and for the better or for the worse?

Tara wasn't paying much attention to Karrubi when she was wrenched into the present moment by Georgie launching himself at Karrubi's face, claws scissoring the man's skin, cat voice snarling. To Tara's horror, Karrubi grabbed her beloved cat and threw open the car door.

"This bloody cat!" he screamed. Blood dripped down his face, and his expensive suit was shredded as he struggled to hold the furious, writhing cat.

"Nooooo!" Tara shrieked in a drawn-out wail of agony.

"*I'm not afraid*," said Georgie's mind-voice, though he was squirming and clawing and doing a good impression of being terrified. "*This is meant to be.*"

Just as the traffic light turned green, Karrubi forcefully flung the cat out into the traffic.

Tara screamed and beat the man with her fists, and clawed at his bloody face with her long nails, just like the cat. But it was too late.

Both drivers, who had started to accelerate, threw on their brakes, and to their credit they tried to avoid the poor cat.

Tara heard a sickening crunch and a cat scream, at the same time her head hit hard against the metal window frame as the two limos slid into each other with a bang.

Oblivious to her bruises, her nausea, her torn clothes and ripped stockings, she wrenched open the damaged door and stepped out into the traffic screaming for her cat. "Georgie! Georgie!"

It was the stuff of a thousand nightmares since childhood, failing to rescue a cat, failing to rescue a child. And where was Leona? Would she at least make it back to 2050 to live out whatever life she and Janus could have?

Tara had no doubt that they had failed. What a mess. She frantically looked under the crumpled cars for Georgie's body, hyperventilating, tears streaming down her face. Why did such an innocent have to die for nothing? Why did she have to lose him too, after all the other losses?

Tara had no idea whether she still looked like a beautiful middle-aged Afghan woman or like the 96-year-old crone she really was. On the pavement she saw a flash of red, but all she found was Georgie's severed red patent leather leash, and a little pool of blood…

Just as something shifted, and the ground tilted beneath her. She was seized by severe spinning vertigo, and was vaguely aware that she had hit her head hard. But something undefinable felt different. As if from the end of a long tunnel she could hear Karrubi screaming at the top of his lungs at Bush and Casey, who were screaming obscenities back with equal rage.

"No surprise from the Great Satan!" Karrubi shouted hoarsely in English. "Unspeakable arrogance! Imperialism!"

"Well you can just tell your Mullahs to forget about those Israeli arms then," screamed George Bush in a nasal voice. "We'll arm the fucking Iraqis instead."

Tara felt a pull, an irresistible pull, a dizziness much like the first time she had teleported. She felt her gorge rising and was pretty sure that she threw up all over the limo's hood before she was pulled into the Time Travel vortex. Dimly, she was aware of something hard and sharp hitting her right shoulder as she was pulled away into swirling rainbows.

Chapter 40

22 December, 2050

Stonehenge, England

I t was…snowing?

Tara felt the soft sting of cold on her face as she lay on her back, staring up at a misty, barely lightening sky. The familiar bulk of the great standing stones of Stonehenge loomed in the pre-dawn darkness, somehow comforting.

Even more comforting was the insistent furry nudge at her face, the soft meow, the loud purring.

She sat up, and the earth didn't spin. She was in the center of the stone circle, having landed right on one of the spirals that had been burned into the grass, a couple of months ago and a minute ago. Georgie nudged his way under her woolen cloak.

Georgie?

She pulled the charcoal gray wool, beaded with melted snowdrops, over her feline companion and held him close. "Georgie, are you okay?"

A plaintive mew. "*Mostly. Missing part of my tail. Hurts like hell. Some people don't know that the penalty for harming a cat in the old days in Egypt was death.*" He popped his head out from the folds of her cloak and stared at her with big green eyes. "*But it was worth it. Look!*"

Snow swirled amongst the standing stones, beginning to stick on the sere grass. Tara stood up, cradling Georgie in her arms. The palm trees that had grown up nearby were…not covered in snow, but just gone, as if they'd never existed. Tara realized that they hadn't. It had worked! But where were the others?

Yeshi and Sitara popped into form on one of the other spirals, holding each other and dancing in joyous circles. Both had tears running down their faces and were shouting over and over, "It worked! It worked!"

In the midst of her great relief and gratitude, Tara felt a strange, achy sense of being…"left out" was the best way she could describe it. She was an outsider. She didn't fit in with the Time Travelers from the future, even after they had all gone through so much together.

Jonah, Leona, and Janus all materialized on the third spiral, holding each other close in a warm, quiet embrace.

Georgie extended his claws and dug them into Tara's arm to get her attention. "*Could you, or someone else, please attend to my sore tail? We've got visitors about to arrive.*"

As Tara crouched down and made a tent of her cloak, she saw that about half of Georgie's tail was missing, and it had a raw wound where it had been severed. She felt a pang of pain for her loyal companion, as if she had a tail and it was her own that was wounded.

Yeshi and Sitara broke away from their rapturous victory dance and came over to see how the little cat was doing.

"Sitara, can you restore his tail?" asked Tara. "It's only molecules, right?"

The tall, fair woman shook her head. "We can't undo what was done there. It was so delicate. But we can heal the wound."

"*Well would you hurry up?*" asked Georgie indignantly. "*And no Manx jokes!*"

"Please," echoed Tara. "He's in pain."

Sitara produced a powder out of the pocket of her own cloak and gently put it on Georgie's wound. He began to purr.

"What's in it?" asked Tara.

"Catnip, for one thing. And some healing herbs. I will leave some with you, but he should soon be well."

"Leave some?"

"Our work is done here."

Tara felt startled by the realization. Had any of it been real? But the proof was there, snowing on her.

"What day is it?" Tara asked.

"December 22nd, Winter Solstice. Same year as we left, 2050 of your…no, not your Timeline anymore, *our* shared Timeline. Order has been restored."

"I feel like a stranger," said Tara. "How about you, Leona, Janus?"

The young couple approached her, seeming far more mature than they had when they first left the Timeline in October. Leona shook her head as if to clear it. "I dunno, Gran. I hear a rushing inside my head."

"Me too," said Janus. "It's like I have two streams roaring in my two ears."

"We're in a different Timeline now, a healed one," said Tara. "But so far all I remember is the old Timeline, and our travels. Shouldn't my life be different? Shouldn't I have different memories?"

And for a moment she caught her breath. Could Xander still be alive in this Timeline? She looked down at herself—the hands of an old woman, but not an ancient one. Her hair, braided, white, but not thin and falling out. She felt her face. Mature, but not a nest of wrinkles. She felt strong, but suddenly very, very tired, as if she could fall asleep and pass into another world, rather as she had been doing for the last few months, or minutes.

The sun had not yet risen, but vehicle lights cut through the darkness and swirling snow about a mile away. Tara automatically tensed up.

"Wait and see," said Yeshi gently.

"But all I have are the old memories. I don't know what to expect, or how to act."

"Give us a moment to catch up to ourselves," said Sitara, a trifle brusquely. "The data is flooding in. That's the sound you hear."

"My Mum and Dad are alive!" squealed Leona. "And I feel them nearby. I think they're with this group who are coming. It's like I have two memories… one in which they died when I was tiny, and now this other one, this life, in which they are still here and gave me a great education. And Janus, we met anyway!"

The young man shook his head, almost like a lion himself. Snow flew from his dreadlocks. "I've got the two memory streams too! I'm so glad we still met, we're still in love. Apparently we met at uni and I've got an advanced degree and we're doing all these amazing things."

Tara looked at Yeshi, a pain stabbing her heart. "Xander's still gone, isn't he?"

"Yes, I died...he died in your arms, at the same time he did in the other Timeline, but not of Plague. He just went peacefully of old age, slipping into the Light."

Tara gasped, a sharp intake of breath as she saw what her soul had known all along, etched on the face of this Tibetan-looking man from the future. "You...you're Xander in a future incarnation!"

He smiled gently, and she saw his face morph into Xander, and many other faces, all somehow known and beloved to her.

"When did you know?" she asked.

"Just now. Like you. But sometimes I wondered. You seemed so familiar, and many times I wanted to touch you, to hold you. But our mission had to be completed before I could even allow myself to wonder about these things."

"Yeshi...Xander...what do we do now? Do I lose you again?"

"We have a couple of choices," he said. "Wait. I'll explain. But first, we have friends to greet."

An official-looking procession was winding its way towards the Henge as the wintry sky lightened. Sitara led the Time Travelers outside the circle, to a waiting area, so they'd be less conspicuous. Subtly, their clothing transformed to match that of the approaching visitors.

Tara felt elated to notice that many in the visiting delegation did not seem happy about the snow and cold. That meant that winter had never disappeared, and was still something of an annoyance at times.

"Who are they?" she whispered to Sitara.

"A delegation of women leaders meeting at a conference in London. They've come to observe the sunrise here as a special treat. Let yourself flow into your memories of your life in this Timeline, and you'll know it all, and remember why you yourself are here."

Tara felt split into two, as her memories simultaneously flowed through her brain and body. Part of her wished that she only remembered the new, altered Timeline, and another part was glad that she had both.

The part of her in the altered Timeline remembered being invited by Xander's cousin Fauzia, the president-emeritus of Afghanistan, to meet the delegation here. Her own vehicle, Leona's and Janus' car, had arrived a bit earlier than the others and they had walked on up to the Henge in the snow, along with the three Professors who were their close friends, Yeshi, Jonah, and Sitara.

Tara was pleased to see Fauzia, who must be about her own age, clomping through the snow with a spry gait. Fauzia had aged well, having steered her country on a course towards permanent peace and equality. Next to her walked a stately middle-aged woman, her head covered with a Kashmiri shawl. Tara knew it was President Malala of Pakistan, the young Nobel Peace Prize winner who had been shot by the Taliban in her youth for being a leader for girls' rights and education. Malala linked arms with her best friend, Prime Minister Sita of India. Tara knew that though both countries took pride in their cultures and histories, the borders for all intents and purposes no longer existed. The population had leveled off due to increased education of girls and women. Most had chosen to have one or at most two children, while many others had chosen to adopt or to remain childless and nurture the children of others.

Tara suppressed a smile as the next group of women arrived in the circle, and she "remembered" in a flash who they were: Prime Minister Halima al-Sayed of the Republic of Arabia; President Ferishte Khalili of Iran; the newly elected first woman and first Quechua president of Peru, Doña Bernardina; and the now elderly stateswoman who had become the first woman president of China, Chiang Fan.

Bringing up the rear was another set of best friends, Israeli Prime Minister Rachel Lubow, who tromped through the drifting snow arm in arm with Palestinian President Habiba Hakim. Tara smiled at the obvious affection the two young women held for one another, like sisters. No wonder they had been able to work together so harmoniously to end millennia of strife, bringing about not only true peace but the radical solution of sharing a capital, the holy city of Jerusalem.

The part of Tara that remembered the other, broken Timeline marveled. All this because President Carter had been re-elected? Events and alternate history tumbled through her brain instantaneously. Oil drilling had been stopped, fracking technology had never been developed, coal mining had been stopped in time. Renewable energy had grown by leaps and bounds, so pollution had never sucked the life out of the atmosphere. Governments had banded together to regulate banks and corporations for the public good, and plagues had been stopped before they became epidemics, let alone pandemics.

A tall Tibetan woman in traditional wraparound *chuba* and colorfully striped apron broke out of the procession and hurried towards Tara and her friends. Tara knew it was Prime Minister Drolma Tsering, the elected leader of Tibet. When Tibet became free after China embraced democracy as the result of a devastating earthquake that had brought people of all nationalities and ethnic groups together, His Holiness the 14th Dalai Lama had been able to return home in the last year of his life. True to his word, he had refused all political positions, calling on the Tibetan people to form a constitution based on the Parliamentary democracy they had been developing in exile in India. Drolma Tsering was now the second Prime Minister of free Tibet.

The Prime Minister made her way step by step through the thickening snow, laughing as she stumbled a little. "*Tashi Delek!*" she greeted them, and then prostrated herself in the snow before Leona. "Rinpoche, we've found you at last."

Still on her knees, the Prime Minister reached out and handed Leona a well-used prayer wheel that looked very familiar to Tara, with its unique rainbow crystal weight.

"Rinpoche?" whispered Tara. Leona had been born well after her teacher had died, but she'd never thought…But of course, now it all made sense, in some strange way. It would be just like Rinpoche, with all his teachings of the oneness of all traditions, to come back as a female of mixed Tibetan-Afghan-Scottish-Zulu parentage.

Leona beamed humbly, realizing the fact of her past incarnation for the first time herself, gently twirling the prayer wheel. "I'm a Tulku?" she asked, stilling the prayer wheel so she could clasp the Prime Minister's hands and raise her to standing.

"You always did sit with us when we were meditating, from the earliest age," said Tara. She simultaneously remembered the tiny one-year-old grieving orphan and the child of this Timeline who had grown up with her loving parents…

Who were here. At the end of the line walked a middle-aged couple, clearly the older versions of Dechen and Kennedy, proud parents of their accomplished daughter who was already at Oxford at age 16, and now was revealed to be a spiritual leader as well. Somehow this latter fact didn't seem to surprise them much.

Dechen and Kennedy embraced Tara with affection and respect. "Joy and Dawa send their best," Dechen said. "I wish they could have been here but they couldn't get away from their work in Lhasa. And I really wish Granddad could have been here to see this," she said. "But he'll be back, one day."

Tara stole a sidelong glance at Professor Yeshi. One day. But here? Or elsewhere, or else-when?

The clouds lifted just long enough for a reddish sun to lift over the horizon and shine through the stones of the ancient calendar. Then everyone hurried back to their vehicles, eager to get to a warm breakfast in the village nearby, where there was a hotel with a welcoming fire and the excellent, wholesome, locally-sourced food that was now the norm.

Tara enjoyed the breakfast, particularly the coffee and orange juice, eating with a gusto belying her chronological age. She shared memories of Xander with Fauzia, and asked how the leadership conference was going. They all stood up when the English and Scottish Prime Ministers, who had been delayed by the snow, arrived together, accompanied by their husbands. Tara thought that the Prime Minister of England's husband looked somehow familiar. As she shook Mr. Clive Baker's hand, a fleeting memory from another Timeline almost made her flinch, then smile. Her interlocutor, the unquestioning corporate minion, had married well in this Timeline, and was as accomplished as his wife. Both were known for their skill at leading the nation in the post-industrial economy, and their compassion.

One accident, one half of a cat's tail, made this much difference?

Georgie had been quiet. He was clearly feeling much better, and had been contentedly snuggling in a large interior pocket inside her spacious cloak all this time, popping his head out for a treat now and again. Did he too have double memories?

"*Do cats like catnip?*" came the familiar voice. "*I remember every bit of it, as well as a pleasant parallel life as your beloved animal companion in which I have been prodigiously spoiled.*"

"*So you talk in this Timeline too?*"

"*Most cats do. If humans would only listen. More and more are, you know, in this Timeline. There's a lot more respect for all non-humans.*"

"So what are the choices?" asked Tara later, alone with Yeshi in what in this Timeline was her home, a cozy, well-appointed cottage on the outskirts of Avebury. She looked out the window at the snow coming down in fairy swirls, now quite thick upon the earth.

"Well, this is unprecedented," he said. "So we're kind of winging it."

"Xander…Yeshi…what does that mean? Can I just go with you now, 300 years into the future?"

"You could." He sounded uncertain. "But would you want to?"

"I don't know," she said hesitantly. "I'm still 96, and you're…I have no idea."

"I'm 44 in my Time. Hardly a third into my expected lifespan."

"And I'd be 96 if I came with you to the Portal and jumped forward into your Time?"

"You'd be 96. You wouldn't necessarily look or feel 96, just as you don't now. But there would be an age difference between us, and your life span would end well before mine."

She looked doubtful. "It's one thing to be an older woman, but another to rob the cradle." She smiled at his bemusement. "An old expression, a joke."

"I love you beyond time," he said. "I will welcome whatever your choice. What a privilege this has been, coming together in this strange way at a pivotal time that has truly changed the course of the planet, if not the universe."

"Indeed," she reflected. "What a strange destiny."

The two sat silently in the darkening room, holding hands, feeling deep and simple gratitude as they looked through the leaded glass windows at the wintry scene outside.

"Yeshi, what is the other choice?"

He cleared his throat. "To die naturally, at the end of this lifetime in this body. And to trust that we will meet again in another incarnation, if that is truly for our highest good."

"Wait a minute. You mean it's not guaranteed?"

He shrugged. "In this Enlightenment game, we're not supposed to be attached. We've taken that Bodhisattva Vow somewhere along the line, so our first priority is to be of service to all sentient beings. We may or may not meet again."

"A love beyond time, distance, and universes," she said. "And yet we two individuals may not actually meet, 300 years in the future or ever. Do we have any choice over this matter?"

"It is said we do. It is taught. It is a paradox. If you have no attachment, then you have choice, but then you don't have the attachment and it doesn't matter."

"Rinpoche used to say, remember, that you can still enjoy things, feel love, love your family, beauty, art, food, as long as you don't grasp on them."

"True." He let go of her hand and they looked into each other's eyes, questioning, memorizing. "I never in a million years expected to meet you again this way, through Time Travel. So who knows what's in store for us?"

The two sat in silence for a long time, their heads bent together, their breaths becoming one.

"Yeshi, I've decided," she said at last. "Go now, with Sitara and Jonah. Your loved ones in your own Time will be wanting to see you, whether it seems you've been gone a moment or years. Let me live out my lifespan here naturally."

Georgie, who was sleeping quietly in her lap, began to purr, and moved his half-tail slightly, kneading his claws into her leg.

"Should I stay longer?" he asked. "To be with you when you make your transition, just as you were with me when I was Xander?"

"Heavens, no! I've practiced the *Phowa*. All cultures have it, the Tibetans had just developed it to a fine art. I'm not afraid. I'm just not quite ready. Leona will be with me, as we were with her…him…when she was our Rinpoche." She touched his cheek. "Go now. No good-byes. I'll see you soon, if that is for the highest good, and Sitara and Jonah too. I'll have the memories of both of these alternate lifetimes, and perhaps remember them, or perhaps forget them in future incarnations. Anyway, it is good."

Yeshi kissed her gently on the lips, and scratched Georgie's ears. He left the room silently, walking through the snow instead of teleporting, to conserve energy for the long and instant journey home to his own Time.

Tara lived out the next days, she stopped counting how many, in the joy of each moment. There was Christmas, which she had always loved, there was video-linking with her sister Christina, still alive and living in Taos, and her daughter, granddaughter, and adopted great-grandchildren. There were New Year fireworks in London on a clear winter night, and there was delicious snow in endless supply.

People in this Timeline had begun to grumble, initially good-naturedly, at the inconvenience of so much snow. But they all said it was good for the land, that the crops would grow well in the spring. There was no such word as "organic" anymore, Tara noticed, as all food was grown without pesticides and chemical fertilizers, and the soil was regularly enhanced and deeply loved and respected.

Sometime in the middle of February, Leona said she would spend the night with her Gran. The two talked for awhile, played with Georgie, and then meditated together.

Tara suddenly felt very, very tired, and energized at the same time. She held her body upright, her spine straight, and rose above her body in a spiral of rainbow light, much like teleporting, much like Time Travel.

She had the sensation of breathing, but realized she was no longer in her body, and with the dissolution of the silver cord that bound her to her body, no longer attached to that body, that incarnation.

"*Everything is fine, as it should be*," whispered a feline mind-voice. "*No good-byes.*"

As Tara floated farther into the bright light, which now surrounded her, she looked back and down at her body. It still sat upright, a gray cat in her lap. Leona had her palm on Tara's body's white crown. When she let go, Tara soared.

AFTERWARDS

Galactic Date 2351

Alcyon University,
Pleiades Star System

Alexandra strode confidently through the crowds in the crystalline corridor, excited to be at the First Inter-Galactic Time Travel Conference. At age 44, she was barely into the prime of her life, just finished with her doctorate in Inter-species Studies, and hoping to lead an adventurous life in this promising universe.

She was glad to have her feline companion, Bastet, sharing this particular adventure with her. Bastet was a graceful, sleek golden creature who rode upon Alexandra's shoulders everywhere she went. She'd named her after the cat goddess of Ancient Egypt, and the cat lived up to the name, mind-speaking in erudite terms, and keeping up with every meditation teaching that Alexandra had taken from any lineage, human or otherwise.

Alexandra's first experience of inter-galactic space travel had proved to be effortless. It required none of the mineral materials mined at great human expense in earlier eras that Alexandra had studied, nearly 400 years ago at the dawn of human space travel. No long rockets in stages, no exploding fuels and thundering noise. Just a portal and an intention, and there you were.

Maybe a little disoriented the first few times, she'd heard, as if one had been twirling in a dance, but that soon passed. Bastet, with her superior feline balance, hardly seemed to notice, and had arrived grooming her paws and face to look her best.

Time Travel. Alexandra certainly believed it was possible, but humans hadn't proven its efficacy, or necessity, until now. It held all kinds of possibilities, but at the same time raised thorny ethical issues. After all, one couldn't just go around randomly changing Timelines.

The rumor was that something really big was about to be revealed, that the guest speakers had a riveting story to tell. Alexandra had noticed that life had seemed unsettled in the last bit of time, while she was completing her dissertation. People had been aggressive and angry, and interpersonal conflicts that felt like they could even lead to violence had surfaced more often. People's egos seemed emphasized, and there were groups of men who said that it was better to be in a male incarnation, and groups of women who said it was better to be female—contrary to all that they had been taught.

Time Travel was a matter for consensus decision, though initially throughout the Sentient Planets there had been anything but consensus. Many holo-commentators had speculated that the unusual lack of consensus, coupled with the desire for domination and personal attention, was the result of a Timeline Bleedthrough from a Timeline somewhere in the past where humanity and other sentient beings had not learned to live in harmony, but persisted in conflict.

Alexandra had studied history extensively, and in addition had had many dreams that the Elders told her were dreams of previous incarnations in various Timelines. All of one's incarnations weren't in a single Timeline. A soul could jump around, seeking experience, and if advanced, seeking to help evolution, from Timeline to Timeline. It was entirely possible to have had simultaneous incarnations in two or more Timelines, one leading to this Time, and the others perhaps petering out, if humans had made unwise and selfish decisions regarding war and/or their planetary environment.

All this was something that couldn't be studied purely academically and intellectually, but had to be looked at with the heart, with intuition. Perhaps that's why Alexandra had excelled in her studies and had been chosen as an Earth-based delegate to the Time Travel conference.

Something felt familiar about the crystalline corridors lit with softly changing colors. Something felt familiar about the crowd of people waiting to get into the conference hall.

"*Me too,*" murmured Bastet. "*It's as if we've been here before. Or known someone who has been and seen it through their eyes.*"

Alexandra scanned the crowd, looking for someone she might know from her studies on Earth, but didn't see anyone. She felt a bit alone, suddenly shy. She was glad Bastet was with her. Quite a number of people had cats riding on their shoulders, and Bastet looked around with interest, wondering if she also might find some friends.

Slowly they made their way into the hall. The speakers were introduced: Yeshi, a man about her age with the high cheekbones and slanted eyes of Old Tibet on Earth; Sitara, a youngish woman who seemed to shimmer and change and then settle into an appearance for awhile, and then change again; and Jonah, a solid slightly older man whose genes mostly seemed to be from Old Africa on Earth.

Alexandra listened with rapt attention, as did Bastet, as the three presented a holo-story of their recent Time Travel experience.

Alexandra's mind and heart stirred as she saw pictures of Old Earth, from centuries before she was born. She'd studied the holos, but they hadn't looked quite like the ones she and the hushed crowd were viewing. The ancient calendar of Stonehenge—but with tropical palm trees growing as tall as the stones? Rice paddies where the Crop Circle communications from other species in the galaxy had been?

She shifted in the liquid crystal chair that conformed to her shape, and Bastet dug in her claws to keep her balance.

"*Nice looking cat,*" said Bastet, looking at the holo-image of Georgie, the First Time-Traveling Cat.

Alexandra felt as if she herself were living the Time Travel experience that had successfully stopped the Bleedthrough into their own Timeline. A huge sigh of relief rippled through the room as everyone collectively realized the degree of disaster that had been averted. Alexandra reflected that the situation was much like she had read about in historical documents from the 21st century, when humans had finally realized how many times nuclear war had been averted, and how often their galactic siblings had helped them to do so—even though only a few indigenous shamans and well-developed intuitives were able to perceive them, and fewer still to communicate with them.

The presentation ended to thunderous applause and full-throated ululations of joy. Yeshi, Sitara, and Jonah bowed humbly to the crowd, their hands in the ancient prayer offering position. Alexandra stood with the crowd, clapping and ululating, wistfully wishing she could have just a few minutes to talk to such illustrious personages, the heroes who had restored the Timeline's integrity. But she was just one among many admirers, and realized that she had little chance of even meeting their gazes.

So she and Bastet together concentrated on sending them all love, and deep gratitude, and letting go of their own ego-thoughts. How wonderful that someone had been able to do what they did. How wonderful that she was there at the conference to learn about it.

Seeking a quiet moment, she sat alone on a dark terrace with her cat in her lap. Together, the two of them gazed at the spectacular display of colors in the indigo sky above them, brighter and more complex than the most vivid auroras on Old Earth that Alexandra had sometimes seen when visiting the Sami side of her family.

She was mesmerized by the beauty of the light, and it took her awhile to become aware of another human presence. She was startled to see that Yeshi, the Time Traveler, sat beside her and gazed into infinity. Improbably, he took her hand. She turned towards him.

And saw the aurora reflected in his dark eyes, his familiar eyes, his eyes with the light of a particular consciousness that spanned centuries and millennia. "I knew you'd come," he said.

Suddenly she understood why Tara, and Georgie, had seemed so familiar. "How does it happen?" she asked. "How do people find each other?"

Yeshi laughed, looking up at the sky. "That way, I guess. Magnetics of the soul."

"I..." she hesitated. "I'm Alexandra."

"Who was Tara. I left you just a minute ago, in time. And I am Yeshi, who was Xander."

"*And I'm Bastet, who was Georgie,*" said the feline mind-voice rather insistently.

"*We've got work to do,*" said the three, all at once, knowing they'd been reunited for a reason.

Acknowledgements

Deep and abiding thanks to Jeannine Seymour for her perceptive insights into the manuscript and her joyful editing. Thanks to Susan McDuffie for reading an early draft and giving me notes which greatly improved the story. Thanks to CJ Ondek for her comments and editing skills, and to David Michie and NV Baker for reading and commenting on the book. Thanks to Tara W. Lumpkin for reading the manuscript, and to my late mother, Maria Denker, for her encouragement, curiosity, and enthusiastic response to the part of the manuscript that she read.

Great thanks are due to Marla Phillips for her beautiful and creative cover design, and to Max Underwood for the author photo and cat photography.

Many others have discussed the narrative with me, including Cindy O'Connell, Maryann De Stefano, Lisa Jackson, and Janna Chandler. Special thanks to Lisa for helping me rescue the short-haired gray time-traveling cat, the very image of Georgie, who appeared outside my house on Christmas Eve and made me wonder if the story is really taking place in some alternate Timeline.

Thanks to my new sisters and brothers from Experience Week at Findhorn Foundation for opening their hearts and listening to me talking about my novel.

Thanks for encouraging purrs and inspiration to my three feline muses, Dorjee Purr-ba, Yeshe Gyalpo, and Samadhi Timewalker.

About the Author

Debra Denker has been writing stories since she learned to read. Although novels and poetry were her first loves, she turned her talent to journalism in the '70s and '80s, writing about Afghanistan and the refugee situation in Pakistan for *National Geographic* and many leading newspapers. She has specialized in social documentation utilizing journalism, photography, and film to convey the experiences of people in war torn areas, with the intention of stimulating the empathy necessary for humans to stop violence against people and planet.

Denker is the author of two published books, the non-fiction literary memoir *Sisters on the Bridge of Fire: One Woman's Journeys in Afghanistan, Pakistan, and India*, and the novel *War in the Land of Cain*—a story of love, war, and moral choices set during the Soviet-Afghan war of the 1980's.

Denker now writes for the award-winning conservation media website, Voices for Biodiversity, raising consciousness to help ward off the Sixth Great Extinction.

She currently lives in Santa Fe with her family of cats, Dorjee Purr-ba, Yeshe Gyalpo, and Samadhi Timewalker, but travels frequently in earthly space, and hopes to travel in time and galactic space.

The novel's website is www.weathermenders.com.

Her personal blog www.mysticresistance.com explores a range of spiritual, social, and political issues and their intersection with sacred activism.

Author & Samadhi cat photo by Max Underwood;
Yeshe by Debra Denker;
Dorjee by Max Underwood

38509515R00181

Printed in Poland
by Amazon Fulfillment
Poland Sp. z o.o., Wrocław